# AWAKENING DESIRES

Jo blushed as she bathed her sleeping patient. His skin glowed bronze in the half-light of the tent, and she had a sudden urge to touch him—to feel his flesh beneath her fingers. She laid her hand on his bare chest. It was warm, not hot.

She lifted her eyes to his face.

His eyes were open, electric blue, and very much aware.

"Somewhere, in the back of my head, I have a distinct impression that you told me you were a man. A doctor?"

She released her breath and swallowed. "I never said I was a man. I said I was a doctor."

His intense blue eyes swept across her body. In the wet shirt, without the protection of a coat, it was easy enough to see she was a woman. Jo blushed scarlet as his bemused gaze paused, then traveled on to her belt-cinched waist and breeches.

His hand touched hers lightly. She was astonished at her own swift, burning reaction.

"I'm glad you turned out to be a woman," he said . . .

# A DOCTOR'S HEART

## JEANNE FELLDIN

**ZEBRA BOOKS**
**KENSINGTON PUBLISHING CORP.**

ZEBRA BOOKS

are published by

Kensington Publishing Corp.
475 Park Avenue South
New York, NY 10016

First printing: October 1987

Printed in the United States of America

*For my husband whose belief came too late
and for my mother who has always believed*

# PROLOGUE

*July 18, 1856*

Another baby. With twisting heart, the young girl crouched over the stinking straw mattress and took her mother's hand. Times past infected Jody's mind with mounting horror—times when she had been forced to leave the room to the sound of her mother's screams. Eight times Jody could remember. Eight trips up the hill behind the sod house to lay another little box in the rich, black soil of Ireland. And after each baby, Mama had been a little weaker, a little slower to climb from her bed, a little softer of speech and gentler of smile. Jody's lips quivered. Other women had babies. Mama had pain and little boxes.

A woman, a stranger, pulled back the stained blanket Pa had hung. The temporary screen gave little privacy. Instead, it bolstered the heat and accentuated the stench of herring that had been with them for almost six weeks, now blended with the acrid odor of her mother's misery. "How bad is she?" asked the woman. "Come away, child, and let me see."

Jody wanted to scream, No. Don't send me away again. I want to help. But her words were soft: "Please—please let me stay."

"Whist now. Your Mama's fixin' to have a baby."

7

Bracing herself against the pitch of the old sailing ship, the woman grasped Jody's arm.

On the makeshift gray curtain, reflections from her mother's gold earrings cavorted gaily. They can't chase me out now, thought Jody. I won't let them.

She shook the woman's hand loose, and her voice took on a hard edge. "I *know* she's having a baby. But I'm old enough to stay this time. I'm thirteen and I want to help."

Swiping her sweaty face with the back of her hand, the woman peered into the blackness beyond the blanket. "Take the girl out of here," she said to someone Jody couldn't see. "Find her father and see if they'll let him take her topside for a bit of air. They'll not, but he kin try."

"Why ain't he here? Where is he?"

"Like my ol' man and all the rest of 'em. Took off as soon as she got the first pain."

"Sure 'n he wud be gone. Knock 'er up, then can't stomach t' watch."

"Well, he can't be far off. There's no place for him to go. He's a little bloke with red hair." The woman's grimy hand came to rest on Jody's shoulder. "What's your pa's name, child?"

"Jonathan. Jonathan Gates."

"I'll find him and bring him back," the other woman promised. The blanket dropped into place, hanging slightly askew and swaying with the motion of the ship.

Suddenly her mother's eyes stretched, wide and staring.

Fright boiled up in Jody. "Mama? Mama?"

Her mother's body tensed, jerked. She grasped Jody's hand in a crushing grip.

"Mama, you're hurting me." But the words were lost in the cry of pain wrenched from her mother's cracked lips. Sweat dripped from her brow. Her eyes bulged

8

and her thin frame arched with strain. With her patched dress hiked up almost to her knees, her legs looked to be sticklike and startlingly white in the flickering lantern glow. Her other hand flew like a claw to grasp Jody's shoulder; she bit down hard on her lip and drew blood, yet the second scream tore from the depths of her soul and echoed through the bowels of the old sailing ship.

From the other side of the blanket came a stirring of bodies, moans, and hundreds of rasping coughs, some stifled, some not, plus several angry curses.

The woman tried again to pull Jody aside. "Here, child. Let me at her."

"I can't." In spite of herself, Jody felt tears well behind her hot lids. "She won't let go."

The woman knelt to reach around Jody. She laid her hands on Edith's shoulders to shove her down again. "Here, lovey," she said, pushing a bit of rags at the laboring woman. "Let go your girl and pull on this."

Then Jody saw her mother's hazel eyes grow peaceful. The hard, biting fingers dropped away. Edith looked happy, as she had been in Ballareen before the blight struck. Jody was too young to remember back before the potato stalks turned black and began to smell, but she could remember how Mama was before they'd left Ireland and gone to Liverpool where it had been so dark and dirty and smoky. Mama hated dirt— but even Liverpool hadn't been dirty like this stinking ship.

"Oh, Mama," Jody whispered, "I wish you didn't hurt so. I wish I knew what to do for you." Mama shouldn't have to suffer like this, she thought. Why did God send babies one after the other—so fast that Mama never had a chance to get better before she was screaming with the birth of another?

And it wasn't only Mama. Jody had heard other

women scream, too.

She leaned close and stroked her mother's graying hair. "Someday, Mama," she whispered. "Someday I'll find a way so this won't happen anymore. I promise. Somehow . . . someday . . ." Her chest ached with the fullness—the fierceness—the rightness of her promise. Her body shook, and she felt as if she had been running a race, as if she had hurtled through time and space to drink at the well of truth.

When she could speak again, she leaned forward. "It's like you always said, Mama: 'However long the road there comes a turning.' Well, I'm going to make a turning for women. I will. I promise I will."

Jody's mind went back to the time when she had suggested that her mother ask God to stop sending babies. "If you told Him how bad you felt—how much you hurt—He wouldn't keep on sending them, would He?" she had asked.

"God made women to have babies, darling," her mother had replied. "It isn't our place to question His authority."

Now Jody leaned over and spoke earnestly: "I'm not questioning God, Mama. All I'm going to do is look for a way to help women. I know babies are wonderful, but we need to fix it somehow so we don't have to accept *all* those babies He sends. That's what I'm going to do. If I find a way, won't that mean He put it there for me to find?" She peered anxiously at her mother's haggard face.

"Oh, if you could just hear me, Mama, I know you'd tell me I'm right—I know you'd never laugh at me for thinking I could make a difference for women. Mama—can you hear me?"

She wanted so much to hear her mother's voice, to hear her speak and laugh again. Her mother had never laughed often, but she always had a kind of easy way

10

about her that made Jody feel good. And before all the potato plants died, her mother used to sing—soft little songs, half humming, half words. Jody hadn't heard her mother sing for a long, long time now.

"You feel better, Mama?" the girl asked, encouraged by the ethereal glow on her mother's thin face.

"Oh, Holy Mother of God!" The woman beside her made the sign across her bosom, and her voice took on a singsong chant: "Hail, Mary, Full of Grace . . ."

Jody followed the line of the woman's eyes. In the wavering light from the pitching lantern, a red river flowed down her mother's legs, spread over the mattress ticking, and mingled with the unnameable filth on the steerage floor.

"Mama . . ."

With the barest whisper of a sigh and a gentle smile, the light left her mother's eyes.

The ship's bell sounded twice. From a far corner of the steerage came the steady drone of snoring, and behind the creaking timbers, the scurrying of rats.

# PART I
# NEW YORK CITY

# 1

*July 7, 1857*

"I'll have yer rent, missy. If ye kin no' pay, it's out ye go."

Jody's mind whirled. For three days now she hadn't been able to think straight. She stared at the landlady, desperately wishing she could tell the old witch what to do with her hole of a room, but it was the only home Jody had known since she and her pa had arrived in New York a year before. "I'm on my way to get the rent money now," she said, hoping it would work out that way. "I'll be back in a couple hours."

"If you're not here by the time they start comin' off the boats, I'll throw yer stuff into the street."

The old hag would sell it, is what she would do. Sell their few bits of furniture, then swear she had thrown them out. Jody had seen it happen before.

The young girl turned away, half-formed ideas swirling in her head. It wouldn't help to get work in a mill, even if she could. They paid at the end of a week, and she had to have the rent money this very day. She could clean houses—be a maid—but in New York City even domestic positions were closed to the Irish unless you knew the right people.

Reluctantly she turned her steps toward Tammany

15

Hall and the odious ward heeler, Teddy Cassidy. He could get her a job if he would. She had put off going to him for help, hoping another way out would occur to her, but when the slovenly landlady stopped her in the tenement doorway, Jody knew her time had run out. There was only Cassidy left. Maybe he would give her a bit of a loan, and she could climb onto a ferryboat and leave this rotten, teeming city—maybe go West somewhere.

She was dreaming and she knew it. Still, there was nowhere else to turn.

Hurrying across the triangle of mud where five streets converged to form the miserably misnamed Paradise Square, Jody was scarcely aware of the pigs and the foul-smelling gutters and clapboard hovels, or the drunks and the groggeries that even sold to children; or the stinking outhouses and rag collectors and pickpockets and garbage rooters; or of the sickness and crime and filth that was Five Points.

It was all there, but she rarely saw it. Long ago she had learned to shut out the squalor of her surroundings and escape into a lovely valley of her own conjuring. It was a trick her mother had taught her back in Liverpool. They had lived on Tithebarn Street then, in a slum almost as filthy as Five Points. Having fled the potato famine in Ireland and gone to England to earn passage money for America, her father took work as a horse trainer on an estate in the country and came home only once each fortnight. Her mother was a carder at the mill. That left Jody alone all day, six days a week. It was early, during those eight years in Liverpool, that Jody's mother taught her the valley trick. "You must empty your mind, darling," Mama had explained. "Make your mind an empty shell. And when your mind is a nice clean slate, then start to put things back. Put back only pretty things—the things

16

you like—flowers in the springtime, warm breezes and birds, and the sky a plate of blue . . ."

Over the years Jody had created a sweet valley where she drifted in her own land of dreams whenever the world around her reared too harsh and ugly.

When her mother died, her father had suddenly become alert to the dangers of leaving her alone in the city while he was off at the firehouse. Even when he was drunk, he had drummed at her. "Listen, lovey," he had said over and over, "if any man—or any boy—grabs ye, ye got t' know how t' pertect yerself." Then he had taught her how, if a man grabbed her from behind, to slip down between his arms to escape; if she was attacked from the front or the side, how to bring her knee up quick in a hard jab to the groin. Jody hadn't been forced to use that last bit yet, but she had become quite adept with a fast kick to the shins or an elbow to the midsection. And she had developed a rapid, convincing patter about her pa and his terrible temper, and how he had killed a man for trying to mess with his only daughter. Pretty as she was, Jody was rarely accosted. Pa was little and scrawny, and often drunk, but he was also a known member of the Dead Rabbits, and that was enough to put fear of the devil into any man.

For years, with her mother's magic, and then her father's coaching in self-defense, the girl had walked untouched through the vile debauchery of Tithebarn Street and Five Points. A newspaper article concerning starvation and disease saddened her far more than the crimes she brushed past every day. These two specters, said the paper, brought death to over a thousand infants in New York City each month, and Jody found this much more disturbing than the drunken brute who grabbed her ankle as she passed and received a kick in the face for his trouble. She would have liked to help

17

the whole world, but had learned that self-preservation came first, compassion second.

Now, as always, it was a treat for Jody to leave the Square. Her steps slowed as she caught a glimpse of the big packets in the harbor to the south. The days of sail were almost over, and the old ships were Jody's last link with her mother and her childhood. She tried to forget the change in her father after they came to America. He would never have shrunk so if Mama had lived. It was for Mama that he had strutted like a rooster and crowed like a cock at first light. After Mama died, he had no one to strut for and nothing to crow about.

Jody crossed Reade and Chambers, her heart beating faster as she approached City Hall. It was an imposing marble building with twin staircases, perched in the middle of a pretty park, surrounded by a wrought-iron fence, and topped by a clock tower and a marble statue of Justice. Across the street, Tammany Hall—the bastion of the Irish political machine—rose in majestic four-storied splendor.

This was the first time since the day they had arrived in New York that Jody had been inside Tammany Hall. It was here Teddy Cassidy had brought them that first day—fresh off the boat—a huge group of Irish immigrants, to naturalize all the men so they would be eligible to vote come election day.

Cassidy was just as she remembered: black haired and florid, with a broad smile and a paunch to match. She didn't like his gold-toothed smile, the way he leered at her, the slither of his eyes. He made her feel dirty somehow. "You're the Gates gel, right?"

"Yes, sir." She bobbed, surprised that he remembered her.

He rose and moved from behind the desk, his eyes feigning sympathy. "I hear yer pa got hisself killed in th'

18

riots down t' Five Points."

She swallowed painfully. It was three days now since her father had died, and she still couldn't accept it. Not that his death had hit her like the bottomless pit her gentle mother's passing had left. No, much as she had loved her loud, brawling father, he had changed so drastically this past year, he wasn't like the old lovable Pa at all. What gnawed at Jody now was the frightening realization that she was totally alone in this cold city, alone and at the mercy of this slimy little ward heeler.

She wished he would stay behind his desk. She fastened her eyes on the glistening gem in his stickpin as it crawled closer. It came to a halt just inches from her chest. "Too bad about yer pa," he said.

He stood too close. Jody's heart pounded. She had heard stories about this man; whispers she didn't even understand. He was supposed to be the owner of Lettie's Place, the house next to Flannigan's warehouse. There were lots of windows in Lettie's Place and in the summertime, a woman hung from every window. Jody had seen them today when she came past. They had painted faces and low-cut dresses. Bold and brazen as brass, they laughed and gestured and called down to the men in the street.

"I had a mass said for Pa," Jody murmured now, swallowing a stab of fear. She stared at Cassidy's gleaming stickpin. Why had she come to him after what he had done to Pa?

It was Cassidy who had started Pa off with the Dead Rabbits, the worst gang in all the city—worse, the papers said, than the Bowery Boys or the Pug Uglies, or any of the others. And it was the Dead Rabbit riot that had killed Pa.

Now she raised her eyes, her lips tightening with determination. "I need your help, Mr. Cassidy. If you remember, you got us a room in Flannigan's old warehouse last year when we first came over. Now . . . with Pa gone . . . I'm in desperate need of a job. Pa . . . he wouldn't let me work before, but now . . . Well, the mass for Pa took the last of our money and our rent is up today. Mrs. Flannigan's about to throw me into the street."

Cassidy's eyes narrowed. The girl had tied her red-gold hair in pigtails with a piece of frayed green ribbon. Her faded calico dress stretched across barely budding young breasts and scarcely reached her well-turned ankles. Slowly his gaze meandered back to the lovely oval face, the challenging hazel eyes punctuated by straight, dark brows. A smile curved his fleshy lips. "How old are ye?"

"Fourteen."

"Sure an' you're a pretty colleen. An' ye'll soon be fillin' out." His eyes gleamed. "How come ye didn't go across th' square t' th' Home Mission when yer pa got hisself killed?"

In spite of herself, Jody's lips quivered. The Five Points Mission School had been a sore spot all year. She missed her mother's daily lessons and had never passed the mission without wanting to go inside to find out what subjects they taught. But Pa had told her it was run by Protestants with no liking for what they called "foreign Papists."

"But I'm not Catholic," she had protested. "You are, but I'm not."

"Try t' tell them that!" roared Jonathan. "We both got th' map o' Ireland on our faces, puss. One look at us and yer goose'd be proper cooked."

Now Cassidy's voice dragged her back to the present. "How come ye're here lookin' fer a handout instead of over t' th' mission?" he demanded again.

"I'm not looking for a handout," she declared

stoutly. "I'm looking for a job."

"So how come ye don't prance over t' th' Goody Twoshoes house?" He sucked on his teeth. "They'd at least take ye in and feed ye—if ye ain't particular what ye eats."

She curbed her temper. "I've heard tell . . . when children go in, they don't come out sometimes."

He laughed then, a short bark of derision. "Sure an' ye ain't a child no more, Jody Gates. Ye afraid they'll serve ye up fer Sunday supper along with th' leftovers they collects from th' rich folks' tables?"

"No," she flared. "I'm afraid they'll plunk me in the Juvenile Asylum or send me to the Almshouse Department, and I'll not get out until I'm full grown."

His eyes slid down slowly, insolently. "Sure an' I'd say ye're almost full growed now." She forced herself not to cringe as he laid a pudgy finger on her cheek. His smile came suddenly then, and the gleam in his eye was no less bright than the gold crown on his front tooth. "Well, maybe I kin help ye after all." His stickpin winked at her. "Do you know Lettie's Place down t' Five Points?"

"Yes, of course." Jody shivered. It was like he had read her mind. Snakes of St. Patrick, she thought, don't let him send me to Lettie's. She didn't know what went on inside that house, but Pa had told her to steer clear of it—that "bad women" lived there.

"Lettie Gillispie jest happens t' be a friend o' mine. Ye take yourself 'round t' Lettie an' tell 'er I sent ye."

"Begging your pardon, Mr. Cassidy, but I need some money today, or Mrs. Flannigan will throw me into the street."

"You do like I tell ye—go see Lettie. She'll take care o' ye."

Jody's mind worked quickly. If Pa said only bad women lived at Lettie's, then she couldn't go there.

21

Even without Pa's warning, one look at those women was enough to tell her she didn't belong with them.

There *must* be something else—some other place Cassidy could send her for work. He knew everyone in the city—all the bigwigs—the mayor—everybody. Why, he could even get her work with a *doctor* if he wanted. Jody's heart leaped. Now that Pa was gone and she was alone, she could start on the promise she had made to Mama that night on the ship. She had promised to find a way to make birthing babies easier, and a deathbed promise was not something to take lightly.

Even now, when she remembered that night, Jody's heart swelled with the blaze of truth—the strength of the promise she had made—the promise that was an unbreakable cord binding her to her mother's memory. And even if she hadn't promised, the memory of her mother's suffering, the memory of those little black boxes remained with her.

Her mother used to say, "A wise woman is better than a foolish doctor," but Jody was sure that doctors were the only ones who knew the right way to go about having babies. If I could just get a job with a doctor, thought Jody. As a scullery maid—anything. Cassidy must know a doctor somewhere. He must.

She licked her lips nervously, trying to find the words. "Mr. Cassidy . . . there is something . . ."

He grinned and the gold tooth blazed at her. "Ye're a good-lookin' lass. Take yerself down t' Lettie's and git yerself into a decent dress. Sure an' there's lots like 'em young an' tight like you. I'll wager ye'll be able t' name yer own price afore long—pretty colleen like you." He patted her cheek. "I'll be down t' see ye meself once ye git a bit more meat on ye."

Jody didn't understand his smirks and winks, but she smiled at him tremulously. "You're so good to help me," she whispered, almost gagging on the words. "But I was hoping—"

"If it's a place o' yer own ye're tryin' t' wangle, I might think on it. But not till after ye git a bit o' experience, understand. Lettie kin train ye good. Then maybe I'll see about settin' ye up some place."

Still Jody didn't understand. She only knew she must ask about a position with a doctor before Cassidy suddenly shuffled her out of the office and on her way back to Five Points. "It's something I've never told anybody before . . ." she began again.

"Ye kin talk t' me about anything," he said unctuously. His foot shot out to kick the door closed and his arm crawled around her waist.

The urge to elbow his fat paunch was strong, but she forced herself to stand quietly. "I've . . . I've set my heart on working for a doctor, Mr. Cassidy." Seeing his mouth drop in astonishment, she hurried on before she lost her nerve: "You see, it's a promise I made my mama on her deathbed. She died birthing a new baby, Mr. Cassidy, and I promised I'd find a way to make it easier for women—easier to have their babies maybe." Suddenly realizing that having babies was something one didn't discuss with a man, Jody bowed her head in mock humility. I don't care, she thought rebelliously. As long as he helps me, I don't care.

Her heart tripped against her ribs as she tilted her head, peering at him hopefully, her pink lower lip caught between white, even teeth. "I thought if I could get work with a doctor," she whispered. "I'll do anything—cook's helper—maid—clean up after the patients . . ."

His arm dropped like a stone and he backed away, staring at her, black brows drawn into a heavy vee between hard gray eyes. She tried to look very young and helpless.

23

Suddenly he began to chuckle. "I'll say this fer ye, lass: Ye're an original. 'Tis th' first time I've iver bin turned down in favor of a bedpan." He was still laughing ruefully as he crossed to the desk and sat down. "A deathbed promise t' yer ma, be it? Sure an' ye'll not be wantin' t' break that now, will ye?"

She shook her head, hope dinning in her ears as he dipped his quill into the inkwell.

"Yer pa used t' brag on how you cud read an' write. If he was tellin' th' truth, you'll have no trouble locatin' th' doctor's house. An' ye kin say I sent ye." He chuckled again as he held out the paper. "Of course, if yer pa was lyin', ye kin always go t' Lettie's Place."

Happiness brimming, Jody grasped the proffered sheet. As she sped toward the door, she heard him mutter something, but her flying feet did not pause.

Ten minutes later, Cassidy was still talking to himself: "Ye're a goddamn jackass, man, lettin' that one git away. 'Tis yourself be needin' the doctor!"

By this time, Jody's flying feet were carrying her back to Paradise Square, back to Flannigan's to collect her only treasured possession: the carpetbag that held her mother's books.

The girl stood before the dark, forbidding brownstone, bolstering nerve to mount the steps and ring the bell. Dusk deepened and night shadows crawled across the face of the house. One-sixty Chambers Street. She peered at the paper again, unable to read it now in the darkness, but knowing what it said. It was the right address—it just didn't fit with where she would have expected Cassidy to send her for a job. Chambers Street, just beyond City Hall, was quiet and orderly. The house looked almost too respectable. For some inexplicable reason, Jody shivered.

While she stood indecisively on the sidewalk, a hired hack pulled up and a woman emerged, face hidden by a heavy veil and figure covered by a closely held cloak. Jody couldn't tell whether the newcomer was old or young. The woman looked about cautiously, then mounted the steps and was swallowed into the sudden shaft of brightness from the briefly opened door. Again Jody waited. The woman did not come out.

Jody bit her lip. Something told her not to go inside, but if she ever was to escape Five Points, it had to be now—right now. Now, with Pa gone, there was a sudden drive in her, a thirst for knowledge, a determination to learn so that she could, as she had promised, somehow ease the pain and frequency of childbirth.

Resolutely, the girl mounted the steps and rang the bell.

## 2

The door opened just a crack, as though the cheery light from inside was too precious to waste on the caller. A woman's stout form blocked the meager opening. "Yes?"

"I'm here to see the doctor," Jody said breathlessly. "Mr. Cassidy sent me."

"Come in." The door swung, then quickly slammed as the girl stepped inside. Her eyes widened in appreciation as she looked around the spacious entrance hall.

"This way." The maid had dark hair and wore a white starched apron and cap, and her stomach preceded her like the prow of a ship. She wasn't much older than Jody, but she was heavy with child and wheezed as she walked.

Following her through the first door on the left, Jody took the indicated chair. "The doctor will be with you soon." The door closed firmly.

She wanted to pinch herself. She was actually going to meet a real doctor tonight—speak to him—hear him speak. The only time she had ever seen a doctor up close was at a fire a few months back. A boy, trapped by flames on the second floor, had jumped onto the cobblestones. As he lay there, writhing in pain, a man in a black frockcoat had appeared, and the crowd opened before him like the Red Sea parting for the Jews. A doctor!

Jody had watched in wonder as he opened his black leather bag and pulled out what looked to be a long needle. Someone moved in front of her just then, and she couldn't see it all, but she caught a brief glimpse of the needle slipping into the boy's arm. And she saw peace fall upon the child as his screams stopped. A miracle. A real miracle.

From then on, Jody's fuzzy daydreams became a definite reality. She saw herself a full-grown woman, a doctor—just like the man in the frockcoat. And she saved people's lives. Like Mama. And the boy who had jumped from the window. And little babies. As a doctor she would do all these things. In her black doctor's bag, she would have a salve to take away all the horrible scabs and running sores—although she suspected that soap and water might cure a lot of those.

Stuck between the pages of Mama's books were notes on how to treat various diseases. After Jody saw the doctor with the miracle needle, she had read the notes over and over. Some of the entries were funny, especially the comments her mother had written in the margins.

One remedy was The Green Plaster. It was for skin infections and called for two pence worth each of beeswax, burgundy pitch, hog's lard, verdigris, and white resin to be boiled together, then stirred with one glass of sweet oil. A note in Mama's neat hand said, "This does nothing for infections, but it is wonderful for sore feet."

There were several cures for whooping cough, including a piece of red flannel to be put on the chest by the patient's godfather, and another that recommended the patient drink a mixture of sheep droppings and milk. Mama had added a huge question mark on

27

this latter one.

Piles were supposedly cured by squatting over a bucket in which a piece of tarred rope had been set afire and was exuding a hearty cloud of black smoke. Mama's note said, "This did nothing for Jonathan except scorch his bottom. I treated the burn with a mixture of buttermilk and bread soda. The piles disappeared by themselves when he stayed away from the pub for a week."

Jody loved reading her mother's notes, but she wished she had a real doctor book to study. Now, perhaps it was about to come true—the dream that had been festering in the back of her head ever since that day at the fire. Now, actually here, waiting to meet the doctor, she couldn't believe her own good fortune.

The office was very grand. There was a flowered carpet and tassels on velvet curtains. There was a real fireplace—the first she had seen since she left Ireland—marble with a brass clock on the mantel. Light from the gaslamp on the doctor's open writing cabinet made the brass clock gleam, and gaslight glinted off engravings on the flowered paper walls.

The door opened and a tall, imposing woman entered. "Good evening. I am Madame Restell, the physician."

The doctor was a woman! In all Jody's dreams, she really had never believed it could happen. Only men were physicians, she thought.

The doctor's black, glossy hair was parted in the middle, looped over her ears, and pulled into a neat snood at the nape of her neck. A white muslin fichu, edged in lace, covered her sloping shoulders. Her face was austere, cold, with heavy black brows and a chin so strong and prominent that it gave her a mannish look. Deep fissures radiated downward from the sides of her sturdy nose and lent a sad, half-angry air to her compressed lips. But her wide-set eyes wore a steady intensity that Jody found reassuring.

Madame Restell's deep eyes searched Jody's face for a moment, then came to rest on the girl's slender waist. "You're here to arrange for your lying-in?"

Jody smiled. Only married ladies had babies. It was funny, the doctor thinking Jody was a married woman. "Oh, no, ma'am," she said quickly. "I'm Jody Gates. Mr. Cassidy sent me."

"You're obviously still in your first trimester. Is it pills you're wanting?"

"No, ma'am. I'm not sick."

The doctor looked annoyed. "You must know this is a lying-in asylum, Mrs. Gates. Do you want to room with us until the baby is delivered? Is that it?"

Jody stifled a nervous giggle. "I'm not married, ma'am. Mr. Cassidy sent me. I'm . . . I'm looking for a position." She swallowed and hurried on. "You see, my pa was killed three days ago. In the riots at Five Points. So now I have to go to work. I'm a hard worker, Madame Restell. I can cook and sew and clean. I'm a regular tyrant on dirt. And I'm honest. I asked Mr. Cassidy special to send me to work for a doctor because someday, I'd like to be a doctor, too." Her rushing words ground to a sudden, embarrassed halt.

"Well. What's your name again, child?"

"Jody. Jody Gates."

"And how old are you?"

"Fourteen last March."

"Turn your face to the light and let me look at you."

Jody turned her head toward the lamp on the desk. The doctor was quiet a long time before she spoke again: "Your mother? Where is she?"

"She died on the ship, trying to have a baby."

The doctor's eyes sharpened. "Did that frighten you, Jody?"

29

"It scared me that Mama hurt so bad—that I couldn't help her. And it scared me that she might die like so many women do when the baby tries to come."

"You're not squeamish at the sight of blood then?"

"No, ma'am."

"I thought not." Definitely, her eyes were warm now. "If you could help ladies, like your mama—would you?"

"Oh, yes, ma'am. I want that more than anything. I'd like to help bring live babies instead of dead ones in little boxes like Mama always had."

The doctor's lips clamped tight and she turned her back with an abruptness that made Jody wonder if she had said something wrong.

At last Madame Restell swung to face her again. "Well. And how many dead babies did your mama have, Jody Gates?"

"Eight that I can remember. But I think maybe there were more before that."

"Well." She sat at the desk, her hands quiet in the folds of her bombazine dress. "Did you see any of the deliveries?"

"No, ma'am. They always chased me out—except that last time, on the ship." Jody bit her lip, waiting, hoping, yet not daring to hope.

"Well. Usually the girls who work here are waiting for their lying-in, but it just happens one of the girls left this morning, and I've no one to replace her yet. Perhaps you could fill in until another pregnancy arrives."

"Oh, yes, ma'am. Anything."

Madame Restell rose and moved to a bellpull in the corner. From the far reaches of the house, Jody heard a soft tinkle. "Are there clothes you'll need to pick up?"

"No, ma'am. I've everything right here in my carpetbag," Jody replied, ashamed to admit that her only clothes were the rags she wore.

The girl in the stiff white wraparound apron stood in the doorway.

"Kathleen, this is Jody. She'll be working here. Take her up to her bed now and find her a uniform."

Jody jumped to her feet. "Thank you, Madame Restell. Oh, I do thank you."

"Mind, it may not be for long. I have only six beds in the attic." Jody's heart fluttered. Another little hole of a room like the one she and Pa had slept in this past year? "The beds are for the poor girls like Kathleen, here, who have nowhere to turn in time of trouble. These girls work for their keep and the delivery of their babies. In your case, since you have no baby to deliver . . ." The doctor's eyes flashed an unspoken order to Kathleen, "You'll be given room and board and two dollars a month. You'll have Mondays off. Your duties will be mostly on the first floor. Kathleen, here, is getting a bit far along for the front door, but she'll continue to assist me in the surgery at present. You're nice and slim, Jody, and you speak well. You'll answer the door and show the patients into the office. Most ladies come at night. In the morning hours you will clean the first floor rooms, and in the afternoons you will assist Dr. Morceau in his mail business."

Jody felt firecrackers and sparklers explode within her. One day, she vowed, after the doctor had found out what a hard worker she was, she would get to "assist in the surgery."

## 3

Jody's first day began well enough. She was to sweep the floor and wash up any blood or "other mess" found there. Then she must wipe the instruments and lay them on a fresh cloth. She was to put a clean sheet on the surgery table and the cot, if needed, then scrub the table, the cabinet, and not forget the baseboards. She was to remove the dirty linens. The wicker basket in the corner was not to be emptied before doctor's surgery hours, but after. Dr. Restell was in surgery almost every morning. At one o'clock, just before dinner, Jody was to empty the basket.

The surgery was hidden beneath a massive staircase, just three steps across the narrow part of the back hall to the "first floor rear."

The first floor rear had once been a billiard room. On one side, near the ceiling, the score counters still stretched, but the billiard table and side chairs were gone. Now the large, dim room served as a hospital ward with sixteen narrow cots.

Jody stood in the doorway, holding the soiled linens, looking for the laundry-shoot door. Seven beds were occupied this first morning, four of them by wan, dull-eyed women who scarcely noticed when the door opened. Then there was a girl of about fourteen who looked very frightened and spoke to no one, and two pert young women who sat bolt upright in bed, chatting and laughing loudly. They stopped as Jody entered the ward. "When's she gonna be ready for me?" one of the women demanded.

"I don't know, ma'am. Kathleen could probably tell you about that. I'm just here to clean the ward."

"*You* can't be too far along," said the woman, eyeing Jody's slender figure speculatively. "You know, that old witch tried to get me to stay here and have this kid, but I told her nothing doing. She probably works you to death, don't she?"

"This is my first day," confided Jody, not bothering to contradict the woman about the reason she was here. It was flattering to have everyone think she was all grown up and married. "I know I'm going to like it," she said as she dumped the soiled linens down the chute. "I sleep with the other girls up in the attic under the eaves—but it's dry and nice with two dormer windows cut through the roof. We each have our own bed and a drawer, just like when I was home in Ballareen."

"Gee, that don't sound half bad. I got a friend who's thataway, too. She might be interested if the work ain't too hard. How many works here anyhow?"

"There's six of us girls. And Cook. And Perry, the handyman. And Mr. Trow and Dr. Morceau, but I haven't met them yet."

"Is your food as good as ours? Or do you get what's left over, like I do where I work?"

Jody began to strip the first of the sheets from four blood-soaked beds. "Oh, it's good. For breakfast this morning I got a whole egg and a bit of fried pork and tea. Cook said the ladies on the second floor get milk every day and whenever there's any left over, I can have it since I'm the youngest."

"My God, Mabel, you've got her wound up like an

eight day clock," the other woman said.

"I'm lucky to get this job," confided Jody. "I keep pinching myself to make sure it's true." She hurried to the chute with the bedclothes, then looked inside the clothes press for fresh linens. "I get up at five and start in the surgery at five-thirty. Have you seen the surgery yet?"

"Not yet." The two women glanced at each other.

"It's so beautiful! I have the surgery and the front five rooms, plus the hall, to clean. The steps, kitchen, and all—they're done by Emily, one of the girls who's waiting to have her baby."

"Working for her keep—like the old witch wanted me to do, I suppose."

"I guess. Emily's baby is due next week." Jody looked up from the sheet she was tucking neatly under the stained mattress. "How soon is your time?"

The girl called Mabel made a rude, snorting sound. "My time? Why we're both havin' our babies this morning, ain't we, Charity?" She winked at her friend. "You know what I think? I think we found us a real innocent."

"Why don't you leave her alone?" demanded the woman in the end bed. "If you were more like her, maybe you wouldn't be here."

"Mind your own business," snapped Mabel. "If I was as innocent as her, I'd have been here years ago!" She flounced onto her stomach.

The woman in the end bed looked at Jody sympathetically. "I went to surgery yesterday," she said. "But my baby died."

"Oh, I'm sorry," said Jody, ignoring another snort from Mabel's bed. Mama never had a doctor, she thought. If she'd had a real doctor, maybe she wouldn't have died.

"You're first, Mrs. Hartley." Kathleen spoke from

34

the doorway.

Mabel climbed out of bed. Her stomach curved gently beneath the white nightgown. Jody eyed her doubtfully. Each of the girls in the attic was heavy with child. Didn't all women get big and fat before the baby came? Mabel didn't look very big at all. What Mabel looked, suddenly, was very young and very scared. Jody touched her arm as she shuffled past. "If it's a girl, I hope she's as pretty as you are." Mabel didn't answer.

Jody hurriedly dressed the other beds and was soon back in the hallway. Each door she opened held new and glorious wonders. A pianoforte. A loo table. Twin mirrors edged in gilt. Then she opened the library door and gasped with joy. Shelf after shelf of books rose from wainscot to ceiling. On all four walls. Books everywhere. Oh, how she wished she had more time. This first day she really had to rush, because it was all so new, but she vowed that tomorrow she would take time to look at the books, maybe even read some.

Suddenly Jody remembered where she was. The clock on the mantel said five after one. She was supposed to be finished already and sitting down to midday supper with the other help. Well, even if she was late, she would sneak into the ward first to see Mabel's baby. She could hardly wait. She opened the ward door and peeked inside.

No babies? Where were the new babies kept? All seven women lay pale and listless now—even Mabel and the other girl who had been so lively this morning. Mabel's dark hair spread across the pillow, framing her still, white face. As Jody watched, she turned slightly, her mouth twisting in pain.

Jody touched her arm with a gentle hand. "Are you all right?"

The answer was a hoarse croak. "I'm okay."

"Where's your baby?"

Mabel's lids clanged shut. "The baby died."

"Oh!" Jody stroked the work-roughened hand. "I'm so sorry. Is there anything I can do?"

Mabel's head moved just once and lay still. Jody slipped out silently. Poor baby. Poor Mabel. To have her baby die like so many of Mama's. And even the doctor not able to help.

Jody had closed the ward door behind her and started down the hall when she remembered—she still had to empty the wicker basket. If she didn't hurry, she'd miss lunch.

She dashed down the back hall and skidded into the kitchen. The help was already seated around a large, circular table. She could smell beans and fresh-baked bread.

"Where are the newspapers? I forget where you said."

"In the pantry, behind the door," replied the Cook. "Slow down, child. Your supper'll be here when you get through."

"Be right back!"

The surgery was no longer clean and shiny as Jody had left it this morning at six-thirty. Now there was blood, like a hog killing—on the instruments—the floor—splattered across the padded table. Well, that was tomorrow's job. All Jody had to do now was wrap the garbage in newspapers and take it down to the cellar.

She found a clean spot on the floor to spread the papers and untied the burlap cover on the close-weave wicker basket.

She had thrown the burlap back and her hands had reached inside before she saw what lay at the bottom.

Her eyes bulged. Fierce pain twisted through her head. Then, just standing there, it was as if she moved out of her own body and became three separate people: one who stood back and watched it all happen, as in a picture; one who stared into the basket and saw the tangle of tiny arms and legs; and one who stood and screamed, and finally backed away, fingers clawing at distended eyes to rend the horror from them.

It was late afternoon when Jody awoke. A dull gray twilight peered through the dormer window above her cot. Her head ached. Her tongue furred in her mouth. She had a vague recollection of Kathie bending over her, forcing her to drink.

"I know it's hard the first time." Kathie's voice was sympathetic. "I should have told you. I never thought about you not knowing."

"At home . . ." stammered Jody, "in Ballareen . . . Pa put our babies in little boxes to bury them . . ." Most folks had used the churchyard, she remembered, but Mama's babies were always buried on the hill behind the house. Mama wanted them nearby, "not off with a lot of strangers."

Jody's hazel eyes crawled with pain. "I know things are done different here in America. But don't they have any place . . . to bury the poor little things?" A whimpering cry escaped, like the mewling of a kitten. She rolled toward the wall.

*Empty your mind, love.* It was Mama's voice, as real and clear as if she spoke straight into Jody's ear. *Make your mind an empty shell.*

She tried. But vivid, full-color pictures of the basket and its contents cavorted behind her hot lids. She lifted her hand to cover her eyes, and one tear crept down her smooth cheek. After a long time, she slept.

When she opened her eyes again, Kathie was

37

bending over her, shaking her shoulder. "Jody. The madame wants to see you in the office before supper."

Wearily, the girl rose to change. Hot and sweaty, she splashed her face with water and smoothed her red-gold hair.

The five young women who shared the garret with her were subdued this evening. Last night they had laughed and joked, like at an Irish wake. Tonight the wake had ended.

Jody made her way down the narrow, poorly lighted back stairs and through the back hall into the bright front entry. She knocked softly on the office door.

"Come." The doctor's voice was quiet, stern. She was seated at her writing desk, quill in hand. Jody stood just inside the door and waited.

At last Madame Restell swung about. Her face was in shadow. "Well. Have you quite recovered from your start?"

The girl didn't know how to answer. She had stopped screaming out loud if that was what the doctor meant by "recovered," but silent screams still pounded behind Jody's eyeballs and echoed in the chambers of her heart.

"I thought you had been toughened by all that has happened to you. Obviously I was wrong." Dr. Restell waited.

Jody could think of nothing to say.

"Well. If that's the way of it, so be it. You can leave at the end of the week. Until then you'll continue with your work, with the exception of the surgery. Kathleen can do that."

"Thank you, ma'am." Jody turned away. Inside her chest, her heart felt sore and hard. She thought it would squeeze in half and clatter to the floor. "I'm sorry, ma'am," she whispered.

"It's all right, child. You're young. You'll toughen in time."

Jody dragged herself through two more days before her appetite came back and she could manage a wan smile and a friendly word for the still suffering Mabel.

It was Friday and there was fried fish for supper, a great heaping platter of it. This was company night for the lying-in help, and there was much laughing and joking around the big kitchen table.

This evening, Emily's "young man" was to visit—for the first time in the five months she had been there. She was so anxious to see him, she overflowed her teacup and then dropped a bite of fish into it.

"How'd you expect me to act?" she demanded. "That blasted railroad thinks they owns my Frank. Like as not they'll want special dispensation from the pope afore he gits another night off."

Jody laughed with the others. As she looked around the table, she suddenly realized how much she would miss this friendly banter.

Meals at home, in Ballareen, had been such a happy time. She could still remember the easy talk, the feeling of closeness, the caring of those she loved, who loved her.

Now she was alone. Her only link with the past was her determination to keep her promise and become a physician. Was she going to turn tail now and run? As soon as she discovered something she didn't like about being a doctor? No! She had promised Mama. This was her chance to start on that promise—not the time to turn squeamish and creep off to hide her head as she used to do when she was a kid in Liverpool.

After supper, before taking her place on the small gilt chair beside the front door, Jody squared her slender shoulders and crossed swiftly to the doctor's office. Her knock was timid but determined.

"Come."

Jody's heart pounded unmercifully.

"Well."

"Madame Restell . . ." She wet her lips and began anew. "Madame Restell . . . I've come to ask . . . may I please stay?"

"Well. Why the change of heart?"

"I . . . I've *got* to be a doctor, that's why. I've just *got* to stay if you'll have me. I'm sorry for the way I carried on this morning. I'd like to stay. Really. I like it here."

The deep-set eyes bored into hers. "Well. Your hysteria certainly didn't indicate a liking, my dear."

"No, ma'am. I don't like that part of it."

"You want to talk about how you feel?"

"Well, you see . . . in Ireland . . . we buried our wee dead babies." Her eyes pleaded. "Can't you bury the wee ones here in New York?"

"Is *that* what troubled you?"

"Oh, yes, ma'am. I'm not Catholic like Pa who thought babies should be laid to rest in the churchyard. But Mama . . . and me . . . we always wanted them to rest easy, close by under the wild cherry trees behind the house. This way . . . here . . . I mean, it's like they . . ." Her voice sank to a soft sigh. "Like they were . . . garbage."

The doctor cleared her throat. "Yes. Well." She could sure put a lot of meaning into that one word, thought Jody. "Would you be content to work as we originally agreed—except for the basket?"

"Oh, yes, ma'am. I want to help the ladies."

"Very well." She cleared her throat again. "Whenever there is anything in the basket in the future, Perry will take care of it."

"Thank you, ma'am." Jody dropped a small curtsy and hurried to answer the bell. The first patient of the

40

evening had arrived.

As Jody showed the shy, cloak-wrapped woman into the doctor's office, she realized that Dr. Restell had not promised to bury any dead babies. All she had said was that in the future, Perry would empty the basket.

Jody shivered in the hot closeness of the office.

# 4

Jody fell quickly into the routine of Dr. Restell's establishment. By five-thirty each morning, dressed in her gray and white striped muslin uniform, she was ready to begin.

Once she had cleaned the surgery and left the haunting memories of the wicker basket behind, work went smoothly. She had one hour to tidy each room with fifteen minutes for tea at ten o'clock, but she skipped tea and rushed her cleaning to steal a few extra minutes in the library. After lunch she reported to Dr. Morceau, Madame Restell's husband, in the basement laboratory.

The laboratory consisted of one huge room with four long tables and several straight-backed chairs. A wall of shelves held an assortment of bottles, boxes, and jars. It wasn't long before Jody knew exactly which of the vials held Madame Restell's medicines and which were Dr. Morceau's. Madame's medicines were the interesting ones. Jody slid the magic-sounding words around her tongue: slippery elm, belladonna, ergot. Someday, she vowed. Some day.

When Jody arrived in the laboratory each afternoon, Mr. Trow, Madame Restell's brother, was busily gluing on labels while Dr. Morceau opened mail and separated it into stacks of orders and money.

Jody was a pill roller. The pills began with loaves of bread the cook gave her after lunch each day. It came fresh from the oven and smelled wonderful. Jody looked forward to this part of her job because she was permitted to eat the golden brown crust, and although she had just finished her noon meal, she could always eat more. "You've a hollow leg and no mistake," the cook would tease, laughing at the girl's healthy appetite.

"I've got a lot of catching up to do," Jody would reply.

She became quite adept at pinching exactly the right amount of dough from the soft white loaf and rolling it between her thumb and forefinger to produce small, even, pill-like pellets, which she then saturated with a peppermint-scented liquid.

Fourteen green bread pills and a set of directions went into each little brown box. The label on top, printed by the doctor and attached by Mr. Trow, read Dr. Morceau's Female Remedy. Jody was doubtful about the curative powers of anything that looked so pretty and smelled so heavenly.

By the time she climbed the stairs for supper each night, she was bone tired, with an evening of greeting patients and showing them into the office still ahead of her.

The nice part about the evening was that she got to sit in the hallway while she waited for the front doorbell to ring. The gilt chair was small and uncomfortable, but she used the time well.

She began at the left-hand corner of the lowest shelf in the library, and was systematically reading every book. By the end of the first week, she had read four. Then she began squeezing a few extra minutes each morning and taking books to the attic for a few treasured moments at night. By the end of the second week she had read ten. She had a long way to go.

The bell rarely rang during daylight hours. The few patients who arrived in the daytime came in elegant landaus pulled by horses in fancy harnesses. These ladies wore lovely gowns, feathered bonnets, and furs. They were inevitably haughty and accompanied by a loud bear of a man who was rude to Jody, and sometimes even to Madame Restell.

These rich day-ladies were ensconced in elaborate, silk-paneled rooms on the second floor. They often stayed a month or more and Susan, who worked up there, said they were real pains. "First it's water, then the chamber pot. And if it ain't the pot, it's to fluff their pillows. In the middle of the night even, they'll want bonbons or oysters, would ye believe. Always something." Each night Susan had stories to tell about something one of the "rich bitches" had said or done.

The other women, those who came after dark, were usually alone. They arrived on foot or in hired carriages. Whether well dressed or plain, they wore heavy veils and spoke softly in frightened voices, and were obviously grateful for the doctor's attentions.

Some of these well-dressed ladies stayed several months on the second floor before delivering their babies; some were sent to the first floor rear with the poorer women. None of the ward patients ever stayed more than a few days. And they always crept out at night, as they had come, silent and pale.

Rich day-ladies each took home a baby. Those who came at night did not.

All the babies were kept in the second-floor front. Jody heard them cry sometimes, but not often. There didn't seem to be many babies.

She quizzed Kathie about why the ward patients came at night and why they never slept upstairs and why their babies never lived, but Kathie told her to get on about her business. "You ask more questions than anybody I ever met," she said, pressing her fingers to the small of her back.

"How am I to learn unless I ask? It wouldn't hurt you to tell me, Kathie. Most of those women in the ward don't even look pregnant. And I've never seen any of them take a baby home. How come, Kathie?"

"They're sick, is why." She brushed the sweat from her forehead with the back of a puffy hand. "They're sick and they can't carry their babies full term. Now leave off with the questions, will you? You'll find out for yourself one of these days." She turned away, looking almost angry.

After Emily went home, an elegantly dressed lady came with her husband and disappeared into Madame Restell's office. They stayed a long time. Finally the doctor rang and asked to have Kathleen bring Emily's baby. As Jody turned to leave, she saw a huge pile of money on the doctor's desk.

Kathie came down the front steps and carried the baby boy into the office. Soon the couple came out, the woman holding the baby and cooing into his face. Emily's baby had been adopted, but Jody didn't know why.

She didn't understand why the girls in the attic always gave their babies up for adoption. She knew now that Emily and Frank hadn't been married, and she supposed Emily's husband had died after she got the baby in her stomach, but Jody couldn't be rude enough to ask. She did question Kathie about her own husband, but Kathie only looked at her strangely and snapped out, "Oh, don't be so daft, Jody!" and stomped off, furious.

Jody felt especially sorry for the young women in the first floor rear. She wondered how the doctor always knew ahead of time that the baby wasn't going to live.

45

Each time Madame Restell said to Jody, "Take Mrs. Smith to the first floor rear," Jody knew the woman's baby would be born dead, and her heart was wrung with wanting to help and not being able.

Only one visitor came regularly to Dr. Restell's establishment. The first time she met him, Jody had been working there almost a month. She was on her knees, scrubbing the front hall when the bell rang. Quickly hiding the bucket behind the gilt chair, she smoothed the gray and white striped skirt and hurried to the door.

The first thing she noticed about their caller was how white his muttonchop whiskers looked against his black broadcloth coat.

"Well, well, well. What have we here?" The man's cheeks puffed out beside his great red beak of a nose, and his little black eyes squinted as he let out a merry chuckle.

"Good morning, sir."

"I am Nicholas Quimby, Madame Restell's lawyer. I have an appointment. And who might you be, little lady?"

"Jody Gates, sir."

"Not one of the madame's patients, surely."

Jody had to smile. "Oh, no, sir. I'm not married." She dropped her eyes as he continued to study her. "This way, sir."

Quimby was with Madame Restell almost an hour, and when he came out, Jody was sitting at the long library table, reading. She didn't hear the door open and didn't realize he was there until he let out an elfinlike chuckle. She jumped to her feet, cheeks scarlet, and hid the book behind her back.

Quimby thought he had never seen such a pretty little piece in all his life. "I'm not married," she had said, as though marriage were a prerequisite for

46

Saturday night fun. What a sweet innocent morsel this one would be. No pockmarks either. The girl had skin like an apricot, creamy peach in color and smooth beyond description. His fingers itched to tangle in those long, sleek, red-gold curls. "Is that a book you're hiding?"

"I finished my work early, sir. It's fifteen minutes yet till I go upstairs." She pulled the book from behind her back and quickly restored it to the shelf. "I didn't mean any harm."

"Don't apologize, child. 'Tis a real pleasure to see a youngen who likes to read. My Anne, now—she's about your age and we can't get her near a book."

The girl stared at him, her hazel eyes wide. What a pretty thing she was—tall and slim—just beginning to bud beneath that ugly uniform, he'd wager. "Don't be afraid. I'll not say anything about your reading madame's books." He chuckled again. "Who taught you to read, child?"

"My mother. She gave me lessons." Jody picked up her bucket and cleaning rags.

"How old are you?"

"Fourteen."

He could feel the saliva start up in his mouth. "A year younger than my Anne."

Jody liked his white whiskers and his big red beak of a nose. And she liked his merry laugh and his round belly. And she liked the smell of his thick black cigar. She thought how nice it would be to have a jolly kind of a father like this. Pa had been jolly once. Oh, how Pa used to make her laugh.

Mr. Quimby came often after that, almost always arriving while Madame Restell was still in surgery. "I'll wait," he would say, then hand Jody his walking stick, gloves, and tall silk hat, and watch her place them on the marble-topped hall table.

47

"I'll wait in the library," he would announce, knowing full well by now that she was in the library each day from eleven-fifteen to twelve forty-five. If she had not finished her cleaning, he would sit and watch, one finger gently massaging the inner edge of his parted lips, the other hand kneading his thigh with a delicate, unobtrusive motion.

Jody got used to his being there and the unease she felt at first gradually disappeared.

When she finished her work and gathered her rags and bucket, he would smile his eye-squinty smile and say, "Don't run off, child. Stay a minute and keep an old man company."

Then, while she listened with wide-eyed wonder, he would talk. He had been all over the world, and he told her stories about places and people she had met only in books and newspapers.

Other times he asked about her life—where she had grown up, what it was like in Ireland when the potato blight struck.

"I was little," replied Jody, "but I remember one old man—spread out flat on the ground, he was, foaming green at the mouth from eating grass. I remember I wanted to give him food, but Pa pulled me away and said we didn't have enough for our own mouths."

"And your pa was right. You got to think of yourself sometimes, Jody."

"It was bad everywhere. The English troops came and dragged the O'Neills right out into the road. Meghan O'Neill was my best friend." Jody's face clouded, remembering. "They threw the furze off Meghan's house and tore down the sod walls. And then the O'Neills roofed over the ditch alongside our house and moved into it. Most families had to live in ditches and scalpeens after the troops came."

"Ah, the trouble you've seen for one so young and

sweet." Quimby's eyes never left her face as she talked, and he never interrupted as adults were prone to do, but listened as though her every word were important to him.

He sounded her out about her life at Madame Restell's, and clucked over her long hours and hard labor.

"Oh, I don't mind the work, sir. I'm strong. And I like helping the ladies when they're sick," she said. "Of course, I'd like more time to read. There's so much I don't know. I want to be a doctor someday, like Madame Restell."

"You have a kind heart," he said, twinkling at her.

Sometimes he would compare his new home on Madison Avenue with Madame Restell's house. His library, he said, was three times the size of this one. He wished Jody could see it one day. She wished she could, too.

He talked often about his family. Anne, an only child, had been delicate from birth. Mrs. Quimby spoiled her, he said. Understandable, he supposed, considering Anne's delicate constitution. "Ah, I wish we had been fortunate enough to have two daughters. Then poor Anne wouldn't be so much alone. Someday, perhaps we could arrange something . . ."

Jody didn't remember when he began talking as if she really were going to see his house one day, but suddenly she realized that he was no longer saying "if you could see my house" but "when you come to my house." Not "if you ever meet Anne" but "when you meet Anne."

Mr. Quimby became a frequent visitor, usually never getting past the library where Jody worked. The girl wondered if he really came to see her instead of Madame Restell, then laughed at her own simple vaporings. Why would an old man like Mr. Quimby come to see her?

Time passed quickly, and Emily's bed under the eaves was soon occupied by another pregnant girl named Helen who whined and complained and never did her share of the work.

On the first of September, Susan went home. Her baby was adopted the next day. Mary and Eileen left that same week, without babies. Both cried when they said good-bye. Neither responded to Jody's attempts at comfort.

Then two more couples came to adopt. Though Jody knew the little ones were getting good homes, her heart ached for the mothers who had left empty armed. She supposed they were all so poor, their husbands so down and out, they couldn't even afford one more small mouth to feed. She realized that poverty—real poverty—was no place to bring a child, but when parents couldn't even afford to take them home, why did God send so many babies?

The new girl, the whiner, was more of a hindrance than a help. With all the others gone except Kathie and Jody, work began to pile up. Four patients on the second floor demanded constant attention, and there were nine in the ward. For three days, Jody and Kathie fetched and carried and scrubbed and hustled, from one chore to the next. Seeing that Kathie was near collapse, Jody tried to do more than her share.

On Friday night, two new girls moved into the attic room, and Jody breathed a sigh of relief. Tomorrow things would let up a bit, she thought, never guessing that the heavy lifting and endless trips up the stairs would bring on Kathie's labor.

They had been asleep for hours that night when Kathie cried out. Jody was instantly on her feet, feeling her way across the dark room.

"Kathie? What is it?"

"I got pains. I think my water broke."

Oh, dear Lord! Jody thought. That was what had happened to Mama on the ship. First the water and then that awful flowing of blood.

"Aaaaaah!" It was a sharp cry of utter anguish. Fingers shaking, Jody felt for candle and lucifers.

Kathleen was bent double on the cot, her hands clutching her distended stomach. In the flickering light, her open mouth and ragged heaving breath brought back Mama and the ship in sharp, jolting pictures.

Jody bent over the bed. "Shall I go wake madame? Can you get to the surgery all right?"

"Jody, wait."

She bent close.

Kathie's words came haltingly, interspersed with shallow pants and gasps of pain. "If anything happens . . . to me . . . you take my things. There's nobody else"

"Simple! Nothing's going to happen to you. Anyhow," she said, trying to make a joke, "your clothes wouldn't fit me."

"Promise, Jody . . . I've got nobody else . . . if anything happens, I don't . . . don't want them others . . . pawin' over my things."

"I promise."

Jody lit a second candle, sheltered it with her hand, and ran.

She pelted down the narrow backstairs, almost falling in her haste. She skidded through the second floor back hall and into the front where a wide corridor ran the length of the house, with doors on both sides.

Her candle had long since blown out, but the gaslights in the front halls burned all night in case of emergency. She had never been to the third floor front before, but she slid around the corner and raced up the second flight with no hesitation. She had made the turn

51

on the landing when she heard a noise above. Madame Restell, in a long black robe, looking as neat and prim as ever, was leaning over the railing. In the flickering gaslight she appeared old and grim, like one of the crones at Five Points.

"What is it, Jody?"

"It's Kathie, ma'am. Her water broke. She's on her way down to surgery."

"I'll only be a minute. Go down and light the lamps. You'll have to help me tonight."

"Yes, ma'am." Despite her worry over Kathie, Jody's heart sang. Tonight she would help in surgery. She was on her way.

# 5

"She's not even started to dilate," said Madame. "She'll be hours yet." Having so proclaimed, she went back to bed.

It was Jody who sat on the hard chair beside Kathie's bed in the ward; Jody who lay beside her friend to hold her close; Jody whose hand was pulled and crushed, and with each wrenching pain, bruised until it was swollen almost double in size.

"Don't leave me," Kathie pleaded.

"Shhh. I won't leave."

Often, as Jody sat through the long night and the next day, it was not Kathie's putty-colored face she sponged, but her mother's. Each eye-bulging scream, each plea for water, each punishing pull upon Jody's already swelling hand was a torturous reminder of the old sailing ship and the last hours of her mother's life.

In the past few weeks Jody thought she had become inured to the shrieks that sometimes ripped through the house when madame was in surgery with a ward patient—or when one of the lying-in ladies gave birth, and screams could be heard all the way to the attic. But this was different. This was too much like Mama—too much and too close and too hurtful.

After twenty-two hours of inexpressible torture, with one mighty final push, the dry birth was accomplished, and Kathie breathed her last.

Taking the child from madame and gently wrapping it in a blanket, Jody's heart battled between the sadness of death and the joy of new life. In that moment, holding Kathie's little girl, the deathbed promise Jody made the year before became not a promise to her mother, but a sacred vow unto herself. If she had been to the well of truth when she made the promise, now she was swept to the very headwaters of justice. Something inexplicably fine had come of Kathie's death. Jody had lost a friend but gained a reason for being. No matter what happened from here on out, no matter how impossible it looked now, or how difficult it might prove in the future, Jody knew she would be a doctor.

Feeling the urge to preserve the knowledge she had gained, she slipped out to the stationer's on the corner to buy a journal. That night, she made her first careful entries, recording everything she could remember, everything she had learned and observed during her twenty-two hour vigil at Kathie's side.

With Kathie gone, madame split the surgery duties. Jody would help deliver babies for the rich ladies on the second floor; Helen, and the new girl, would help with ward patients. Jody was sick with disappointment. She ached to know how the doctor relieved the ward ladies of their babies, but all she could do was watch and wait.

"You need a day out," the cook scolded. "You're lookin' pale as blue john." But Jody merely smiled and spent another day off in the library.

September drifted into October. Mrs. Smith gave birth, and Jody made extensive notes in her journal. All her free moments were spent in the library now, devouring books with a single-minded purpose that finally drew comment from Madame Restell: "Go out once in a while and enjoy yourself, girl. You've earned it."

But it was Mr. Quimby, arriving in his blue phaeton with its prancing matched grays and its liveried black coachman, who finally persuaded her. "Come for a ride and soak up a bit of sunshine," he urged.

"Oh, Mr. Quimby, it wouldn't look proper for me to go riding with you." But the temptation to sit in a fine carriage like a fine lady was too great. She already knew she would go.

"Not proper?" he sputtered. "Nonsense! Fresh air and sunshine will put the roses back in your cheeks."

She gazed past him, her eyes drinking in the fine carriage and the black, stiff-spined coachman. "Are you sure you won't be ashamed to have me ride with you?"

"Ashamed?" Quimby's white side whiskers bristled with indignation. "Not a bit of it! I'll be as puffed as a peacock."

"Then I'll just run and change." She had purchased one dress. It wasn't fancy, but it reached the floor and made her feel almost a grown-up lady.

"Hold on there a minute." Quimby's eyes twinkled at her, and she suddenly realized he was concealing something behind his back. "I was afraid you might be too proud to go riding in your own clothes, so I brought you something." He whisked a package from behind him, a large package that a less corpulent man could not have hidden so easily.

Jody gasped. He had bought her a dress! How well she knew she couldn't accept his gift—and how much she wanted to take it.

He sensed her indecision. "Now Jody, child, I know it's improper for a young lady to accept gifts from a man, but this is different. It isn't as though I were a suitor, you know. I look upon you as my second daughter, and I want to be proud of you when we take

55

our outings." She still looked doubtful so he hurried on: "You know how I've been saying that you should meet my girl, Annie? Well, she's agreed to come with us on your day off next Monday. We'll go somewhere special. But I must warn you. Anne's like her mother—given to overestimating the importance of first impressions." His black eyes twinkled. "That's why I want you to look your best. I want to make sure you two girls hit it off." He placed the package in Jody's hesitant arms.

Ten minutes later, when she came back, she had been transformed into a sky-blue nymph with a tight-fitting bodice and a full-hooped skirt. Quimby licked his lips. Beneath a matching blue bonnet, the girl's lovely face shone, more from happiness than from the brisk scrubbing she had given it.

The coachman lowered the steps, and Mr. Quimby handed her into the blue phaeton. She couldn't believe it was happening.

They swirled down Chambers and wheeled into the great roaring thoroughfare that was Broadway. Lumbering wagons vied with sleek coaches and fancy carriages and horse-drawn trolleys. Bulletin wagons advertised Chatham Theatre and Gosling's Restaurant. The sidewalks were rivers of finely dressed gentlemen and beautiful ladies in wide-skirted silk gowns and feathered bonnets. On every corner newsboys hawked their papers.

New York was a gawdy, sprawling metropolis with Broadway running, long and straight, through the center. The dizzily rushing street, glutted with vehicles, invariably made Jody's pulse beat faster. Now she was actually a part of it, and these beautiful people were nodding at Mr. Quimby—and eyeing her with curiosity and—yes, with admiration! She couldn't help being thrilled by all the new sensations—even the malodorous Fulton Fish Market and the oyster bar, which

Mr. Quimby assured her was the latest rage. Jody liked the oyster stew, but the smell of the place brought back memories of the ship and her mother's death.

He took Jody to Third Avenue to watch the pacers and trotters work out on the open dirt road that stretched from above Astor Place all the way to Harlem Bridge. And just before they went home, they stopped to buy hot corn from one of the street vendors, something Jody's mouth had watered for this past year and a half in New York.

It was a full, exciting day, one that was to be repeated, with variations, time and again, over the next several months. Quimby escorted her to Barnum's Museum and to Sweets Restaurant, and twice she waited in the phaeton while he visited different banks and emerged huffing and puffing under the weight of bulging leather bags, which were then deposited in his office on lower Braodway.

Quimby and Parmenter, Attorneys at Law, the gold-lettered window proclaimed. Waiting in the carriage, Jody wondered if his transfer of gold was brought on by the bank closing she had read about in the *Tribune* that morning. She also wondered why the rotund little man no longer talked about his daughter, but she didn't ask either question.

Her life was going too smoothly, and in the back of her mind, an idea germinated: Perhaps Mr. Quimby could arrange an apprenticeship for her with another doctor.

Jody was learning as much as she could from Madame Restell and her library, but it wasn't fast enough. If she was apprenticed to a doctor, she might earn a certificate, she realized. And by now she had begun to suspect there was something strange about Madame Restell's medical practice—and certainly something dishonest about the order-by-mail business conducted in the basement of the old brownstone.

Winter had come and gone, mild spring days given way to the muggy discomfort of summer in the city, when Mr. Quimby finally kept his promise.

"It's a special day, Jody," the lawyer announced as he entered the library where she sat reading, waiting for him. "Annie's with me and we're all going on a picnic."

Jody almost giggled. She couldn't imagine this tubby little man squatting on the grass to eat. She had taken supper with him many times now, and she knew the extent of his appetite, the discrimination of his palate, and his predilection for fine linens and silver and candlelight. "I hope your daughter likes me," she said, stifling the giggle.

Anne, waiting in the carriage, was not at all what Jody had imagined. Instead of thin and languid, Anne Quimby was plump and sturdy, with a stiff back and a persimmon face. She had black, carefully coiffed hair. Her eyes were black too, like her father's, but without his twinkle. Anne's eyes stared resentfully past Jody, two polished ebony stones sliding arrogantly down a prow of a nose, lips compressed so tightly that they were practically nonexistent. Jody's hopes for a friendship plummeted.

"Annie, this is Jody Gates I've been telling you so much about. Jody, this young snippet is my daughter, Anne."

"Hello, Anne."

"How do you do." Anne's voice was no less icy than the lace-mitted fingers that touched Jody's with such obvious distaste.

Jody supposed the other girl's resentment was natural. Anne was a lady—refined—with all the advantages money bought. Jody was a nobody from the slums of Five Points. She climbed miserably into the carriage and wished she were back inside the safe anonymity of the house on Chambers Street.

It fell to Mr. Quimby to carry the conversation, with Jody commenting softly when called upon and Anne speaking not at all.

Jones Woods nodded sleepily in the hot sunlight. Sam, the black coachman, spread a large blanket for the girls to sit upon—and a large chair for the portly barrister.

Then came the food. Hampers stuffed with delicacies: cold lobster aspic, deviled soft roe on squares of dry toast, tiny sandwiches of potted salmon, dates, and fresh fat peaches smothered in cream. It was a feast fit for a king, and if Mr. Quimby was an uneasy monarch, he managed to conceal it admirably as he chuckled and joked and tried to draw the girls into conversation. Anne, with obvious perversity, grew more remote as the afternoon progressed.

Luncheon over, Quimby was beginning to nod over his claret when Anne suddenly jumped to her feet and announced she was going for a walk. Jody looked from one to the other, then stood reluctantly. "I'll go with you," she said.

The two girls crossed the meadow. When they entered the shade of budding maples and tall oaks, Anne stopped abruptly, her face stiff with determination. She whirled about and faced Jody. "Are you sleeping with my father?" she demanded.

Jody gasped. "Am I doing what?"

"Fucking my father. Are you?"

Although she hadn't the faintest idea of Anne's meaning, Jody realized that she had just been accused of something unspeakably vile. She had heard the word before, knew it was something only low people did and nice people didn't even discuss. "Snakes of St.

Patrick," she burst out.

"With all that red hair," Anne said in a voice that dripped contempt, "I should have known you were an Irisher."

Jody's temper flared then: "Yes, and proud of it. Who do you think you are anyhow? Just because you're lucky enough to have a rich . . ." Her voice faded uncertainly as Anne's expression altered.

"You think I'm lucky to have *him* for a father?" Her face congealed with hatred as she stared over her shoulder at her father who nodded benevolently in the sun, white hair stirring lightly in the breeze and muttonchop whiskers splayed across his black collar.

Why, she's unhappy, thought Jody. How could anybody be unhappy when she had so much? "Your father's been very good to me," she said finally.

The other girl made a rude noise in her throat.

"Well, he has. He's taken me riding, and to luncheon sometimes, and Barnum's and the like. But that's *all*. He says he's asked you to come along . . ." Her voice ground to a halt as Anne's black eyes swung resentfully.

"He tell you that you're taking my place because I'm not a good daughter to him? Is that what he's saying? Oh, that bastard! That dirty, lying, toad bastard."

Anne's language shocked Jody. Not that she hadn't heard such words before—they were legion in Five Points—but to hear them pour from the pink lips of this sedate young woman—and her hateful attack on her father who was so kind.

They walked in silence then, each wrapped in her own thoughts. Occasionally Anne cast calculating glances at Jody, as though trying to judge the truth of her relationship with Quimby. "I'm sorry for what I said about you being Irish," she said at last. "I'm Irish descent myself. Half, anyway."

"That's all right," replied Jody grudgingly.

"Papa said you've only lived here two years. How come you don't speak with an Irish brogue? You sound British."

"My mother was English." Jody could have explained that her mother was the daughter of an English lord, that she had eloped with her father's young horse trainer, accompanied him back to his beloved Ireland, and been disowned. But having learned that few people accepted the truth, Jody kept silent now about her ancestry. "Mama taught me to read and write and cipher," she said smiling at the memory. "We only had two books—the Bible and Shakespeare's complete works. I used to read them aloud, over and over, so I could practice speaking like her."

"Is your mother dead?"

Jody nodded, pain knifing through her. "Two years ago."

"My mother might as well be dead, too, for all the good she is to me." Anne's words carried more defiance than regret. "How'd you meet my father?"

"He's the doctor's lawyer—the doctor I work for."

"That where we picked you up?"

Jody nodded. "Madame Restell gives me Mondays off—"

"Who's Madame Restell? The doctor's wife?"

"No, she's the doctor. At the lying-in hospital where you picked me up."

Ann stopped in her tracks and turned an incredulous face. "You work for *Madame Killer?*"

"I work at a lying-in asylum. I don't know what you mean. Who's Madame Killer?"

"Madame Killer—Madame Restell—everybody knows about her. Why, she's no doctor. She's an abortionist. I've heard the servants talk. All the ladies

61

go to Madame Killer when they want to get rid of their babies. I've heard tell her backyard is stuffed full of bodies."

Jody's heart pounded against her ribs. "What's an abortionist?" she demanded.

"She cuts the babies up and pulls them out of women's stomachs. Then she buries them in her backyard—all the babies and the women who don't live through her doctoring. That's why they call her Madame Killer."

Shock and denial were physical blows, yet with sudden clarity, Jody knew the other girl spoke the truth. Not about the backyard, but about the babies. It was so obvious now: the women who came and went only by dark; those in the ward who never took babies home; the wicker basket.

No wonder no one would tell me anything, thought Jody. They're all ashamed of what they do. Madame Restell hasn't found the magic secret for helping women—she's found the magic formula for making money.

"Jody . . ." Anne's black eyes were wary, but warming slightly now with sympathy. "Don't cry."

"I'm not going to cry." Jody clamped her teeth hard on her lower lip.

"I am sorry," Anne said. "I've got a big mouth and no mistake. Ryecroft's been telling me that for years. I didn't mean to get you all upset."

Anne's voice went on and on, but Jody was fighting her own demons. Had Madame Restell actually killed all those babies? Is that what went on in the surgery? Why had they kept it secret from her—all the long string of girls who had shared the attic room with her this past year? In a whole year, why had she never guessed? How could she have been so stupid? And how could she stay at the house on Chambers Street now that she knew?

Anne was still talking. "You're not responsible for what Madame Killer does, you know. It's not like you're doing the abortions. You just work there. What kind of work do you do for her anyhow?"

"I'm sorry. What?"

"What kind of work do you do?"

"I help deliver babies. And I—"

"You help with the babies?" Incredulity now, mixed with a grudging admiration.

"The *live* ones." Jody's voice was bitter. "I thought I could learn doctoring from her. I didn't know about the rest of it."

"Well, it's like I said—you're not responsible for what she does. Nobody is responsible for what others do. We're not even responsible for what others make us do sometimes. That's what I think. Sometimes we have to do things we know are bad, but we don't have any choice 'cause they're forced on us. You believe that, don't you, Jody?"

Through her own worry, Jody could sense the plea in the other girl's voice. Anne was asking for herself—begging Jody to understand and accept something that had nothing at all to do with Madame Restell and her activities. "Yes, of course," she agreed automatically.

"I'm sorry I was so nasty before," Anne said. "I thought—well, it doesn't matter what I thought—I'm glad I came today. I hope we see each other again, Jody."

"What? Oh, I'm sure we will. Your father comes every Monday." Her eyes clouded. "Only maybe I won't be there after today. How can I work there now that I know? I want to help women, but I don't want to kill babies." The wicker basket flared in her mind, and she fought a hot rush of angry tears.

Before the other girl could answer, they heard a

63

rustling in the woods behind them. Turning, Jody quickly dried her eyes as she saw Sam coming toward them.

"Mr. Quimby, he says to come on now. He's ready to go, Miss Anne."

"We're just coming." Anne squeezed Jody's hand consolingly. "Don't you worry," she whispered as they recrossed the meadow. "It's not your fault what Madame Killer does."

Hampers and blankets and chair were already repacked, Quimby waiting impatiently. "Come, girls," he said, hustling them into the carriage. "We have a big afternoon ahead of us."

The blue phaeton with its prancing matched grays and its liveried black coachman swept impressively back toward the city, but Jody's pleasure in the day was not to be rekindled. "Mr. Quimby, I know you've gone to a lot of trouble to plan a nice day for Anne and me, but if you don't mind, I'd like to go home now."

"Did this youngen of mine say something—"

"I told her about Madame Killer," interrupted Anne sharply.

His eyes narrowed. "Why you young—I'll take care of you when we get home," he snapped, his black eyes smoldering.

"For telling the truth?" Anne's voice was harsh.

"I'm sorry to cause so much trouble," said Jody. "But I'd really like to go back now. I have to talk to the—to Madame Restell."

Half an hour later, she stood before the office door, trying to collect her thoughts before knocking.

"Come." The doctor looked up, placidity giving way to consternation as she saw Jody's white face. "What is it? Sit down, child. You look positively ill."

Jody lowered herself stiffly to the edge of the sofa. Her hands twisted in her lap. "I know I've no right to ask you any question, madame. But last year when you saved Kathie's baby . . . I thought you were the most wonderful person in the world. I've thought so ever since. I vowed then that when I became a doctor, I'd be just like you." Her hand flew up to cover her mouth, and she turned her head away sharply.

"Well. You have heard something that made you change your mind?"

Their eyes met and there was regret in the madame's eyes, but no shame.

"They call you Madame Killer!" The words burst from Jody, more a plea than an accusation.

"And flock to me for help." Quick bitterness and anger loomed, a black cloud in the sunny room. "What would you have a woman do when she finds out she's pregnant with a child she can't possibly support? Or when she knows her father will throw her out of the house—and 'nice' ladies pull their skirts aside when she passes."

Jody didn't know exactly what she meant, but it didn't matter. All that mattered were the babies in the basket. "They could do like Emily," she said. "And like Susan and Eileen. They could go full term. Then you could put the babies up for adoption. You could do it that way. Oh, Madame Restell, I want to understand. What is it you do to the ward patients?"

The doctor lifted her chin. "I abort the fetus." She saw the uncertainty on Jody's face. "Cause the fetus to be expelled before its time."

"Why? Are they sick? Would they die like Mama if you didn't . . . abort the fetus? Is that why, Madame Restell?"

"I told you why. Because they come to me to get rid of their mistakes. Now you've asked, I'll not lie to you. It's time you learned—time you grew up and faced facts."

65

There was silence in the room as Jody's thoughts tumbled.

The doctor sat down. "Listen," she said, leaning forward earnestly, "young as you are, you have a way about you that most girls don't have. You're good with the ladies. You're quick and you're willing. Now you say you want to be a doctor. Well, I tell you that you can stay here and work with me if you want." She laid her hand on Jody's skirt. "I need an assistant. I'm going to build a big lying-in hospital soon. Uptown. Right in the middle of all those women who come to me for help and then turn up their noses when they pass me on the street. I'm going to put my hospital on Fifth Avenue. Right in the middle of their fancy houses. Are you listening, Jody?"

"The ladies in the ward *aren't* sick as Kathie said, are they? They'd have live babies if you just left them alone, wouldn't they?"

"Of course they would." Madam sounded annoyed now. "But they can't take their woods colts home. That's why they come to me." She rubbed her long nose with impatient fingers. "It's time you grew up, Jody. You're such an innocent. I can see now it was a mistake to keep you that way so long. You say you want to be a doctor? Well, here's your chance."

Jody fought the scream that rose in her throat. "What is it you do to those women in the ward?" she demanded.

"I'll tell you what I do. Then you tell me if you want to be my assistant and move out of the attic and into a nice room on the third floor front. With a good raise in pay." Her voice low and emotionless, the doctor explained in detail about the "crochet" and exactly how it was used to extract the fetus from the birth canal, and how to pack the vagina with alum paste, and dose the patient with laudanum.

Jody's head ached. The sun had gone behind a cloud and the room crawled with dirty, dun-colored shadows. Over and over the refrain slashed through her head. She *did* kill those babies. She cut them up just like Anne said—with her crochet, her curette.

A small, unwelcome question nagged deep in Jody's mind. *No*, she answered fiercely. No, this *couldn't* be the way God had sent for her to find. Could it?

And even as her heart rejected, her mind registered Madame Restell's words, filed away the techniques of abortion—the instruments—the drugs—

"Well? Would you like to learn my trade? You'll be a rich woman one day."

"But they're babies. Real babies. And you *did* kill them." Jody was screaming now, but she didn't care. "How could you, Madame Restell? How *could* you?"

The abortionist reared back as though struck. "They're not babies until the quickening," she snapped. Then she talked on, her voice hard as she explained about trimesters and the fetus and the child that is not yet a child because it has not yet quickened.

"But I saw them."

"I'll not defend myself before a fifteen-year-old chit of a girl," the doctor exclaimed. She smoothed her bombazine dress with agitated fingers. "If you don't like my offer, you can take your impertinent questions and get out."

The room pulsed with her anger as she waited for Jody to speak. But Jody had no words to express her horror.

"Well," said Madame Restell at last. "Quimby's been after me for a year to give you to him. He can jolly well have you. Just don't come back to me when you've a brat in your belly." She opened a drawer and pulled out

67

a paper banknote. "Here's your week's wages and more. Go and good riddance." She turned a stiff, proud back and stared into the dust-swirled street.

The white-haired lawyer was perched on the hall settee, hat and stick in hand. Jody was grateful that he had waited.

He moved toward her. "Was it bad?"

"She gave me the sack."

His eyes gleamed; he appeared almost happy. "Why don't you just come home to Quimby House with Anne and me?"

She looked full at him then, her eyes on a level with his, for she was tall and he was not. She swallowed and the sound was loud in the empty hall. "What about your wife? What would she say if you brought home a stray like me?"

"Mrs. Quimby's in Newport for the summer, taking the waters. There's only Anne and me—and with her mother away, Anne could use the company."

"But Madame Restell—will she dismiss you because of me?"

"Lord no, child." His voice dropped to a conspiratorial whisper. "She needs me. She'll be back in court one of these days. She's been there before, you know."

"Could you wait while I get my things and say good-bye to the cook and Perry?"

"I'll wait in the carriage. When Mrs. Quimby's out of town, we have no set schedule."

He's too kind, said the little voice within her—too happy about her predicament—too willing to help.

But she couldn't stay here, that much was certain. She had learned all she wanted to learn from Madame Restell. It was time to move on.

When Jody returned with her mother's carpetbag, stuffed now with Kathie's things as well as her own, Quimby took it with an exaggerated gallantry and escorted her to the waiting carriage.

"Jody's going home with us to Quimby House," he told his daughter as Sam lowered the steps. "She's going to stay with us awhile."

Anne stared from one to the other, and her eyes widened in horror.

# 6

Quimby House towered above the southeast corner of Madison and Thirty-fifth, a two-storied, hip-roofed Amazon, ruler of all it surveyed. Its green-lawned skirts were hemmed with a wrought-iron fence. One set of steps mounted to plant-laced grass, another to a Greek-columned portico. Mullioned sidelights framed carved double doors, and graceful pillars supported a balcony on the second level.

Inside, a huge entry hall, twenty-eight feet high, was surrounded by a balcony and dominated by a lead-crystal chandelier. Dozens of candles highlighted the exquisite Aubusson carpet centered on the white marble floor. Four marble columns flanked a magnificent marble stairway which curved away from the landing on each side and formed two separate sets of steps to the next level. The large landing, overlooking a lovely box-garden, was illuminated by gaslights set into pale blue damask walls.

Jody's room—her very own—was the first door at the top of the left staircase. Anne's was directly across the wide hall.

Past the chandelier, on the other side of the balcony-rimmed cathedral ceiling, were separate bedrooms for Mr. and Mrs. Quimby, accessible by the other staircase or the balcony.

Water closets graced every floor, and speaking tubes connected each room with the kitchen and servants' quarters. Jody thought she had never seen nor heard of anything so grand.

"This is my room," Anne announced, flinging open a door.

Jody gasped. The elaborately carved furniture fairly exploded in varying colors of rosewood—from dark red to sunset orange. But it was Anne's doll collection that drew Jody's astonished eyes. Dolls were strewn about the room—dozens of them—from every country in the world, dressed in rich, colorful costumes.

"This one's papier-mâché from Paris, made by Madame Lebas." Anne pointed. "And here—this is one of Wickelpuppen's *poupards*." She laughed. "Wow, that's hard to say!"

"They're all so lovely."

Jody gazed so long and so longingly at one beautifully dressed kid doll that Anne picked it up. "I call this one Amelia, after my mother. That's because she has so many dresses. Here." She held the doll out to Jody. "You can have her if you want."

"Oh, I couldn't do that," Jody said, looking wistfully at the pretty porcelain face. "She's beautiful, but I couldn't keep her."

Ann stared distastefully at the doll then tossed it carelessly aside. "Mama bought all of these—I don't know why she doesn't just keep them. But she collects thimbles."

"What does your father collect?" She smiled. "Strays like me?"

"He collects paperweights." Anne's face tightened.

Jody looked around the room. "Where does that door go?" she asked, pointing.

"To the front balcony. It looks out on Madison Avenue. Come on, you'll want to see your room."

71

"Will your mother be away long?" Jody asked as they walked across the hall.

"Until Thanksgiving. She takes the waters in Newport all summer, then goes to visit Aunt Helen in Boston."

Anne threw open the other door, and Jody emitted a long sigh of pure delight. "Ooooh!"

The walls were pale pink silk patterned with tiny leaf sprigs and periwinkles. The same blue floral design, in crewel embroidery, was etched on champagne-colored drapes, bedspread, and canopy. There was a serpentine-fronted dressing chest topped with white marble, an elegant toilet table with an adjustable looking-glass above, and a small upholstered couch.

"Like it?"

"Oh, it's beautiful! And so big—so roomy."

"It has to be. With dresses like these, we couldn't even move without lots of space." Ann spun and her wide skirts swirled. "You'll need some new clothes, Jody. Why, I bet you don't have any more than five petticoats under that skimpy skirt."

"Four."

"You couldn't even make cheese!"

"What do you mean, make cheese?"

"Don't you know? Watch." Anne dimpled as she twirled, skirts and petticoats flaring, then sat quickly to form a pretty circle of her garments, like a wheel of cheese. "Nice girls don't do that in front of boys anymore. But boys will still try to get you to do it so they can see your ankles."

Anne was a different person when not with her father. Now that she was no longer playing the haughty young heiress, her eyes were merry, and she fairly danced with good humor and the pleasure of Jody's company.

It came as a surprise then, when they went down to

dinner that evening, to see Anne turn quiet and moody again, and to see her pick at the delicious food.

The long pedestal dining table had been set with Quimby at the head, Anne and Jody at each side, about halfway down; but he promptly ordered the serving girl to move the settings closer, so that they were all together at one end. "No sense in shouting at each other." He twinkled at Jody.

Miniature roses patterned the china plates. The water goblet, deeply hand cut in smoky gray crystal, drew Jody's admiring fingers.

"They're from Ireland," said Quimby. "Waterford glass. Pretty, ain't they?"

"Beautiful."

Supper was served by a thin, pale girl, not as old as Jody, who sidled in and out of the room. A huge tureen of thick hot asparagus soup with fat-sliced leeks floating on top, roast duck stuffed with oysters riding on a silver platter, and great silver bowls of steaming vegetables were all placed on the sideboard, then served by the trembling child.

The girl had cleared the entree plates and was nervously placing a plum torte in front of Mr. Quimby when her hand accidently struck a piece of silver and sent it clattering to the floor. He rounded on her with a nasty growl. "If you can't serve a meal properly, Tina, we'll jolly well get someone who can."

"Yes, sir. Sorry, sir." She bobbed a curtsy and hurriedly obtained another teaspoon from the sideboard. There were tears in her eyes as she scurried from the room.

Jody was surprised at Quimby's outburst and felt sorry for the thin child, but what shocked her most was the vehement expression that flared in Anne's black eyes. The look she threw her father was shot with pure hatred.

Jody shifted uneasily in her chair. There was something strange about this house and the people in it. The fear on the little serving girl's face was deep seated, frantic, irrational, certainly not stemming from a dropped spoon and a few gruff words. Then there had been the matter of Jody's room: "As long as my wife is away," Quimby had said, "how would you like to sleep in her room for a few nights?"

It was Anne who had answered so quickly and decisively. "Jody's sleeping in the room across from me. She's here to be my companion. That's what you said."

His chuckle was forced. "I did, I did. Still, a few nights in Mrs. Quimby's room would be a real treat for the girl. She's had a rough time, Anne."

"If she is here to be *my* companion, she can sleep in the pink room. If she's to be *your* companion, then by all means, put her in Mama's room."

"Anne, such a temper!" His black eyes had raked his daughter, then twinkled at Jody as though to say, "See? Didn't I tell you she was spoiled?"

After supper, Quimby asked if Jody would like to see the library.

"Oh, yes, sir. Do you have a dictionary? I've never seen one, but Mama always said you could look up any word in the English language and find the meaning." Madame Restell's words still rang in Jody's ears, and though she had written all she could remember in her journal, she was still vague on many points.

"Then to the dictionary it is." He rose and ceremoniously pulled back her chair. "Anne, before you go up to your room, ask Tina to serve our coffee in the library." He took Jody's arm and led her toward the door.

Anne jumped to her feet and reached for the small Sevres bell that sat beside her father's place when

74

her mother was in Newport. She had no intention of letting her father get Jody off alone.

I should have warned Jody this afternoon, she thought. I had my chance there in Jones Woods, but Jody was so upset when she found out about Madame Killer. What would she think, Anne wondered, if she knew the truth about the old fart who had just escorted her off to the library. Talk about leaping from the frying pan into the fire!

Anne gave the bell a second ring just as the door swung inward. "Tina, we'll have coffee in the library." If he thought he was going to have it easy with Jody the way he did with all the others, he had another thing coming.

Anne's face twisted into an ugly mask of determination as she hurried from the room.

# 7

Three weeks had passed and a real friendship had developed between the two girls. Anne didn't know what to do. She was torn between her shame and the knowledge that Jody must move on. She didn't want to confess the hidden truth about her father, but she must.

More and more, her father was contriving to be alone with the pretty, red-haired girl. In the last week, he had twice sent Anne to her room on trumped-up punishments. He wasn't going to wait much longer. She had to tell Jody before it was too late.

She went to Jody's room after breakfast one morning. Rapping on the door, she stuck her head inside. "Busy?"

Jody looked up from her toilet table with shining, happy eyes and a spate of gratitude: "Oh, Anne, I'm glad you're here. I've just been thinking—if it weren't for wanting so hard to be a doctor, I could just stay here all my life if you'd have me. You know, I'm fifteen and this is the first time I've ever had a room of my own? I can come in here and close the door, and just listen to the silence." She laughed happily. "I'm actually getting to know myself." Suddenly she realized that Anne looked troubled. "What's wrong? Is there something you wanted to tell me?"

"No. Nothing." Anne gave her a little squeeze before

76

flouncing on the bed. "I just wondered if you wanted to do something special today since Papa's gone to his office."

Anne's averted face contradicted her light words, and Jody experienced another sharp stab of disquiet. There was nothing she could put her finger on, yet something sinister stalked the halls of this beautiful house. She didn't like the fright she saw in the little serving girl, Tina, or the housekeeper's bland coldness, or the way Anne looked at her father. And the way Quimby looked at Jody sometimes—it made her flesh crawl. Like an undertaker measuring her for a casket.

It had been a strange three weeks—a disconcerting mixture of pleasure and displeasure.

With Anne always present, whether invited or not, Quimby had taken Jody to A. T. Stewart's retail palace for a completely new wardrobe, from the skin out: Irish linen chemises and embroidered drawers, crinoline petticoats, skirts, habit shirts, bodices, jackets, gowns, lace berthas and linen fichus, shawls, mitts, parasols, snoods and bonnets, high button shoes that actually fit, a dozen pair of lisle thread stockings, and even dancing slippers.

When Jody protested, he only said it made him happy to buy for her—and surprisingly, Anne backed him up. "You need clothes," she said. "Here, try this one. It goes with your hazel eyes."

No match for the two of them, Jody finally relaxed and let it happen.

"Oh, look, Anne!" she exclaimed on one of their shopping tours. "Wouldn't my mother have loved this warm shawl." Then she saw the price and gasped. "Two thousand dollars!"

"It's cashmere, my dear," chuckled Quimby.

"Well, for two thousand dollars, Mama could have had two thousand shawls," declared the practical Jody.

From then on she ignored the outlandish prices and her conscience and reveled in the lovely things Quimby purchased for her. Irish point lace. An ebony hairbrush with inlaid mother of pearl. Even nightdresses—two of them—of the finest silk.

They went to the Lafayette Bazaar for perfume and to Tiffany's for a hand-painted fan, which Anne taught her how to use—how to snap open to show displeasure, to peek flirtatiously across its fluted edge, and to flutter with false modesty. It was all great fun.

When no other activity was planned, Jody spent her spare time curled up with a book. Her world of poverty had been so narrow; now a whole new existence unfolded. Nights were mental orgies as she fed her mind, and days were visual restoratives as she absorbed the fascinating sights of the city. But in the back of her head, never far from conscious thought, was her nagging desire to become a doctor and her worry about how to broach the subject to Anne's father.

In two months, Mrs. Quimby would return from her sister's in Boston. The portrait of Anne's mother in the drawing room told Jody, more than words, that life might not be so pleasant once Mrs. Quimby was back in residence. The picture showed hard brown eyes and a self-important, smirking mouth. The girl promised herself that before Anne's mother came home from Boston, she would approach Quimby about helping her obtain an apprenticeship with a doctor. In the meantime, she was having fun.

Jody liked it best when she and Anne went out alone in Anne's pony cart. Or when Sam drove them downtown and they paraded up and down Broadway with all the swells, as Pa used to call the elegant ladies and gentlemen.

Quimby took the girls to the theatre to see *All That Glitters is Not Gold*, Edwin Booth as *Othello*—which was wonderful!—and Harriet Beecher Stowe's *Uncle Tom's Cabin*. Mrs. Stowe's play was upsetting, especially in light of all Mama had told Jody about slavery. From what Mama had said, the girl strongly suspected that it was from the slave trade that the first Lord Herndon, her very own great-grandfather, had made his fortune.

Holding a horror of slavery as her mother had, Jody asked if the wretchedness depicted by the play was true. Quimby assured her it wasn't. "Nonsense. That Stowe woman ought to be run out of town. They should never have passed a law against slavery in the first place."

"But if there's a law against it, how come there are still slaves?"

"Lord, pretty girl, there's no law against *owning* slaves—just against *importing* them. In fact, black-birding is a highly profitable endeavor these days."

There was a hard twist to Anne's pink lips. "Even a field hand brings eighteen hundred dollars. Right, Papa?"

He licked his lips, failing to hear the irony in her voice. "Everything that's illegal is profitable, my dear."

It was the sudden disappearance of Tina that started Jody's fears up again. It all began at breakfast when Ryecroft came in to announce that the young serving girl had disappeared. Quimby took another huge bite of ham omelet and chewed placidly. "You take care of hiring someone else, Ryecroft," he ordered, floating a fat slab of butter on his roll.

"Yes, sir."

"What happened to Tina?" demanded Anne.

Mrs. Ryecroft's eyes shifted. "I don't rightly know, miss. She wasn't here when we got up this morning."

"Are her clothes gone?"

Quimby stopped chewing and slapped his napkin on the table. "Really, Anne, there's no call to cross-examine the servants. The girl was worthless anyhow. If she's left us, we'll hire someone else, that's all. You see to it, Ryecroft." He nodded to the housekeeper who disappeared obediently through the swinging doors.

Anne was strangely quiet for the rest of the day, not even wanting to discuss Tina's disappearance. Jody needed someone to talk with, but she couldn't bring herself to tell Anne how uneasy she was feeling about Quimby these days.

Breakfast, the following morning, was served by a pleasant older woman whom Quimby promptly fired. "You'll find somebody suitable or you'll find yourself another place," he snapped at Ryecroft.

Supper, that night, was served by the older woman's replacement, a rosy-cheeked Swedish girl named Gretchen. Jody became more uneasy with each passing day.

On Sunday mornings, they went to what Mr. Quimby called the "little church around the corner on Twenty-ninth." It was built like the small country parish church Jody and her mother had attended in Liverpool, and it made the girl feel right at home. Quimby couldn't be too bad, she rationalized, when she heard him raise his voice in church, loud and clear and fervent.

On week days, when the lawyer made one of his rare visits to his office. Anne and Jody would take the pony cart to tour the northern part of the city. One of their favorite excursions was Croton Water Reservoir on Forty-second and Fifth, only a few blocks from Quimby House. The reservoir was built in the form of an Egyptian temple, with a promenade walk encircling its top edge. From there they could see north past Central Park, all the way to Yorkville and Harlem.

After one circle of the walkway, they always stopped at the Crystal Palace, which had been built for the 1853 World's Fair. The view from the Palace tower was spectacular.

Anne was good company. Having been born and raised in New York City, she was a well of information. The girls spent a lot of time laughing at nothing. It was a carefree, youthful period, the first such Jody had ever known.

She was thinking about her good fortune one morning in late September as she threw back the covers and crossed to the window to look out. The early morning sun cast a pale peach glow over trees shimmering with the first tinges of autumn gold. Below Jody's window a gardener swept and burned. She wished he wouldn't. The falling leaves reminded her that summer was over. Mrs. Quimby would soon be home.

Jody dressed quickly and went down to breakfast.

Gretchen, the new serving girl, had been with them a week now. Already having lost her good nature and taking on what Jody thought of as the "intimidated Tina-look," Gretchen crept about the sunny room in teary silence.

At breakfast, Quimby roared at her twice and finally ordered her from the room "so we don't have to listen to you snivel." His very presence seemed to trigger the poor girl's fright, as it had Tina's, and as it triggered hatred in Anne—yes, and fear as well. Jody was certain now that she had seen both these emotions in Anne's bleak black eyes.

Anne looked pale and picked at her food this morning, as she often did. Suddenly, after no more than two bites, she clamped her hand over her mouth and fled from the room.

Jody started up from her chair, but Quimby waved

81

her back. "She'll be down again in a few minutes," he said. "It'll give us a bit of time to talk." His black eyes twinkled.

She subsided reluctantly. Anne sick, and her father not the least concerned as he swilled down a slab of ham swimming in white sauce.

"Well, what's it to be today, Miss Jody?" He sat back with an expansive sigh and wiped his mouth on a snowy napkin. White muttonchop whiskers puffed from cheeks that glowed with color. "I hoped you would accompany me on a tour of the Daguerrian Miniature Gallery. Then I've planned a special treat for you while I take care of a bit of business downtown . . ."

As usual, he ignored his daughter who had returned quietly to her place at the table. Anne, now pasty faced and subdued, was forced to invite herself.

After the tour of Brady's Gallery and a visit to John Taylor's new ice-cream saloon, the girls settled in the phaeton outside Sweets Restaurant to wait for Quimby and to enjoy the passing parade of people.

They had not been parked long when a closed carriage pulled up beside them and two gentlemen stepped out. They were well dressed, affluent, one wearing a tall D'Orsay hat, the other a Regent. They stopped directly beside the blue phaeton and continued their conversation in low tones.

Anne, eyes twinkling, held a warning finger to her lips. The men's conversation, though guarded, was clearly audible: ". . . several of them," said the D'Orsay. "On Greene Street mostly. White *and* black."

"Where's he get the niggers? He got somebody buying for him?" the Regent asked.

"Hell, no. He runs his own show. He's still got shares in slavers, for Chrissake."

"You think he'll go for it?" asked the Regent.

"Quimby's hard as a gig whip," replied the other. "But he'll bite—especially if we sweeten the pot with a young—" The rumble of a trade cart buried the D'Orsay's final words.

With stricken face, Jody stared at Sam's stiff back.

Anne's grin was twisted. Now maybe Jody would begin to realize what a toad Mr. Nicholas Quimby really was beneath that deceiving chuckle of his. Oh, how Anne hated that bubbly laugh. Vicious, perverted toad.

Quimby was not laughing when he finally reappeared. "They weren't buying—they were trying to unload. What do they take me for anyhow?" He fell heavily into the seat opposite. "Uptown, Sam," he snapped, without his usual precise instructions.

It was Jody who first became aware of the new route they had taken. Instead of the usual trip up Broadway through snarled afternoon traffic, Sam had tooled the team smartly onto Canal Street, then slowed the horses to an amble as they started up Greene.

This was the street, Jody remembered, that the two men had been discussing. She had never been here before, and her eyes widened as she studied the houses. From every window hung a scantily clad woman. Along the sidewalk, women accosted men with bold glances and soft words. Snakes of St. Patrick! A whole street of "bad women." Jody cast a swift glance at Anne who had turned pale and was staring about with frightened eyes. Quimby appeared lost in his own angry reverie.

"Hey, old man, since when you been slummin' this far down Greene?" The strident voice came from a second-story window. All three of the carriage occupants looked up. "Yeah, you! You come to see where we wind up when you're through with us at your fancy uptown houses?" The woman had gaudy gold hair and

83

a hard, painted face. She spat out the window and made a crude gesture with the middle finger of her right hand.

Jody dropped her head—and looked straight into the eyes of young Tina, a serving girl no longer. She wore a stained red satin gown with the bodice cut low across her childish bosom. Hanging onto the arm of a burly, half-drunken sailor, she appeared frozen in the act of leading him into one of the houses. A childish parody of a seductive smile hung on the girl's painted face. It died as her eyes met Jody's.

"Sam!" roared Quimby. "Get the hell off this street! Whatever possessed you, boy!"

As they whirled smartly across Bleecker, Anne turned to stare back over her shoulder. Her face was white, and her fingers picked nervously at her black lace mitts.

"Anne!" roared her father. "You forget you're a lady? Gawkin' over your shoulder."

An hour later, when they sat down to supper, Anne had recovered her composure, but her father was roaring at her again. "Have you had your bonnet off, you young snippet? Your face looks like a lobster! When your mother sees that, she'll skin you proper."

"It'll all be gone by the time Mama gets home," murmured Anne.

"Oh, you think so? Well, think again, Miss Smarty!"

Anne's heart jumped. Was Mama coming home? Was that it? Of course. Mama was coming home early from Aunt Helen's. Oh no, she thought. Wait till Mama hears that Jody is sleeping upstairs in one of the guest rooms! She'll have a fit. She'll throw Jody right out into the street.

Anne's feelings were mixed. On one hand, she nearly died at the thought of losing her friend, but on the other was the blessed relief that Jody would be safe.

84

"Mama always stays until Thanksgiving," she said aloud. "Why is she coming home early?"

His fist hit the table with a resounding thud. "Stop your clapper-clawing, girl! You take too much on yourself. It's none of your affair why your mama's coming home. You think you're privy to everything that goes on in this house? You're spoiled rotten, that's your trouble. That's what I get for giving in to your whims and letting you galavant all over town in that pony cart." He was working himself into a towering rage.

"I'm sorry, Papa. I didn't mean anything. Honest I didn't."

"Don't give me none of your beer-garden jaw! Think you're something special, do you, missy? Well, we'll see how special you are!" His face was turning an ugly puce. A black vein pulsed in his neck. "Gretchen!" he bawled. "Where are you?"

The girl scrambled into the room and stood trembling before him.

"Get Ryecroft in here. Now!"

"Yes, sir." She scuttled away, not pausing to curtsy.

The housekeeper straightened from her listening crouch and moved quickly through the doorway, smoothing her hands over her black cotton uniform. This had the makings of a bad night, she thought. One of them girls was in for it, and no mistake. She hoped it wasn't Miss Anne again. She was fond of Miss Anne. "Yes, sir?"

"Take 'er to her room and lock 'er in. Miss Jody will have coffee with me in my office."

"Yes, sir." So that was it. Ryecroft breathed a silent sigh of relief. She liked Miss Jody, but if it had to be one of them, she was glad it wouldn't be Miss Anne. The missus was coming home sooner than His Lordship planned, and it looked like he was going to have to speed things up. A letter from the missus had come by special messenger early that afternoon, and the master had been in a real snit ever since he opened it. He had vanished into his office and reappeared only when supper was announced. The missus coming home would sure put a crimp in his plans, thought Ryecroft complacently. Messing with Miss Anne and the help—that was one thing, but keeping a pretty toy in one of the guest rooms—the missus wouldn't stand for that.

"When will Mama be home?" demanded Anne. The fat was already in the fire, she thought. She might as well find out all she could.

"None of your business! Get off to your room like I said. And no supper. Ryecroft, lock her in and see she has *nothing* to eat. And nothing to drink. *Nothing."*

"Yes, sir." She fingered the ring of keys at her waist. "When is Mama coming? I know she's coming or you wouldn't be so mad. At least tell me when she's coming."

"You shut your bone box and get out of here." He half rose in his chair and his fist hit the table. The silver jumped from the force of the blow. Anne flinched.

"Come on, Miss Anne." Ryecroft nudged the girl's arm.

Anne went quietly, but as soon as the door closed behind them she began to plead. "Please, Ryecroft. Don't do this. You must know what will happen if you do this. Please. Please."

"Now, Miss Anne, you been locked in before. It will soon be morning."

All the way up the steps, the girl begged. "Please, Ryecroft. I don't care about myself anymore. It's Jody. Just don't let this happen to Jody. Oh, please don't. I'll find some way to stop him if you just don't lock my door."

Ryecroft's heart was sorely moved. "It's my job, Miss

86

Anne. You know that. If I don't do what himself orders, I'll lose my job." Times like this she could wish she was a Catholic so she could go off to confession and clear her soul, no matter what kind of mischief she'd been forced into.

She closed the door on the pitiful, tear-stained face and turned the key, her mind working. There was a big revival meeting in a tent up on Sixth Avenue, she remembered. A revival would be sort of like church. Maybe it would ease her soul a bit—if she could just get up nerve to ask for the night off. It would get her out of the house, and then she wouldn't have to sleep with her head under her pillow again. Not that she had ever actually heard anything, but with all the goings-on in this house, you could never tell when you might.

"Ryecroft! Ryecroft!" She could hear him bellowing as soon as her foot touched the landing.

"Yes, sir?" Her gaze was fixed on his watch chain, yet she couldn't help but be aware of how stiff and still the pretty red-haired girl sat.

"My daughter is not to be let out of her room till I come down in the morning. You hear? No matter what happens, she is to stay locked in until I say to let her out. And she's not to use the speaking tube. If she speaks to you, you'll not reply. No matter what she says or what story she invents."

"Yes, sir." Ryecroft's glance fell on a paperweight, which lay beside the master's place. It was the latest in his prized collection: a geometric design with white-enameled decoration on clear turquoise. He must have been so upset over the missus coming home that he'd carried it with him to the table without thinking. If he knocked it off now and broke it with his ranting and raving, she'd be the one he'd lay the blame to. He was like that. "Would you like me to put the paperweight in the cabinet in your office, sir?"

87

"No! I don't want you to do a thing except get it straight about Miss Anne."

"Yes, sir." Mrs. Ryecroft shifted uneasily on her feet. Her lips worked as she tried to summon her courage.

"Well, what is it? What is it?"

"There's a revival tonight, sir, and I thought if you wouldn't be needing me . . ."

His little black pig eyes gleamed. "Go! Go right now. And take that whole crew with you." His arm waved in the direction of the kitchen.

"Take . . . who, sir?"

"All of 'em. Every last mother's son of 'em. Sam can drive you in the coach. He can go, too."

"But . . ."

"No buts. Take 'em all."

"Briget . . . she's Catholic, sir."

"If she don't want to go, then give her notice. Same goes for everyone else. I want every last mother's son of you gone! I'm sick of all of you. Get out before I give you all the sack!" He was standing now, his face purple with rage.

"Yes, sir. Right now, sir." Mrs. Ryecroft wished she hadn't mentioned the revival. She was the one needing solace, not the rest of the help. Now, with him sending them all off— She cast a furtive, pitying glance at Jody before gliding hurriedly from the room.

Quimby ate stolidly, ploughing his way through roast of lamb with mint sauce, carrot timbale, and a jellied salad of green asparagus and egg slices.

Jody pushed at the food on the flowered plate and worried about Anne. And about Mrs. Quimby coming home early—and still nothing settled about an apprenticeship with a doctor.

Quimby's high color slowly receded to its natural rosy hue. The wonder of it, Jody thought, was that he hadn't fallen over dead like Meghan O'Neill's granddad, in Ballareen. Pa had said it was old man O'Neill's temper that had finally done him in, and now Jody wondered if Mr. Quimby was all right after his outburst. Well, if he wasn't, it would serve him right, punishing Anne like that just because she had gotten hot waiting in the sun outside Sweets and had slipped off her bonnet.

Quimby wiped his lips. He shoved back his chair slowly. "I'm not feeling at all well, Jody."

She jumped to her feet. "Can I help?" She wasn't comfortable with him now, yet felt obliged to offer. "Can I do anything?"

"Yes, child, you can." He suddenly seemed to droop, scarcely able to hold the paperweight he had picked up from the table. "Take this back to the office for me, will you? Just put it on the shelf with the rest of the collection."

"Yes, sir."

"Oh, and while you're there, one more little thing . . ."

"Yes, sir?"

"Fetch me the decanter and glass. They're on the little tray on my desk. Just bring tray and all. It was foolish of me to send the servants away like that, but you don't mind helping an old man, now, do you, child?"

"No, sir." She took the heavy paperweight from his hand, happy to have an excuse to escape, wondering if she would be able to whisper to Anne through her bedroom door without his hearing—maybe after he settled down with his brandy.

"Jody, I'm really not well at all." He passed an unsteady hand over his eyes. "I believe I'll go up to my room. You can bring the tray to me there. Will you do that for me, child?"

"Oh, yes, sir." If he went to bed, she'd surely be able

to talk to Anne through the door. "Do you need help to get upstairs?"

He was tempted, but knew that once he touched her, he might lose control. He wanted her in the bedroom where he could lock the door and she couldn't get away. She was one sweet morsel, this slim Irish lass with her red-gold curls and her tip-tilted nose. He had waited too long for this one. But she was worth it. "No, no, child," he assured her. "I can make it by myself." He crossed the room. "Mind, now, don't hurry. Take your time. Come up the stairs slow like, so you won't drop the decanter. I wouldn't want it broken."

Maybe I'll have a chance to ask him about an apprenticeship—if he isn't too sick, she thought. "I'll be careful," she said aloud.

# 8

Upstairs, Anne saw the light appear in her father's room. The outside balcony, above the portico, could be reached by two glass doors: one from her room, one from her father's. Tonight she had pulled back one of her curtains and tied it with the sash so she could watch for the lamp to come on in his room. Luckily his drapes weren't pulled tightly, and now a rim of light flickered across the blackness of the balcony. Was it Papa? Anne gnawed her lower lip. Supper no sooner over and Papa already in his room? What was he up too?

Her eyes fell on the skeleton key in the French door. Maybe it would fit the hall door—maybe she could get out of here. Why hadn't that ever occurred to her before?

The key didn't fit. Bouncing it thoughtfully, the girl carried it back across the room.

She looked out into the night, studying the matching glass door, and a grim smile twisted her young face. The key might not let her into the hall, but what opened one glass door would undoubtedly open its twin. Gingerly, silently, she turned the key in the lock and pushed the door outward.

The night air was crisp and cold, the stars bright gems set in black velvet. A quarter moon mounted the night sky, casting thick shadows onto the walk below, but Anne had eyes only for the furrow of light in the space between her father's curtains.

She crept across the gallery and pressed her eye to the narrow slit. All she could see was a small piece of scroll-carved ornamentation on one side of her father's bed.

Placing her hand on the knob, she turned it cautiously. Locked. She'd try the key. It was dark, and she had to bend close to see what she was doing.

There was no keyhole.

Then she remembered. Just after the house was completed last year, burglars, using a skeleton key, had entered through one of the balcony doors and cleaned out her father's office safe. He'd nearly had apoplexy—accused the builder of using inferior locks that would yield to such a key, and threatened to sue. The builder had changed all the locks in the house except those in the offending balcony doors, which Quimby ordered sealed from the outside. For the first time, Anne realized what it must have cost him to have those locks sealed. He had planned on using those doors between her room and his, but fear of burglars had won. Now the doors could be unlocked from the inside only. He couldn't sneak from his room into hers, but neither could she use his room as an escape route.

Oh, Jody, she thought, what have I done to you? I let him bring you here. I knew what would happen. Why didn't I tell you everything that day in Jones Woods?

She pressed her ear to the glass door. Footsteps. Drawers opening and closing. She strained to hear. Someone was rushing about in there. Papa? Or maybe Becky, the upstairs maid?

Suddenly her father passed in front of the glass, just inches from her startled eyes. Anne leaped back, then pressed quickly forward again. He was wearing a robe and slippers. He appeared to be turning down the bed.

The girl frowned. Retiring this early? With her finally out of the way and Jody his for the taking? And turning down his own bed?

Something was wrong.

Had Jody come up early, too? Anne crept back into the house and pressed her ear to the hall door.

Nothing.

She felt so helpless.

Would he have the nerve to try anything with all the servants in the house? Of course he would. He'd done it with her and with Tina and Gretchen and all the others, hadn't he? Then shipped them off to one of those houses like he was always threatening to do with Anne.

Today had been a revelation—he really *did* own that string of whorehouses on Greene Street where he said he would send Anne if she didn't do what he wanted. Her stomach flipped in a sickening jolt.

Maybe his temper tantrum tonight had been too much for him, she thought hopefully. Maybe it had made him sick, bellowing at her like that. Maybe he *was* going to bed early.

No, he hadn't locked her in her room for nothing, she knew that. And it wasn't Anne he intended to fuck tonight. Oh, if she could just catch Jody as she came upstairs to her room—call to her through the door— warn her to lock it and brace a chair against it. Sure as thunder it was going to be tonight.

She ran to the speaking tube and blew into it. "Ryecroft. Ryecroft! Are you there? Becky? Oh, please. Won't somebody answer me?"

She waited.

Nothing.

"Nellie? Gissing? Please. Gretchen. Gretchen, if you're there, please answer me. Don't let this happen to Jody. Ryecroft!"

Then it hit her. Nobody was going to answer. There

was nobody there. Becky wasn't turning down the bed because Becky was gone. There was nobody in the kitchen. There was nobody in the house but the three of them. Somehow, he had gotten rid of all the servants.

Mama was probably coming home tomorrow. That explained the near case of apoplexy he'd had at dinner. Mama was coming home tomorrow, so it had to be tonight.

Mama turned a blind eye to Papa's abuse of his own daughter and all the servant girls, but she'd never stand for him keeping a doxy in one of the guestrooms. And he knew it. No, it had to be tonight.

Anne could feel the memories begin to crawl inside her head. She tried to force them away, but they were a fiery carnage behind her lids. Hot irons in her loins. As real, as horrible, as that first time.

She had been eight years old, and as she collapsed in a mountain of pain, he had told her of houses he owned where only women lived. And where men came to do things to them—things like he had just done to her.

Shivering, rubbing her arms. Anne paced distractedly across the room. From the settee, a china face stared at her—Amelia—the doll she had named for her mother. She snatched up the doll and shook it furiously. "You!" she screamed at the painted face. "You could have stopped him if you wanted. I tried to tell you, If you'd only listened . . ."

She had been eight years old. Pain writhed within her. Terror rode her mind and squeezed her heart. She didn't know what she had done to make her father punish her so, or what he would do to her now for telling, but she was torn and bleeding, and barely able to walk. She crept into her mother's room. "Mama . . ." she said, the tears streaming down her face.

And her mother had stared down at her with

distaste. "Not now, darling," she said. "Today's my loo day and I'm already late." She turned to the mirror to pin her hat in place. "If you have a problem, tell Ryecroft about it."

She had been eight years old. Now she was sixteen. Eight years of hell. Afraid to lock her own door against him—afraid to wedge a chair to keep him out—afraid of what new perversions the dirty toad bastard might force her into next.

But Jody could wedge her door shut, Anne thought now. If I can just warn her. Suddenly Anne's head snapped up, listening. A noise on the stairs. Somebody coming up. Jody? Anne pushed her ear against the door panel.

Then, from the other side of the hall balcony, echoing off the domed ceiling, came a distinct click.

*His bedroom door.*

On cat feet, Anne dashed back across the room and onto the balcony. The lamp was still lit.

Who had opened and closed his door? Had he gone back downstairs? Had Jody come up? Did he have her in there now?

Anne peered frantically through the chink in the curtains, her eyes pressed to the glass. She couldn't see anything but the edge of his bed.

Was that a voice she heard, or just the sighing of the wind in the trees? Was Jody in there with him? Oh, what was happening?

Then, from the other side of the glass door, she heard her father chuckle—that low, throaty chortle she knew so well.

A tide of hot, rippling nausea welled in Anne's throat. She squeezed her eyes shut, but the laugh was still there—coming from the bedroom—echoing in her mind.

In utter frustration, she brought up her fists and beat

them in palsied helplessness against the sides of her head. Amelia's legs flopped on her shoulder as she pounded the doll frantically against her throbbing temple.

Inside her head was a scream. All those years she had wanted to scream and couldn't came suddenly to fruition. The scream inside her head was very real. Shrill, unmitigated terror. Scream after scream after scream.

Then she knew. The terror was not in her own head. It came from her father's room.

With more reflex than plan, Amelia's china face struck the door pane with all the force Anne could muster. The glass shattered. She thrust the doll through the jagged edge, then dropped it to feel for the key.

Jody was still screaming. He had her on the bed, his fat belly pressing her down, his hands tearing at her bodice.

Anne cast frantic eyes around the room. There, on the drum table, sat a tray—a tray with a decanter, a glass, and a paperweight. She grabbed the closest object.

The heavy paperweight was geometrically shaped with sharp, hard points. It was one of those points Anne embedded in the back of her father's head.

# 9

How quiet the big kitchen was, frightening in the stillness where servants should bustle. Chill bumps stood on Jody's arms. Sweat stung her eyes. Her fingers plucked restlessly at her torn bodice, pulling at the tear, worrying the severed cloth. Her head was a pulsing, quivering mass. If she could just stop shaking.

She tried to shove the ragged pieces of her mind back from the cliff of finality—away from the edge, the end of her endurance. Where was the calmness Mama had taught?

Pictures of past horrors loomed in her mind's eyes: her mother's death, the sudden loss of her father, the street killings, the boy who had leaped from the burning building, the mangled little girl pulled from the loom in Liverpool, Kathie's death, the babies in the wicker basket. And now, that man—the attack—and the horribly still body upstairs on the bed.

One after another, tormenting pictures rose to cavort through Jody's brain. She wanted to cry—scream—run shrieking from this house of horrors. Every nerve ending in her body raced headlong to the brink of a cliff, wanting to fling out into space and be lost forever in the fall.

For the third time, she crept to the sink and scrubbed her hands until they were raw. She wanted to strip and soap her whole body. Oh, that dirty, *dirty* old man. What had he wanted of her? Jody shuddered. What had he been about to do with his tearing fingers and his hard, pressing body and his disgusting laugh and rattling breath? And how had such a fat old man— He was so fast. What happened to her knee and the kick Pa had taught? There'd been no time. How had he— Oh, God, if it weren't for Anne—

She raised her eyes to look at the other girl, and revulsion stirred deep within her. His daughter. Flesh of his flesh. Yet it was Anne who had saved her. She couldn't hold Anne accountable for her father's evil.

Suddenly Jody realized how strange Anne looked. Blank. Calmly stirring the fire. Placidly setting the kettle to boil. It was she who had suggested tea and led the way to the kitchen, just as composedly as if her father's body didn't lie upstairs in his bedroom with a fancy paperweight buried in his head.

Anne moved smoothly about the kitchen, looking as sweet and innocent as the organist at the church they attended. Yet she had just killed her own father. How could she be so passive? So unconcerned? Jody remembered the look of pure hate on Anne's face as she had stared down at his body, the heavy paperweight deep in the back of his skull. Now she set tea to steep and placed cups on the table with nauseating coolness.

Yet, if it weren't for Anne— Here Jody's thoughts skidded to a halt. She didn't know exactly what Quimby would have done to her if Anne hadn't burst into the bedroom. She didn't even want to know.

She leaned over the table and dropped her head in her arms. Dry sobs racked her slim body as fear, shock, and a deep, wrenching disgust battled hard within her. Her head threatened to split, her eyeballs to roll to the back of their sockets.

"Here," said Anne, her voice serene. "Drink this. I

put some of Nellie's cooking sherry in it. Ryecroft always laced Papa's tea with brandy, but that's all locked up. Except for the bottle in his office." She looked puzzled for a moment. "Anyhow, I put in cooking sherry and sugar."

Jody thought about the bottle of brandy upstairs on the tray—the brandy he had asked her to bring to his bedroom. Oh, how could she have been so stupid? How could she have ever thought he was nice? How could she have liked that jolly laugh and that evil, red-veined face? The picture of him on the bed, as she had last seen him, loomed in her mind: his white, chalky legs protruding from a red brocade robe, the turquoise paperweight growing like a great green mushroom from his fluffy white hair.

Jody fought back nausea and tried to think.

Where had the paperweight come from. She had carried it to his office as he asked, to replace it in the cabinet. Had Anne gone into the office later and picked it up? No, that didn't make sense; Anne was locked in her room.

Then Jody realized that she must not have done as he asked. She must have put the paperweight on the tray instead of in the cabinet. She must have carried it to his bedroom by mistake. And it was there when Anne broke through the door and reached for a weapon.

Anne was placidly drinking her sherry-laced tea. Jody lifted her own cup. Her hand shook and tea sloshed onto the table.

What were they to do now? What did you do when your only friend has just killed her own father? They couldn't just stay here and wait for the police to come and cart Anne off to the Tombs.

"Last year, when we were robbed," said the other girl conversationally, "Ryecroft fixed tea with brandy for all three of us." She smiled. "I had two cups, and Mama

99

had to send me to my room because it made me silly."
Her lack of concern was unbelievable.

Jody shut out the cool voice and tried to concentrate.
The servants would come home soon. They'd find the
body and Ryecroft would call the police. If Jody had
learned anything from her year in Five Points, it was
that you didn't hang around and wait for the cops, no
matter what. You ran before the cops got there.

Money—that was the answer. To get away, they had
to have money, and she didn't own even a half dime.
Everything she had earned at Madame Restell's had
been spent on clothes and writing materials.

"Anne, listen to me," Jody said, her street sense
finally beginning to stir. "Last year your father took
lots of gold out of the bank. I'm sure it was gold. He put
it in his office downtown, I remember. Does he maybe
have a safe here, too?"

"Of course."

Jody's heart leaped with hope. "Do you know where
it is?"

"Sure. Why?"

"We've got to get out of here before the servants
come back. And we need money."

"Why do we have to run away?" Anne's eyes were
clear, though puzzled. Didn't she realize she'd be held
for murder?

"Your father's dead, Anne. They'll take us off and
lock us up in the Tombs. It's an awful place, like
nothing you've ever imagined." Everybody in Five
Points knew about the Tombs—the disease, the filth—
where ten or twelve people died every day. "Take my
word for it, Annie, we've got to get out of here."

"But I had to do it. He was trying to—"

"Don't! Please don't talk about that." Jody didn't
understand what Quimby had been about to do to her,
but if she dwelled on that part she knew she would

come to pieces, and she had to be strong—for both of them. If only she could stop shaking. "Come on. Show me the safe," Jody urged, tugging at the other girl's hand.

The safe was in his office, hidden behind a painting. It had numbers surrounding a small round dial. Jody bit her lower lip. "Do you know how to open it?"

"No. He was the only one who knew the combination. But that didn't help any when the robbers came. They opened it anyhow."

Jody whirled the dial back and forth. "Oh, Anne," she moaned. "Don't you have any money?"

"Maybe enough for a dish of ice cream. Why do we need money?"

For the first time, Jody realized there was something seriously wrong with her friend. Anne's eyes wore a frozen, dead look that Jody had seen twice before. Pa had looked like that when Mama died. The look had never quite left him. Mrs. Amato had looked like that when they laid her dead son in her arms after the Bowery Boys had finished with him. Mrs. Amato had worn her still, quiet look for two days before she had slashed her own wrists with a butcher knife.

That couldn't be Anne's problem though, reasoned Jody; she hadn't loved her father. No, for some reason, she had hated him.

Jody put down the lamp and took her friend's face in her hands. "Look at me, Annie. Listen to me." The black eyes that stared into her own didn't quite focus. Jody shook the other girl's arm. "We're in trouble and we've got to get out of here. You've got to help me. Think, Annie, think! Is there any money anywhere? Household money? Anything?"

"There's still some of the gold he took out of the banks before they closed. He didn't store all of it at the office. He brought a lot of it back here. And he won't

101

need it now."

"But you don't know the combination."

"Oh, he doesn't keep gold in the safe anymore. That's what was robbed last year. That's the first place thieves look, the architect said."

Jody was almost afraid to ask. "Where does he keep it? Do you know?"

Anne smiled, the smile of a superior adult reasoning with a somewhat backward child. "Of course. In those fake books. Up there." She pointed behind the desk where a wall of books was partially covered by a royal-blue velvet drape. Crossing the room, she moved a stepstool into position and stood on it to reach a row of gold-embossed encyclopedias. Her small figure cast a huge black shadow across the blue velvet. She pulled out a book. The weight tore it from her fingers and it flew open, scattering double eagles like huge bright teardrops across the carpet.

"Oh, Anne. So many."

"There's more. Probably every book in this set is full of gold. And more in his bedroom. He thought nobody knew about his hiding places, and I guess nobody does now but me." She pulled out another volume and watched with interest as more coins cascaded to the floor.

Jody's mind was working rapidly: With this money they could leave town, get out of New York right now—tonight.

She looked up. Anne was still standing on the stool, her eyes fixed, unseeing, on the cabinet of paper-weights. "Help me, Annie," she urged. "We've got to get out of here. And we've got to make it look like a robbery." She grapped Anne's unresponsive shoulders and shook. "Listen to me. We've got to make it look like robbery and murder. And a kidnapping." She was improvising as she talked, ideas tumbling faster than

102

words. "We have to make it look as if the robbers killed your father and then kidnapped us. We'll have to drag his body downstairs to the office as if they brought him here and then forced him to open the safe . . ."

The blankness left Anne's eyes in a rush of terror. "You mean move him . . ." Her voice was a hoarse whisper.

"I'll do it. You don't have to help," Jody said quickly.

With quivering chin, Anne collapsed into the leather chair. Tears rolled down her cheeks, and her body shook as Jody's had shaken just minutes before.

Oh, Lord, not now, Jody thought. Don't let her fall apart now. "Come on," she cried urgently. She reached for Anne's hand, but her eyes were caught by a thin red line of blood. "You've cut yourself. You've cut your wrist."

Anne stared blindly at the blood. Tremors shook her body as she rocked back and forth.

"Come on," said Jody. "I'll take care of him while you wash that cut and find a traveling bag of some kind. Something old—a carpetbag if you have one. Then wait for me in your room."

"Don't make me go upstairs. Please, Jody—please don't make me go up there."

"Don't fall apart now, Annie. I'll be along in a minute. Just find an old traveling bag, that's all." She bent to retrieve the gold as Anne shuffled reluctantly toward the door.

Alone, Jody stood in the center of the room, shaking, knowing the body was next. She had to go upstairs, too. She had to move Quimby down here and fix the office so it looked as if the murder was the outcome of a robbery. In a rush of determination she moved into the hall.

Trying to outrun the ogres that lurked in shadowed corners, she raced up the stairway. Her footsteps

103

slowed as she moved around the balcony toward Quimby's door. She had never been upset by the sight of blood before, but for some reason the idea of his lying there in his own clotting blood—where she had fought him just a short time before—where she had fought as his hands tore at her bodice while his little black pig eyes laughed at her terror—

The bedroom door was open. Her deep, shuddering breath evoked a sick squeak, frightening in the utter stillness of the domed entry. Jody twisted away and leaned over the balcony. She gripped the railing. *I won't be sick,* she vowed. *I won't.* She got a quick picture of herself throwing up and vomit splattering on the marble floor twelve feet or more below. Her eyes squeezed shut, and her face ground into a tight knot of determination.

This was not the time to be sick. This was the time to steel herself against the reality of what she must do. She pushed herself into the room and stood swaying against the doorjamb.

She swallowed again and opened her eyes. Still there. But no blood on the sheet. Only a small stain on the soft white hair around the buried paperweight. She averted her eyes.

She set the lamp on the table beside the brandy tray.

How can I get him downstairs alone? I told Anne I'd do it. But how?

Her eyes lit on a gold and green afghan, neatly folded across a chair back.

She moved quickly then, smoothing the Berlin-wool afghan beside him on the bed. She was going to have to touch him once—roll him onto the afghan. Her hands poised over the body.

Her slender frame rocked as she tried to prime herself.

She remembered his heavy paunch pressing into her,

those pudgy fingers tearing at her dress. She gagged. The taste of vomit rose in her throat, acid hot. She couldn't touch him.

"Empty your mind. Empty your mind." She realized she was saying the words aloud, over and over. Oh, Lord, she thought. If I can't do it now, I'll never have another chance. Oh, Mama, where are you? I need you. I need you.

Minutes stretched as the girl stared at the patterned robe and waited for her mother's soft voice to take command of her thoughts.

Gradually the room disappeared, became a bright field of daisies nodding in the summer sunlight. Flowers swayed in a soft warm breeze, gold and red against a bright blue sky. The dell was alive with the song of birds and the flash of wings beneath the trees.

And there, barring the path through her dream valley, lay a rotten log.

Jody's outstretched hands struck the log with a determined rush. She caught a glimpse of Quimby's eyes, black and bulging, as his body made one complete revolution and ended facedown in the center of the afghan. Without thought, she was around the bed, tugging on the closely knit woolen coverlet. She braced her feet and gave a tremendous yank. Off it flew with its loathsome burden, the brocade robe a crimson slash across the green and gold spread.

Jody closed her eyes to recall the field of flowers, the bright sky. She reinforced her vision with a glistening waterfall, added a soft early morning mist to cool her fever. Then with ragged breath, she grasped the edges of the afghan to haul the body toward the door. The picture in her head faltered. Who would have thought he could weigh so much?

She maneuvered him out of the room.

Wiping the sweat from her brow, she looked around,

astonished to see that nothing had changed. The chandelier still hung from the domed ceiling, highlighting the Aubusson carpet and the polished marble below. Globed gas jets still cast a wavering glow on the mahogany stair rail, and shadows still swirled on the blue silk walls. All looked the same—as though nothing had happened. Yet her entire world had turned upside down. Jody's legs buckled suddenly, and she had to grasp the railing for support.

A sound behind her made her jump. She swung about.

Anne, carrying a carpetbag, was coming through Quimby's door. Of course—with her own door locked, poor Anne had been forced to go past her father's body and across the balcony to get into her own room.

In the candlelight from the crystal chandelier, Anne's black eyes glistened with terror. Her lips trembled as she dropped the bag and reached for a corner of the afghan.

"You don't have to help, Annie." Jody's voice reverberated with sepulcherlike intensity against the marble dome. "Go on downstairs."

"You can't do it alone." Anne's face was a white mask.

Without another word, Jody bent to grasp the other corner. They pulled quickly. Only the rasp of ragged breath sounded against the eerie silence of the great hall.

Jody thought she would die when the body bumped down that first marble step. It was a hard bump that echoed in the empty hallway. Unable to look at the dead man, she glued her eyes to his white legs. Broken capillaries. Thighs veined like the old mirror on the wall of the room in Liverpool. Gay red brocade slippers exquisitely embroidered in green.

*Thump* went his head. Then the echo: thump-thump. *Thump*. Thump-thump.

Ten thumps to the landing, each one louder than the last. Each with its own *thump-thump* echo.

Across the landing, vulnerable against tall staring windows.

Thump. Thump-thump.

Ten thumps to the polished hallway. Ten echoes.

There was a frantic rush to their movements now as they dragged their burden, intent with the need to be finished.

"Over here," panted Jody, indicating the office fireplace. But the body had ground to a sudden halt, and she couldn't budge it. She glanced up, startled. Anne lay on the carpet beside her father, her face drained of color, her eyes closed.

Bless her, thought Jody. She came through when I needed her. Tugging at the coverlet, feeling the sweat run below her armpits, feeling her muscles ache with strain, Jody inched the body across the room and rolled it onto the hearth. There was blood on the afghan now, from the bulbous nose and the step-battered face. If he had died here, on the hearth, there would have been blood here, too, she realized. She had to make him bleed more.

But could she touch him again? She stared down at him. His robe had twisted around his putty white legs, and she could see his bare buttocks. Suddenly she had no need to summon her mother's help. She didn't know why he was nude beneath his robe, but his hairy repulsiveness provided all the incentive necessary.

Straddling his body, Jody lifted his head in ruthless hands and let it drop. His face hit the brick hearth like the popping of an overripe melon.

She stared at the crimson blotch on the afghan.

107

They'd have to take it with them and get rid of it later. She folded it carefully and laid it in the doorway. Behind her, the other girl was stirring. "Are you all right, Anne?"

"Yes." She cleared her throat, passed her hand across her eyes.

Jody tugged at her. "Come on. There's not much time left. We have to change clothes." She looked down at the torn watered silk, her favorite of all the dresses Quimby had bought. She could never wear it again, never wear any of those beautiful things again. A slice of heaven had been dumped in her lap, then snatched away.

Jody raked distracted fingers through her tousled curls. "How long does a revival meeting last?"

"Three—four hours." There was no curiosity in Anne's voice, and her eyes were dull. "They're usually over by ten, I think."

"Come on. We've got to hurry."

Upstairs, as she changed into one of the cheap dresses purchased from her wages last year, Jody wondered where Anne had gone.

Jody was just buttoning her shoes when the other girl reappeared, a doll in her hand. The china head had been smashed, but Jody immediately recognized the bright blue dress. "That's Amelia. What happened to her?"

"She's what I broke the glass door with. I picked up all the pieces, but left the glass on the floor to make it look like a burglar broke in." She held out her hand, displaying the bits of china. Two baby-blue eyes looked particularly obscene in her small palm. "And I broke the glass on my balcony door—from the outside, just like his—so it would look like burglars broke in through his door, then through mine. Ryecroft locked me in, remember? Nobody could kidnap me with both my doors locked."

"Good girl!" Jody was amazed by Anne's quick thinking. There was a toughness in the other girl Jody would never have suspected. I've got to be tough, too, she thought. But her knees felt like water, and her hand shook as she took her mother's precious books from the drawer. "You've got to have some old clothes, Anne. We have to look like maids, not rich ladies out for a lark."

"I don't have any clothes that would make me look like a maid."

Suddenly Jody clapped her hands in relief and dropped to her knees to paw through the bottom drawer.

"Oh, thank you, Kathie," she whispered when the bundle of Kathie's meager belongings was spread over the bed. "Put this on," she ordered, handing Anne a clean but worn gray dress. "You can keep your own stockings and crinolines and drawers and stuff. And your own shoes. They'll be hidden by your skirts."

The gray muslin was obviously from before Kathie's pregnancy. Luckily she and Anne were fairly close in size and build.

Jody grabbed one last regretful look around the room. "I have to go back to the office for the money," she told Anne finally. "Give me your bag and wait by the front door."

Avoiding the body in front of the fireplace, she stuffed the two bags full of gold coins, then padded them with petticoats and drawers so they wouldn't rattle.

Five minutes later, the two girls stood together in the vast, silent hallway. Anne, like Jody, had draped a shawl over her head. Her face was pale and set, yet

109

there was no resemblance to the haughty girl Jody had met three months earlier in the carriage on Chambers Street.

For the first time since she had knocked at Quimby's bedroom door with the tray two hours before, Jody smiled. "We'll do, you know." Anne's answering smile was wan and uncertain.

The front door closed behind them with a soft click. To Jody it had the final, deep, reverberation of doom.

# PART II
# ST. LOUIS, MISSOURI

# 10

*October 4, 1858*

It was late afternoon. They had spent the entire day walking the streets of St. Louis, searching for signs in windows and inspecting squalid rooms. With drooping spirits, the footsore girls mounted the steps to yet another narrow brick house and turned the bell ringer.

The door flung wide and they were accosted by a red-haired beauty of about thirty-five years who plunked her hands on her curving hips and glared at them. In a bright green dress, with smooth white skin and green eyes, she was a study of contrasts: all red and white and green, punctuated by a velvety black mole just to the right of her tight red lips.

"If you've come about the room, you're welcome. But if you're here about Jeremy again, you can take your complaints and stuff 'em in your hoops. The boy's all boy, that's all. Full of mischief, he is."

Anne stepped back, intimidated by the unexpected attack.

Even Jody hesitated before speaking: "We're here about the room."

"Well, then!" Lush red lips spread in a smile as genuine as the irritation displayed a moment before. "I'm Meg O'Gerity and I'm happy to welcome you to my home." She stepped back, a theatrical wave of her hand inviting them to enter.

"I'm Jody Gates. And this is my friend Anne. Anne O'Neill." It was Jody who suggested *O'Neill* when Anne refused to use her own name. They had talked for hours on the train and both were determined to put New York, and all that had happened there, behind them. They would begin new lives in St. Louis, Jody with her own name, which the servants probably wouldn't remember anyhow, and Anne with a new one.

"You two girls alone?" The green eyes were friendly, but sharp.

"Yes, ma'am. We've just come from Boston and we'll be looking for work." If Anne doesn't get sick again, Jody thought. If that happens, I'll be the only one looking for a job.

"I have a nice big room on the third floor front." Meg's diction was good, but Jody could hear the faint cadence that would have given away her heritage even if her name and red hair had not.

The room, overlooking the quiet street, was delightful. It reminded Jody of a stage setting, and when Meg O'Gerity swept into the room and raised the shade to admit the pale October sunlight, it was as though the curtain had just gone up on the first act.

Anne giggled as she closed the door on their new landlady's swaying skirts. "That woman is a character straight out of Dickens," she whispered.

"I like her. She didn't have to put two beds and an extra chair in here for us." Jody pulled the pins from her hat and gazed about the bedroom with satisfaction.

"If that carrot top of hers is natural, I'm Queen Victoria."

"She did say she had been on the stage."

"Well, she's theatrical enough or I don't know how many beans make five." Anne bounced on the bed. "I'll take this one. It's nearest the washstand."

"Now you listen to me, Annie. You're not going to need the washstand in a hurry anymore, you hear? You're all through being sick. It wasn't anything but train sickness. From the motion of the train, that's all."

"I'm not so sure. I'd been sick a few times at home, too. Anyhow, I'm not taking any chances. I want the bed closest the washbasin and the top two drawers of the dresser and the right side of the closet."

"That's fine."

Anne winced as she removed her shoes. "I've got blisters something awful."

"I didn't want us to take just anything. We'll probably stay in St. Louis awhile."

"But we didn't have to spend the whole day walking. We could have taken our time and stayed at a hotel while we looked."

"Oh, no! I'm not letting you near any more hotel stationery." They had stayed one night in Baltimore and Anne, in a fit of pique Jody still didn't understand, had written to her mother on hotel stationery. By the time Jody found out, the letter was already mailed and the damage done. They had fled Baltimore on the first available train.

Now, in St. Louis, Jody eyed her friend intently. "You won't write your mother again, will you?"

"No. I got it off my chest. I had to do it that once, though. I couldn't let her think she had gotten away with . . . with . . . well, with what she did all those years."

There it was again, that curtain Anne drew whenever the subject of her parents arose. Jody knew Anne was bitter because her mother had not protected her from her father. But what he had done to Anne was still not clear. He had apparently attacked her as he had attacked Jody. But what had he done next? What had

115

he been about to do when Anne broke in and struck him with the paperweight?

Jody was plagued with nightmares in which she could see Quimby's red-veined face bear down on hers. She could hear his excited chortle and see his black eyes gleam with unholy anticipation—feel his wet mouth and the surprising hardness of a body that had looked so soft and round and pudgy. Nightmares dramatized the turquoised paperweight buried in his white hair, magnified the drum of his head on the stairs, illuminated his sticklike legs and those ridiculously pointed red slippers, and emphasized his bare, hairy bottom beneath the red brocade robe.

Anne had nightmares, too. She sometimes woke screaming with terror, and Jody would hold her and whisper comforting words until Anne relaxed and slept again. But when morning came, except for an embarrassed evasiveness, it was as though Anne's nightmares had never been.

In their new room, their meager belongings put away, the girls barely had time to freshen up before they heard a harsh clanging sound.

"Is that the supper bell already?" Anne rushed into the hall to look down the stairwell. There stood Meg, a cowbell clutched in her shapely hand, swinging her arm in a wide, exaggerated gesture.

"A cowbell," Anne whispered to Jody as the two girls answered the summons. "Can you imagine?"

Meals in the O'Gerity boardinghouse were boisterous. Food was plentiful, conversation loud and animated. The paying guests, with the exception of the two girls, were composed entirely of actors and actresses with whom Meg had once "trod the boards."

"I gave it up sixteen years ago," the red-haired beauty said with a fond smile at her son, Jeremy.

"And has regretted it ever since," announced a

116

languid blonde with aging bedroom eyes.

"Not for one minute," declared Meg stoutly. "Jody—Anne, that rude baggage is Nella Boone, female lead in Thompson's Stock Company. Moving on around the table, we have Charlie Townsend who performs a wonderful Uncle Tom—Magdaline Celano, character actress of renown—Will Cottle, as versatile an actor as ever trod the boards—Annette Arnold, leading ingenue of the company, who in real life is Mrs. Thompson—and Mr. Phineas Thompson himself, entrepreneur and leading man."

"You must have the whole company living here."

"Every time they come through town," said Meg with obvious pride. "That's why we have supper so early; they have to get to the theatre by six. They open tonight in *Uncle Tom's Cabin,* and I'll bet if you smile at Phinny he'll give you free tickets for tonight's performance."

Jody smiled at Meg's words, and the florid Phineas Thompson promptly whipped out a pair of tickets. "If you've a mind to go on stage, my dear, I shall be only too happy to give you an audition," he told her gallantly.

"Down, Phinny," said his wife, her dry tone at odds with her little-girl voice. "You already have one ingenue. Remember me?"

"I simply meant that the little lady has a lovely contralto voice. We could use her as a young boy as well as a young woman. Egad, my dear, you accuse where no accusations are warranted."

Annette looked Jody up and down. "I can see *exactly* what you meant, Phinny." Then she smiled grimly. "Take the tickets, dear child. Phinny has dozens of free seats for tonight's performance. He has to pack the theatre with sympathetic customers or we might all be killed." She swung resentful eyes on her husband. "I

117

still say it's idiotic, bringing *Uncle Tom's Cabin* to a slave state like Missouri. At the very least we'll be pelted with rotten tomatoes."

Meg's green eyes looked concerned. "She may be right, Phinny. I passed out tickets to every Free Stater on the block, but even if you pack the theatre, the proslavers will likely wait for you at the stage door. I don't see why you were so set on bringing *Uncle Tom's Cabin* to St. Louis."

"He's apparently tired of panting over Nella and me. The shine has worn off." Annette Arnold's glance at her husband was anything but ingenuish. "Besides, he likes playing Simon Legree. Phinny loves to crack a whip."

The man's already florid face reddened as he turned back to Jody. "Pay no attention to this jaded ingenue, my dear—she speaks with a forked tongue. You need not fear to attend tonight's performance, although the theatre has *not* been packed, as my sweet wife suggests. The police have assured me they'll keep the crowd in good order, so all will go splendidly."

"We'll take them," said Anne, her hand darting out to relieve Thompson of the tickets. "Thank you."

Jody was seated next to Jeremy, the landlady's son. He was sixteen, not tall, but muscular. He had Meg's green eyes with a hint of malice lurking in their mischievous depths, and he kept up a lively conversation throughout supper.

Even Anne's unpredictable appetite perked up in the congenial atmosphere, but she was to suffer for it later that night when a sudden dizzy spell prevented their attending the theatre. "I must have eaten too much," she moaned, wiping the perspiration from her clammy forehead.

The next morning, barely awake, she suddenly

clamped her hand to her mouth and scrambled from the bed to the basin. Jody ran to hold her head. "Oh, Anne, not again. Just when we thought you were getting better."

Whey faced and shaky, Anne finally allowed herself to be led back to bed where she curled into a frightened little ball. "What's wrong with me, Jo?" she groaned.

"I don't know. But I think you'd better see a doctor."

"I'm not going to any doctor. I can't stand those horrid leeches."

Jody sat on the edge of the bed, biting her lips with indecision. "I don't see how you could go anyhow, Anne. Suppose the police are looking for you? They can't have a picture of me, but they sure could have some of you. Suppose they saw through our kidnapping scheme and have your picture on one of those Wanted posters or something?"

"Oh!" Anne's black eyes opened wide. "I never thought of that."

"I've been thinking about it ever since you wrote that letter to your mother."

"Oh!" Anne's eyes were giant jellyfish swimming in a sea of regret. "After what I said in that letter, it would be just like her to send the police after us. If they weren't looking for us before, they sure will be now. They won't know I . . . I did it to save you; they'll think I did it because of what he did to me. Oh," she wailed, "I'll bet my picture is plastered in every post office and every bank from New York to San Francisco. Oh. Oh!" This last was a cry of anguish mixed with another wave of nausea as she dashed for the basin.

An hour passed before Anne's stomach, fortified now with a piece of dry toast from the kitchen, settled sufficiently for the two girls to discuss their dilemma. Thoroughly frightened by having vomited twice in one

119

morning, Anne was finally convinced of the need for a doctor. Only the question of how remained.

Neither had any idea about police procedures, but both girls expected the worst. "Even if your picture isn't posted, the police may be showing it around," Jody said.

Back and forth they seesawed between Anne's need for a doctor and the danger of her being recognized.

Suddenly a dimple creased Anne's plump cheek as she clutched Jody's arm. "I've got it! *You* go to the doctor. They don't have your picture. You can go to the doctor and tell him *you're* sick. You know all my symptoms. Just tell him you're sick at your stomach every morning, how it sort of comes in waves. It's awful. Tell him that. And that you feel a bit faint sometimes."

Something jiggled at the rear of Jody's memory. She could hear her mother's voice: "It's nothing, dear, just a bit faint is all."

"It's only been twice," continued Anne. "Just a little dizziness, and it passes almost as soon as it comes. The doctor will ask questions and you'll need to know what to say."

"You don't suppose he'll want to bleed me, do you? I won't go if he's going to do that. If there's any bleeding to be done, you can blame well go yourself."

"Don't let him. Tell him you need pills. Just bring home something to make me better."

"I guess I can handle that." Jody grinned. "If I'm any good at impersonating you, I just might audition for Mr. Thompson and go on the stage. We could use the extra money." She struck a dramatic pose with the back of one hand across her brow and the other hand thrown up in simulated fear. "No, no, Mr. Villain. You cannot force me to go with you—"

"I'm sick and you're clowning." Disgust laced Anne's voice.

Jody laughed. "I'll go ask Meg about a doctor."


Doctor Adams's office occupied the second floor of an old limestone building on the corner of the levee and Chestnut Street. The waiting room reeked of sweat and overflowed with four crying children and their impatient mothers, several stoic laborers in dirty work clothes, plus one young woman who looked almost as ill at ease as Jody felt. The shawl-draped women scolded their offspring in several different languages, punctuating each reprimand with a shake or slap.

At last Jody occupied the number one seat and took her turn through the sacred door.

Kindly eyes, on a level with hers, smiled with tired interest. The doctor wiped his hands on his soiled white coat and rolled down his shirt sleeves, as though to lend formality to the interview. "Now suppose you sit here and tell me what's wrong."

Jody sat nervously. "Well, I've been sick at my stomach every morning for almost a month now, and I've been feeling faint—or I did twice—and I need to be cured so I can go out and look for a job." She drew a deep breath and looked up at him, glad to have gotten it over with.

His lined face broke into an amused smile. "Whoa, there. Let's start with a name, Mrs. . . . ."

"It's Miss. Miss Jody Gates."

He cleared his throat and swiveled the desk chair about to face her, his eyes soaked in pity. "Tell me, Miss Jody, how many of your monthly turns have you already missed?" He made a pyramid of his fingers and scrutinized them intently.

"I don't understand . . ." she began. Then his meaning hit her with embarrassing suddenness. She could feel her face pink and was grateful when he didn't look at her. "Oh, you mean . . . Oh, my." She wet her lips. She didn't know how to answer the question except to be honest about herself. "I . . . I haven't missed any." She had no idea if Anne had missed any, but she, Jody, had just gotten her first monthly period last week, and it was still a ripe, unpleasant memory. She had thought she was dying—that Quimby's lying on top of her had somehow made her pregnant even though they weren't married, and that she was bleeding to death as Mama had done. Anne had laughed at her. "You mean you're fifteen and this is the first time?" she hooted. Then, still laughing, she had explained about monthly menstrual periods. It had been most embarrassing. After all Jody's reading—after working at Madame Restell's for a year— Well, now she knew it all, she thought. From now on there wouldn't be any more surprises.

But now the doctor looked startled, as though her not having missed a monthly turn was unusual. She had the uneasy feeling that she and Anne had not discussed this thing fully enough before she had agreed to the masquerade. She bowed her head and watched her own fingers fumble nervously with her handkerchief.

"Tell me a bit more about your morning sickness."

"There isn't much to tell. I usually feel all right until I start to get out of bed in the morning," she said, trying to remember Anne's words. "Then it comes over me like I'd been stuffing myself with green apples or something. But if I eat a bit of toast, it usually goes away and then I can get up." Her voice slowed as she listened to what she had just said. *Morning sickness.* That was what Mama used to get. Jody's stomach began a strange, uncomfortable jig.

"Have you actually thrown up?"

"Four times," she said, dragging her mind back to his question. "Twice this morning. It comes in waves, kind of." She could hear her mother's voice. *It's just morning sickness. It will be gone soon.*

"When is your next menstrual discharge due?"

Jody's mind leaped to attention. Snakes of St. Patrick, this man was determined to embarrass her. If it came once a month, when did he think it would be due, for Paddy's sake? "This month," she muttered.

"And when was your last one?"

"Last month!" Was this doctor obsessed with the subject of her monthly turns? Did doctors always ask such personal questions?

His lips twitched. "Was it a normal flow?"

"I suppose so. If you can call such a mess normal," she muttered. Then she clamped her hand across her mouth, aghast at her own temerity.

There was a long silence while he digested her reply.

"Miss Jody . . ." He paused and she could feel his eyes on her now. "Do you live with your parents?"

What did that have to do with being sick at her stomach? she wondered. "My parents are dead."

"I see." He seemed to be making up his mind about something. She wished he would get on with it; she wanted nothing more than to get out of here and mull over the wild thoughts spinning through her head and knotting her stomach.

"Have you been with a man since the last time you came sick?"

Jody frowned in puzzlement. He asked the strangest questions. She didn't understand what being with men had to do with anything, but she was delighted to have a change of subject. "Last night," she answered quickly. "I was with two men—that is if you don't count Jeremy."

123

Now it was Adams's turn to look startled. He could scarcely believe this sweet young thing was a whore. She blushed when he spoke of her menstrual discharge—as all well-brought-up girls should do—yet there she sat, brazen as brass, saying she'd had two customers last night—not counting Jeremy, whoever that might be.

Jody, happy to have a change of subject, would have continued to talk about the ladies and gentlemen of the stock company, but Adams forestalled her. "Why should we not count this Jeremy?" he demanded, his heavy brows rushing together.

"Well, he's only sixteen—hardly a man. I thought you wanted to know . . . about men . . ." She stammered to a halt before his obvious disapproval.

"He was man enough for your purposes last night, I take it." The doctor's voice rumbled deep in his chest. She wondered what she had done to upset him, but since she did not understand what he meant by, "for your purposes," she kept still.

"Has your bosom been tender to the touch?"

Jody couldn't believe her ears. What did her—or Anne's—bosom have to do with being sick at her stomach? "No." Then she remembered. She had felt a little sore just before the bleeding started last week. "Yes. I mean, yes. I guess I . . . it was a little."

"I'll have to examine you to be certain. Go behind that screen and remove your underclothing."

"I'll do no such thing!" Jody bounced to her feet then, indignation pouring from her slender frame. Madame Restell's examinations of other women had been routine procedure, but after all, Madame Restell was a woman. This whole thing had gotten out of hand. This was definitely carrying her friendship for Anne too far.

Adams stifled a smile. He shuffled the papers on his

124

desk and peered at her from beneath shaggy brows. "Perhaps I'd best explain the situation to you," he said finally. He wondered if she was new in the business—she seemed such a contradictory mixture of brazen professionalism and little-girl innocence. "Your symptoms point to one conclusion—that you are with child." He saw the shock and denial on her face as she sank onto the chair once more.

He was saying Anne was pregnant, thought Jody with alarm. But that was impossible. A woman had to be married to get that way.

"However," continued the doctor, "the normal state is for your monthly discharges to cease with pregnancy." Now he saw interest overcome her natural embarrassment. She leaned toward him, as though to move closer to this fount of knowledge. She was a strange one; he didn't know what to make of her. "You're certain you have not missed any of your monthlies?"

"I haven't." She wondered if maybe Anne had, but all Jody could do now was be honest about herself. "Please go on, doctor."

"Morning sickness and occasional vapors are a normal part of pregnancy. However, as I said, in the natural course of events, your monthlies would also have ceased. Of course, it's not unheard of for a woman to continue a little monthly staining and still bear a healthy, active baby. But . . ." He settled back in his chair and stared at her from beneath beetling brows. "Understand the circumstances, the only way I can be certain is to examine you. For that, you must remove your underclothing."

She blushed again. It was most becoming, he thought. He watched as she gathered her composure about her in a protective cloak.

"Can't you just give me some medicine so I won't be

125

sick mornings?"

He studied her. She was neatly dressed, exuding the faint scent of violets; well groomed in an inexpensive cotton dress; a lovely young woman with wide hazel eyes, straight dark brows, and a full but stubborn mouth. She sat quite stiffly, as though the news of her pregnancy had been totally unexpected, a real blow. He wondered how she could still be so innocent; what had caused her to take to the streets, and how long it would be before that beautiful face turned hard and coarse.

"I can give you something," he said, reaching into a cabinet for a vial of green pills. "Take two of these each morning before arising. If you are with child, the morning sickness should pass by the fourth month." He noticed that Jody was staring doubtfully at the pills, as though she knew they were nothing but rolled bread doused in a syrupy mint solution.

She left the office in disgust. Much as she had liked Meg's Doc Adams, he was full of prunes when he said Anne was pregnant. Morning sickness or not, Anne couldn't be pregnant. Jody might not know much, but she knew that much. She realized the doctor was at a disadvantage, not having the real patient there, but doctors were supposed to know about sickness, and he should have been able to do more than give her these dumb bread pills. She pulled the cork and sniffed. Just as she suspected.

Jody expected Anne to laugh at the story of her visit to Doc Adams, but Anne's face went white when she got to the part about her being "with child."

"Then he said the only way he could tell for sure if I was pregnant was if I took off my drawers and let him examine me!"

126

Still Anne didn't laugh. She stared past Jody from bleak eyes, and her mouth pulled into a hard pink knot.

Desperately, trying to ward off something—she didn't know what—Jody rushed on. "You haven't heard the funniest part yet—"

"I guess I'll have to go see him." Anne interrupted, her voice sounding like it had been dredged from the bottom of a well. "What's he like?"

Jody dropped her forced gaiety. "Nice. Tired looking. Kind. At least he was until I told him about supper last night."

Anne frowned, trying to concentrate on Jody's words. "Supper?"

"He asked if I'd been with any men and I told him about the two men last night—not counting Jeremy because he isn't really a man yet. But it seemed to make the doctor mad that I wasn't counting Jeremy, because he said sixteen is a man, too—or it was 'for my purposes'—whatever he meant by that."

Now Anne laughed. Laughed and cried all at the same time. "Oh, Jody, you're such a ninny." The tears flowed freely then as Anne explained what was meant by "being with a man."

Between hiccoughing sobs, she blurted out the story of the years of agony her father had put her through. The horror. The pain. The fear. The humiliation.

At last Jody understood. At last she knew what Nicholas Quimby had been about to do when Anne burst through the door. Rape had been just a word to her, its meaning unknown, but as Anne talked, it became a horrifying reality.

In the hushed room, Quimby lived again that night. Jody cried for the childhood Anne had sacrificed to her father's evil brutality. She walked with Anne—the frightened child creeping fearfully to her mother's room for help—and saw Amelia push her away, foist

127

her onto Ryecroft who didn't want to be bothered either. Then all the later doubts and uncertainties—Anne told it all—how she had agonized over the possibility that she had somehow brought this horror on herself: the long trail of young maids her mother had hired; the awareness of what was happening to them.

And still, in the dead of night, Quimby had come to her room. For eight interminable years she had suffered his brutal attacks and his vile threats.

"He said there were ten thousand whores in New York City and if I ever told, I'd just be one more."

"Oh, Anne."

"He used to talk about the whorehouses he owned on Greene Street and how much money they brought in. Once I asked him why he didn't just go to Greene Street and leave me alone. You know what he said?"

Jody shook her head, her heart breaking for her friend.

"He said there were seventy-five thousand cases of the French disease in New York—enough to contaminate all the men in the United States." Anne's eyes wore a haunted look. "He said he'd rather have me anyhow. Me and the 'sweet virgins' Mama supplied." Her eyes sharpened. "That's how I knew what was going to happen to you, Jody. That's why I broke the door. I had to kill him . . . I had to!"

Jody held her close, so horror-stricken she could find no words of comfort. A father who committed such atrocities on the body and mind of his own child!

"And now," Anne concluded in a fresh burst of sobs, "now . . . if I . . . if I'm going to have a baby . . . *his* baby . . . Oh, God, Jody! If I have a baby, it will be my own sister!"

# 11

Anne insisted on visiting the doctor alone. "You didn't see any Wanted posters of me, did you?" she demanded.

"No. But I didn't see any Wanted posters of anybody, so that doesn't prove anything."

"I'll probably be all right then. But if the police are looking for me, there's no sense letting them catch you at the same time." Nothing Jody could say would change Anne's mind. "I won't go unless I go alone," she repeated stubbornly.

Waiting, not knowing, was the worst part, Jody decided. If Adams's office was as crowded today as it had been yesterday, Anne wouldn't be back for hours.

Restless, Jody wandered downstairs. In the parlor, a deep voice rose and fell dramatically. Jody stuck her head around the archway and discovered Phineas Thompson prancing up and down. In one hand he held a dog-eared script while the other flourished in wide, melodramatic gestures, and his face screwed up with heartfelt anguish.

She started to back away but familiar words held her fast:

Then you must speak
Of one that loved not wisely, but too well . . .

129

*Othello*. One of Jody's favorites. She mouthed the suicide scene with Thompson, her mind traveling back to her childhood when she had read Shakespeare aloud and played all the parts. Unaware of his audience, Phinny emoted on to the end of the speech and concluded, "I took by th' throat the circumcised dog/ And smote him—thus." He stabbed himself with an imaginary dagger and staggered majestically.

"O bloody period!" Jody intoned from the doorway. "All that's spoke is marred."

Phinny's eyes flashed appreciation. His stagger flourished with unbelievable elegance as he enacted Othello's final speech:

I kissed thee ere I killed thee. No way but this, Killing myself, to die upon a kiss.

He fell upon the couch and expired with painful quiverings. Jody was hard put not to laugh. Having loved Shakespeare from childhood, and having seen Edwin Booth's portrayal in New York, she was amused by Phinny's stilted performance. On stage Phineas Thompson might be an impressive Moor, but close up, his Othello was pathetically overplayed.

After what he deemed a decent interval for death, he raised himself on one arm and peered at her, his face creased in an exaggerated smile. "Just what I needed— someone to cue me. Unbelievable, in a hole like this, to find a young beauty with such a thorough knowledge of the immortal bard. What a Desdemona you would make to my Othello!" he cried.

Jody had no desire to play Desdemona to his Othello. She didn't particularly like the man; he reminded her of Teddy Cassidy. Regretting now that she had let her presence be known, she smiled politely and turned to leave.

"Don't go, my dear." He jumped to his feet. "I am so sorry you missed our opening night."

"Anne was ill. In fact, that's where she is now—at the doctor's."

"How terribly unfortunate. But the tickets I gave you are good for any night this week, so you've not lost your opportunity to see me as Simon Legree. It went splendidly, you know. No problem at all with rowdies."

Meg had said the police were cracking heads outside the theatre when she arrived, and Jody wondered just what Thompson's version of "splendidly" was.

"Next week we do *Ten Nights in a Barroom.* Then I'm *Rip Van Winkle,* and the last week, *Othello.* We've not done *Othello* since last year in Atlanta. Hence my need for rehearsal." He waved the well-thumbed script.

She wished she had stayed in her room.

"I was serious about an audition, my dear. With your face and figure, you could go far on the boards."

Jody had filled out this past year, as Teddy Cassidy had predicted. She no longer looked like a child, and she didn't like the way Thompson examined her "figure" with his eyes.

"Ah, shades of youth," breathed the aging thespian. "Would that I could play Romeo to thy sweet Juliet!" He studied her face. "We pick up our bit players from among the locals, you know. I could really use you if you are interested. Not as a female in *Othello,* of course." This last with overacted regret.

Jody suspected that Mrs. Thompson, the snippy little Annette Arnold, held this would-be Romeo on a tight leash.

"But you could play a young man," he continued. "Your voice, with a bit of training, would be excellent for male juveniles."

Jody laughed and was startled by the sound of her own voice, aware for the first time of its low, husky quality. If someone wasn't looking at her, she supposed she could be mistaken for a young fellow of about Jeremy's age. Of course, Jeremy's voice was deep and manly, but lots of young men didn't have voices any huskier than her own. Her appearance was something else, however. Jody didn't think she could pass for a boy if they were looking at her.

"What would I do, wear a bag over my head?" she asked.

"Indeed not. If we cut your hair or put a wig on you—with breeches and a waistcoat, no one could tell the difference—not after I got through with you."

She eyed him curiously. "You really think so?"

"My dear, I am certain of it. There are several bit parts in *Othello* you could play. One of the three gentlemen, for example. Or the clown. Or the messenger. Here, walk for me." He sat down, relinquishing the center of the room.

"Oh, Mr. Thompson."

"Walk," he commanded. "This is no time for false modesty, my dear. Majesty and arrogance rule the boards. The stage is a hard and jealous taskmaster, but a generous one as you may be destined to discover. Now walk."

Jody moved self-consciously toward the far windows.

"Egad, that's nice. Oh, yes, very nice." Then he caught himself and cleared his throat abruptly. "You walk like a beautiful woman—as you should, of course. You walk like this—" He rose and minced toward her, one hand hanging limply from an upraised wrist. Jody laughed.

"Your walk is charming to be sure, but hardly the walk of a man or a boy. A man—" Here he sucked in his sagging stomach and thrust out his chest. "A man has muscles." Thompson placed his hand on the fleshy portion under his armpit. "These muscles thrust his arms away from his body. A young man swings his shoulders. He swaggers. He struts. Long strides. As though to conquer the world." Thompson strutted across the room while Jody watched in amazement. He looked, at least from the back, like a virile young Bowery "Bhoy" out for a night of deviltry.

"Now you try it."

It looked like fun, she thought. She strode across the room, arms swinging, chest high and swaying, imaginary muscles bulging beneath her arms.

"My Gawd!" Nella Boone's awed tones came from the doorway. "If you weren't wearing hoops and crinolines, I swear I'd smuggle you upstairs to my bed."

Before Jody could reply, she heard the front door open. She dashed into the front hall to find Anne already on the stairs. Jody followed.

Anne threw herself onto the bed and her body shook. "I'm pregnant all right. Two months, he thinks." Dry sobs tore her throat. She sat up, gagging. "He says . . . it'll be . . . about the middle of May." Her face twisted, shredded with terror. "Oh, Jody . . . what are we to do now?"

Unbidden, Madame Restell's abortion mill flew into Jody's mind. She was horrified at herself for even thinking such a thing. Abortion was wrong. She knew that. In the very depths of her being, she knew it. Unable to look at Anne, she moved to the window, lifted the curtain, and peered distractedly into the street. Fallen leaves eddied on the wet cobblestones. Clouds of migrating birds blackened the sky, and the trees shivered with cold. Jody's heart was as frigid as the swirling leaves.

"What am I going to do?" Anne moaned behind her. "What can I do? I can't believe . . . Oh, God, what'll I do now?"

It was a question she was to ask over and over as the night wore into dawn. "Shhh. It'll be all right, Anne. It'll be all right." It was no answer, but it was the only answer Jody had.

The room grew cold. Jody climbed into bed with her friend to hold her close. They slept that way, Anne's dark head cradled on Jody's shoulder and her tears drying slowly on Jody's gown.

It was almost dawn when Jody dozed off, still dark when she was awakened by an insistent shaking. "What is it? What's wrong?"

"Jo, I've been thinking. You have to do the abortion. Madame Restell explained it to you. I mean . . . about how abortions are done and all. So you can do it. I know you can."

All night Jody's conscience had been a bomb waiting to explode. Now Anne's hateful whisper had lighted the fuse.

"It'll be easy for you, Jody. It won't be much different from delivering a baby, will it?" Again the shake on the shoulder. "Jody! Are you awake? Are you listening?"

"I heard you."

"You will do it for me, won't you?" Anne's voice was a pitiful plea in the darkness. "Oh, I feel so much better. I can't have this baby, Jody. I just can't. I couldn't ever look at it without remembering. I . . . I hate it as much as I hated him."

The bomb exploded. "Don't you ask that of me! Don't you dare ask me to do that."

"You've got to. I can't have his baby. You know that. You've just got to do the abortion . . . the way Madame Restell told you. You've got to help me."

"No. Oh, no, no." Mama had said it was wrong to challenge God's authority, and that's exactly what abortion did. Abortion wasn't the way God meant for

134

Jody to help women. Abortion wasn't what He had put here for her to find.

"Jody, you don't know what it was like . . . you don't know how I hated him . . . the awful things he did to me."

"I don't want to hear any more." She clapped her hands over her ears, but Anne's voice went on:

"The awful things he made me do. I can't have his baby, Jody . . . I can't. You got to help."

"I won't do it. You've no right to ask me. That's a baby you've got in there, Anne. I couldn't kill a baby, no matter what." She pulled away from Anne's plucking fingers and made a dash for her own bed.

"Jody—"

"It isn't fair of you to ask," she gritted into the darkness. "You know how much I want to be a doctor, Anne. It's all I ever think of. But I walked out of Madame Restell's. Because of the abortions, I walked out. I couldn't even stay there and learn. Do you think I'd have left there if I could have stayed?"

"I know, but—"

"I want to help women . . . not kill babies."

"It's not a baby yet. Not until it's born. You told me that's what she said."

"She lied. I saw . . ."

"Oh, Jo, just this once. This is different."

Jo burrowed beneath the covers.

"He *raped* me, dammit. This baby's not like those at the lying-in hospital. My father *raped* me."

Jody's head shot out. "It's a baby you're carrying, no matter how it got there. You know I'd help if I could. But it's wrong. I can't do it. And I won't listen to any more." She buried her head under the covers and turned her back.

Behind her, Anne's voice went on and on, explaining, cajoling, pleading, but Jody had closed her out. Secure in the absolute knowledge that she was right, Jody had escaped to her private valley where her tears watered the wildflowers, and the wind in the trees was but a sigh of regret in her heart.

As daylight crept across the worn carpet, Anne began again. "Help me, Jody. I won't ever ask anything of you again. As long as I live I won't ask anything else. Only this."

In her own bed, Jody tried to conjure her valley.

"You *owe* me!" Anne yelled finally. "If I hadn't hit him with that paperweight, my father would have raped you, too. Suppose he'd made *you* pregnant, then what would you do? Where'd you be then? Maybe then you wouldn't be so sure abortion is wrong. You listen to me, Jody Gates. *You owe me.*"

Jody's gorge rose. "I'll be damned if I do!" she yelled, swinging to face Anne. "You can't make me do what I know is wrong. Sure you saved me. Sure I owe you— and I'll spend my life being a friend to you and your baby. But you're asking me to kill! I'll not kill for you, Anne."

"Why not?" Anne's voice was thick with venom. *I killed for you.*"

The words hung in the air between them.

How could she be so cruel? Jody thought resentfully. It's not fair to bring up Quimby's death like it was my fault. You killed him, not me. You're the one who hated him. You hated him and you killed him. Jody jumped out of bed and paced across the room, so upset she thought she would choke. "Don't you ever throw that up to me again." Her breath quivered and her voice shook. "You remember what you said the day we met? You said we're not responsible for what others do. So don't expect me to go through life feeling responsible for what you *or* your father did. No, as far as I'm concerned, you can forget about your abortion. I

136

don't want to hear any more about it. If you'd told me about your miserable old man in the first place, I'd never have gone to live at your house. Then he'd never have had the chance to get me alone in his bedroom . . . and you'd never have had to . . . kill for me, as you say."

The anger had drained from Anne's face and she looked like a frightened child.

Jody felt immediate remorse. "Oh, Annie, I'm sorry. I know you don't want the baby. We're having our first fight. I'm sorry. But I can't do what I know in my heart is wrong. That's why I left Madame Restell's. I couldn't do it then and I can't do it now. Not even for you."

Anne suddenly leaped from the bed and ran for the washbasin. After one startled glance, Jody ran to hold her head.

Half an hour later, having dutifully chewed the bread pills, Anne said she did feel better.

"You understand why I can't do the abortion, don't you?" Jody asked, determined to settle the question once and for all.

Anne sighed. "I understand."

"It's just that I feel so strongly—"

"I said I understand."

"Then," she said hesitantly, "you won't go to anybody else . . . will you?"

"No, I won't go to anybody else." Her voice was very soft and sad. "I'd trust you to do it, Jody, but I'd be afraid to go to someone else."

Jody gave her a quick hug. "You wait," she said, relief surging through her. "You'll start to want this baby. I saw it happen more than once at Madame Restell's. A girl would come in wanting nothing more than to have her baby and give it up for adoption, but then a funny thing would happen: After the baby quickened, then she would feel different, and when

137

time for adoption came, she didn't want to give it up at all. Of course she had to, because I guess she . . . she wasn't married." Jody stopped, astonished at how innocent she had been. "You just wait, Annie," she finished. "You'll love your baby once it starts to kick."

Anne's eyes were inscrutable black wells. "The girls you're talking about couldn't have been raped," she said quietly.

Jody had no reply.

When she came back from breakfast later in the morning, Anne was dressed and sitting on the edge of the bed. "I think I know where I can get a job," she said abruptly.

"You? How can you go out to work now that you're pregnant?"

"I wouldn't have to go out. Listen and see what you think: I heard Jeremy tell his mother that Phinny Thompson had offered him a place in the acting company. If it works out, Jeremy said he was going with them when they move on to Salt Lake City."

"When did you hear all this?"

"When they came into the dining room the first night. I was in the kitchen filching a piece of bread and jam. I couldn't get out without walking right past them so I just stayed put."

"After being so sick you couldn't go to the play; you were downstairs stuffing your face with bread and jam?"

Anne smiled, but the old impishness was gone. "Meg said all Jeremy did was spit on the floor and spread the spit with his toe, but he was better than nothing, and she'd have to replace him if he left. Anyhow, I'm going to ask Meg if I can work here when Jeremy leaves. The only thing I know how to do is clean house. I've never actually done it, but I've spent half my life watching and listening. I can probably clean house as

138

well as most."

"Anne, that's wonderful." Jody thought she had never known anyone so brave.

"I couldn't be seen in public anyhow when I . . . get big. I was just waiting to see what you thought before I asked Meg."

"I think it's great."

When Anne had gone downstairs in search of their landlady, Jody settled into a brown study. It had just occurred to her that she didn't actually want to work in a doctor's office. She wanted to enroll in a school—a real medical school. She wouldn't be a quack doctor like Madame Restell. She would have a proper medical certificate—be a real doctor. That was the only way to keep her promise to her mother.

"Jeremy's already tried out and it's all settled," announced Anne, closing the door quietly behind her. "Phinny says he's good, and Meg told me I can start work today." There was only a hint of the old exuberance.

"What are you supposed to do?" Jody couldn't imagine Anne cleaning house. If she was in a room five minutes it looked like Flannigan's front stoop. Anne may have seen a house cleaned, but Jody was willing to wager she had no conception of how to do it.

"First I'm to wash the third floor halls and all the steps. I'll earn two dollars a week plus room and board. Where's that old dress of Kathie's? It'll do just fine for scrubbing floors."

"Annie, I'm so proud of you." Jody gave her a hug. "I've decided what I'm going to do, too."

"Tell me."

"I'll tell you about it when I come back. Oh, Anne, we're going to do just fine—you wait and see if we don't."

There was no answering enthusiasm from Anne.

# 12

Jody fumed all the way home. St. Louis Medical College had turned her away with the simple explanation that it was an all male school—which was bad enough—but at the Dutton School of Medicine they not only turned her down, they laughed at her. Actually laughed! Women were getting above themselves, the registration clerk snickered.

His attitude was insulting enough, but when Jody demanded to see someone in authority, she was destined for even ruder treatment.

"Females," declared the stuffed fop who interviewed her next, "belong in the home. That Nightingale woman has put outrageous ideas into women's heads. First women nurses, now wanting to be doctors." He rolled his eyes. "We'll have none of that nonsense here at Dutton. What you need, young lady, is a husband."

"He was a rude, show-offish jackass," Jody told Anne later. "I've heard there are lots of men who practice without a license." Anyone with a bit of acting ability and a chunk of audacity could carry it off, she thought resentfully. After the acting lesson Phinny Thompson had given her, if she had her hair cut and put on men's pantaloons, as he suggested, she could probably march right up to that snooty registration clerk and be accepted without question. Thinking about it, she laughed.

"If something's funny, tell me," said Anne.

"I was just thinking that if I dressed up like a man, I bet they'd accept me in medical school."

"Sure they would. They're like Nella," Anne said, her voice bitter. "They'll take anything in pants. I heard Meg tell Jeremy that if he didn't stay away from Nella he'd get himself peppered off."

"What did she mean by that?"

"That he'd get the French disease, I guess. Anyhow, Jeremy laughed and said he wasn't taking turpentine pills yet, but if he had to, it would be worth it. And then Meg laughed, too, and said he was no good at all—just like his father."

Jody's mind wandered back to the insulting men at the medical school. She wondered if Dr. Adams held the same narrow views. "When you went to the doctor, Anne, did you tell him about me? Did you tell him that I was just taking your place when I went to see him?"

"No. I had enough trouble getting up nerve to go into his office without trying to explain about you."

"You know what I'm going to do? I'm going back there."

"What for? Are you sick?"

"Sick with wanting to be a doctor. Oh, Annie—do you suppose he would take me on as an apprentice? A lot of men still earn certificates that way, you know. They don't all go to medical school. If I studied with him and got a certificate, then maybe we could go West where there aren't enough doctors and where they'd be happy to have me—even if I am a woman."

She was dreaming out loud this time, letting her dreams run away with her common sense. But hadn't Mama told her that dreams come before reality? "If you dream about your valley often enough," Mama had said, "it will be more real to you than all the

141

squalor around you. Your valley can be real, darling, if you work hard enough." Suddenly Jody's dell took on a new dimension. Always before, it had been pure and untarnished by mankind. Now she saw a country lane and a pretty little white house and a shiny new sign with black letters: *Dr. Jody Gates.*

The vision of that sign stayed with her all night and transported her into Dr. Adams's office early the next morning.

From the doctor's waiting room, she could see the busy levee and a row of steamboats belching black smoke. One day she would be a passenger on a steamboat, she vowed. She would go West, is what she would do—go West and be a real doctor. She tapped her boot nervously as the room began to fill.

Finally the inner door opened and Adams stood in the doorway, less impressive in his once white doctor's coat than she would have wished. "Who's first?" he asked.

She jumped up.

"Miss Gates, isn't it?" He was surprised to see her again so soon.

"I'm glad you remember me."

He smiled. Refreshing, he thought, for a beautiful woman to be so innocently unaware of the effect her beauty had on men. Then he remembered why she had come to him in the first place and how blatantly she had exposed her sexual conquests. "Have you other complications?" He asked, turning his eyes away from her fresh young loveliness.

"No, sir. Could we talk a few minutes?"

He indicated a chair and took his place behind the scarred desk.

"Do you remember Anne O'Neill who came in to see you yesterday?"

"Mrs. O'Neill—dark-haired young lady?"

142

Jody nodded. "She's my friend—and if you remember, she is pregnant. But we didn't know what was wrong with her, and she was afraid to come on her own, so I came in her place. And when I told you her symptoms, you said I was . . . was expecting a baby."

"You mean you're not . . . it was . . ." He digested it slowly, feeling a chuckle grow deep within him. No wonder she had been so vehement in her denials. He burst into a mighty guffaw and Jody joined him. His laugh was straight from the belly, hers shy, embarrassed.

"And when I said I'd . . . I'd been with two men," she stammered, determined to clear matters between them, "I . . . I meant there were two men at dinner with us the night before. We live in a boardinghouse."

Adams wiped his streaming eyes. "And Jeremy?" he asked, surprised that he remembered the name of the one who "didn't count because he wasn't a man yet."

"Jeremy is the landlady's son."

The doctor took out a red bandana and blew his nose resoundingly. "Ho! Won't Mrs. Adams get a howl out of that one." He wiped his eyes again. "Now tell me why you've come back. Much as I appreciate a good story, I'm sure you didn't come here just to amuse me."

"Dr. Adams, I don't know how to say this except to just come right out with it. I . . . I want so badly to be a doctor. I went to the medical college and to Dutton, but they only laughed at me. They said women belong in the home. They said my . . . my monthly turns make me unclean, that even if I was allowed to become a doctor, I still wouldn't be able to care for my patients at that time of month. That isn't true, is it?" Jody didn't know why she trusted this man when others had been so unfeeling, but she placed her dream in his hands and waited, hoping against hope that he, too, would not trample it.

143

His countenance had sobered, and she saw the multitude of tired lines surrounding the deep pity of his eyes.

She stood abruptly, her knuckles white on the strings of her purse. She didn't need his pity.

"As far as we know," he said, clearing his throat, "the menstrual discharge prepares the uterine system for conception. Therefore, there should be no connection between your monthly turns and your ability to care for patients." He had answered properly and seriously, but a tiny gleam in his eye betrayed his amusement.

Damn him, she didn't want to be laughed at either. "I'm sorry I troubled you." She turned to leave.

"Hold on there a minute." His bushy brows shot together and his voice was brusk. "Suppose you sit down, young lady, and tell me *why* you want to be a doctor."

Was he going to listen? Really listen? She sat down again, her heart beating with faint hope.

"For as long as I can remember," she said slowly, feeling for the proper words, "I've seen pain that no one could ease. In Ballareen, people died of starvation. I'll never forget their swollen bellies—the way their cheekbones stuck out and the way their eyes stared from their sockets. In Liverpool, when Mama had another miscarriage, I had to go to work in a linen factory. I saw a little boy's hand crushed in a loom. I wanted to help, but I was only nine years old." Now the amusement was gone from his eyes. Her voice strengthened. "My own mother—I couldn't help her either. She'd had so many miscarriages—too many. She finally died in childbirth." Jody bowed her head, then raised it swiftly, and her voice flattened. "I had a friend who suffered through twenty-two hours of labor. I helped deliver her baby—but she died, too.

"And then," Jody said, leaning forward in her chair,

"when I held Kathie's new baby in my arms, something happened. It was like there was hope for the whole world. Oh, Dr. Adams, a baby is such a miraculous thing. I want to be a part of it—I want to be a part of making it easier for women to bring babies into the world."

"Then be a midwife."

"It isn't enough," she burst out. "I worked for a . . . a midwife in New York for a year and I could have stayed there. But being a midwife isn't enough. I want more. I want to help people—really help. Women and children especially . . ."

He was only a man. How could she make him understand? "My mother had eight miscarriages in eight years—and who knows how many more that I can't remember? Oh, there's got to be some way to keep that from happening—to keep women from becoming pregnant when their bodies are still too weak—"

"What do you propose?" His voice rustled with dry humor. "To halt the natural flow of nature?"

"I don't know what I propose." She bit her lip but refused to be embarrassed by his baiting. "All I know is I want to help. Dr. Adams, I saw a boy jump from a burning building, his ragged clothes a mass of flames. When they got the fire out, he just lay there in the street, screaming with pain. And then a doctor came along—and what he did was a miracle. He put a needle into the boy's arm and the pain went away—"

"I've heard of that," interrupted Adams, sitting forward on the edge of his chair. "He must have injected morphine through a hollow needle attached to a syringe. What did it look like—the thing he used?"

"I was too far away to see. I'm sorry."

"Where'd you see this needle thing? Here in St. Louis?"

"No, back in New York City."

"Hmmmmph." He leaned his chair back on its legs and examined a framed certificate on the wall. Jody stared at his certificate and despair gnawed at her. He wasn't going to help. That much was obvious.

"You know," he said, his voice reflective, "there weren't any medical schools when I was a young man with aspirations to become a physician." He waggled a blunt finger at the certificate. "I got my medical education by private instruction from Dr. Turner. He's dead now, rest his soul." Adams swung his eyes and studied the girl's intent face. "Of course, you couldn't do that, not being a man."

Her heart, just beginning to pound with hope, scraped to slow defeat.

He pulled the wrinkled bandana from his pocket and blew his nose. One hand came up to rub his chin and his eyes were thoughtful. "I'm going to write some of the supply houses in New York to see if they carry that syringe and needle," he said finally. His chair legs hit the floor with a bang. "You write a legible hand?"

"Yes."

He frowned at her. "Understand now, I don't condone women doctors. It goes against nature." He lifted his hand as she began to protest. "Still—it'd be a pity for so much eagerness to be wasted. Suppose I let you work as my nurse? It'll be hard work, but we can give it a try if you're willing."

"I'm not afraid of hard work," she said, her spirits soaring. It wasn't what she wanted, but after nothing but ridicule at the medical school, it was more than she had dared hope.

"It's a dirty job," he warned.

"That's part of what I'd like to change," she said, leaning forward eagerly. "If people could be taught to keep themselves clean, wouldn't there be less sickness?"

"Ye gods. A do-gooder with a cleanliness phobia."

146

He shook his head in disgust as he pulled a wrinkled garment from a rack in the corner. "Here, put this on."

She slipped into the smocklike coat. It could have wrapped around her twice. It was as stained as the one he wore, and she vowed to herself that she would wash them both at the first opportunity. Then he rummaged in the bottom desk drawer to produce a long tube which he fitted to Jody's ear.

"What is it?" she asked.

"A stethoscope. Set it against my chest and listen." He watched as a look of pleased amazement lit her lovely features.

"Is that your heart I hear?" Her own heart pounded with the wonder of listening to his.

He nodded.

"Why is the tube so long?"

"So the doctor doesn't have to get too close to the patient. Can't you see what it would do to my practice if I went around plunking my ear down on a woman's bosom so I could hear her heart beat?"

Jody smiled.

"How much schooling have you had?" he asked abruptly.

"No formal education at all. My mother taught me, and I've read a lot."

"It won't matter. You can't ever hope for a doctor's license; you got to face that. Even if you had formal schooling, your being a woman would make it impossible for you to ever become a physician." His eyes were intent. "You understand?"

She swallowed and nodded. She didn't understand and she wouldn't accept—but if he wanted to think he had killed her hopes, let him think that way. Just as long as she could work with him and learn.

"You've got a dream to be a doctor, and I've got a dream to own a hospital someday. Looks like we'll neither of us fulfill our dreams." He chuckled good-naturedly and slapped his knee. "You know, you're going to come in right handy when another of these confounded women expects me to deliver her baby while she's blanketed from chin to ankle." He stood suddenly and clapped his big hands together. "Now, suppose you admit our first patient."

The morning fled past. She could scarcely believe she was a part of it all.

"Do you speak Italian and German and all these other languages?" she asked during a two-minute respite.

"Of course not."

"Then how do you understand your patients?"

"Sickness is a universal language, Jo. Besides, there are only so many known cures. I can't go too far wrong, no matter what the complaint." He chuckled. "I just do the best I can and hope my mistakes are little ones."

The steeple bells of the old church at Second and Walnut had already rung the noon hour when Jody ushered the last of the patients to the door. She turned back to find Doc Adams opening a box lunch and solemnly dividing the contents.

"Mrs. Adams didn't know she'd be feeding two today, but she packs enough for an army anyhow."

Jody went to the basin to wash her hands as she had done several times during the morning. He munched on a pear and watched.

Lunch was delicious, and Jody could just picture the apple dumpling little woman who had packed it so lovingly.

They closed the office then, to make afternoon rounds. For Jo, the house calls in the city were a haunting return to Five Points. The familiar sounds and smells dredged up the misery of that first year in New York—and especially the night her father was killed.

148

"You all right?" asked Adams.

Her smile was thin lipped. "I'm fine," she assured him as they closed another door on the strong smell of boiled cabbage. "Just a bad case of memories."

It was a source of amazement to Jody that the poor of the area called on Doc Adams as frequently as they did. She thought about her mother's carefully written remedies and remembered how reluctant the poor were to fetch a medical man. Doctors were *so* expensive, and their treatment was often worse than the illness. People treated themselves until they really got scared; only then did they call the doctor.

Jo decided Doc's reluctance to bleed patients or use leeches was a big reason for his popularity. In an age when blistering, blood-letting, cathartics, and tartar emetics were standard, no matter what the illness, Doc Adams's mild treatments were an anathema to his fellow practitioners, a godsend to his patients. Jody questioned Doc about why the poor called him so often, and his explanation was simple: "I've been here twenty years. They know I'll come whether they can pay or not."

He was pleased with her work and before the week was out, she was applying dressings and administering medications. He gave her simple medical books to read, then quizzed her on their contents.

From the very beginning, it was obvious that Jo had a way with their women patients. They trusted her, and before the end of the first week, they had begun to call her "Dr. Jo." Adams found it amusing and, with a wink at Jody, soon was introducing her that way.

"They shouldn't call me doctor," she protested, but was pleased.

"It's only a complimentary title—they know that. They realize you're just a nurse, but they like you, and they know you're here to help."

Doc Adams and Dr. Jo, in their open black buggy,

149

soon became an accepted twosome, their visits always welcome. Even in the poorest of households, a steaming cup of mocha awaited the Doc. And before long, a washbasin with a bit of soft soap awaited the dirt-chasing Dr. Jo.

At first Adams teased her about her "cleanliness phobia," and her initial, bristling reaction gradually mellowed as she realized he enjoyed baiting her. He was a monstrous tease, but liked getting back as good as he delivered—a man who enjoyed a good argument and didn't much care which side he took as long as his opponent was quick with a sharp retort.

"When you're making rounds, you can't expect to wash your hands whenever the urge strikes," he said.

"I'll soon change that," she told him. "If your patients can get used to you wanting coffee as soon as you walk in the door, they'll soon get used to me washing my hands."

He snorted with disgust. "You'll wear the skin off!"

"Doc, have you ever heard of Semmelweiss?"

"What's that, some kind of soap?"

"He's a doctor in Europe somewhere. I read about him in a New York paper. He has a theory that doctors carry diseases from one patient to the next."

"Well, we're not weighted down with money, that's for sure. We might as well put something in our pockets to carry from one place to another."

"Don't you think it's possible that we carry germs?"

"If diseases were spread by touching diseased people, I'd be dead twenty times a day," declared Doc.

"But Semmelweis proved that puerperal fever is carried by doctors. He made everybody wash—"

"You want to work for me?"

"Of course."

"Then stop beating a dead horse."

As the days passed, Jody learned to keep her ideas on

150

cleanliness to herself. She continued to scrub her hands and to take their white coats home to launder, but she kept a curb on her tongue.

"He's not like anybody I ever met before," she said at the supper table one night. "He can't help doing good deeds, but he hopes nobody will notice. If you accused him of being kindhearted, he'd deny it with his last breath."

"He just seemed like a cranky old man to me," retorted Anne, pushing her plate away with a sigh.

"You talking about Doc Adams?" inquired Meg who arrived just then with a platter of thickly sliced gingerbread cake. "He's a lovable old coot. Give you the shirt right off his back and then swear on a stack of Bibles it wasn't his shirt. It was Doc delivered Jeremy, you know."

Jody was constantly surprised at the freedom of expression around Meg's table. No subject was taboo, nothing sacred.

"Me, a scared young actress left behind when the troupe moved on," continued Meg blithely. "So big with child I couldn't hide it anymore with high waistlines and piles of petticoats." She glanced at Anne, and Jody wondered if she knew about the expected baby. Had Anne told her?

"You were the sweetest Juliet this Romeo ever loved," declared Phinny gallantly. There was a small sound from the other end of the table. "With the exception of my dear Annette, of course," he added hastily.

Jeremy leaned toward Jody and whispered, "If Annette wore horns and a tail, she'd make Phinny swear they were beauty marks."

Jody looked into his dancing green eyes. "How are rehearsals going?"

"Splendidly." His imitation of the flowery Phinny

151

was very convincing. "Nella says I'm good. *Othello* is next week and I'm taking three parts: the Messenger, the Second Gentleman, and the Herald."

"Then you have quite a few speeches."

"One of these days, I'll play Othello himself," Jeremy bragged. "And Romeo. And I'll have my own company." He was nearing the end of his first week on stage and feeling very cocky.

Jody noticed Nella's gaze rest on the boy's animated face. Something dark and glittering moved in the depths of her sleepy eyes. Jeremy seemed unaware of her interest as he leaned toward Jody. "Phinny's still holding tryouts for some of the smaller *Othello* parts. I've heard him say more than once that you could pass for a man. Why don't you?"

"I couldn't be in a play even if I wanted to," laughed Jody. "We don't get through rounds until six or seven. You know I usually don't get home until after supper is over. Tonight's an exception."

"Well, I know Phinny's getting worried. He says if he doesn't cast all the parts soon he'll have to rewrite and give me extra speeches. Of course, I could handle it with no problem, but he's saving that as a last resort. Why don't you? You'd have fun."

"He's right, my dear," interjected Thompson, who had apparently been listening. "If you would agree to filling in as the Sailor and the First Gentleman, I'd have my *Othello* cast all set. What do you say?"

"I say I'm not that softheaded." In spite of her protest, Jody was flattered that Phinny should want her. She thought about what fun it had been, striding so freely across the parlor, pretending to be a man; how wickedly delicious it would be to don Shakespearean tights and strut about on a stage before hundreds of anonymous eyes.

Phinny sensed the weakening and quickly baited the

hook. "You'd make two dollars for the week. You could use a little extra, I'll wager. And I'll wager you already know the parts." He cast his eyes up and launched into the sailor's cue line: "Now, what's the business?"

"The Turkish preparation makes for Rhodes," replied Jody promptly. "So I was bid report here to the state by Signior Angelo."

There was a ripple of applause around the table.

"What from the cape can you discern at sea?" demanded Jeremy, cuing her for the First Gentleman.

"Nothing at all: it is a high-wrought flood," replied Jody, the lines flowing back as readily as if she had the old leather copy of Shakespeare open before her on the table. "I cannot 'twixt the heaven and the main Descry a sail."

"Bravo, my dear! Bravo!" Phinny was on his feet and even Annette looked approving.

"Come on, Jody, why don't you do it?" Meg urged, taking her seat at the head of the table. "Doc Adams could let you off early. It's only for one week."

Amid all the urgings, Jody found herself agreeing. "But only if it's all right with Doc," she insisted. "And only for this one play."

"*Othello* is our last appearance in St. Louis this year anyhow," said Annette, pursing her prim mouth. "After that we move on to Salt Lake City where Nella gets to sample her own version of heaven." She cast a withering glance at the other woman.

"Maybe you ought to sample a few of the saints yourself," drawled Nella good-naturedly. "It's probably the closest you'll ever come to the pearly gates."

153

# 13

Doc pulled a long face when Jo approached him about going on stage with the Thompson Company for a week. "You'll not be running off to be one of them professional actors, will you?"

"No, you're stuck with me whether you like it or not," she laughed. "Phinny—Mr. Thompson—says I could rehearse nights after they get home. So I'd be at work every day as usual. I'd just have to get off early that one week so I could be at the theatre by six each night."

"You'll be dropping for want of sleep."

"I'll not do it if you really object."

"Don't put the blame on me. If you want to go on stage in men's pants, go ahead. But if you fall asleep in the buggy just once, I'll roll you out on your hoops and leave you in the middle of the road."

"You would, too."

"You're right, I would."

Every day he asked how rehearsals were going, and she knew he was angling for an invitation. He wanted to see the play, but wanted her to invite him. It was childish, but she loved him for it.

Phinny had given her two free tickets, and she was saving them until the day before the *Othello* opening when she planned to slip them in Doc's lunch box with a note to Mrs. Adams saying how much she hoped they could attend, and that they could meet backstage after the play.

Every day now, the doctor's wife sent special treats marked, "Hands off, Archibald Adams! This is for Dr. Jo." Or, "Don't let Dr. Adams get hold of this, Jo. He's already too fat." Jo couldn't wait to meet the doctor's wife whom she pictured as a round little woman with tight springy curls and bright blue eyes.

Rehearsals were going well, except that Jo was having trouble with the Second Gentleman, who was no gentleman. Jeremy kept touching her, holding her hand or putting his arm around her. It was most disconcerting when he was so attractive, and she was trying so hard to act like a man.

For the first three nights, after the troupe returned from the theatre, Phinny had coached Jo on her walk, her stage presence, and the delivery of her lines. He proclaimed her diction: "Splendid!" And her husky voice: "Splendid! Splendid!"

On the fourth night, Jo met the rest of the *Othello* cast at the theatre and walked through her two scenes with Jeremy and the other actors. Phinny spent an hour coaching her on how to walk and how to project her voice across the footlights into the back rows.

The stage, with the empty space beyond, was awe inspiring and more than a little frightening, but Phinny was so pleased with Jo's progress that he said she could rehearse alone from then on. Sunday there would be a full dress rehearsal at the theatre with the entire cast.

Meg, offering to supply her costumes, took Jo to the attic. "Actors aren't the most reliable of boarders," she said as she threw open the musty trunk. "This collection represents thirteen years of friends skipping out on their room rent. This is where most of my furniture comes from, you know." She waved her hand at a pile of scenery and several boxes of props and smiled as she sank to the floor to paw through an assortment of gowns and waistcoats. "Comes in handy at times like this, though."

Having practically poured Jo into what she called "the gentleman's suit," she stood back to admire the results. Jo frowned, aghast at the way the tights clung to her legs. "But that's the way they should look," Meg assured her.

Jo gazed doubtfully at her own legs. What had made her agree to this dumb idea? "Even if I could wear these tights, what about my hair?" she asked miserably. "Mr. Thompson said he might cut it, but I don't want my hair cut."

Meg rummaged again, discarding several ratty-looking hairpieces before she came up with a present-able man's wig. "Here, this ought to do the trick."

The blond wig was fine and Jo was amazed at the transformation. Now if only the tights weren't so tight.

She mentioned her reservations to Jeremy later.

"Why don't you come down to the theatre again tonight," he suggested. "Wear the tights and I'll ask Phinny to hold a late rehearsal so you can get the feel of them onstage. If they're really too snug, it's better to find out now instead of waiting until it's too late to do anything about it."

Jo arrived backstage, modestly covered with a flowing black cape, just in time to watch from the wings as Annette and Phinny took their curtain calls, bowing and smiling.

The curtain closed and the bright smile promptly died on Annette's face. She swung on her husband in anger. "You deliberately upstaged me, you bastard!" Her little-girl voice quivered with rage.

"Now, Annette, baby, you know I wouldn't do that."

"Get the hell out of my way!" She stormed past Jo

and Jeremy, her small bosom swelling in its fury to soprano fullness. Her husband trotted behind her, futilely protesting his innocence.

Within a few minutes, the troupe had all departed, leaving the two young people alone in the wings.

"Where did everybody go?" asked Jo in alarm. "Aren't they staying to rehearse?"

"I guess Annette's tantrum took care of that."

"Oh, fiddlesticks."

"We can run through your scenes anyway."

"That's good. I really feel ridiculous in these tights." She peered through a hole in the curtain, amazed at how rapidly the barnlike theatre could be emptied of several hundred people. But the real shocker came when a stagehand appeared and began to extinguish the footlights.

"Tell him to stop," she said, starting forward. "Don't they know we're going to rehearse?"

Jeremy grabbed her arm. "Phinny must have forgotten to tell them," he whispered. "It's all right. As soon as they've gone, I'll light the foots again."

All over the theatre gaslights, turned up for departing patrons, were now being extinguished. Soon the entire theatre was dark, and there came a distant clang as the stage door slammed behind the last stagehand.

"They've gone," said Jo nervously. "Light the lamps."

"I'll open the act curtain first and raise the drop." Jeremy was very proud of his stage talk. He ran lightly across the darkened boards, and soon the heavy curtain beside Jo bunched together. Next the act drop swished above her, baring the stage.

"What from the cape can you discern at sea?" called Jeremy, cuing her with Montano's line as he came toward her.

157

She forgot the footlights as she dropped her cloak, and was glad now for the darkness. How would she ever get up enough nerve to go on a lighted stage with her legs hanging out like this?

"What from the cape can you discern at sea?" demanded Jeremy again.

Jo opened her mouth, let her words flow from her diaphragm as Phinny had taught her, and felt the role take over. Her voice, deep and full and husky, rolled into the empty recesses of the theatre with a carrying quality she had not known she possessed until Phinny had explained about the diaphragm and proper breathing.

They ran through the scene, Jeremy playing all the characters except hers. When he came to Desdemona's entrance, he didn't want to stop. "Come on, Jo, you know all the parts," he pleaded. "You be the women and I'll be everyone else."

"I can't even see you. Light the foots so we can at least see."

"I'm here." He moved close and touched her shoulder. "Come on, you be Desdemona and Emilia . . .

> Hail to thee, lady! and the grace of heaven,
> Before, behind thee, and on every hand,
> Enwheel thee round!"

Entering into the spirit of adventure projected by the insistent Jeremy, Jo recited Desdemona's lines, replying to his Cassio. It was when Cassio spoke to Emilia that Jo began to feel ill at ease.

"Welcome, mistress," he began—just as she remembered that this particular speech ended with a kiss. Jo backed away from the sound of Jeremy's voice, but his hand caught her arm.

> 'Tis my breeding
> That gives me this bold show of courtesy . . .

Then Jo felt his breath hot against her cheek. His arms went around her and his mouth found hers. Her heart pounded. His lips were hesitant, then suddenly firm. His hands moved across her back, past her narrow waist, to grasp her pantaloon-encased buttocks and pull her close against him.

She gasped. Immediately, his tongue took advantage of her loosened lips. Snakes of St. Patrick what was he doing?

Without thought or malice, she instinctively did as Pa had taught. She brought her knee up in one quick sharp jab between Jeremy's spread legs. He gave a yelp of pain and hunched over, holding himself in silent anguish.

She backed away then and huddled against the traveler, waiting for him to get his voice back. He was silent so long that she finally crept cautiously toward him.

"Jeremy?" She hadn't meant to really hurt him. Her eyes had adjusted to the dimness now and she could see him bent over, holding his groin and groaning in anguish. She hadn't expected her father's training to prove so effective. "Are you all right?"

"Lot you care." The words wrenched from him like a rusty nail from a board.

"I'm sorry. I didn't mean to hurt you so badly."

"Christ, it was only a kiss."

"I said I was sorry."

"Lot of good that does me now. Christ, you might have wrecked me for life."

She didn't know how to answer.

"Are you really sorry?"

"I said I was."

"Want to kiss it and make it better?" He moved close again, but she noticed with amusement that he didn't turn his body toward her, only his head.

Her heart still beat with hard insistence, and her lips still burned where his had pressed. And she could still feel a strange tingling between her legs. But she wasn't about to let him know how she had been affected. "You want another of the same?" she countered.

He edged away in alarm. "You ain't natural!"

"You ready to rehearse now?"

"You know what I want to do," he grumbled.

"If that means we're not going to rehearse anymore, then I'm going home. I have to be up at seven in the morning." She thought he might relent and offer to run through her scenes once more, but he didn't. He even let her take the reins while he sulked in the corner of the buggy.

She didn't see Jeremy again until dress rehearsal Sunday when he played the big, professional actor to the hilt, his green eyes studiously ignoring her. Well, she supposed she deserved his scorn. Looking back, she guessed what he had done wasn't so bad, but after her experience with Quimby and Anne's confidences—everything was too raw in her mind. A kiss was one thing, but how was a girl supposed to know where a kiss might leave off and rape begin?

From then on, Jeremy avoided her. When they actually stood together onstage on opening night, he still did not meet her eye, but Jo was too caught up in her own acting to care. Not once did she remember the tights and her exposed limbs—not even when the final curtain had fallen and Doc Adams brought his wife backstage.

Jo had so looked forward to meeting Mrs. Adams, but now, as they came toward her, Jo's heart twisted in aching disbelief. Sally Adams was an invalid.

160

Doc pushed his wife's wheelchair toward Jo, his brows knotted above a hard stare, as though daring her to show pity. With obvious effort, Sally Adams held herself erect, her wasted body and gaunt face mute evidence of her pain-wracked existence.

"Dr. Jo—Mrs. Adams." He glared at Jo.

"Call me Sally." The thin face lit with a sweet smile. "The doctor had told me so much about you, Jo. I feel we are already friends."

"I feel the same way."

Sally Adams turned reproving eyes on her husband. "You told me she was beautiful—you never mentioned that she has the smile of an angel."

"Hmmmmph!" Doc looked away in mock disgust.

"You were marvelous, Jo," said Sally. "Watching you on stage, I even forgot you were a woman, you were so convincing."

"Thank you. It was great fun."

"Hmmmmph!" Doc glared at her. "I suppose now you'll decide to go traipsing off with them actor fellows."

Jo grinned at him. "I told you I wouldn't. You'll not get rid of me that easily." Then she saw the strain on Sally's face and her smile faded.

Immediately sensitive to his wife's needs, Doc bent over her and touched her shoulder. "I'm sorry to cut your evening short, Mrs. Adams, but it has been a long day for me." He straightened and glared at Jo. "We'll say good night now. See that you are on time in the morning."


*Othello* ran its week and was a marked success, but the pleasure was gone for Jo. Meeting Sally Adams had placed a damper on Jo's normally good spirits, and Jeremy's continued coldness was the final straw. His

161

reaction to the way she had protected herself was a bit excessive, Jo thought. After all, he was the one who had been too forward. All she did was protect herself from advances she hadn't asked for and didn't want. Although that last might not be completely true. If she was being honest, she'd have to admit she had enjoyed the feel of his lips. But after Quimby's attempted rape, men made her nervous.

Jeremy and the Thompson Company were to depart for Salt Lake City on Saturday, but since Butterfield's Overland Coach didn't leave until ten in the morning, Meg had prepared a late Friday night supper, replete with squab, French champagne, and rattle boxes.

"It isn't every day one bids adieu to one's only child," she declared. She put up a gay front, but often her eyes rested on her handsome son and her smile came brighter as she fought her tears.

Jeremy's laugh grew boisterous as the evening progressed, his eyes a deeper, more devilish green, as he indulged in the sparkling beverage. Phinny, too, had partaken freely of the wine. His leonine head rolled, too heavy to support. He appeared not to notice when Jeremy's arm rested lightly across Annette's slender shoulders with fingers trailing teasingly over the exposed upper portion of her breast. But Jo saw, and Nella saw, and Meg saw.

Meg's smile was indulgent, Nella's grim. Jo turned away in disgust, thinking that he hadn't been very interested in her if he could immediately take up with this faded, middle-aged ingenue with her kohl-lined eyes and her painted cupid's bow mouth.

"Anne, I'm going up to bed. Are you coming?"

"Yes." Anne's eyes also rested on Jeremy. Jo saw the fright in them and knew that Anne was remembering past nights when her father's hand had clutched her breast. "Come on. They'll never miss us."

They got as far as the archway into the hall when Charles Townsend impaled them with his baritone. "Not sneaking out without a final good-bye, I hope."

"And a final toast," called Meg. "Here, Anne, Jo—let me fill your glasses. We'll drink to Jeremy's success."

The girls turned reluctantly to accept the proffered drinks.

"To Jeremy O'Gerity—may his star rise to the heavens and his name be sung throughout the world." Meg raised her glass high, her eyes glowing with love and glistening with the knowledge that she had lost her son.

"Hear! Hear!"

"Egad. 'Tis time for toasts." Phinny lifted his glass to Jo with tipsy gallantry. "To the first First Gentleman who ever sported an apple dumpling shop!" It was an expression Jo had never heard before, but his meaning was clear as his bloodshot eyes swept across her small, firm breasts. "And the sweetest apple dumpling shop a man could ever put his mouth to, too!"

She felt herself flush.

"Mind your tongue, Phinny, before your cockney ancestry begins to show," ordered Meg with a good-natured laugh. "And make your proper farewells to your First Gentleman. She's off to bed."

"Farewell, my dear. Parting is such sweet sorrow . . ." He aimed his kiss at her cheek, but it skidded lightly off her ear.

Will Cottle smiled and nodded; the two women waggled graceful fingers. Charles Townsend stepped forward then and took her hand with old-fashioned grace. "Your presence on the stage tonight was felt by all of us, Miss Jo. You were a grand First Gentleman, and it has been a real pleasure."

"For me too, Charlie."

Past Charlie's ear, she saw Jeremy waiting, his eyes agleam with the old mischief. "You've not said good-bye to me," he declared. Stepping forward quickly, he clasped her to him. His mouth was hard and insistent this time, his arms imprisoning bands.

Damn him, he was deliberately taking advantage of the watching company, knowing she couldn't knee him again while his mother stood there smiling. The kiss went on and on while her body grew hot and her face began to burn. His tongue probed tentatively, then with forceful demand. Jo felt that tingling again—that sudden quickening of muscles in her lower abdomen and between her legs. Her breath came faster. Her heart pounded unmercifully.

Jeremy released her at last, his green eyes triumphant. He knew full well she had enjoyed the kiss in spite of the circumstances.

Jo felt Anne's comforting hand slip into hers. She squeezed it gratefully. It gave her courage as she lifted her head. "You have all been so kind to me," she said, forcing her eyes to travel slowly around the room. "I enjoyed being a small part of your Company."

She looked last at Jeremy. Her voice was even, and the smile on her bruised lips was defiant. "As for you, Jeremy O'Gerity, if you ever try that again you'll be crawling for a week."

She read reluctant admiration in the dancing green depths of his eyes as he raised his hand in a final salute. "'Bye, Red. If you ever change your mind, come look me up. I'll be waiting in the wings any time you're ready."

Jeremy and the Thompson Company departed on Saturday. On Sunday, the Mark Webster Company moved in, but by then Jo had settled down to the serious study of medicine. Doc Adams had lent her another medical book, and Jo was curled up on her bed, Jeremy forgotten as she studied the illustrations and struggled to follow the text.

In the months that followed, Jo became a sponge, a bottomless pit into which all manner of information was poured. Where she had once been an ostrich, she was now a ferret. Her eyes missed nothing; her ears stretched to catch the slightest nuance. There was so much to learn.

At Doc's amused suggestion, Jo found a man's suit in the attic trunk and attended several lectures at Dutton School of Medicine. He had thought she wouldn't do it, but she fooled him. Posing as a man, she managed to watch four operations and two dissections.

Everything, all her observations, were carefully sorted and evaluated. As her mother had taught, Jo applied her mind to the facts, then searched out her own conclusions—but Edith Gates would have been considerably shocked at some of the conclusions her daughter now entered in her fattening notebook.

"You never have time for me anymore," Anne

complained. But Jo, deep into the mysteries of medical science, continued her studies.

At first, she worked hard to obtain an overall knowledge, but as time wore on, her focus narrowed until the plight of women claimed her concentrated attention.

Women with consumption, honey-sweet diabetes, severe asthma, or a dropped womb—nothing deterred the parade of children these unfortunates were forced to bring forth on an average of one a year. These repeated, life-draining pregnancies were what had led Jo to medicine in the first place, and the more she worked with these unfortunates, the more determined she became to find a way to help them.

Fenella Brady, thirty-eight, with sixteen pregnancies and seven miscarriages behind her, had tried to abort her baby with a knitting needle. She was hemorrhaging badly when they arrived. It took all night and all Doc's skill to save her.

When he left, Jo stayed to fix breakfast for the bevy of small tots still at home. Fenella watched from her pallet in the corner.

"Dr. Jo," she whispered, "Can't you give me something so I won't have no more kids?"

Jo had no answer.

One day a girl about Jo's age came alone to the office. She had missed two menstrual periods, she said.

"Looks like you're in a family way, Leona," the doctor told her after he had asked all the usual questions and examined her breasts. This, in itself, was a first for Jo who was shocked at the girl's utter lack of modesty.

"That's what I was afraid of. You sure, Doc?" Leona asked, buttoning her bodice.

"As sure as I can be without further examination."

"You mean there's another way to find out?"

166

"Yes, I could examine you internally."

"Then let's get on with it. If I'm thataway, I gotta know it so I can do somethin' about it."

"There isn't anything you *can* do, Leona. At least not without great danger to your life."

"You let me worry about that, Doc. All I wanta know from you is, am I for sure carryin' a kid?"

The doctor sighed. "Step behind the screen and remove your undergarments," he said.

The girl did as he directed, then climbed obligingly onto the table, her skirt hoisted over wide-spread knees. After one startled look, Jo moved closer. Doc turned his head, his lips automatically compressed with disapproval. Then, at her pleading look, he reluctantly moved aside so she could get a better view. And he began to explain exactly what he was doing—and why.

Then the girl was gone. Jo, her face blazing with embarrassment, busied herself at the washbasin.

"If you're going to work with me," Doc said implacably, "you'll have to get over that unprofessional modesty."

She swung about and glared into his amused face. "I'll get over it, don't you worry."

"If you're embarrassed, it makes your patients feel the same way."

"Not her. Not that one who just left. What's wrong with her that she has no modesty?"

Doc grinned. "Leona is one of the girls at Claire's Sporting Parlor. For your information, that's a high-class whorehouse. Which means I give the girls a checkup every once in awhile." He examined her face with a knowing grin. "And now that you've seen how free and open Leona is, I suppose you'll be wanting to come along next time I have a house call at Claire's. You'll probably learn more in a brothel in one afternoon than you'll learn in six months of

167

treating ladies."

He was right. Jo learned about the female douche and the use of strong purgatives like those she had seen in the basement laboratory at Madame Restell's. But several of the women had children, she discovered, some off at school, some being raised in the country. So their douches and cathartics obviously didn't work too well.

Jo read far into the night, every night, searching for answers.

"Listen to this," she said to Anne one evening, "'In 1542 physicians believed that eating lettuce killed sexual desire.'" She turned the book upside-down on her stomach and stared at her friend. "What do you think? Do you suppose what men eat affects how often they want to . . . to . . . you know . . ."

Anne didn't look up from the pink bootie slowly taking form beneath the flashing needles. "Not likely." Her voice was tight. "If other men are like my father, they're ready to do it anytime, anyplace."

Discussion of sexual matters seemed to disturb Anne, so Jo stopped sharing her discoveries, but when she found her first reference to a condom, she was so excited that she had to tell someone. She raced downstairs to disclose her monumental discovery to Meg.

Jo burst through the door where the red-haired landlady was setting bread to rise, her face flushed with the warmth of the kitchen.

"Listen to what it says here, Meg. The first condom, a linen sheath, was invented in 1560, following a syphilis epidemic."

"Bless us, girl, what are you reading?"

"It's a medical history. It says here that the male sperm wasn't discovered until 1677, and it was another hundred years more before they found out that it was the male sperm that made a woman pregnant."

"Merciful heavens."

Jo giggled. "You know how they found out? They put some kind of pantaloons on a frog and when they mated him . . ."

"How could frogs get together if they was wearin' breeches?" demanded Meg, her brogue growing with her agitation.

"I don't know—but they did. And they found out that none of the female eggs got fertilized."

"What's a female egg?"

"That's what the baby starts with—an egg inside the woman or inside the frog—"

"You mean like a chicken?"

"Well, sort of. Like a chicken egg without a shell, I guess."

"You're trying to tell me Jeremy came out of something like a chicken egg?"

"No, I'm trying to tell you that the frog eggs weren't fertile when the frogs wore pantaloons. So they scraped off the semen from the inside of the breeches and injected it into the female frog and she got pregnant."

Meg sniffed. "You can't tell me Jeremy come from an egg."

Jo laughed. "I'm telling you what the book says, Meg. Why, they've even injected a man's sperm into a woman and she had a baby."

"Saints preserve us!" the other woman squealed. "Where'd you get that dirty book?"

"Doc Adams lent it to me. But it's not a dirty book. It's a medical history."

"A young woman like you has no right reading filth like that. What's come over Doc that he'd give you such trash to read?"

Jo couldn't believe Meg was such a prude. Here was a woman who had begat an illegitimate child yet thought it wrong to discuss how a woman became pregnant. She couldn't believe it.

"I'm going to be a doctor one day," she said. "I have to know about things like this."

"Well, if you have to know it, then you'd best keep it to yourself. No nice woman will ever admit she knows about such things. And certainly no lady would ever talk about them."

As Meg washed her hands and dried them on her apron, her gaze kept straying to the book Jo held.

"Well," she burst out finally, "you've already read it—and you've already told me part—you might as well tell me the rest. Where'd they get this 'semen' they stuck into that woman's—into that woman?"

"The man masturbated."

"Holy Mother of God." Meg crossed herself. "That's a sin!"

## 15

It was Marlene Schmidt's ninth pregnancy but only her fifth live child, and it was the first time the doctor had ever been summoned. Her husband, refusing to pay for even a midwife, had always delivered their children himself. Cheap whiskey and inept bungling had brought the death of four of his children and the near death of his wife, but that had not stopped Karl Schmidt's brutal deliveries. This time, fortunately for Marlene, her husband was out of town when her labor pains began. A neighbor had summoned Doc Adams, but it was Jo who answered the call. She had already delivered fourteen babies without Doc's staring over her shoulder, and now considered herself as good as any midwife in the city.

Three hours later, she delivered number fifteen, a little girl, dainty and thin, with a full head of dark fuzz. The grateful mother named the child Jody Gates Schmidt. Dr. Jo was ridiculously proud of the wee, red-faced namesake.

"You should see her try to hold up her head," she told Anne later. "And the way her little hand curls around my finger. It's like she knows me."

Anne turned away, her face clouded. Jo soon stopped talking about the Schmidt baby. Anne wasn't getting used to the idea of her own pregnancy as Jo had

171

hoped. If anything, her friend grew moodier and more surly with each passing day.

Finally, one winter evening, Jo brought her stethoscope home to let Anne listen to her own heart. Then, almost imperceptibly, she slid the tube down to Anne's swollen belly. The girl jerked away, then stopped and slowly replaced the tube. A strange, alert look sprang into her black eyes, and her mouth opened in gentle wonder. "That's . . . is that . . . is that my baby?" She grasped the tube in both hands, her face breaking into an awed smile. "It is! I can hear her heartbeat! So strong . . ."

"What makes you so sure it's a girl?" teased Jo. It was the first interest Anne had shown in months. Jo felt tears of relief sting her lids.

Anne's laugh rang out and her eyes were bright. "She wouldn't dare be a boy!"

As the days wore on, Anne threw off the cloud that had been her companion for so long now. She began to ask questions about the nearing delivery, and once Jo overheard her talking with Meg about the possibility of restoring an old crib in the attic. Jo relaxed, secure at last in the knowledge that she had been right to refuse to do the abortion. Not that she would have done it anyway, but she was glad to be vindicated, happy that Anne now accepted the coming baby, even looked forward to it.

Although months had passed, the possibility that the police might be hunting for them still haunted the two girls, and now they began to make plans to put more distance between themselves and the New York police. Their plans would come to fruition, they decided, after the baby was born and after Doc Adams had relented and presented Jo with a medical certificate.

"When I've learned all I can from Doc, and when the baby's big enough to travel, that's when we'll go West,"

Jo promised.

"We can go as a family," interposed Anne who loved make-believe. "You can wear that man's suit you wear to the operations—the one you borrowed from Meg. No one would recognize us then. They'd never be looking for a mother and a father and a baby."

"Never mind making me over into a man," said Jo. "When we go West, I'm going as a woman, same as you. We can be sisters if you want, but just because I'll be a doctor doesn't mean I can't be a woman, too. I'm going to marry someday and have a big family. I just have to get my certificate first." Her grin was confident. "I know Doc will give me a certificate. He said he wouldn't, but I know he will when the time comes."

"Of course he will." Anne glowed with good health these days. She had taken to housework like a bird to nest building. She sang now, as she worked, in a clear, sweet voice that could be heard throughout the house. She had apparently closed the door on all that had gone before and immersed herself in planning for the baby.

She named the expected child Jody Anne, and she carried high, which Meg assured her meant a girl. When Jody Anne kicked, Anne's face lighted with joy.

Jo congratulated herself often. Smartest thing I ever did, she thought, bringing that stethoscope home.

The winter passed in a busy blur. Anne's pile of handmade baby clothes grew. The old spool crib was hauled from the attic, and Anne scraped and sanded and painted. Now it stood waiting in the corner of their room, a pink and white reminder of the happily awaited event.

Sauntering home from the livery stable one evening, Jo filled her lungs with moist April air and laughed at the bluejay jawing from the linden tree in Meg's front yard. It was spring and good to be alive.

173

It was too dark to see the watch pinned to her bodice, but Jo knew it was getting on toward six. The new people should be pouring out the door any minute now on their way to the theatre.

Jo wondered what the new batch of thespians would be like. Over the past months, she had played a French maid and drew laughs with her perky "oo la la!"—had a few lines in *The Taming of the Shrew*—and was a swashbuckling buccaneer in the *The Pirate* once when a musical company was in residence, but now she had made up her mind not to become involved with acting anymore, much as she enjoyed it.

Anne had also enjoyed Jo's excursions into the theatre, and despite her expanding girth, whenever Jo was on stage, had always occupied a seat in the front row.

Doc and Sally Adams had not come to the theatre after that first time, but Jo knew that the older woman suffered such pain she was no longer able to go out in public. Once a month Jo and Anne were invited to Sunday supper at the Adams's home on Manchester Road. It was a handsome brick house with wide verandas and white pillars. She loved the quiet times spent there, but it broke her heart to see Sally's obviously worsening condition. Entertaining, even in this simple fashion, was a terrible drain on the failing woman, and Jo had finally spoken to Doc about it. "It's too much for her. I don't think we should come anymore."

"Nonsense. It's all she has to look forward to. If it bothers you to see her suffer, that's too bad. You'll just have to put up with it."

"You know I didn't mean that."

"We'll not discuss it." Doc's temper was thin these days, and his normally lovable irascibility had taken on an unhealthy edge. His suffering and Sally's increasing

174

pain were the only flaws in Jo's growing well of content, but large as they loomed, they could not overshadow the satisfaction her expanding medical expertise afforded.

One after the other, she had exhausted Doc's slim supply of medical books. The last set he lent her had come from the Dutton School Library. It dealt exclusively with malformed children and the suspected causes of such tragedies. Jo had waded through two volumes before she came across a reference to incest and the deformed or retarded children who often resulted from such unions.

"Dr. Howe," the book said, "has examined almost all cases of idiocy in Massachusetts and found (in all but four) that the *parents* of the idiots were either intemperate, addicted to sensual vices, scrofulous, predisposed to insanity, or had intermarried with blood relations."

Then it delved into specific cases of known incest and the resulting deformities.

Horrified, Jo read that chapter over and over, not wanting to believe, yet faced with undeniable evidence in the case studies presented.

Sick at heart, she laid the book aside, unable to read further. Finally, just today, she had gotten up enough nerve to discuss it with Doc. He had never asked about the father of Anne's child, and now Jo could see the tired lines deepen in his face as he listened. There was a long silence when she finished. "Will Anne's baby be like those in the book?" she asked haltingly.

His answer came slowly: "Listen to me, Jo—most imperfect embryos abort early. We see malformed *embryos* all the time—but full-term babies usually aren't defective. The fact that Anne has carried this long is undoubtedly a good sign. She only has two weeks to go now. Chances are her baby will be fine."

Then, just as Jo was about to say good night, Doc had thrust another book at her. "Here," he said roughly, "see what you make of this one. Bring that other set back and study this one awhile."

It wasn't until she was outside that she had looked down at the book and her heart began to thump. Doc had actually relinquished his brand-new, prized copy of *Gray's Anatomy* for her to study.

Jo's arm closed over the precious book. She couldn't wait to get home and begin to read. Tonight, she decided, she would skip the cold supper Anne always saved for her and go straight up.

She glanced up at their bedroom window now, surprised to see lamplight shining through the lace curtains. Anne shouldn't be up there now. She ought to be downstairs, helping clean up after supper.

With the book clutched tightly to her, drinking in the fresh April breeze, Jo mounted the steps to the narrow brick boardinghouse and pushed her key into the lock.

From inside came a high-pitched, wavy reverberation. A scream. Somewhere inside, a woman in absolute terror was screaming.

Jo's flesh turned to fire. She pushed open the door.

The scene before her might have been staged. A mob scene, with bit players crowded at the steps, staring upward. Coated, ready to leave for the theatre, they froze in place, as though posing for a linotype advertisement for a new show.

From the second floor rang an endless, mindless shriek of pure terror. "Oh God oh no oh God no no . . ."

Jo's breath stopped. Her heart swelled. Threatened to choke her. She thrust through the boarders, ran up the steps, knowing—yet denying with every fibre of her being.

Meg stood in the doorway, green eyes distended, red

176

mouth stretched in horror.

It was all there—easy to see. Anne lay across the bed, her slashed wrists turned up as though in supplication. Beneath her white cheek, barely touched by the girl's congealed blood, lay an open book.

Even from here Jo could read the bold black letters of the chapter heading: *Incidence of Malformation in Cases of Incest*, it said. *Case Histories*.

# 16

It rained the day of the funeral, a mild, steady May rain that bogged the cemetery in a grove of mud. There were only four mourners: Jo, Meg, Doc, and Sally. The pain in Jo's heart was so intense she scarcely recognized the physical pain in Sally's gaunt face and scarcely heard the words of love and regret her friends expressed.

Sally Adams touched Jo's arm. "Come home with us tonight, Jo."

"I can't. I can't." Blinded by tears that gathered but would not fall, she shook off Sally's hand and walked rapidly away. She heard Meg behind her, calling, but she plodded on. She had to be alone, find a quiet place.

If Doc had never lent me that set of books— If I had never taken them home— If I had aborted the child as Anne begged me to do— If— If—

Jo's feet moved, but one wet cobbled street looked much like another. She must have closed her umbrella for her coat and dress were soon soaked through, but she had no recollection.

Dusk was descending when Jo's wanderings came to an end. What made her look up, she didn't know, but when she raised her eyes, she was standing in front of a small church. A place to sit. Solitude. She pushed the heavy door open.

It was almost dark inside, the half-glow through stained glass windows fading as the day wore into evening. The church smelled of lilies. There were white candles on the altar. She felt the hush of the chapel seep into the depths of her soul where neither rain, with its steady fingers, nor the concern of friends had reached. She knelt in the last pew and rested her head against the seat in front. Her mind was a quivering malignancy of memories, yet void of thought. She knelt a long time before she realized she was not alone.

Through the dull drum of rain on the roof came a low-pitched drone, an insistent hum like a litany—a prayer repeated over and over in a monotone.

Perhaps she made some small noise, she didn't know, but the voice ceased and a black shadow detached itself from the shadows at the altar and glided toward her.

She shrunk into the pew. Footsteps whispered in the empty chapel, stopped beside her. She could see a long black robe. A priest.

"Can I help?" When she did not answer, he crouched beside her. "If you tell me to go away, I will. But if you need someone to listen, I'm here."

*If*, he said. *If*.

She lifted her head. He couldn't see her face, but he felt the anguish in the hunched shoulders and the still, withdrawn body. "It helps sometimes to talk about it," he said.

The fingers on the roof ceased, and silence drifted between them. The independent person in her resented his intrusion and wanted to be alone; the woman in her longed to bury her head in the black robe and the deep velvet of his voice, and somehow ease her unbearable burden.

Anne's suicide was beyond bearing—beyond—beyond anything. It was as though all the deaths that had gone before—Mama, Pa, Kathie, yes, even

179

Nicholas Quimby—had combined in this one overwhelming catastrophe to break Jo's rebellious spirit.

Desperately, she tried to summon her valley, but she had lost the path. A low moan escaped her taut throat, and her body shook.

"You're shivering." His hand touched her shoulder.

He leaned toward her then, and his face passed through a waning shaft of light from a multifoiled window on the west side of the chapel. She had the impression of burning eyes in a white face.

"You're soaked through," he said. Under his hand, the woman continued to shake with cold. He wondered if she were dumb and unable to speak. "Come. There's always a fire in Father Lucien's study." He drew her to her feet and was surprised when the crumpled figure rose straight and tall beside him. He had thought her elderly.

He hoped to find the study empty. Father Lucien was not a particularly sympathetic man, and this woman needed a sensitive ear. He was glad to have a fire to offer, but as they passed the confessionals, his conscience smote him. "Would you prefer to go into the confessional?" Immediately he felt her withdrawal and knew the question was a mistake.

"I am not a Catholic, Father." Her words were a mere whisper.

"Then the fire it is," he said, drawing her past the curtained cubicles to a small door at the back of the chancel, and through the garden to the rectory.

There was no reply when he rapped on the door of Lucien's study. Good, he thought. The old priest had gone out.

The room was depressingly hot, as usual, a great fire leaping in the fireplace and the drapes tightly drawn. The senior priest claimed his bones needed more heat than young bones. He kept the small study so hot, winter and summer, that Father Fabian dreaded their Tuesday night meetings.

Now he welcomed the dry discomfort of the room for the sake of the woman who would soon be physically warm and comfortable. It was easier to reach a troubled spirit, he thought, when the body didn't suffer as well.

He drew the woman toward the fire. "Let's get you out of that wet hat and coat."

She allowed him to remove the wrap from her shoulders, then lifted slender arms to unpin her dripping hat. Her red-blond hair was a mass of heavy wet curls. "I'll see if I can find a towel," he said, abruptly heading for the door.

When he returned, she had knelt before the fire. She raised her head, and firelight danced across her face, high cheekbones and bruised hazel eyes set in a softly tinted oval; dark straight brows and a rebellious mouth, tremulous now in grief. With her skirt bunched about her like great darkened leaves, her slender waist a stem that swelled and blossomed, she was a vision of young loveliness, a flower in first bud.

He recognized her, of course, although he had never seen her up close before. They called her Dr. Jo, and all the parish women talked about her, the one who was telling them they shouldn't have one child after another—that it was bad for their health—that it was even unfair to the children, when another mouth to feed meant slow starvation for the entire family.

Fabian crossed himself and held out the towel.

"Thank you." Her voice was husky and laced with pain.

*Why Anne*? Over and over the question roared through her mind. What finger had crept from the heavens and touched Anne just when she had begun to reach out for a bit of happiness? The same cruel finger

181

that had cut down Mama just when they were about to land in America, the dream Mama had worked toward for ten years or more. Why, cried Jo's heart, why?

"Would you like to tell me about it?"

She looked at him for the first time then: Father Fabian—the young priest she had seen so often on rounds. A man of God. A man who believed in the goodness of God—the God who had taken Mama just when she was about to realize her life's dream. The God who had swept Anne away just when she had accepted her baby and glowed with joy for the upcoming birth.

"How can you believe in a God of mercy and goodness?" Jo burst out. "He's cruel and He's evil. He sits up there in his cloud castle and watches, and when He sees somebody about to be happy, He says, 'That's enough for you, sister. You've had a bucketful of misery and that's all you're entitled to. Let's end it before you get a taste of actual happiness.'" She broke into great gulping sobs and her voice rose hysterically. "He says, 'Misery . . . that's all . . . all you're going to get!'" Tears flooded her pale cheeks, and her lips twisted in the tight, ugly strain of grief.

"Man brought sorrow and pain and death into the world," the priest said softly. "That was not God's doing."

"Man couldn't have done it without God's consent," she screamed at him.

Fabian's hand went toward her, but he quickly drew it back to grasp his cross. What could he say to this Dr. Jo, a woman so strong in her beliefs, so determined to help other women that she was making trouble for all the parish—yet so defeated by death that she could not accept it. How could he comfort her?

After a bit, her sobs abated and she used the towel to wipe her face, then rummaged in her purse for a

182

handkerchief and blew her nose with no ladylike pretenses.

He sat on the floor beside her. "Was she a relative or friend?"

"A dear friend. About to have a baby," she told him, her voice breaking. "A fifteen-year-old girl who had been raped by her own father. A sweet young girl whose early life was hell, but who had finally found happiness in the baby she carried. For the first time in her life she was content—at peace. And then your God looked down and saw her happiness and snatched it away." If Anne had never read the book, she thought. If I could have done as Anne asked. But I couldn't.

The priest's eyes gripped hers. When he began to speak it was as though he held her heart in his hands and massaged it with gentle fingers. "The one left behind is the one who really suffers," he said. "Your friend is with our Father now. If He called her just when her life seemed to be unfolding, at the peak of her happiness, it may have been to spare her later, even greater pain—"

"But He didn't call her!" Jo was sobbing openly now, thinking of the blood—Anne's slender wrists. "You don't understand—"

"You are in pain," he said, his voice a velvet, restful relief. "And in your pain, you deny our Lord and His wisdom. But He can see the future. Perhaps your friend's child, conceived as it was in violence and incest, was already malformed—"

Jo started back in horror. "No. Oh, no. Don't you say that to me."

"Perhaps He spared your friend that grief. I don't suggest that I can see what was in His mind when He called your friend, but I do know that His call did not come from cruelty. Nor anger. Nor evil. And certainly

183

not as a whim. He called your friend because that was best for her. And best for you. Now it's up to you to accept your loss—to understand it—to let it work for you. Our Father hasn't forgotten that you, too, are suffering. He has sent this trial, this pain. In the name of Christ, you must endure it, let it strengthen you. God may have need of you later in your life. He may want you to be ready and able when He calls upon your strength."

Father Fabian's eyes were great glowing coals of fire, and she felt the power pass through him into her. Could it be true that Anne was better off? To Jo, whose life was dedicated to saving others, it was a shattering idea. That anyone could be better off dead than alive went against everything in which she believed. And what this priest didn't know was that Anne had taken her own life—and that she wouldn't have died if Jo had helped her—if Jo had aborted the baby as Anne had begged.

But Jo couldn't think about that now. She wouldn't think of that night when Anne had pleaded with her—

*It wasn't fair of Anne to ask me to do the abortion. It wasn't.*

If only she hadn't found that particular chapter, Jo thought.

Anne had been so happy about the baby lately—looking forward to it, loving it—

Did this priest make sense, even though he didn't know it was suicide? Was Anne, in death, spared even greater unhappiness?

Jo and the priest sat side by side, each wrapped in thought. At last she rose and stretched her hands to the blaze. He stood beside her.

"Thank you, Father." She smiled then, a determined little smile that touched his heart even more than her tears had done.

184

"You're Dr. Jo, aren't you?"

"How did you know?" The hypnotic glow had drained from his eyes, and she saw what a handsome man he was.

"My parishioners talk about you," he said.

She rotated her head and rubbed at the ache between her shoulder blades. "Your parishioners say something nice, I hope."

"They think you're a bit touched on the subject of soap and water, but they love you. Even those whose language I don't speak have a way of expressing their high regard for you."

"They do?"

"When I visit a sick woman in one of the foreign communities and find her getting well, I'll always say something like, 'Good! Good!' and she'll nod and smile and pat herself and say, 'Good! Dr. Jo,' and then she'll laugh and rub her hands together with a scrubbing motion." He made washing movements with his hands to demonstrate what the women did.

She smiled again, and this time her smile was tender. He could see why her patients trusted her.

"I must go." She moved toward the door. "I hope we meet again, Father."

"I'm sure we will. If ever you'd like to talk, I'll be here." He looked around the cramped office with distaste. "Well, not here exactly. This is Father Lucien's office. My office—such as it is—is outside. I use the garden in nice weather, the chapel when it's raining."

"Father Lucien? Then this is St. Anne's."

"Yes. You know the father?"

"Only by reputation. I hear he doesn't like my outspokenness on family limitation."

In the depths of the young priest's eyes, she could

185

see a quick spark. "Perhaps what he objects to is outspokenness concerning Catholic doctrine, by a non-Catholic."

"Religion has nothing to do with it," she said in a tired voice. "I talk about family limitation to women who are dying because of repeated pregnancies. If I offend Catholicism, Father, I'm sorry. But your religion dictates that women continue to bear children in the face of certain death. Women should have the right to limit their families, that's all. There should be a way to prevent pregnancy. If there were, Anne would still be alive." Or if I could have done as she asked, Jo thought as she turned wearily away.

He felt sorry for her, but her attack could not be ignored. "The doctrines of the Holy Church are not open to question," he told her quietly.

"Does the Church have so little feeling," she flared at him, "that women must die in order to perpetuate Catholicism?"

Before he could answer there was a sound of a carriage outside a second door.

"It's Father Lucien," he said quickly. Somehow, although Fabian didn't approve of her meddling in church affairs, neither did he want her subjected to Lucien's wrath. At least not just now, while she was fighting her grief.

"I'll be going," she said.

He picked up her wrap and hat, followed her into the hall, and quickly closed the office door.

She pinned her hat in place. "One thing I would like to tell you," she said softly. "Surely something—or someone—guided my footsteps to St. Anne's today. My friend's name was Anne."

# 17

In the weeks that followed the funeral, Jo tried hard to settle back into the niche she had carved for herself among the ailing women of the city, but her patience was thin and her tongue sharp. She had little sympathy now for a mother of fourteen, seven of them dead, who found herself with child again. The woman damn well knew how she got that way. All she had to do was say no when her husband demanded his rights.

*His* rights, sneered Jo. What about the wife's rights? Even women didn't seem to understand that they were due any privileges. Before a woman married, she was ruled by her father, afterward by her husband. She couldn't win. Nationality, education, class, money—none of these seemed to change the views of either men or women. The man was the master, the woman little better than a slave.

Dr. Jo was hard put to curb her tongue when a woman poured forth problems that could only be solved through abstinence, withdrawal, or possibly by the use of condoms. Jo wanted to tell her patients about the linen sheaths that had been invented to prevent syphilis, but she didn't know much about them.

About this time, Doc Adams gave her a beautifully descriptive little book written by Dr. Charles Knowlton of Ashfield, Massachusetts. It was called *Fruits of Philosophy: the Private Companion of Young Married People*. "Maybe this will keep you from pesterin' me with questions," Adams said, thrusting his gift at her with a gruffness she knew was more assumed than real.

The book addressed itself to the specifics of family limitation, and Jo learned more about her own internal organs from this one small book than she had from *Gray's Anatomy* or the dozens of other tomes through which she had waded.

After worrying her way through all the theories on conception, Jo concluded that the whole argument about *how* implantation took place was secondary to where it took place. If something could be inserted into the woman *without the husband's knowledge*—something like a new, tough hymen that fit over the cervix. But what? And how?

One snowy February day, Jo paid a visit to her namesake, little Jody Gates Schmidt, and found Mrs. Schmidt expecting again. Jo exploded: "You knew you shouldn't get with child again. You know another pregnancy could kill you."

Marlene hung her head. "Karl tells me I can't say no. He says if I talk about it, he'll leave me and go to California. How can I raise four kids if Karl leaves me?" she whined.

"Didn't you tell him what I said about your health?"

"I told him, Dr. Jo. He says you should mind your own business. He says you meddle anymore, he'll come after you with his meat hook." Karl Schmidt was an ex-boxer turned butcher, and Jo had no reason to doubt his threat. Doc had already treated two men who had crossed Schmidt's path: one for a broken jaw and cracked ribs, the other for a gash on his cheek, laid open to the bone by Schmidt's hook.

Jo stormed from the house, her face red with fury.

"Who in hell does he think he is?" she thundered at the startled Dr. Adams. "Take his meat hook to me will he? I'd like to take his cleaver and cut off his bawbles!" She stopped, surprised at the crude Five Points expression she had not even been aware she knew until it popped out.

Doc chuckled. "Whose bawbles are you preparing to sever?"

"Karl Schmidt. He's got his wife pregnant again! Snakes of St. Patrick, when will these women learn?" Grasping the reins, she brought them down sharply on Annabelle's back.

"No need to take it out on the horse because a man impregnates his wife," Doc said mildly.

"You don't like the way I handle your horse? Then you drive," she snapped. Damn Marlene Schmidt's whining acceptance! Damn Karl Schmidt and his carnal demands!

"There's no point getting yourself all worked up about women," said Doc. "When you been around as long as I have, you'll come to accept things the way they are and not go battering your head against a chimney block. Sickness and death and birthing—that's the lot of womenfolk. It's all they know."

Sometimes Doc said the dumbest things. "There's *got* to be a way to keep women from having one baby after another," she insisted. "If it was a man had the babies, they'd sure find a way in a hurry." And then the question just popped out of nowhere—full blown, demanding an answer: "Doc, did you ever see one of those sheaths—those condoms? I know they're used to prevent the French disease, but if a man wore a condom, wouldn't it be like the frog's pantaloons? Wouldn't it keep a woman from getting pregnant?"

It took a great deal to shock the doctor, and this was the first time Jo had ever seen him at a loss for words.

His face turned red, then white, then red again as he sputtered helplessly. "A . . . you're asking me about a . . . what's got into you, Jo Gates? Them things are not only immoral, they're illegal. Give me the reins. I *will* drive." And he cracked the reins down even harder on poor Annabelle's back.

Jo seethed in silence. Doc was always telling her she couldn't go around preaching family limitation—that it was a crime to give out such information. The crime, she thought, was bringing babies into the world when they were doomed to misery and premature deaths—and when their birth often condemned the mother to death as well.

All right, thought Jo. There were more ways than one to skin a tabby. If Doc wouldn't tell her about sheaths, she'd just buy one of the blasted things and find out for herself.

Inscribing Doc's name with what she hoped was a reasonable facsimile of his illegible signature, Jo dashed off letters to medical supply houses in New York and Philadelphia, plus one to Joseph Trow at 160 Chambers Street. If the medical houses refused to supply information regarding these illegal devices so that Dr. Adams could "prepare a paper for the *Journal of the American Medical Association,*" as Jo had written, then surely Madame Restell's brother would supply some condoms to turn a fast fiver.

While she waited for answers, Jo chafed with the knowledge that even if the condoms were effective and if husbands would wear them, they would come too late for some of her patients.

It was already too late for Mrs. Higbee who had tried to rid herself of an unwanted child and had perforated the uterus. Jo cooked a pot of soup for the motherless children and fed them one last time before they were taken away by the juvenile authorities.

After Mrs. Higbee's death, Jo speeded up her information bank. She made extensive notes in her journal and spent extra time with each woman, explaining, cajoling. Somehow she had to make them understand that by giving in to their husband's demands, they were literally committing suicide.

One day in early spring, when Jo was alone in the office, Father Lucien came storming up the stairs. He burst through the waiting room door, Father Fabian trailing quietly behind.

"You are the handmaiden of the devil," screamed the irate priest. "Preaching onanism to Catholics, ye are!"

Jo's mouth dropped open. "But God didn't say onanism was wrong," she protested. "He only said Onan was wrong." She was glad Doc wasn't here yet. She had a feeling he wouldn't like this conversation.

"The only reason for marital intercourse is for procreation," yelled the priest. "What you're teaching is a mortal sin. If women follow you, they'll be denied the sacraments and condemned to eternal damnation." A red vein throbbed in his forehead. "You're the devil's own daughter and you'll burn in hell. You're a she-devil—preaching mortal sin to God-fearing Catholics."

Although Jo's father had been Catholic, Jo had been raised a Protestant and was never exposed to any priest except the mild-mannered Father Anselm in Ballareen. She was unprepared for this fire-breathing black dragon. Moreover, she resented his attack. It was all she could do to hold her tongue.

"You can't mess with the doctrines of the Catholic church," screamed the furious priest shaking his fist in her face. "You keep your evil nose out of the Church's business, or you'll take the consequences!"

Jo was still forming her reply when he spun on his heel and marched from the office.

Father Fabian's face was thoughtful. He knew Lucien was right and the young midwife wrong, yet he couldn't believe Dr. Jo's actions were evil. Misdirected, perhaps, but surely one so fair couldn't be the handmaiden of the devil. Trailing the fuming senior priest back down the narrow stairs, Fabian resolved to talk further with the young lady. Perhaps he could persuade her of the error of her ways before she got herself into deep trouble.

Often Fabian's rounds of sick calls crossed hers. Following Lucien's angry visit, Dr. Jo was decidedly cool toward the young priest when they met, but over the next few weeks she relented and her greetings became warm and friendly again.

It was late May when Fabian knew he must take the devil by the horns and talk with Dr. Jo. She had finally done it—finally persuaded one of his parishioners to refuse her husband his conjugal rights. Although the husband had accepted the new way of things, the wife felt so guilty, she had confessed her sin to Father Fabian. If the senior priest ever got wind of this there'd be the devil to pay.

The difficulty in Fabian's talking with Dr. Jo lay in finding a place to talk. If it were anyone else, he would have invited her to his garden, in full view of the rectory, but due to Lucien's unbending attitude toward the young woman, that wasn't possible.

At last Fabian caught up with her, without Doc, descending the steps of a hovel on Cherry Street.

"Aren't you afraid to go into places like this alone?" he asked, coming up behind her.

"Aren't you the one who told me whatever God decrees will happen anyhow?" she countered with a tight smile.

"I don't think He means us to tempt Him."

"Why not? He doesn't act on whim—or so you said."

"Are my words always to be hurled back at me?"

"Don't you stand on your own words?"

He grimaced. "You're worse than Doc Adams."

"Heaven forbid." She laughed then.

"Dr. Jo, I must talk with you in private. I obviously can't invite you to my office . . ." A small rueful smile here. "So I wonder if you would join me in a picnic sometime soon?"

Her eyes opened in astonishment, and he suddenly looked very young and shy. "I can't think of anyplace where we could talk—and not be seen—except out in the country," he explained.

"I do declare, Father, if you weren't wearing that collar, I'd think you had ulterior designs upon my person." She teased, but when she saw his expression she was immediately sorry. "You're being nice and I'm teasing," she said with a smile. "Look, when I finish here, I have two calls way out on Gravois Road. You can come along if you like. We'd have lots of time to talk on the way out and back."

"That would be fine. I'll wait here for you."

"Where's your buggy?"

"Right here." He pointed to his feet and laughed. "Not very fast. But reliable."

Father Fabian took the reins. She was glad to let him drive. They left the city streets behind, and she felt a sense of comfort at his nearness, a tender, tentative easing of the tension and pain she had borne this past month since Anne's death.

It was a lovely May day, one of those mild, balmy days when the breeze is as light as a whisper, the sky a plate of blue with great lumps of puffy white clouds, the sun warm on your cheek, and the whole world soft and fresh and new.

Jo unpinned her hat and the spring breeze ruffled her long bright curls. Fabian glanced at her, then quickly away.

He told himself he was ill at ease because he didn't know how to begin. She was a headstrong young lady, there was no mistake about that. It wouldn't be easy to convince her she could be in for real trouble if she persisted in her present course.

Jo glanced at the young priest. Since that day in church, she had seen him frequently. She noticed he always came quickly when called and was often there ahead of the doctor. They would find him heating milk for a baby or spooning soup into a toothless old woman down with pneumonia, and more than once she had seen him step between a cowering woman and her husband's fist. His eyes would flash then and his voice take on the rumbling of an angry heaven, and more often than not, he subdued the unruly wife beater. Jo had developed a tremendous respect for the father's activities and had finally said as much to him, but he had replied that no credit was due him; all credit went to the Church.

"My father was Catholic," Jo told him now as they left the city behind. "Mama was Church of England, but we lived in Ireland and didn't go to church. Pa went, of course, and he sometimes tried to convert me—"

"So you're familiar with Catholic doctrines."

"Like th' back o' me hand."

"Then you know that what you're teaching is a mortal sin."

"But forgivable by the priest after confession and penance," she said quickly.

"The confessional must never be used as an excuse to sin."

"But that's the way it *is* used. How many drunkards do you think confess their overindulgence, then really go forth and sin no more? Don't talk to me about your

194

confessional, Father. It's a license to sin, that's what it is."

He looked pained. "Abuse of the confessional by the penitent in no way diminishes the *intent* of the confessional."

She looked disgusted. "You're not a stuffy old man; why do you talk like one? You know that as soon as a man confesses, he feels free to go out and do it all over. You're just giving him a license to get drunk and beat his wife or—or rape his daughter," she finished. Her chin tilted defiantly. "He knows all he has to do is confess and say a few Hail Marys."

"You're pointing to a misuse of Catholic doctrine, not a flaw in the doctrine itself. Furthermore, you're condemning a man for taking advantage of forgiveness, yet you want to condone a woman's actions when she does the same thing. You think a woman should take steps to prevent childbirth, which will totally alienate her from God and condemn her to everlasting punishment, yet you think it's all right for *her* to go to confession and then be free to sin again."

"Wait a minute!" Jo's face broke into a delighted grin. "Are you saying some of my patients have confessed to denying their husbands? Is that what this talk is all about?"

She had a beautiful smile. He turned his eyes back to the road. "I'm not saying anything of the kind," he replied stiffly. "You must know anything revealed in the confessional is confidential."

"Who was it? Oh, I'm sorry. I know I mustn't ask, and you wouldn't tell me anyhow." She chuckled happily. "I can't believe any of them actually had the nerve! I thought my only near success was one poor woman whose husband threatened to leave her and go to California if she ever mentioned abstention again."

Fabian was decidedly uneasy. Beside him sat a

young woman who sought to undermine the very foundation of the Church, and instead of recoiling in horror, he was enjoying the drive and the conversation. It wasn't natural.

Then Jo began to speak of her childhood, and Fabian forgot his discomfort. She described the horrors of Tithebarn Street in Liverpool and Five Points in New York, and he saw that her spirit had never been immersed in the filth that had surrounded her, that she had somehow been deeply touched by the pathos, yet not tainted by the depravity. In spite of her views on what she called "family limitation," he sensed a beauty within her as strong and bright as the loveliness of her face and figure.

Then Fabian told her about his childhood in an orphanage in Detroit, and of his sister, Mary, who had died of consumption when she was twelve. "You remind me of Mary," he said simply. Then he talked about his call to the priesthood after Mary's death, and of the peace it brought him.

When he spoke of his calling, Fabian's eyes glowed as they had that first day in the chapel, and Jo thought again what a beautiful man he was. He had curling black hair; his eyes were brown and large, and she felt she could lose herself in their warm full depths.

Their afternoon in the sun ended all too soon. Fabian stopped the carriage several blocks from the church, in a German neighborhood where St. Anne's had no communicants.

He passed the reins to Jo and looked up at her. "Could we do it again sometime?"

Her smile was wide, innocent. "Doc takes off every Monday now," she said. "We only have two patients out on Gravois Road, and Doc lets me visit them alone. If you just happen to be near Gravois and Arsenal about two o'clock on a Monday, I'm sure to pass by."

"If I do happen to be near there on a Monday, I'll look for you," he said casually.

They both knew she would drive past that corner just at two o'clock next Monday. And they both knew he would be waiting. And each reflected on how wonderful it was to have a new friend.

197

# 18

Through the gentle springtime, Monday came to be a special day. If Jo dressed her hair with greater care, she told herself it was because she had just washed it and it was more unmanageable than usual, or because she could see the trees bending in the breeze outside her window and her hair took special pinning lest it blow in the wind.

But when Fabian joined her and they reached the long stretch of the plank road where the trees whispered overhead in a gauzelike canopy of shimmering veils and Annabelle slowed to a placid amble, Jo always removed her hat and let the gentle breeze have its way.

When she splurged on a new yellow dress at Wainright's, she assured herself it was only because she was filling out and dresses from her earlier days were a bit snug. That was true, but when Fabian's eyes revealed how pretty she looked in her new yellow cotton, her heart swelled with shy pleasure.

Once, in the heat of discussion, when Fabian completely forgot the reins, Annabelle drifted to a stop and began to nibble placidly at the tasty sprigs of spring growth along the roadside. Jo jumped impulsively from the buggy, drawn by the soft green of new grass, the silky gold of buttercups, and the lodestar call of songbirds. There was an almost imperceptible hum in the air, and it was warm and overlaid with a smooth patina of peace and serenity.

The grass was sweet underfoot, untrodden, fresh. She wanted to remove her shoes to dance through the velvety tufts, then lie on her back and run her fingers through the fluffy white clouds that looked so near she just knew she could reach up and touch them.

Fabian followed, pulled by her sweet innocence, and his eyes were as naive and clear as the bright spring day.

After that they often paused for a stroll through flower-strewn fields, or under a rustling umbrella of wide green boughs.

Then as spring crept into summer and the sun grew hot and the air dry, he would guide Doc's buggy over the covered bridge, across the field to a little bubbling brook where they clambered over rocks to a tree-shaded mound of moss. And there they whiled away their Monday afternoons, talking, arguing theology, teasing, trembling on the edge of discovery, bewitched by an emotion they neither, in their innocence, understood nor acknowledged.

"I'll see you next week?" he would ask as he stepped from the carriage.

"I'll be looking for you," she would reply.

Jo was grateful that the subject of family limitation did not rise often between them. She was feeling guilty these days about the box of dried sheep gut condoms she had finally received from Joseph Trow, plus the fact that she had actually succeeded in convincing two of her patients to have their husbands try the illegal devices. True, the two women weren't Catholic; nevertheless, she had trouble meeting Fabian's clear trusting eyes when the subject of family limitation did arise.

Her friendship with Father Fabian was very important to her now. When there was illness neither she nor Doc could cure—or a case of extreme poverty—Jo would pour out her troubles, and always Fabian was there to console and hearten. He was so positive in his beliefs, so trusting in his simplistic approach to life. He acted as a balm to her impatient needs.

She looked forward to their Monday afternoons with innocent eagerness, planning things to discuss with him, saving the occasional funny events of the week, for they were few and therefore precious.

She often talked about their cases—like the outbreak of smallpox and Doc's concentrated vaccination program. It had lasted one week and at the height of it, they vaccinated over one hundred people in one day. "We're finally getting some important medical advances," she told Fabian happily. "If only they'd all come to be vaccinated . . ."

Then there was little Eve Henderson, a beautiful child who came down with chicken pox. Because so many were pockmarked, and chicken pox such a mild disease, Jo had always accepted it with little concern. Now she balked. She could not accept Eve's once lovely face, scarred now almost beyond recognition.

"There must be some way to avoid the pitting," she wailed to Fabian the following Monday. "If they just didn't scratch the scabs off and get dirt in them—"

"Can't you put something on that would stop the itching?" he asked.

"That's what Doc's bread soda's supposed to do. Oh, Fabian, people shouldn't have to go through life scarred like that. There's just got to be a way."

She began her campaign by cutting the fingernails of each chicken pox patient and scrubbing them with a brush and harsh, yellow soap. Then, looking for a better medication, she pulled out her mother's hand-written notes. And there it was—just as she remembered—a recipe for chicken pox salve.

Fabian helped her. They spent one whole Monday cutting rushes, and Jo arrived home that afternoon with a buggyful of weeds. She burned the rushes in a bucket in the backyard and produced a fine carbon, which she mixed with gunpowder and hog lard, begged from Meg.

Jo's chicken pox patients were ugly beyond belief when blackened with her concoction, but when the disease had run its course, there were few if any pockmarks. Jo thought she would fly with happiness when Doc Adams asked what she had used.

"Can you believe it?" she crowed to Fabian. "Doc actually asked *me.*"

"First thing you know you'll be a full-fledged physician and opening your own office."

"You really think so? You really think he'll give me a certificate some day?"

Fabian smiled at her intensity. "One day you'll be so famous you won't even speak to me anymore."

She laughed at his nonsense, and her laugh was young and carefree.

Dear Jo, he thought—she felt so strongly, wanted so much. She was like a greedy child, reaching for the sun with both pudgy hands and crying with heartbreak when only the moon fell into her lap.

Fabian stuck a blade of grass between his teeth and lay back on the mossy knoll. Overhead, the sky was black with migrating birds, and a few bright leaves skittered in the wind. Summer would soon be gone. He was very conscious of the lovely young lady at his side. She had become such an important part of his life—more important than he cared to admit.

She must have felt his eyes on her then, for she turned and smiled. Such wide, trusting eyes. And her fine-bones, oval face, framed by wind-tossed, red-gold

201

curls. Abruptly he raised himself on his elbow. "It's time to be heading back," he said.


Jo glowed these days with an inner joy. Doc mentioned it to Sally. "The girl looks like she just discovered a cure for malaria," he told his wife. "Floats around like a firefly, all lit up and giddy. If I didn't know how busy she was, I'd swear some young buck was sparking her."

Sally laughed—an infrequent sound in their home these days. "It's probably one of those actor fellows," she said, trying not to let her relief creep into her voice. She, too, had noticed Jo's glow when she came for Sunday supper each month, but it seemed to Sally that the girl shone more brightly whenever she looked at Archibald. Silly old woman, Sally thought, seeing goblins where there's none to see.

Meg, too, had noticed Jo's inner glow. The lengthy stages of grief following Anne's funeral had left Jo solitary and thin. For a time there, it was as if she had maggots in her head, Meg thought. Jo had waggled her tongue at the wrong time, spilling sharp words that turned friends away, and was never home for supper— worked long hours and began to lose weight.

Then suddenly, that spring, everything had changed. Meg could remember so well one day in May when Jo came home with that funny little smile on her face—the first real smile Meg had seen from her in over a month. From then on, the girl seemed to bloom like a butterfly emerging from its cocoon.

It was a real puzzle. Meg knew Jo wasn't sweet on any of the actors. There had been several who had tried, but Jo scarcely passed the time of day now with any of the transients. From what Meg could learn, there was nothing but work in her life. Meg was happy

202

for the change, but unable to explain it. Jo was in love, that was for sure—but with whom?

It was late summer before Meg finally admitted to herself that there was only one explanation. Jo was practicing the good old trade of basket making with Doc Adams. She spent all her time with him. Yes, much as Meg hated to accept it, that dirty old man had knocked Jo for sure! That was what came from reading all them dirty books together.

Meg wouldn't have believed it of either of them, for she had known and respected Doc for many years, and Jo was like a daughter to her—but Meg knew the signs. That look in Jo's eyes told the story. The girl was in love. And happiness that complete didn't come with chastity, Meg was certain of that. But with a married man—and an old man at that. Somebody had to explain the facts of life to the poor girl, and distasteful as it was, it looked as if Meg were elected.

She planned her campaign with care. Sunday was the only day Jo was around the house much, the day she washed her hair and her clothes, and did her mending. This coming Sunday, she would be at Doc's for supper, so Meg's talk would have to wait for the following weekend. That would work out well because the current crop of players would move out Saturday morning, and the new batch didn't arrive until late that night. Meg would have the afternoon alone with Jo.

She planned what she would say and how she would say it. It was a delicate matter, sticking your nose into someone else's love life, particularly when the love affair was between a headstrong girl and an old married roué.

She was thinking about Jo and Doc again as she climbed into a hired hack to visit her friend, Flossie, who had married and moved to the country, southwest of St. Louis.

203

How could that sweet Jo have the nerve to go right into Doc's house once a month and sit down to dinner with him and his wife? And her in a wheelchair to boot. It was beyond Meg's understanding. Besides which, Jo didn't realize she was throwing her life away on a married man.

Meg could sympathize with her, though. After all, hadn't Meg herself lost her head the same way? Of course, Meg's Jerry hadn't been an old stick like Adams. Jerry had been so handsome. So dashing. Fond memories brought a curve to Meg's lips. Even if Jerry had walked out on her, leaving her pregnant and broke, she couldn't fault him. He had been some chunk of man, that one. And her Jeremy just like him, she thought proudly. A real chip off the old block.

It was late, afternoon. The day had turned cool. Mullion and goldenrod still tinted the sun-browned fields, and a nip of fall held the air. Meg was glad for the closed carriage.

She ought to get out more often, she thought. It was no good being tied to the house day in and day out. The only place she ever went, other than St. Anne's on Sunday, was to see Flossie, and this was the first time in months she had done even that. She was looking forward to Flossie's rum omelet.

In the distance, an open carriage moved lazily through a meadow of tall brown weeds. Meg chuckled. Lovers coming back from a tryst in the woods, she'd wager. She remembered that little brook, right back through the meadow, behind the big oak, where she and Jerry had made love. That soft hillock of moss. That long-ago summer.

Yes, there were two of them in the buggy all right. Meg smiled indulgently.

Then her green eyes sharpened and she leaned forward with a fierce intake of breath. That looked like

204

Doc's buggy—and Jo driving. But surely that wasn't Doc in the buggy with her?

The other carriage had entered the covered bridge, and Meg pulled to one side, listening to the wheels rumble over the wooden planks, and waiting for it to come out again.

It passed within three feet of Meg's shocked gaze. Jo and Father Fabian, deep in conversation, had eyes only for each other. They didn't see the hard green glare directed upon them.

Messing with a married man was one thing, thought Meg as shock and righteous anger filled her. But messing with a priest was beyond all sense of decency. And Father Fabian at that.

The Catholic in Meg was aghast; the woman in her avidly curious and more than a little jealous.

# 19

Jo's heart sang. It had been a lovely afternoon with a crisp, invigorating bite in the air. Her lips curved in an unconscious smile as she deposited the buggy at the livery stable and strolled slowly toward the boardinghouse.

This afternoon had been, as usual, the bright spot in Jo's week. She loved her work, but Monday afternoons were glowing gems of happiness that cheered her through all the defeating, depressing days—and there had been many of those. There was no doubt about it: Fabian's company was good for her.

She hummed softly as she mounted the steps to the boardinghouse.

Before she could insert the key, the door was flung wide and Meg stood before her, hands on hips, green eyes flashing, and a sneer twisting her full red lips. "So here's the divlish piece. Home from her divilment is she?" Her brogue was as thick as the day she had stepped off the boat.

"What are you talking about?"

"Arrah now! See what an innocent she is. And her as common as the barber's chair. Wasn't I after seein' ye with me own two eyes?"

"Seeing me do what?" Jo's face was a study in bewilderment.

"Prancin' across the field, the two of ye. The Faather with his tongue still hangin' out."

"Father Fabian? You mean when we were down by the stream talking?"

"Don't try to bamboozle me," flared the irate Meg. "Ye can't tell me he's like the butcher's dog, lyin' by the beef without touchin' it."

"Meg!" Jo was shocked, almost as much by the vehemence of the attack as by the accusation itself.

"I'm not one for kissin' the pope's feet, but let me tell ye, there's a limit. I've seen ye with that snide smirk on yer face, like you'd licked all the cream off the top of the can. Arrah, Jo, how could ye do it with a priest? Ye'll roast in hell—and rightly so."

"Meg O'Gerity, you stop that! There's never been a thing between me and Father Fabian but friendship." But even as she said it, Jo's heart lurched with knowledge that there had been more. Friendship didn't foster the sweet happiness she had known these past months. Friendship didn't bring an ache to one's heart, make one glory in the play of emotions across that friend's dear face—with an almost uncontrollable urge to reach out and touch—to smooth the furrowed brow, to trace the firm lips. It was wrong to dream of a priest. She didn't have to be Catholic to know that. Oh, how could she have been so blind?

And Fabian—what of him? She remembered now how he looked at her sometimes, regret blazing deep in bleak brown eyes, the curve of his lips tightening as he turned away. Oh, poor darling. Did he feel it, too? This wild sweet pull that was like the first strawberries, fresh and dewy as the morning—

Ruined now. The truth was a tumult in her breast, a storm that struck with sudden fury and plunged her heart into despair.

Watching realization sweep across Jo's face, Meg's

207

spite drained away. She knew that instead of calling a halt to an impossible situation, her accusations had simply bared reality to the poor child. You're a blatherskite and no mistake, Meg O'Gerity, she scolded herself. 'Twasn't enough the child lost Anne—now your big mouth has spoiled her friendship with the young priest.

But it would never have remained a friendship; Meg knew that. There was no denying the look of a woman in love. Oh, was there to be no peace for this sweet young colleen?

Meg put her arm around Jo. "Come into the kitchen, me darlin', and I'll fix us a nice cuppa tea."

Jo told herself nothing had really changed, but she knew better. With the realization that what she felt for Fabian was more than friendship, her belief in herself had suffered a staggering blow. If she had lied to herself about her feelings for Fabian, how else might she deceive herself to gain her own desires?

How devious the human mind, she thought. Or was it only the mind of woman? Then her heart contracted as she remembered Fabian's open glances of admiration, so quickly quelled, and the way his dark eyes deepened when their hands touched accidentally—yet his naturalness when they talked, the quiet strength of his velvety voice when he spoke of God and of his utter faith in the power of the cross. No, it was not only she who deceived herself. It was not a fault confined to women.

She wished Meg had never spoken, never raised the curtain on what must now be the final act of her friendship with Fabian.

The following Monday she did not drive past Gravois and Arsenal, but went by way of Miami instead. It was cowardly, but she didn't know how to tell him. Perhaps, with winter coming on, it could break off naturally. Surely he wouldn't come when the snow began to fly? Yet she knew he would.

This past summer, when it rained and she had to take Doc's closed carriage and the rain beat on the roof, how often had she thought to put off her rounds in the country until the next day; but always she had gone, knowing how foolish it was to expect him to be there, yet hoping. And the leap of joy within her when she had spied his tall black figure, hunched against the rain, waiting for her. Always waiting.

No. Rain hadn't deterred him. Neither would snow.

Another week dragged by. As the following Monday approached, Jo still fought her conscience. She feared they would meet accidentally as she and Doc made rounds in the city, and they wouldn't be able to talk with others around. She had no choice but to meet him alone one more time.

She rehearsed her speech, practiced a light, carefree laugh, and wished she didn't have to go through with it.

It was a warm October day, though windy. The final fling of summer, thought Fabian, as he watched the carriages and drays wheel past. She was late. Or had he come early? He had no watch so he couldn't be certain. Surely she would come today. If she didn't come, he would go to her office to inquire. Perhaps she was sick. At that thought, he closed his eyes and whispered a brief prayer for her well-being and safety.

When he opened them again, there she was—all white and gold, in a dress as sunny as the day. The sight of her brought a glad smile to his lips, and he murmured a quick thanks to God that she was well and safe—and here to spend the afternoon with him. His heart was very full as he leaped lightly into the carriage and took the reins.

"I was afraid you weren't coming again."

"I almost didn't. But I had to talk to you, Father—"

"Father? What happened to Fabian?" he teased.

There was no answering smile, and he pulled the carriage to the side of the road, sudden concern biting at him. "You *are* ill. What is it, Jo? Tell me." Only sickness or deep sorrow would cause her to close up against him like this. He reached for her hands, twisting in her lap. "Jo, look at me."

She was handling this all wrong, but she couldn't seem to help herself. She had meant to be so light and gay. She had meant to laugh when she told him that people were beginning to talk. She had thought they could laugh together at the narrow-minded people who couldn't understand a friendship between a priest and a woman. And then they would decide that, foolish as the notion was, perhaps it would be better to call a halt to their Monday afternoons.

Ah, but hers was the foolish notion. How could she have been so stupid as to think they could laugh about their summer and their feelings for each other?

She couldn't tell him that people were talking about them. She couldn't hurt him that way. She blurted out the first thing that came to mind. "It's just a bit of silliness." There was a sob in the laugh that had sounded so gay and carefree when she practiced it earlier. "Doc told me today that he won't be taking Mondays off anymore, and I guess I was thinking how much I'll miss our afternoons."

He pulled his hands from hers as though scalded. He flushed. He looked away. Jo could only sit, silent and miserable, knowing what he was feeling, for she felt it, too.

"Well," he said finally, "if this is to be our last afternoon, then we had best make the most of it." He

210

snapped the reins and Annabelle broke into a reluctant amble.

"I don't have time to stop by the creek today," Jo lied. "I . . . actually, I'm not going out Gravois Road at all today. I . . . I have two more calls to make in town." Better to break it quickly, she thought. She saw the hurt in his face, and a fierce resentment burned in her. Their afternoons were a sacrifice to the stupidity of little people, yet the anger in Meg's green eyes—and Meg a friend—told Jo, more than words, how the rest of St. Louis would react. She couldn't let that happen to Fabian.

He broke the uneasy silence between them with a simple acceptance that shriveled Jo's heart. "I'll miss our afternoons," he said. "You've become very dear to me, Jo, like the sister I lost. But you needn't try to hide the truth from me. I know how cruel people can be. They don't understand that a man and woman may be as brother and sister and have a love between them that is pure and clean. It was only a matter of time before they began to talk."

"I suppose so," she murmured miserably.

"Jo, you're so very young . . ."

"And you're an old man with a gray beard, I suppose." She tried to laugh, but her voice broke.

"There's one thing I want you to remember. In these past months I've come to know your mind and how it works. I admire you. I admire your pluck and your dedication and your intelligence—and your tremendous capacity for compassion. I disagree with your ideas on childbirth checks, yet I can't help but admire your deep concern for women." His fingers moved jerkily across the edges of the cross, and his voice roughened. "I worry about you, Jo. About your stubborn determination to help others." He was

211

looking at her now, his eyes dark and burning with a richness she remembered from that first day in the church. "People will doubt your intentions, you know. You'll be attacked—by perfectly well-meaning people. By jealous people. Careless people. By those you love and those you're hard put to like." His eyes searched hers. "Do you understand what I'm saying, Jo? If you have a fault, it's your headstrong determination to help others no matter what the cost or the outcome; no matter what they want or need, you'll try to help them anyhow." He took a deep breath. "What I'm saying is that perhaps you could temper your beliefs to fit the need. Perhaps not 'do unto others as you would have them do unto you,' but *do unto others as they would have you do unto them*.

"And above all, try not to let the world sour your love for it. You have such a capacity for giving, Jo. Don't let the small people of this world diminish that greatness."

How beautiful everything was with him beside her. The sun warmer. The sky brighter. The birds singing more sweetly. The breeze caressing with a gentleness beyond description. Later she would look back on his words and take them to her heart, cherishing the love implied in them, but for now it was only important to press the day between the leaves of her memory. For now, she must let herself feel, not think—feel and hear and smell, and touch the heart of the autumn day, for it would be their last one together.

## 20

"Who the hell do you think you are?" roared Doc as he paced the office. "Whenever you treat a patient, young lady, you represent me. Folks take it for granted that your actions carry my stamp of approval. Now I find out you've been rousing my women patients—telling 'em not to sleep with their husbands. Jesus H. Christ, I knew you were headstrong but I didn't expect a knife in the back!"

Doc had been roaring and pacing the small office for twenty minutes. Jo wished he would stop long enough for her to apologize. She shouldn't have to apologize, of course. She was right and he was wrong, but that didn't matter. If she wanted to continue working with him, she would have to eat crow.

"You want to preach women's rights?" steamed Doc. "Then put on a pair of them consarned bloomers and go stomping around the country and give lectures on how a wife can keep her husband out of her bed. But don't go behind my back and tell it to my patients!"

He stood glaring at her and she realized he had finally run down. "I'm sorry, Doc," she said quickly.

"Hmmmmph. A lot of good that would do if one of them husbands came gunning for us. My God, Jo, don't you know men will kill for less than that? You can't meddle in a man's bedroom. From what I hear,

213

you been preaching that women not only *can* say no, they *should* say no."

Why didn't he just let it alone? He'd made his position clear; she'd said she was sorry. Now why didn't he drop it before she lost her temper and blurted what she really thought?

"'I'm sorry,'" he mimicked. "'I'm sorry,' she says now, like butter wouldn't melt in her mouth."

"I'm not sorry for what I told them," Jo flared, unable to hold her tongue any longer, but immediately hauling her voice back to a rational level: "But I *am* sorry I involved you. I shouldn't have told them what I did. Not because it's wrong, mind you—but because I work for you. What I say reflects on you and puts you on the same stage as me, I know that."

"Puts me in the same pigsty."

"I'm sorry."

He glared at her in disgust. "You've been spouting that nonsense ever since you walked into this office over a year ago. I just never realized how far you'd actually go with it. When are you going to grow up, girl? When are you going to face facts and admit you can't change man's nature just to suit your own ideas of right and wrong? Man has a carnal nature. Face that and we'll get along better. You can't change it anyhow."

"Doc, I've been thinking—if the sperm could be destroyed chemically—"

"There you go again. My God, girl, giving out information about family limitation is not only illegal, it's immoral! You ought to know that much."

Now *he* had gone too far. "Immoral!" She shouted the word. "How can a *truth* be immoral? Everyone has a right to knowledge, Doc. It isn't the knowledge that's immoral, it's the misuse of it. You can't suggest it's wrong for me to know about rape as long as there are

214

men like Nicholas Quimby walking around."

"You sound like one of them crusading females," he spat in disgust. "Why don't you get yourself a pair of bloomers and take your speeches on tour? I'll not have you spreading vicious lies to my patients."

"They're *not* lies. They're not." In spite of her good intentions, her voice had risen several octaves. She made an effort to control it by speaking slowly. "I'm sorry I put you in a bad light by talking about health to your patients. Because that's exactly what I did—I talked about women's *health.* Women's rights only came into it because it's the lack of their rights that's ruining their health." She took a deep breath. "Now you apparently can't see that. All right. I work for you and I've got to do as you say—and from now on I will. I'm sorry I talked about *health* to your women patients, doctor." She blinked back sudden tears. "And if you'll still have me, I'll not do it again—not while I work for you."

"Don't you dare cry, Jo Gates. How does it happen that I am suddenly on the defensive? We start with you having done something wrong and by the time you get through with it, you've twisted it all around to make out you're the martyr and I'm Simon Legree. That's what comes of trying to have an intelligent conversation with a woman. She winds up twisting words and facts until there's no resemblance left to what you set out to talk about."

He was going to let her stay. She grinned tremulously, her threatening tears forgotten. "Maybe that's because women *do* have brains after all," she said sweetly.

"Get your bonnet. We'll make rounds. We'll not have lunch today, thanks to you. You've got me in such a stew, that cold pork supper would curdle before it ever reached my stomach." He clapped his hat on his head, staring at her from beneath beetling brows. "But there's one more thing needs saying before we drop the subject: You do it once more," he proclaimed, pointing an irate finger, "and you're out on your hoop in the street."

She knew he was serious. She must stop preaching family limitation if she was to stay on with Doc. But the *cap,* she thought with sinking heart. Snakes of St. Patrick, what if Doc ever found out about the *cap?*

Jo's female cap, as she called it, was formed of delicate sponge with elastic to hold it in place over the curve of the cervix. The beauty of her new invention was that the men didn't have to cooperate. The cap could be soaked in chemical checks first, then inserted without the knowledge of the husband, and removed the following morning. It wasn't too different from the ineffective bit of sponge women had been using for years, the major improvement being in the chemicals and the fact that her cap was a concave circle that nestled snugly over the cervix.

Jo had been working on the caps for months. The first to try them had been prostitutes, and by now, all the girls at Claire's Sporting House, plus four other patients used them regularly. Each was supplied with three sponges, careful instructions on their insertion and cleansing, plus a goodly supply of alum and sulfate of zinc.

It's a sour note in hell, she thought, when one person is made to feel guilty for saving another person's life.

All right, she thought, I'll keep my promise to Doc, but I'll go on reading and working. When I get my license, then I'll be able to work full time on family limitation.

The more Jo learned, the more she realized how little she knew. Yet, inadequate as she sometimes felt, what really disturbed her was the realization of how little even full-fledged doctors knew about the art of healing. Doc, for example, was one of the better physicians, yet there were days when Jo could positively have wept at his stupidity—like when he went from a sour, pus-filled wound to a sweet new baby with never a thought of soap and water between.

The more she saw of squalid living conditions, the more certain Jo became that simple cleanliness would halt much of the illness of the world.

Thrush, a white-patched fungus that infected the lining of mouth and tongue, occurred most often in nursing children. Jo was sure that if the mother would wash her breast before letting the baby suckle, thrush would never appear. Eight of her patients followed this advice, and their babies did *not* get the nasty fungus, but it was too small a sampling to prove her theory. She noted each small victory in her journal and plodded on.

Impetigo, with oozing pustules and yellowish crusts, was another disease she thought might be dirt related and passed from one to the other within a family. She recommended careful cleansing with warm water before applying Doc's ointment of mercury, and that each person should use a separate cloth. She was pleased to see that *her* patients rarely passed on the infection. Doc's almost always did. Yet she daren't mention her triumphs because her "cleanliness phobia" was still a sore subject with him.

Jo was fuming inwardly over Doc's blind spots when she arrived at the boardinghouse one evening and found Jeremy back in residence.

"Jo, you sweet thing!" He spanned her slender waist with his hands and swung her around. He had apparently forgiven her for the episode in the darkened theatre; now he was testing her forgiveness of him. Her skirts swirled and his green eyes laughed into her startled hazel ones.

217

In his brocaded velvet vest and satin tie, he was even better looking than she remembered. He had filled out and grown in stature and assurance. "Put me down, you idiot."

"Doesn't he look wonderful?" Meg beamed at her son with pride. "Can you imagine a handsome beard like that at eighteen? His father was a hairy brute, too."

Jo silently admitted that Jeremy's good looks were enhanced by the dark beard and mustache. He undoubtedly fluttered many a maiden's heart—and didn't he know it though.

"Did you miss me?" he demanded as he planted a noisy buss on her cheek.

"Daily." Her voice was dry but with no remaining rancor.

"Good. Then you'll come to the races at the Fairgrounds with us Sunday."

"I'm going, too," interposed Meg. "With Duncan. I'm having a new dress made especially." Duncan was the leading man currently in residence. "Do come with us, Jo. It's great fun."

The St. Louis Fair was an institution of many years' standing. It attracted the best horses in the country and was attended by the finest families of the city. A day at the fair was one of the highlights of the season, and Jo had never been.

"We'll have supper at Planter's Hotel afterward," promised Jeremy. "I'm celebrating and I want you to come celebrate with us."

"What's the big event?"

"Jeremy has left Phinny's company and is on his way to New York." Meg was so proud of her son that the row of ruffles quivered across her ample breasts.

Meg quivered all through the races on Sunday, too, but from excitement this time. Her new dress, a vivid green to match her eyes, was revealingly low cut, and her exuberant antics kept the men in surrounding boxes spellbound throughout the afternoon.

Jeremy was equally grand in a three-piece, easy-fitting Tweedside, short and square of cut, in a flecked material, with a sacklike jacket fastened by the top button. He was in fine fettle all afternoon and all through supper at Planter's House, flattering Jo outrageously, flirting with the saloon girls, and being generally young and carefree, and very male.

They feasted on creole gumbo with diced chicken and rice, a salad, and candied oranges, and drank a new potion invented by the house, called Planter's Punch.

Jo enjoyed herself to the point of accepting Jeremy's invitation the next evening to see the moving pictures. "See the glorious West unfold before your very eyes," said the advertisements. It turned out to be a huge roll of continuous paintings of western scenes that scrolled across the stage in a moving panorama. Even the amateurish painting could not diminish the vibrant color and majesty of the snow-capped mountains, the glory of the desert, or the stark beauty of the canyons.

Jo came away awe-stricken. "Anne and I used to talk of going West," she told Jeremy. "But we never dreamed how beautiful it would be." She grasped his arm. "Oh, Jeremy, I am going West someday—just as we planned. When I've learned all I can from Doc and he's given me a certificate, that's when I'll go." Perhaps I'll even find my valley, she thought.

She was so set up by her daydreams that she allowed Jeremy to kiss her good night outside her door. It was a surprisingly chaste kiss from the young man who had flirted all evening with every skirt in sight.

He pressed his lips to hers lightly, quickly, with an embarrassed little laugh. "Was that better than the last time?" he asked.

Her smile was impish. "It's always better when your

219

partner is willing to dance, and you don't have to drag her around the floor."

He toyed with her coppery curls and let one finger trail lightly across her neck. "I always thought stolen goodies were best."

"So did your father!" she replied tartly as she pulled away from his hand. "And look where that got your mother."

His laugh was good-natured as he backed away, his hands lifted in such a comic gesture of surrender that she had to laugh with him.

The next evening, encouraged by their good night scene, Jeremy caught Jo as she came in from work to invite her on a trip down the moonlit river Saturday evening. "There's a boat trip that goes south, down past Kennet's Folly," he said. "I'll even put off leaving for New York if you'll come sailing with me."

Jo declined firmly and with no regret.

She had been glad to see Jeremy—now she was glad to see him leave. She didn't need moonlight excursions or good night kisses. Not anymore. All she needed in her life now was her career. There was no space now for men or the frivolities that went with male companionship. She had made a deathbed promise to her mother and was impatient to get on with it.

Despite her surprisingly giant steps this past year, Doc's ultimatum concerning family limitation had been a serious setback. Suddenly Jo was resenting the time spent under Doc's tutelage. She couldn't wait to get her certificate and start a practice of her own. Then she wouldn't be hemmed in by Doc's narrow outlook.

She promptly resumed her male masquerade and began to monitor operations once more. Each time she donned men's breeches, she feared she would be exposed. Doc laughed at her deception the first few

220

times, then finally told her she was playing with fire. "If you're caught," he said, "I'll deny I knew anything about it. If you're caught, you're through in St. Louis, you know. No decent woman will ever let you treat her again if they find out you're traipsing about in men's pantaloons."

Her trouble, Jo decided, was that she didn't have a schedule—a timetable. She thought long and hard about how much more time was reasonable to allow as an apprentice physician before approaching Doc again about a certificate.

She had been studying with him over a year now. Another six months maybe—that would be March.

Jo's eyes lit with sudden inspiration. Next March, she would be seventeen. On her birthday, she would ask Doc Adams for her license. She had no doubt now that he would give her one. She had proved her ability.

On her seventeenth birthday, she would become a licensed physician, she promised herself.

221

# 21

There was an old Irish saying: "A green Christmas makes a fat churchyard." In a dry Irish winter, the turf they burned for heat was plentiful, but when a winter was mild and damp and the turf stayed green and unburnable, colds quickly developed into congestion and pneumonia. In mild winters, with no turf to burn, Irish wakes were frequent and the population of church cemeteries soared.

In St. Louis it was just the opposite. Particularly the poor were vulnerable during frigid months when inadequate food and no heat became forerunners to pneumonia, bronchitis, pleurisy, and consumption. A cold winter in St. Louis spelled death among the destitute, especially for the very young and very old.

Unfortunately, as Doc said, they had many medications but few cures. Even a simple ailment like chilblains thwarted Jo's efforts at first. Doc Adams's remedy for the swelling and itching caused by exposure to cold was ridiculously simple and disgustingly crude. It angered Jo that his earthy prescription was a valid one. "Just piss on it," Doc would advise. She tried a more civilized version, but many of their patients knew only rudimentary English, and "urinate" was obviously not part of their limited vocabulary. At last Jo was forced to quote Doc verbatim. She carried an empty bottle in her doctor bag to make explanations easier.

She pointed to the patient: "You—*piss*—in the bottle."
She pointed then to the bottle. "And rub on." She
made rubbing motions in the air over the affected area.
After a few such demonstrations, Jo's blush was cured.
So were the chilblains.

On December second, old John Brown was hanged
and folks were saying there was going to be a war
between the states, but Jo's worries were closer at hand.
Her slender savings were soon spent to help her ailing
patients. After buying coats and shoes and the makings
for soup, her wages scarcely stretched to cover her own
toothpaste. Jo's heart broke with wanting to help,
needing to help, and finding her funds desperately
inadequate.

Christmas came and went in an unhappy blur. Even
the holiday celebration with Doc and Sally was
painful, for Sally was taken with a bad spell halfway
through the meal and had to be sedated and put to bed.
Jo and Doc finished their plum pudding alone, in
brooding silence.

Afterward, Jo wandered back to the boardinghouse
and sat in the kitchen with Meg who was celebrating
Christmas alone and had already made steady inroads
into a bottle of wine. Jo had several glasses and felt a
comfortable glow when she finally zigzagged up to bed.

Pa might have had the right idea, she thought as she
drifted off. This gentle swimming sensation beat
worrying all hollow. But the next morning when the
top of her head threatened to secede from the rest of
her, she decided Pa hadn't been so smart after all.

She faced 1860 with grim determination to make it
better than the year before, though how, she didn't
know.

Amid her winter doldrums, there were only two
bright spots: her occasional trips to the hospital to
observe, and her wee namesake, Jody Gates Schmidt.
The little girl was thirteen months old now, a pretty

223

baby with chubby cheeks and large blue eyes. Her mother was convalescing after another miscarriage, this one almost having cost her life. It was Marlene Schmidt's second miscarriage in a year, and it was concern over her that finally caused Jo to break her promise to Doc.

Marlene was convinced now that she would not survive another pregnancy. "Please, Dr. Jo," she pleaded. "Do something for me. Help me."

"You know what you have to do," Jo replied tartly.

"I can't keep Karl out of my bed. You know I can't. I tried that before. When he gets home this time he'll be all over me like a bear on a honey hive. You gotta think o' somethin' afore he gets back."

"Where is he?"

"Over in Kansas with the Blue Lodges." She clamped her hand over her mouth. "Oh, I shouldn't have said that. Don't you tell noboby, Dr. Jo. Karl would kill me if he knowed I told."

"That's one of those secret pro-slavery societies, isn't it?"

Marlene nodded, her dirty hair falling in limp strings about her pale face. "He's been gone a whole week now. When he gets back he'll be all over me. He ain't never waited a whole week before."

"You mean *never?* Not even when you're pregnant or when you've just miscarried?"

Marlene dropped her eyes and shook her head. "He's a mighty man, my Karl." She sounded almost proud, thought Jo with disgust. "I don't mind when I'm thataway," the woman continued. "It's when I've lost another baby, like now, that I get worried. I'm so weak and kinda wide open like. I'll get thataway again for sure, first time he docks me."

"Why can't you say no?" Jo demanded in exasperation.

"He'd only force me. He done it before. That's how I come to blurt out that it was you told me I should say no. I'm right sorry about that, Dr. Jo. I'd never of told if he hadn't been beatin' on me and forcin' me."

Jo couldn't help comparing Karl Schmidt's treatment of his wife with Nicholas Quimby's rape of his daughter. A man would hoot with laughter at her idea that he could rape his own wife, but Jo knew with certainty that it did happen.

She tried not to look at Marlene, tried to avoid the pinched face, the pleading eyes. She wanted to open her bag and pull out the Female Cap that could be Marlene's salvation—but she couldn't take a chance.

Not being able to dispense her female cap was particularly infuriating in light of the fact that it seemed to be working. Not one of the seven women who used the cap had become pregnant. It wouldn't hurt to help Marlene, yet she knew she mustn't. It was only two months until her birthday. Only two months left until she would ask Doc for a medical certificate. She wanted that license—had to have it.

Damn Doc anyhow. How could he have put her in such a position? If she didn't give Marlene the cap, the woman would be dead before the year was out. It was a miracle she was still alive after this last miscarriage.

When Marlene lay dead and there was no one to take care of her children, who would have murdered her? The unfeeling brute who had raped her because he claimed it as his right? Or the unfeeling doctor who had known the rape would occur, yet had refused to supply the cap?

In the bottom of Jo's doctor bag lay the small black box she always carried with her despite the promise to Doc. Opening the box, she removed a small sponge and began to explain its use.

Marlene bent forward to listen.

225

## 22

A blustery March wind tore at Jo's gray bonnet and shawl. She pulled the robe over her knees and picked up the reins, glad she had taken the closed carriage in spite of the deceptive sunshine.

The tumult in her breast did not dissipate quickly. That Karl Schmidt was one mean devil! If she had known he was at home, of course she wouldn't have stopped to see Marlene. Jo's being there for no reason had aroused his suspicions; she saw it in the way he had looked at her and then at his wife—looked back and forth from one to the other.

Oh, thought Jo, don't let there be trouble again. Don't let him find out about the cap and make trouble. If he went to Doc Adams—

Marlene had been using the cap for two months now, and Jo had dropped in today just to make sure the woman was cleansing the cap carefully and using the chemicals. Jo had just finished entering notes in her journal when Marlene's husband walked in.

Schmidt's unexpected presence and his suspicious glances had made Jo nervous. Blast the man anyhow! It shouldn't be necessary to sneak behind his back. Did he want his wife dead, his children motherless?

Jo had fled the Schmidt's rooms as quickly as possible—almost run from the man and his accusing glances. In the carriage, driving away, she reflected that it was no wonder Marlene couldn't say no. She was probably scared to death of that brute she had married.

Marlene Schmidt was only twenty-four, yet looked forty. The ragged remnants of a pretty face gazed from weary blue eyes that had long since given up hope. Twenty-four. Only seven years older than Jo, for Jo's birthday was coming up Friday.

Most women were married long before they reached seventeen, she reflected. In two or three years, if she hadn't married, she'd be considered an old maid. The thought amused her. Doctoring was an all-consuming passion that left no space for such shallow pastimes as love and marriage.

If she kept to her schedule, in four days she would have her certificate. Doc couldn't refuse now. He knew she was capable. He couldn't let the fact that she was a woman stand in the way now that she had proven herself.

Crossing Adelle, Jo turned the buggy into Jefferson Avenue. Seventeen, she thought. She could scarcely believe it. So much had happened to her. It seemed a whole lifetime ago that Mama had whispered to her, "Never mind, my darling, one day you will have a fine birthday party with all your friends and family gathered round."

"What's a birthday party, Mama?" she had asked.

And Mama had gathered her close and held her a long time, and tears had coursed down Mama's cheeks.

Ten or more birthdays had passed since that long-ago day. Jo had had no party yet.

A bit of paper swirled across the street in front of the buggy. Up ahead, on the corner of Gravois and Arsenal, a familiar black figure braced against the wind. It couldn't be—but it was.

Jo's lips curved in a delighted welcome. "Oh, you've

come just at the right time," she cried out. "I was feeling sorry for myself."

His bare hands were cold on hers. "You mustn't feel sad, Jo—especially with a seventeenth birthday coming up." He smiled as he held out a small package. His eyes were wonderfully tender.

"For me?" she asked incredulously. "How did you know about my birthday?"

"You told me."

"But how did you ever remember?"

"March eighteenth. The feast day of St. John of God, the patron saint of hospitals."

"You're kidding. Is it really? My birthday?" She was pleased beyond words, not only at his remembering, but to know that her birthday fell on such an auspicious day. Saint's days, she had been taught by her father, were wonderful days, whether you were Catholic or not. And saint's days, in Ireland, had been a time for gaiety and celebration. She had never heard of St. John of God, but to find that he was the patron saint of hospitals was wonderful beyond belief. It was a good omen—her being born on that special day. "Why didn't you tell me before?" she asked.

"I had to look it up to make sure. He's not a very well-known saint."

She smiled softly. It was the first real birthday present she had ever received. "May I open it now?"

"I want you to."

It felt like a book. She untied the string with delicious anticipation. It *was* a book—*The Deerslayer* by James Fenimore Cooper. "Oh, Fabian." In her delight, she leaned forward, meaning to kiss him on the cheek, but just then he turned his head, and her lips touched his. He pulled back as though burned, his dark eyes startled and very aware.

"I'm sorry," she murmured, moving away quickly.

"I . . . I only meant to let you know . . . how . . . pleased I am. I didn't mean . . . I'm sorry, Father."

"Are you pleased with the book, then?" His voice was very low and he didn't look at her.

"Oh, yes. Thank you."

"I'm glad." With sudden decision, he stepped from the carriage. "I won't keep you from your rounds any longer."

She looked squarely at him then. His face was drawn into a closed fist, his eyes hooded against her. "You aren't coming with me on rounds?" she whispered. "I'm going out in the country today. We could stop by the brook—"

"I have pressing business this afternoon," he said abruptly. "Good-bye, Jo." He turned away, his eyes sad beyond description.

She watched until he was lost from sight. With that one impulsive kiss, she had stripped him of his illusions and forced him to face his feelings for her. She had recognized it in his eyes, for it was what she had been feeling these many months. But for him, how much worse it was. For him it was truly a sin. And to him, this particular sin was a pit into which he must not sink lest his calling turn to ashes and he fall from the grace of God.

She wanted to go after him, help him through his time of trouble as he had helped her after Anne's death. But she knew she mustn't. There was no way she could help Fabian now. Perhaps his God could help.

Jo hurried through rounds, leaving old Mrs. Holland more syrup for her chronic winter cough, removing the splint from little Adam Spencer's leg and wishing she had been called before the bone had taken a set like that, listening to the heartbeat of the child Jane Simpson carried and cautioning her not to lift any more heavy laundry baskets.

"There's no way around it, Dr. Jo," protested Mrs. Simpson. "It has to be done."

"You can do the laundry, but carry it to the line one piece at a time. The walking will do you good. It's the lifting I don't want."

Jo finished rounds early, but was not ready to go home. She climbed from the buggy and on impulse, rented a spirited mare for a fast canter. Her inappropriate attire and the cold wind detracted from her pleasure, but it was highly preferable to sitting down to supper with a new troupe of actors. Jo usually looked forward to meeting the new company, but today Fabian's face haunted her.

For over two hours she rode, ignoring her straggling hair and the discomfort of her crinolines bunched out behind her like the hump on a camel. It was dark when she untied the saddle string to remove her doctor bag. She would skip supper tonight, she thought, avoid Meg and the new company, and spend the evening reading the book Fabian had given her for her birthday.

She turned the key and pushed open the door. They were all still seated at the table. She stood in the entrance hall a moment to listen. The happiness in Meg's voice told Jo that there must be special old friends in this batch of thespians. Jo crept up the stairs, careful to avoid the third step from the top because it creaked fit to wake the dead.

She undressed, washed and brushed her hair, quitting after the first fifty strokes instead of the usual hundred as her mother had taught her. Her feet were cold and she pulled on clean cotton stockings.

Then, in her nightgown, she curled up to read about Natty Bumppo, who was called the Deerslayer, the coarse Hurry Harry, and the beautiful Lake Glimmerglass. She had been reading for over an hour when she heard loud voices raised in the lower hall. At first she thought it must be the new company leaving for the theatre; it was about that time. Then she heard, above the ruckus, the roar of a man beside himself with fury. Jo stepped to the door and opened it just a hair.

"I'll kill her! She can't keep her nose out of my business, I'll chop it off! Get the fuck out of my way, woman! I know she's here!"

Shock slapped Jo to attention. The man's voice was familiar. *Chop off.* Snakes of St. Patrick, that was Karl Schmidt. He had found out about the cap.

"I tell you she isn't here . . ."

There was a loud crack and Meg cried out in pain. Then came several halfhearted protests: "I say there . . ."

"Now see here . . ."

"You want some of the same?" demanded Schmidt. "Gimme that fuckin' lamp. I'll find 'er."

Jo blew out her light, grabbed her doctor bag and crept into the hall. Softly. She closed the door behind her. On stockinged feet, she raced up the stairs, praying there were no creaking steps in this flight as there were in the flight below. Her breath rasped, ragged in her chest. She made for the attic door, the only door she knew for sure would be unlocked. Schmidt's heavy boots pounded up the first flight. The third step squealed beneath his weight. His lamp cast eerie shadows against the wall.

"She-wolf! Where are you?"

"Please. She isn't here. I swear she isn't here."

"Which one of these rooms? Which one?" He grabbed the knob of the first door and shook it. "Git up here with the key, woman, or I'll break the shit out of every door in the house."

Jo reached the top of the attic steps. It was pitch black. In the north corner, Jo knew, under the window, stood a big trunk of clothing. She could hide in the

231

trunk. The book under one arm, the doctor bag under the other, she felt her way toward the trunk. Hands outstretched, cautious. Trying to remember what stood between her and the trunk. A pile of drapes and picture frames. Her toe touched the softness of fabric.

Below her, doors slammed. The sound of heavy boots.

Her heart boomed in her ears. If he opened the attic door now, he was sure to hear it. Her fingers touched something. Wood. Knobby. Tall. The pink and white spooled crib. The lump in Jo's throat threatened to dissolve into hysterical sobs. She eased around the small bed and its painful memories.

Her stockinged toe bumped something hard. She gasped, then bent to feel. The trunk.

*Please don't let the lid squeak.*

It whined harshly. Jo held her breath.

Doors slammed, one after the other. He was inspecting each room in turn. He was on the third floor now. Soon he would reach the attic door.

She stepped into the trunk and burrowed beneath the costumes, trying not to disturb the dust. If she sneezed she was dead.

She pulled the old clothing over her. Settled into the trunk.

*Green valley, where are you?* Her mother's voice refused to come. Jo closed her eyes and dragged rancid air into her lungs.

The attic door opened.

"What the hell's up here?" Schmidt.

"Just junk." Meg.

Boots pounded. Something heavy crashed to the floor. The lectern? Lights peeped around a curl of gold braid.

*I'm going to sneeze.* She stuffed her finger under her nose. The musty smell of long-stored costumes nearly choked her. Her nose twitched, and she pushed harder with her finger. Her heart beat like a drum. He would surely hear. She held her breath.

"Shit!" His boot struck the side of the trunk a frustrated thud.

A shuffling of feet.

"She'll show up sooner or later. I'll wait."

Heavy steps as the light moved away. Darkness. Muffled sounds.

Then silence.

Endless time dragged before Jo rose from her bed of rumpled clothing. *Now what?* He must be sitting in the lower hall, right by the front door, just waiting for her to come home. She couldn't go down the steps, couldn't get past him without being seen. Here she was in her nightgown and stockings and dare not even go downstairs for her clothes.

Suppose he caught her like this, in her nightshirt. She thought back over what she had heard about the man. Boxer turned butcher. A man who raped his own wife, and her not yet out of her childbirth bed. A bully that even strong men feared. Member of the Blue Lodges, according to Marlene—secret because of the murders that had occurred on the other side of the border in Kansas Territory. Two men scarred for life by Schmidt's meat hook and cleaver. And how many more, only God knew.

Now that madman was after her. Jo shivered. Marlene must have told him about the cap.

Somehow, she had to get some clothes and get out of here. How?

She couldn't walk out with him parked right there in the hall. There were no back stairs to the kitchen. How? How?

She sat on the edge of the trunk, unconsciously rubbing the fabric between her fingers. Gradually the

233

feel of the cloth came to her and she snapped erect, hope whirling. If she could sneak down to her room and get the man's suit she had worn to the university—maybe—just maybe—she could walk right past him.

As a man.

As a man she could walk out into the street and Karl Schmidt none the wiser.

She put the book Fabian had given her inside the doctor bag and placed the bag on the top step. Perhaps she could come back for them somehow, someday. If not, at least she could write Meg and ask her to return them. Jo didn't know where she would go, but she knew she would never be safe in St. Louis again.

She buried that thought as she crept down the stairs. This was not the time to worry; this was the time to act.

The attic door stood open.

As soon as she stepped into the hallway, she could hear the melee of protest below.

"Don't you understand, man, we have a performance to give."

"Please, you must let us leave."

Placing one stockinged foot in front of the other, Jo inched her way down the second flight and along the hall. On each side of her, doors stood open, gaping black holes where Schmidt had searched.

Fear swelled her throat until she thought she would choke. She opened her mouth to suck air. Her breath wheezed past the blockage in her throat and hurt her lungs.

She wormed her way across her own room and placed trembling fingers on the closet knob, trying to remember whether this door creaked. The tension had built in her until she had a shocking urge to giggle. It was a frightening thought—that she might actually giggle out loud—so frightening that the urge died almost as soon as it was born.

234

The door didn't creak. Her fingers found the suit—the last garments at the back of the narrow closet.

Jody pulled her nightdress over her head and dressed quickly, quietly, concentrating on her own movements, forcing her mind away from the danger at the foot of the stairs, ignoring the voices that rose and fell, and the occasional curse, louder than the rest.

Finally satisfied that she had done the best she could in the faint light, Jo stepped into the hall. Her own bright hair was tucked neatly inside the familiar blond wig and capped by a wide-brimmed black hat.

Gaslight cast her wavering shadow on the wall.

She looked down at herself—black wool and heavy brogans. She'd do. She'd have to do.

The actors were still trying to convince Schmidt: "I tell you, we must get to the theatre."

"Our contract will be canceled if we don't show up."

He had just searched upstairs and found it empty. If he looked up and saw her now, she was dead. Jo took a deep breath and strolled casually down the steps.

His back was turned.

Avoiding the telltale step and hoping no one else could hear the pound of her heart, she joined the group in the hallway. The ladies wore hats and coats, the men held hats in hand, some with greatcoats over their arms. Her own round hat was most apropos, she saw.

Schmidt stood by the front door, ranting to himself. "Bitch. She thinks she can hide out and I'll forgit. I'll not. I'll mark that bitch for life. However long it takes, I'll git 'er." He gave a vicious slash with his hook, and the group jumped back, gasping with alarm. "Shut your bone boxes, the lot of you!" he roared.

Jo could see his flushed face clearly now. His eyes were bloodshot, his words faintly slurred. He'd been drinking, but he wasn't drunk. Had he been rip-snorting, beyond-caring drunk, she might have hoped

235

for him to sleep it off and forget it by morning as Pa used to do. But Schmidt wasn't drunk on liquor; he was drunk on rage. It wouldn't take much to set him off and start him swinging that meat hook.

Suddenly he sprang to the door and flung it open. "Charlie! Charlie! Where the hell are you?"

Another bruiser appeared from the darkness. "Yeah, Karl?"

"She ain't here. You get on over to Doc's house like I told you. Send Curley down to Doc's office on Chestnut. That fucker shows up either place—you bring 'er back here to me."

"I seen her oncet, Karl. She shows up at the Doc's house, I'll have some fun with her first. I bet she' never seen a ten-inch whacker."

Jo's flesh crawled. She clamped her teeth together, holding back the involuntary scream that rose in her throat like sour bile.

"She's mine," Schmidt roared. "You'll bring 'er back to me, you hear?"

The members of the troupe were looking at her strangely now, and Meg flashed them a look of warning. Jo stayed in the shadows at the back of the group as Schmidt swung on them again.

"Awright. Git yer asses out o' here. I'm sick of your yappin'!"

They didn't need a second invitation. Crowding protectively around Jo, they hurried past Schmidt and into the night. Jo felt Meg's eyes, but didn't dare return her good-bye glance.

Outside, with the door closed behind them, the group moved away from Jo as though she were a leper. "Where can we get a hack?" one man demanded.

"This way." She led them, grateful that they were more upset about the late curtain than they were curious about her.

Worrying about Meg back there with that madman, yet knowing there was nothing she could do about it, Jo ordered Doc's closed carriage. There was only one place she could go now. According to what Schmidt said, his cronies were waiting at the office and at Doc's house. That left only St. Anne's and Fabian.

It was almost eight o'clock when she entered the church. Hoping it was Fabian in the confessional tonight, she genuflected and sank nervously into an empty pew to await her turn.

When the last of the penitents had left the church, Jo slipped into the confessional and knelt before the wire window. She could see nothing through the grating, had no way of knowing whether he could see her. "Father, I am in trouble. I need help."

She waited. No sound from the other side of the mesh-covered window.

"Please, Father, my trouble is not for the confessional. My life is threatened and Meg is in danger. Please. May I talk with you?" If it turned out to be Father Lucien— Oh, why didn't he speak, whoever he was?

There was a soft rustle from the other side of the window and the soft click of a door closing.

He hadn't even answered. Yet it had to have been Fabian; Father Lucien would have railed at her. Jo rose and crept disconsolately across the aisle.

Crouched in the pew, she bowed her head, tried to let the hushed peace of the chapel seep into her aching soul. Her life had taken another uprooting twist. And all because she had tried to help Marlene.

Because I tried to help, she thought resentfully, here I am running for my life. If I'd listened to Doc and Fabian and not stuck my nose into Schmidt's bedroom, Marlene might be dead—but I wouldn't be here now, needing help and feeling the pain of

237

Fabian's refusal.

He hadn't said one word. Not one. Just walked away. Now there was nowhere to turn—no one to help.

But even now, with her very life in danger, Jo didn't regret what she had done. For Marlene, yes, because now that her husband had found out, she would submit to his brutish attacks and probably be dead within the year. So Jo hadn't helped her, and for that she was sorry. But the other women with caps *were* being helped, and for them Jo was proud of what she had done.

Suddenly she realized she was no longer alone. She looked up. Fabian stood beside her, tall and stern. She pulled herself erect, grateful that he had come to her, yet not knowing how he could help.

His eyes swept over her, taking in the masculine attire. He frowned. "Come." He led the way past the confessionals as he had that first day—the day of Anne's funeral. Across the bare cold garden toward the same small office.

"Father Lucien?" she asked.

"He's retired early." Fabian opened the office door. "Good. The fire isn't quite out," he said, his eyes carefully avoiding her exposed legs. He poked at the coals and a timid blue flame stretched to life. "You must be cold. Perhaps another log . . ." He tossed a pine knot and poked it into place. It flared brightly. "There. That's better," he said.

She knew he was making small talk and performing small chores because he was nervous. She had never seen him nervous before.

"A man . . ." she began. "The husband of one of my patients . . . is threatening to kill me." She bit her lip. "You told me once that my headstrong ways would get me into trouble. Oh, Fabian, I'm going to have to leave St. Louis. I'm going to have to give up doctoring." Her voice broke.

He stepped quickly to her then and took her cold hands in his warm ones. When he spoke, it was with that same hypnotic conviction she had heard and responded to the day of Anne's funeral.

Carefully he drew the story from her. As she talked, the warmth left his eyes and his face tightened with disapproval. She tossed her head. *I don't care what he thinks. I don't care. I was right to help Marlene, even if it did cause trouble.*

At last the room was quiet. A faint rosy gleam from the fireplace highlighted the priest's tight lips and hooded eyes. She shouldn't have told him about the cap, she realized now.

She stood and turned to leave. "I shouldn't have come to you," she said, her back as stiff as her voice. "I know you don't approve of what I'm doing. I know it goes against everything you believe in."

"Sit down." She could hear softness, laced with resignation and a deep well of sadness. "Do you have anyplace to go, Jo? Do you want to go back to New York?"

"No. Never there—"

"Suppose you think about it awhile," he said before she could continue. "Meanwhile, I'll go to the boardinghouse to get your clothes."

"Will you try to get Meg away from him? Or get him out of there?"

"Don't worry. I will take young Michael Kane with me and leave him to look after your Mrs. O'Gerity." He smiled then, a faint, unwilling smile. "And I'll get the doctor bag and the book I gave you. I'll return the bag to Doc Adams and see if he has any suggestions about where you could go."

"Take the carriage," she said, her spirits lifting. Doc would send her a certificate now. She knew he would. If

239

Fabian went to him and told him what had happened, Doc wouldn't let her leave St. Louis without a certificate. Not after all her work this past year and a half. "The carriage is out front," she said.

"Good. That will speed things up a bit. You'll be safe enough here until I come back."

He was gone almost two hours, but she was so busy with her dreams it seemed only minutes.

"Is Meg all right?" she asked, hugging her arms against the cold blast of air that swirled through the open door.

"She's fine. I left Michael with her."

"Is Schmidt still there?"

"Yes, but Michael will take care of Mrs. O'Gerity. He's a good, strong, solid boy. She'll be safe with him."

"You've brought the doctor bag back with you—didn't you see Doc?"

"I saw him. He wants you to keep the bag. He says you're a fine doctor even if you can't ever hope to hang out your shingle. He wants you to have the bag and everything in it."

*Not hang out her shingle.* She couldn't believe Doc hadn't sent her certificate. She had been so sure.

Damned old fool! She had worked as hard as any man—was as good as any man—but just because she was a woman—

"Now, about where you might go—" began Fabian.

"I know where I'm going," interrupted Jo, her cat's eyes glowing angrily in the firelight. "I'm going West. To Oregon. And somehow, someway, whether Doc Adams or you or anybody else approves, I'm going to be a doctor."

240

# PART III

# THE OREGON TRAIL

# 23

*March 15, 1860*

Walls of limestone rose sharply above the deep valleys through which the train passed. Elderberry bushes, now bare and spindly, lined the tracks. As the train roared westward, windswept fields hung mirage-like in the distance; the few log-house farms were shimmering tapestries in pale March sunlight, there and gone almost before she could distinguish them through the grimy window.

The trip to Jefferson, Missouri, was short in time but endless in emotion as Jo's mind dredged up yesterday's bittersweet pageant. Despite his disappointment in her appearance and his disapproval of her actions, Fabian's censure had been a silent one. He had done all he could for her, and his dark eyes had been soft and loving when he put her on the train.

Doc, on the other hand, had delivered his clear and final protest against women physicians: While willingly sending her the tools of her profession, he had withheld the proof of her ability.

Just yesterday her promise to her mother had burned so brightly—now it was little more than an ephemeral dream, almost more remote than when she made it four years ago. If she went West and found her valley now, what good would it do? If she couldn't keep her promise and have her certificate, there would be no point in finding the valley.

Jo gave a little sniffle, quickly stifled it, and looked around to see if anyone had noticed. Dressed as a man in a train full of men, how would it look to be slouched in a corner crying? Jo stared dolefully out the window.

The train had stopped. Barren grape vineyards stretched on sharp bluffs overlooking the track. *Hermann* proclaimed the sign that swung forlornly from the empty platform. Not much farther to Jefferson, she thought. She squared her shoulders and lifted her chin.


The steamer's lower deck sat almost level with the dirty water. And a tall, railed structure rose three decks high, dominated by two towering, smoke-belching stacks, and crowned with a texas and a rotund pilothouse. It was white with red trim around lacelike railings. It looked like a great big wedding cake, thought Jo, and for some reason the thought made her more miserable than ever.

Squealing, braying, stomping, bellowing animals jammed the lower deck while half a dozen people crowded into every stateroom. She wasn't surprised to discover that she would be sleeping on a mattress on the floor, but she was startled to realize that since she was dressed as a man, she had to share her room with six others of the masculine gender. Snakes of St. Patrick, she thought, what have I let myself in for?

Somehow she had imagined there would be an opportunity to change clothes before she boarded the steamboat, but it hadn't worked out that way. Now here she was steaming up the Missouri toward Leavenworth, stuck in men's breeches with a blond wig on her head, and no way to remedy the situation. She stood at the rail and stared wretchedly at the murky water.

The Missouri was a repulsive stream of flowing mud. Jo heard one nearby passenger say the the silt-filled river was "too thick to swim in but not quite thick enough to walk on." At supper, the water served was so brown it looked as though someone had used it to wash in, but she heard a soldier at the next table assert that it was clean.

"Let it set awhile," he told the pretty girl he had spent the day trying to charm. "In about five minutes that silt will sink to the bottom. You'll maybe get about an inch of mud, but the rest will be clear as the noontime sky on the prairie." Jo stifled a laugh. The lieutenant was spectacularly handsome, in his mid-thirties, with chiseled features and brown hair, beard, and mustache. She wondered how often he had used that line on pretty girls. For a fleeting moment, Jo wished she weren't wearing pantaloons.

"Navigating the Missouri at low water ain't easy," said the soldier later when he came to stand beside Jo at the railing. He must have lost out with the girl, Jo thought.

"It's kind of like putting a ship on dry land," he continued, "then trying to float it by sending a nigger ahead with a sprinkling pot." He paused to light a cheroot and pointed. "Ain't them snags something? Ain't anybody can get up river past them snags but a licensed pilot, and they don't always make it either." He introduced himself as Lt. Philip Templeton and said he was on his way to Fort Leavenworth, "reporting for active duty again after leave in St. Louis."

"I'm Jo Gates," she said in her deepest Shakespearean voice.

He leaned against the rail and rested his foot on the bottom bar. Jo promptly imitated his stance, her lower limbs feeling very exposed. The brisk March wind fluttered her hat brim. She grabbed at it and jammed it tightly onto her head.

"Where you headed, Joe?" asked the lieutenant.

"Leavenworth."

"Going to Pikes Peak to strike it rich?"

"Could be." Jo thought it best not to discuss her past or her uncertain future.

Templeton eyed her with superior amusement. "Listen, kid, if you think you can just waltz out to Pikes Peak and hit pay dirt the first lick or two, you got another thing coming. It's no picnic out there. Just getting from Leavenworth to the diggings is worth your life—even on the new Republican route. You ain't a match for the sort you'll meet on the trail, kid. They're a tough lot."

Jo looked at him, wondering if he was trying to be nice beneath that superior manner. He was almost breath-stoppingly handsome, but she didn't like his exaggerated sense of self-importance.

"Feel that?" asked Templeton as the steamer gave a little shudder.

"What was it?"

"Snag scraping against the keel. You'll feel every snag and every sandbar. This your first trip up the Missouri, kid?"

Jo nodded. Her hat brim flapped violently in the wind, and she felt her coattails fly. She needed three hands. One for her hat, one for her doctor bag, and one to hold her coattails down so her behind wouldn't hang out.

Her portmanteau had been consigned to the cabin, but not her precious leather bag. Not trusting its safety in the crowded stateroom, she kept her doctor bag and money with her at all times. Now it was proving a problem. Jo's one free hand darted from her hat to her coattails, and back again, until finally the lieutenant commented on her dilemma.

"Something wrong, kid?"

"No."

"Too windy for you?"

"A little." She grabbed at her flying coat.

"For Chrissake, kid, either set down your bag or stop grabbing your coattails."

"Perhaps I'll go inside."

He grinned and shook his head as she moved away from the railing.

From the promenade, Jo could hear a man on the bow of the lower deck calling out river depths: "Four and one half. Five feet. Quarter less twain. Mark twain. No bottom." And then the pilot's three-belled whistle rang to indicate the danger was past. Every few minutes, night and day, the man on the bow called out the soundings.

The Big Muddy, as the river was affectionately called, strode due west across Missouri, then made a sharp right angle at the border to serve as the dividing line between the States and the Kansas Territory. Changeable and dangerous, the rive zigzagged through a broad valley and shifted its channel by as much as fifty feet in a single week. It was shallow but fast moving, studded with islands of sand. Dead tree trunks protruded from the dun-drab water like huge spears, and tangled heaps of driftwood sometimes cut the channel by half.

The *Tropic* traveled between low, wooded banks through a vast wilderness. Jo saw only one log house that first day, and two trees hatchet-blazed by some lone traveler.

In daylight, the river was liquid dust—brown,

dreary, turbid, but under the blood-red sky at dusk, and then the silvery moon later, the river shone with translucent beauty, and each tree leaf was stenciled sharply against the clear night sky, weaving an exquisite magic.

When the time came to bed down in the crowded stateroom with six men, Jo couldn't do it. All night she sat on the hurricane deck, shivering in her thin coat and blanket, wondering what would happen now that she was actually going West without a medical certificate. After all her grandiose plans, was she destined to wind up nothing more than a midwife?

She met the morning sun with red-rimmed eyes and trooped into breakfast with little appetite and even less direction.

The steamboat had scraped on sandbars and stopped abruptly almost a dozen times a day, but each time she had easily drifted free. About ten miles upstream from the City of Kansas, the big sidewheeler was less fortunate. With no warning, a huge section of bank gave way and fell into the river. It roared like a mighty waterfall and flung a spray of white water high into the air. The *Tropic* swung wide, trying to avoid the rapidly forming sandbar, but the channel was narrow at that point. A tremendous jolt shook the boat, and it shuddered to a dead stop. Passengers rushed to the railing where they could plainly see the bar on which they hung. Beside them a huge tree toppled and whipped past, driven by the swift current.

"If they just wait," said Templeton, who seemed to know all about everything, "the river will shift enough to move the sand out from under us." That appeared unlikely to Jo. What had been water with a powerful current just a few minutes before was now a solid nest of sand on which the *Tropic* roosted, high and dry.

Apparently the pilot didn't agree with Templeton either, for crewmen soon lowered two tall wooden spars, like crooked legs, on each side of the boat.

"They call it *grasshoppering,*" explained Templeton. "Those lines get power from the capstan and act like hoists. The spars are the pushers. The boat lifts and pushes itself all at the same time. Speeds things up a bit."

Grasshoppering was still not speedy, Jo discovered as the afternoon wore on. "Does this happen often?" she asked.

"We've been right lucky this trip. There's four big dangers on the Missouri, kid. Sandbars like this one. And snags like those—" He pointed to the ugly, twisted limbs protruding from the water. "The snags the pilot really has to watch out for are those just under the surface."

"How can he look out for them if he can't see them?"

"The current swirls around 'em. See up there—that's an underwater tree. You know, a lot of fellas prefer sternwheelers because they ain't so easy to snag, but give me a good pilot and I'll take a sidewheeler every time." He threw his cheroot over the railing. "Like I was saying, there's four dangers: sandbars and snags was the first two. Then there's the boilers. If the boiler goes, it'll blow us all to glory."

He was a walking encyclopedia of disaster, she thought. Not wanting to hear any more, Jo turned her back, but her shoulder didn't rebuff Templeton who continued his list of doom: "And fire. Fire's the worst. These babies burn in minutes. A steamboat has to be light as possible, you know, so it don't draw much water. The *Tropic* don't draw much more'n a dugout canoe. That means all these upper decks are made out of the lightest material they can find. Looks pretty, but it's flimsy as hell. I saw one burn once on the Mississippi. Cinders—stem to stern—in nothing flat."

Jo refused to think about the possibility of fire. Instead she fastened her mind on the partially submerged tree limbs. "Why are they all pointing at us?" she asked. "Why don't some of them point the other way?"

"We're going upriver. The water pulls at the trees until it turns them all in the direction the current flows. They're called *steamboat killers*. Coming downriver ain't half as dangerous as going up."

Jo looked at the spare, sharp-faced man in the pilothouse and wondered how he could be so confident in the face of such overwhelming dangers. But even as she watched, he grew red of face and no longer appeared calm. Jo began to suspect he was a bit of a hothead.

Templeton grinned knowingly. "If there's one thing a river pilot can't stand, it's being passed in mid-river. Look at his face—he is one pissed-off man!" Jo blinked at the soldier's words and stifled a gasp as she realized she was now open to whatever language men used among themselves. It wasn't a pleasant thought. She'd heard it all before in Liverpool and Five Points, of course, but in St. Louis these past two years, she'd been treated as a lady, and she liked it. Although she had been forced to use that particular word so that her patients could understand the treatment of chilblains, she was shocked to have it said aloud to her by a man. Doc was one thing; this soldier was another. She couldn't wait to reach Leavenworth so she could get back into her own clothes.

"If we don't slide free soon, the captain just might have to put the cargo ashore to lighten the load," said Templeton, unaware of Jo's discomfort.

Just then the steamer, *Deliverance*, drew alongside,

250

and the air was thick with rude taunting from its passengers.

Minutes later, the *Tropic* broke free from the bar.

Jo saw the captain speak and the pilot's enraged face as he answered. Then she saw the pilot shout through the pipe—to the engineer, she supposed. A spate of orders was flung down the pipe, and suddenly the boat shuddered, rattled glass, and spurted upriver.

Black smoke poured from the stacks. The *Tropic* surged ahead, thrashed upstream in the wake of the other boat. Apparently the pilot was determined to regain his lead. He soon had a full head of steam and was out to pass the *Deliverance*. Passengers rushed to the rails. They began to shout and cheer.

"That crazy bastard has tied down the safety valves," Templeton muttered, half under his breath.

The *Deliverance* still showed her wake, but the *Tropic* gained slowly, inexorably. Jo squeezed next to the railing beside the lieutenant. Excitement rose in her as white water churned. Sparks flew from the overheated chimneys and spattered on passengers and freight.

"He's burning either pitch or oil." Templeton's voice wore a hard edge. "If them boilers blow . . ." The lieutenant tossed another cheroot over the railing and shot a quick look at the pilot.

Jo heard but didn't understand. She was too caught up in the thrill of the race to care. The boats were drawing abreast now, almost bow to bow. Jo's breath came faster. Her cheeks felt hot. She began to jump up and down and scream. In her excitement, she grabbed Templeton's arm. "We're winning! We're winning!"

Her laughing eyes passed over him and froze. The lieutenant was looking directly into her face and he was smiling, a twisted, knowing smile—the smile of an attracted male. His eyes roved slowly down her body,

251

and his grin broadened as he gazed on her pantaloon-encased legs.

Jo's hand jumped from his arm. A hot blush suffused her features.

Suddenly, before either of them could speak, their world went berserk. With a terrible grinding roar, the steamer came to an abrupt halt.

The bow flung skyward. Jo lurched sideways and Templeton's strong arms enveloped her.

She felt herself lifted off her feet. Then they were flying through the air.

She was still locked in his arms when the water of the icy Missouri closed around them.

Don't breathe, she told herself. Don't breathe. She opened her eyes. The water churned, brown with silt. She felt Templeton tug at the doctor bag, which weighed them down. She resisted his efforts to dislodge it and clung desperately to her future. She thought her lungs would burst. Templeton still held her. She felt, rather than saw, his legs and one arm beating upward. She kicked strongly to help him.

When they broke the surface, the *Deliverance* was well upstream, but slowing. The *Tropic* loomed high above them, the stern underwater, the forward deck spurting steam and fingering the blue sky. The boat was impaled on a huge tree, like a butterfly on a pin.

Screams and curses and moans came from the deck and the muddy water around them. Two lifeless bodies bobbed past.

The death-dealing oak that struck the boat had been completely hidden in the walnut-colored water. It had pierced the *Tropic*'s hull, speared upward through the lower deck, the pantry, and two staterooms, and thrust out at the hurricane roof where Jo had been standing moments before. It was a sturdy oak, bare of leaves and

252

branches, and it had broken the main pipe, deluging the cabin with steam.

The next hours were nightmarish in their stark reality, but the snag which proved fatal to the *Tropic* was the saving of those still aboard. It held the big sidewheeler impaled and motionless while the *Deliverance* backed downstream to effect a rescue.

Templeton assisted Jo aboard the rescue boat and mockingly proffered his army hat so she could hide her long strawberry hair. She thanked him with a nod, too frozen to do more. The March wind whipped through her wet clothes. Her fingers, frigid claws surrounding the bag handle, now refused to function at all. The leather bag clattered to the deck.

The lieutenant bent to retrieve it as a stout little man rushed up to them. "You need dry suits?" he asked, beaming.

"You might say that." Templeton drew his lips back against his teeth, and his breath was white in the chill air.

"I'm a ready-made clothing salesman. I can fit both of you fellers if you can pay."

The man's eagerness drew a cynical grin from Philip. "I been wet before," he said. He had waved the drummer away when he caught sight of the boy-woman at his side. Her teeth chattered; her body shook. Her hair, heavy with river water, had been hurriedly thrust inside his army hat, and now water oozed down her face and squiggled beneath her collar in cold brown rivulets. Even under these miserable circumstances, she was a real looker.

Templeton turned back to the drummer. "You got a suit to fit my friend here?"

"I guess so."

Templeton had soon struck a bargain. "Come on,

253

Miss Joe," he said, grasping her hand. "Let's get you into some dry clothes before you come down with pneumonia."

Jo accepted the clothing numbly and closeted herself in an empty stateroom to change.

Ten minutes later she was dressed in a sturdy gray wool suit. The wig was gone, presumably floating downstream somewhere, but her hair was coiled atop her head and tucked neatly inside a new broad-brimmed black hat.

Five minutes after that, as she surveyed the salon full of injured people, Jo had the passing realization that this was her birthday. Today was the day she had sworn to get her certificate from Doc, she realized with a sharp stab of regret.

Her heart drummed nervously against her rib cage as she knelt beside her first patient. She had treated women and children without Doc's supervision for well over a year now, but suddenly she was frightened, uncertain of Her own abilities.

What am I doing here? she asked herself. I'm a seventeen-year-old woman dressed in men's clothes and pretending to be a doctor. An out-and-out fraud—that's what I am. How can I possibly help these people?

Then the little boy beside her whimpered in pain, and Jo's vision cleared. She saw the shiny lobster-red flesh of the steam-burned child, and her heart thawed as deep compassion swept through her.

She opened her doctor bag and her fingers were quick and deft.

After one startled glance, Philip Templeton bent to assist.

One hour stretched to two and two to three as more burn victims were pulled from the stricken *Tropic*. No one questioned Jo's authority or ability. Her heart breaking with sympathy, she applied tincture of comfrey leaves, gave morphine, set broken limbs, and dressed wounds.

It was almost dark when the pilot concluded that nothing more could be accomplished at the scene of the accident. The roustabouts had salvaged most of the cargo and piled it on shore where it forlornly awaited another steamer.

Jo had long since depleted the small supply of drugs Doc had left in her bag. When she dragged herself from the salon, four bodies lay in the main cabin, along with thirty-three injured. No one knew for sure if all the victims had been recovered from the water. Jo had done all she could, yet her heart was sore within her breast. There was so little she *could* do—so few drugs or ointments really worked.

"About fifty steamboats sink on the Missouri and the Mississippi every year," said Philip, still spreading his message of doom. "I came up the river in '52 about three weeks after the *Saluda* went down, and would you believe they were still pulling out bodies. Had a clothesline rigged up on shore and were stripping the clothes off the corpses before they buried 'em. Right near Lexington it was."

Jo would have moved away from him then, but there was nowhere to go. At his urging, she sat with him on the hurricane deck to drink hot mocha, their backs resting against the texas. She let out a long, weary sigh as he spread a blanket over her. She was bone tired, yet proud of her afternoon's work.

She could sense his eyes and turned her head. "Thank you for helping."

"You looked right efficient." There was grudging admiration in his voice, but speculation, too. "Want to tell me about yourself?"

"There isn't much to tell."

"If I didn't know you were a woman, I'd have thought you were a real doctor."

"I *am* a real doctor," Jo declared, almost choking on the lie that knotted her throat.

He raised a skeptical brow and chuckled. "Doctoring's not proper for a woman. Everybody knows that."

"What, you, too?" She didn't bother to hide her bitterness.

"Is that why you're wearing breeches? To pass yourself off as a man so you can pretend to be a doctor?"

"I'm not pretending."

"You mean you got a medical license and all—just like a real doctor?"

"If my carpetbag hadn't been lost on the *Tropic*, I'd prove it to you." Would he believe her? Jo held her breath.

He chuckled. "But you have been trying to pass as a man. How come?"

"Please, Lieutenant Templeton, I'd rather not discuss the reasons for my unseemly garb."

"Well, whatever your reason, if you run around in pants, you'll have to whack off all that pretty red hair. And that would be a shame."

"There's no need to cut my hair, lieutenant—I don't plan on remaining a man once I get to Leavenworth."

"Good." He paused to light a cheroot and squint at her over the glowing tip. "I've heard tell of women dressing up like men and heading for the gold fields," he said finally. "Some of 'em even get away with it. You sure you ain't planning something like that, pretty lady?"

She shook her head. "I have no intentions of digging for gold, lieutenant. I'm a doctor." Her heart pounded. "I'm going to Oregon to open an office there."

His teeth flashed white in the gathering darkness.

"That so? You sign on with a wagon train yet?"

"No. I understand I can do that in Leavenworth."

"I ain't asking out of idle curiosity, you know. I've got orders to Fort Boise and I'll be leaving with the first wagon train out. Maybe we could go with the same train—maybe I could even help you get signed up . . ."

She wanted to turn him down cold, but he was the one person who might help her now. After all, he had seen her in action as a doctor. He could vouch for her ability and the fact that her luggage had been lost in the river—if he wanted to.

Jo tilted her cat's eyes at him and wished she were wearing a dress and had a fan to flutter as Anne had taught her so long ago. "You wouldn't know of a nice respectable lodging house in Leavenworth, would you, lieutenant?"

His chest expanded as he warmed to her flirting. "There's Mrs. Knox's place on Third and Ottawa. If I didn't have to report to the fort, I'd take you myself."

"Aren't you nice." She smiled up at him again. "How would I go about signing on a wagon train?"

"You might try Angus Drummond. Since he's always the first to jump off in the spring, I'll probably go with him myself."

"And where will I find this Angus Drummond?"

"On the road up to Fort Leavenworth. He's there every spring. Listen, if you wait till Sunday, I'll run you up there myself."

"Do you suppose he could use a doctor on his wagon train?"

"Drummond's always on the lookout for doctors and preachers. They make the trip West a sight easier. But he'd not take kindly to a woman physician, and that's a fact."

"Oh." She fluttered her lashes again. "And after my

suitcase with all my credentials were lost on the *Tropic*! I may need you to vouch for my authenticity, lieutenant."

His eyes narrowed and his smile was very knowing. Suddenly she wondered if she was being smart to flirt with this man—yet she might need his help. She tipped her eyes at him and her smile was warm.

## 24

Leavenworth was a crude five-year-old town that
had grown so fast it had had no time to acquire sophis-
tication. It was one continuous country fair, Jo saw: all
excitement and bustle with the sun beating on muddy
streets that still throbbed with gold fever.

She turned for one last look at the tall-chimneyed
sidewheeler where Philip Templeton watched from the
promenade. He raised his hat, his white teeth outlined
by his full brown beard and mustache. "I'll come look
for you first Sunday I'm free," he called.

She waved, then stepped off the plank into the
slippery red mud. Long wagons, each with six or more
oxen, blocked the levee, and she had to pick her way
between boxes and crates piled high on the wharf,
between buckskin-clad pioneers and Mexicans in wide-
peaked hats and Indians in brightly colored blankets.
Her heart pounded uneasily as three soldiers staggered
past, jostling other pedestrians. There were few women
on the streets, she noticed, and those few were heavily
veiled. Glad to be in pantaloons, Jo averted her face.
Maybe she'd better just keep her masquerade a while
longer, she reflected.

Across the wide esplanade, freighters blocked one
street; she picked the next. Potawatomie was muddy
and uneven, houses and shops having been built before

the street was leveled or the stumps removed.

On one corner a man delivered a speech—something about slavery. He had gathered a small crowd of supporters and several hecklers. The slavery question and the bloody Kansas battle had made daily newspaper reading in St. Louis, but it had seemed so far away and unreal to Jo then, immersed as she had been in her study of medicine. She hurried past the gesturing men.

The frontier town of Leavenworth was unbelievably crude: a church with no belfry—just a bell that hung on a pole before the door, buildings constructed of green cottonwood that had dried and warped in the hot Kansas sun and reminded her of great gray corkscrews. She passed a tailor shop, a saddler, several busy drinking saloons, a hatter, and an eating saloon.

Templeton had warned Jo not to expect much, so she was pleasantly surprised to find that the boardinghouse on Ottowa and Third was two-storied, a gray monstrosity run by a birdlike little lady with a knot of thinning gray hair pulled tightly atop her head.

"Kick the mud off'n your shoes afore you come in," Mrs. Knox ordered. "Mud comes in three colors here: black, red, and clay. You don't keep ahead of it, it'll climb right into bed with you."

The little woman was a dynamo of energy. Within minutes of Jo's arrival, she had been assigned a room, advised of the house rules, and led to the parlor to meet the other paying guests.

The parlor was a delight. Like most of the town's crude homes, the cottonwood shakes, nailed up green, had shrunk in the hot Kansas sun. Daylight danced through the room's newspaper-covered walls and pirouetted across bright, haphazardly scattered throw rugs. What tickled Jo immediately was the incongruity of newspapered walls, lace curtains, the dirt floor, and

260

a piano.

There were three ladies and one man in the sparsely furnished parlor. Mr. Brown, reading a paper in one corner, was as nondescript as his name. The Harrow ladies, well dressed and stylishly coiffed, lent a solid respectability to the strange room.

"Mrs. Harrow. Mrs. Harrow. And Mrs. Harrow," the landlady chirped. "This Mrs. Harrow," she said, indicating a sweet-faced older lady, "is the mother-in-law of these two Mrs. Harrows: Patience and Agnes. Ladies, this here's Joe Gates."

Patience smiled and lowered her eyes. Agnes bridled and batted hers. Jo swallowed and reminded herself that she was supposed to have a well-developed latissimus and an accompanying swagger. She squared her shoulders and spread her arms as Phinny had taught her.

Mrs. Harrow nodded pleasantly. "Are you newly arrived in Leavenworth, Mr. Gates?"

"Just today."

"From where, Mr. Gates, if you don't mind my asking?"

"St. Louis. And you, ma'am?"

"We're from Bangor, Maine. On our way to Oregon to join our menfolk." Jo noticed a sudden tensing about the older woman's mouth, and a shadow behind her eyes.

Patience, the pretty one, patted her mother-in-law's arm. "Now, Mother Harrow, don't you start worrying about Mitch again. He'll get back before jumping-off time." She turned to Jo. "Are you on your way West, too, Mr. Gates?"

Jo nodded, thinking hard. She couldn't let them go on calling her mister. Her heart thumped. "But it's Dr. Gates—not mister. Most folks call me Dr. Jo."

There was a moment's silence as everyone stared at

261

her. Finally Mrs. Harrow spoke: "Forgive our rudeness, doctor. I guess it's your youth that startled us so."

Jo tried to make her smile confident and amused. "I'm used to that reaction," she said, wondering how she had ever expected to carry this off. It was one thing to play a young man on stage, quite another to do it in real life.

"How did you ever manage to become a doctor so young?" queried Agnes in a breathless whisper. "Did you go through medical school and all? Oh my, isn't this wonderful—why you can't be any older than I am . . ."

Jo smiled, her heart pounding with the effort to appear calm. "I was apprenticed to a physician for almost two years."

"A real doctor!" Agnes's voice dripped admiration. "Why, I don't think you're too young to be a doctor at all. What I think is that if you're going to Oregon, like us, you ought to come on our wagon train." Her lashes fluttered and her small white teeth gleamed.

When Mrs. Knox announced supper, Jo was grateful for a chance to escape, but Agnes glued herself to Jo's side and squeezed into the next chair. "Oh, I'm so glad you're sitting here, Dr. Joe," she said, smiling archly. "It'll give us a chance to get better acquainted." She was slightly overweight, with stays so tight that her bosom swelled alarmingly above her low-cut gown. Heavy earbobs swayed as she tilted her head and batted her short pale lashes.

"I think Agnes's idea of you signing on with the Drummond train is a good one, Dr. Gates," said Mrs. Harrow from across the table. "I, personally, would feel much better if we had a doctor along."

Jo looked up quickly. "You're going with Angus Drummond? I met a soldier on the *Tropic* who suggested that train." Her voice came out calm, but her heart was dancing. Mrs. Harrow had called her "doctor." They had accepted her at her word. This was going to be easier than she had ever dreamed. She buttered a biscuit and tried to still her shaking fingers.

"You were on the *Tropic?*" breathed Agnes excitedly. "Why, you must be that doctor the whole town's talking about. You're the one who saved all those people! Oh, do tell us what happened, Dr. Joe."

As Jo talked reluctantly about the sinking of the *Tropic*, she was very aware of Agnes's animated face and of her pink mouth spread in a soft circle of admiration. If ever I get out of these damned pantaloons and into a dress again, vowed Jo silently, I'll never tilt my head, never bat my eyes as Anne once showed me, never hide behind a fluttering fan, and most of all—never, never say in a sweetly simpering voice, "Oh, how terribly interesting!" Yet even in the midst of her distaste, Jo couldn't help realizing that this was possibly the biggest boost her medical career could ever receive. The circle of believers was growing.

After supper everyone returned to the parlor. Agnes, still fluttering and taking deep breaths to swell her breasts, grasped Jo's arm in a proprietary gesture. Jo thought she would die.

Patience, who had a sweet, true voice, was soon pressed into singing, and it wasn't until after her rendition of "Sweet Betsy of Pike" that Jo managed to escape Agnes's bridling attentions and position herself across the room, next to Mrs. Harrow.

"So you're off to Oregon to open your office," said the older woman as the applause abated.

Jo nodded, her heart pumping nervously.

"I guess I'm hopelessly old-fashioned. I come from a big family and just can't get used to young people being completely on their own so early in life."

"Some of us don't have much choice, ma'am."

263

"No, I suppose not. Have you no family, Dr. Joe?"

"No, ma'am, I'm alone."

"How sad. My family has been split for two years now. I'm so happy our separation is about to end. My sons have built homes in Oregon now. Soon we'll all be together again." She followed the direction of Jo's glance. "Neither of my sons were married long when they left for Oregon. Patience and Sam had only been married a year when he left. And Agnes—well, Agnes was fourteen and a bride of just one week. The boys have been gone two years now. These girls will still be newlyweds when we get to Oregon."

"Is your husband waiting there too, ma'am?"

"Mr. Harrow passed away three years ago. That's when the boys decided to resettle. Mitch is the youngest of the three. He came East to sell his lumber business and take us back with him. He had a manager in Bangor these last two years and that didn't work out too well." She looked at Jo. "What is it makes you men want to keep moving West?" She sighed. "Of course, Mitch and the boys have a fine lumber business started on the Thunder River in Oregon now. But it's taken two years. Two years of waiting."

"And then Mitch goes off and leaves us here in this hole of a town!" Agnes had approached unnoticed and now eased herself close to Jo on the sofa. Her hoop skirt tilted up in front, revealing trim ankles encased in bright silk stockings. Anne had said nice girls never showed their ankles, Jo remembered. She looked away as Agnes crossed her small feet. "He'll never get back in time," whined the girl. "We might as well face it."

"Oh, Agnes." Patience's soft voice was mildly reproving. "He hasn't been gone two months yet."

"I don't care. He had no right to leave three defenseless women alone in a strange town with all these gold-crazy men!"

264

Mrs. Harrow picked up her needlework. "If the men are as gold-crazed as you seem to think, Agnes, they won't have much time to chase after us."

The older woman's tone was dry, and her daughter-in-law sniffed indignantly. "Well, if he doesn't get back soon, we'll miss our wagon train."

"Agnes, he said he'd be back in time; he'll *be* back in time. The train doesn't leave until April twenty-second."

"But that's only a month off," wailed the girl. "And you know the train is already starting to rendezvous. Mrs. Knox told me that if we have an early spring, Mr. Drummond won't wait till the twenty-second. He takes supplies to the road ranches along the route, so he has to jump off before all the other trains."

"I know, I heard that, too."

"Mrs. Knox says all it depends on is having enough grass for the animals. And already the grass is green!" Agnes's voice rose angrily. "Mitch'll never make it, I tell you. He'll stay out there digging for gold and we'll be stuck in this godforsaken hole another year!"

Jo thought Agnes sounded more spoiled than worried.

"He knows the date, Agnes," said Patience quietly. "He'll be back in time."

"Mrs. Knox told me anybody who left for Pikes Peak before the middle of March was just asking for trouble. And it was only February when he went. If he got caught in a snowstorm in the mountains . . ."

Mrs. Harrow laid her needlework in her lap. "That's enough, Agnes. You know Mitch brought us early so he could take a run up to the gold fields. And you know he made arrangements for Mr. Peavy to drive our wagon if anything happened that he didn't get back. If he isn't here in time, we'll simply go with Mr. Peavy as Mitch arranged. He provided very well for us

265

if anything should happen to him." Her voice broke on the last words.

"I don't care. It's not right, him leaving us here in a strange town like this with no proper escort. Besides, I don't like that Peavy. He's nothing but a dirty old man."

Mrs. Harrow looked at Jo and smiled faintly. Jo felt obliged to say something. "I suppose it's natural for your daughter-in-law to be worried about her husband," she murmured.

"Agnes worried about Willie?" For a moment Mrs. Harrow looked surprised. Then her face cleared and her smile was broad. "No, you misunderstand. Agnes is married to my oldest son, Willie. He's still in Oregon."

Now Jo was surprised. "I thought . . ."

Patience stifled a giggle, and Mrs. Harrow laughed aloud. "You thought Agnes was married to Mitch? Lordy, no!"

Agnes stiffened.

"Mitch isn't the marrying sort," Mrs. Harrow continued serenely. "He says if he was after a rocky road like most wives give their menfolk, he'd just put a burr under his saddle and let his horse buck him to death."

Patience turned a gentle smile on the older woman. "Now you stop that, Mother Harrow. Mitch will make some girl a wonderful husband."

"I doubt it. No, much as I love him, I don't think the woman's been born who could put up with Mitch's rock-hard independence." She turned to Jo again. "Have you thought about where you'll settle in Oregon, Dr. Gates? We could surely use a physician in Glad Hand."

"Sam says we need one in the lumber camps, too," interjected Patience shyly. Then her voice took on a wistful dreaminess. "My Sam says that timber in

266

Oregon is as thick as the hairs on a hound dog—and the air is sweet, and the rivers jump with salmon, and the soil's so rich and black that I'll be able to grow roses as big as Kansas sunflowers." Patience broke off, embarrassed at the general laugh.

Agnes jumped up, her plump face spiteful. "And if Sam told you one of Mitch's tall tales, like how pigs run around already cooked so all you have to do is cut off a slice when you're hungry—I suppose you'd believe that, too!"

# 25

It was a week later, on Sunday, when an assertive knock at the front door interrupted dessert at the Knox Boardinghouse. "It's for you, Dr. Gates—a Lieutenant Templeton. He's waitin' in the parlor."

"Good!" exclaimed Jo jumping to her feet. "He said he'd drive me up to sign on with the Drummond train." She had been waiting all week, wondering how long it would be before he came looking for her, worrying she would have to face the wagon master alone. Now the lieutenant was here. If she could just get him to drive her up to the rendezvous and introduce her to Drummond, it would go a long way toward establishing her credentials.

Templeton was every bit as handsome as she remembered—devlishly handsome, and very conscious of it. He leaned against the doorjamb, and his eyes slid over her with insolent self-assurance, his thin lips stretching in an appreciative smirk. Jo felt herself flush under the rude scrutiny.

"Hello, lieutenant. I've been hoping you'd come by so I could pay you for this suit."

His roving eyes reached her face then widened in shock at the sight of her shortened strawberry hair. "You've cut it." His voice was a well of disgust, mingled with reluctant admiration.

"I'm glad to see you, too."

"It's kinda pretty at that."

She laughed. "About what I owe you, lieutenant—"

"Come buggy riding with me and we'll call it even."

"I wouldn't mind a buggy ride, but I'm not letting you pay for this suit."

"Then come riding with me and we'll talk about it."

"All right. I'll just get my hat."

"You put me at an awful disadvantage," complained Philip as they crossed the wooden plank to the rig a few minutes later. "I can't even help you into the buggy to show what a gentleman I am."

She grimaced. "How do you think I feel—decked out like this?" As she swung herself up, she could sense his eyes on her snugly encased bottom. She felt hot and uncomfortable.

He sat beside her. Too close. The full length of his muscular leg pressed tightly against hers. "Don't you go anywhere without your doctor bag?" he teased. "Are you expecting another disaster?"

"It's possible. If you don't behave yourself." She shifted her legs and moved to the far side of the buggy.

He laughed as he picked up the reins. "I thought we could ride down to Pilot's Knob and have a picnic. It's got a nice view and a pretty grove of trees that ought to be just starting to flower. I brought a lunch." He indicated a cloth-covered basket at her feet.

"How does a soldier manage that?"

"I bribed the mess sergeant."

"But I've just finished Sunday supper."

"We don't have to eat right away."

"Good. I was hoping you'd take me up to the rendezvous."

"So you've decided to sign on with Drummond? That's great. You found a family to join up with?"

"No. I'm going on my own."

269

His eyebrow lifted. "You can't. You're a woman."

"Where have I heard that before?"

"It's the truth. I know Drummond. He'd never sign on a lone woman."

"Do I *look* like a woman?" she demanded with a short laugh.

He paused to light a cheroot before answering. His eyes passed slowly over her body and came to rest on her face. "You sure look like a woman to me. Yes, ma'am!"

She felt her whole body grow hot under his gaze. "Well, hopefully Mr. Drummond won't see me in the same light."

Philip studied her intently, a speculative look in his brown eyes. "You know, I'm going with Drummond's train."

"No, I didn't know." She wished he would stop looking at her as if he were famished and she were a blueberry tart.

"Seven of us are ordered to Fort Boise. There's been another incident with the Indians, and I'm taking a squad and two ammunition wagons," he said. He grinned at her as he turned the horse north along the river road.

From a distance, the rendezvous was a sea of white tents wrapped in a shell of smoke; up close, it was a cesspool of animals, wagons, tents, shouting children, and barking dogs. There was an appalling racket—the air thick with sound and with the scent of baking bread, coffee, bacon, and smoke from hundreds of fires mixed with the acrid smell of ammonia and sweat.

Many of the wagons had slogans painted on the sides in big sprawling letters: Oregon Or Bust; Heading West From Illinois; and Bound for California.

Jo tried to relax, but knew that the next half hour could mean everything to her. If Drummond accepted her as a doctor and allowed her to go with them to Oregon; if she had enough money for the contract; if this soldier would just vouch for her—

"I'm glad you'll be with the train," she said to Templeton. She smiled tremulously. "That means I'll know four people: you and the Harrow women." She let her thick lashes flutter briefly. His grin was cynical.

He guided the rig toward one side of the camp where several wagons crouched apart from the others. In front of them, papers spread before him, sat a man at a long table.

"That's Drummond."

Jo felt a tightness in her throat. She turned quickly and grasped Templeton's arm. "Lieutenant—Philip—there's one more thing—a favor—"

He looked down at the slender hand and grinned his twisted grin. "Name it."

"I've just *got* to be accepted as a doctor and go with this train . . . but . . . well . . . you know that my carpetbag with my certificate in it was lost when the *Tropic* went down. I don't have anything to prove I'm a doctor now except this . . ." She held up her black satchel. "And you."

He let out a low chuckle. "So you want me to vouch for you? Well, you don't have to sell me on the idea, honey. I want you to come with this train."

"Thanks." She ignored the meaningful leer and jumped from the wagon to stride through the slippery red clay in Templeton's wake.

Drummond stood. He was short and compact with a lump of coal-black hair. He thrust out his hand. "Lieutenant Templeton. What can I do for you?" His voice boomed from the bottom of a barrel chest.

"I've brought you another customer. This here's Dr. Joe Gates. He wants to go to Oregon."

"Horse doctor?"

271

"People doctor."

Drummond's eyes narrowed as he studied her. "A doctor would be a right fine addition to our train," he said slowly. "But you look a mite young."

"I'm older than I look," Jo said, her husky stage voice booming back at him. As a woman that was true; she looked several years older than seventeen. But in a man's suit she looked little more than a beardless youth. Still, she was tall for a woman—almost five feet seven inches—as tall as most men. Surely that would help.

"This here's the doctor from the *Tropic*," Philip interjected. He pulled the bandana from his neck and used it to wipe the sweat from his face. "Doc Gates is the one who pitched in and saved all those people when the *Tropic* hung up on a snag. You must have heard about him."

Templeton's eyes laughed at Jo, but Drummond's eyes narrowed with quick interest. One to lie and one to swear, she thought. Without Templeton to back her up, she hadn't stood a chance.

"You got a wagon, Doc?"

"No. I'll be on horseback."

"You'd be obliged to take on the same duties as the other single men. Bein' a doctor wouldn't let you slack on that."

"That's fine," she said, holding her voice level when what she really wanted to do was jump up and down and shout with jubilation. Her breath came faster, and she had to concentrate on what he was saying.

"Since you're already here, we can knock off five dollars for the boat trip from St. Louie." It had cost Jo ten just from Jefferson, but she wasn't about to argue. "Here's the contract. If it's checkers with you, we got us a deal."

Jo read quickly. *One hundred and fifty dollars . . .*

*each man must supply a gun, ammunition, knife, two
blankets, and a horse . . . each man will stand sentry by
turns . . . procure a sack for his clothes . . . twenty-five
pounds of baggage exclusive of blankets and gun . . .
Drummond & Co. agree to furnish one tent and cooking utensils to each mess . . .*

She calculated swiftly. The money Doc had sent
would just about cover the requirements and some
extra drugs. He hadn't sent her certificate, but he had
sent the means for her to get to Oregon. She looked up.
"This is fine," she said.

The contract signed and the fare paid, Jo fairly
floated back to the wagon. She didn't sink into the
puddles now; she glided right across the surface. She
could scarcely contain her excitement until they got out
of camp.

"I'm going! I'm actually going!"

She yanked off the black hat and sailed it across the
field. Her short red-gold hair spilled out like bright
pennies flying into the wind, a mop of unruly curls that
tinged her laughing face with the glow of apricots
touched with early morning dew.

Philip felt an instant stirring in his loins. His chuckle
came deep in his throat. He pulled the horse to a halt
and jumped from the buggy. "Come on down here!" he
ordered, reaching for her. "You threw that hat—you
can just go with me to get it." His hands spanned her
slender waist. He swung her to the ground and pulled
her tight against him, his eyes hard on hers.

"Whoa, lieutenant. Being accepted on the wagon
train is all the excitement I can take for one day."

He studied her, as though weighing his chances. She
put her hand on his chest and felt her leg twitch. He had
just helped her with Drummond, and she didn't want to
knee him the way she had Jeremy, but she would if she
had to.

273

"I'll get your hat," he said finally.

"How much did you pay for these clothes, lieutenant?"

"What happened to 'Philip'?" he asked as he handed her the hat.

"He lost his rights when he forgot that I am a very respectable doctor." Templeton had to be put in his place, she thought, but her body tingled where it had pressed against his, and her pulse raced. "Now tell me how much I owe you. Then maybe you won't feel you can take advantage of your past kindness." She smiled slightly to remove some of the sting. She wouldn't let him treat her like a loose woman of some kind, yet she didn't want to make him angry either. In fact, she couldn't afford to make him angry. He could give her away to Drummond and wreck her chance to go to Oregon.

"A fiver'll do it," he growled in answer to her question.

"I didn't know army officers were so flush they could waste money like that," she said as she rummaged in her doctor bag.

"I didn't consider it a waste."

She pulled herself onto the wagon and handed him the half eagle. "Maybe you better take me home after all, lieutenant."

"What, no picnic? Listen, after I just vouched for your medical abilities, you owe me a picnic, pretty lady."

"That's blackmail."

"You know, you're right."

Jo thought quickly. Her contract to Oregon, made out to Dr. Joe Gates, was safe in her bag; Templeton had already made his move and been rejected; it was a beautiful day—why not relax and enjoy it? To the south a few rain clouds gathered, but the sky overhead

274

was clear and bright. She ruffled her short hair and welcomed the breeze cool to her neck.

In another hour they were on the other side of Leavenworth, bouncing along the river road toward Pilot's Knob. White, puffy clouds scuttled above the spring grass, and an already blazing sun spoke of the sweltering, unrelenting heat of the summer yet to come.

The Big Muddy was even more dangerous now than it had been when the *Tropic* was snagged two weeks before. Now it was high, swollen with spring rains, as the snow melted along its northern tributaries. Rushing water lifted trees from their beds of sand and cast them downstream like javelins released from the hand of God. Whole sections of seemingly solid bank collapsed and roared off in the swift current, only to be deposited at some lower bend and further alter the course of the constantly shifting riverbed.

Philip pointed out one deserted sod dwelling, then laughed when they passed another that had been built too close to the bank and now rode majestically downstream. "The Big Muddy takes a different course every day," he said knowingly. "Up in St. Joe, on the Missouri side, it used to run along First Street. Now it runs along Fourth. Everything in between has just plain disappeared." He snapped the reins. "You know, a friend of mine bought levee lots right after St. Joe was laid out, and when he came back to build on them last year, they weren't even there. He ordered a survey, and you know where he found his land? Across the river in Elwood, Kansas, that's where."

Jo's mind was busy with her own thoughts, but Philip didn't seem to mind. He kept up his one-sided dissertation all the way to Pilot's Knob, a high knoll from which they could see for miles. Templeton unfolded a colorful Indian blanket and spread it for them to sit. She noticed with amusement that it smelled a bit horsey.

Although she wasn't hungry, she was grateful for his help with Drummond, and she nibbled politely on a burnt chicken leg while he sipped a whiskey and watched her.

"Penny . . ." he offered as the silence between them lengthened.

"Not worth it." Actually she was comparing this drab, muddy stream with the wild white beauty of waves breaking over the Irish coast at Ballareen. If she closed her eyes, she could still conjure up the cherry trees—the fern and heather—the flowering butterwort she hadn't seen in nine years. She felt a rush of nostalgia and an unnameable longing.

Overhead, catkins were beginning to form into long clusters of graceful, cottony flowers. Crimson parakeets with golden heads, green wings, and long, graduated tails flitted among the branches. She could hear the whippoorwills sing. By the time they reached Oregon, she reflected sadly, summer would have come and gone.

"How come you're pretending to be a man, Joe Gates? Are you running from something?"

"I'd rather not talk about it. I have to pretend to be a man now so Drummond will accept me, that's all."

"Well, your misfortune is a bit of luck for me."

"How's that?"

"You ain't gonna have a bunch of young swains nipping at your heels. I'm the only one who knows you are a woman, so I'll have a clear field."

"You may get a bit of unexpected competition from the other women," said Jo wryly. She couldn't help but laugh as she thought about Agnes's persistent flirtations.

It was some time before Philip realized that the wind had quickened. Black clouds gathered swiftly in the

276

southern sky. "We're in for another thunderstorm," he said. "We better head back."

Even as he spoke, the wind stiffened and began to blow swirls of dust in frantic eddies. The sky split in jagged spears of light. "We'll never make it," he prophesied as they tossed the remains of lunch into the basket and ran for the buggy. "It's moving in too fast."

He whipped the horse to a good gait, but they were nowhere near town when the first large drops began to pelt. Within minutes the air had erupted in a solid, beating sheet of water.

"There's that hay tent," he shouted above the roar of the storm. "We'll make for that." Jo squinted, but it was raining so hard she could scarcely see.

By the time they got inside the squat little sod and hay house, the sky was completely black, all trace of daylight having vanished. Jo removed her coat to wring the water from it. She felt as wet as the day Philip had hauled her from the icy Missouri onto the deck of the *Deliverance*, but this was a warm spring rain and she wasn't cold.

She had never been inside what the natives called a "hay tent" before, and whenever the lightning flashed, she tried to see if it was like their sod house in Ireland. It wasn't, she decided.

This was a simple affair, all roof and gable. The roof was two rows of poles brought together at the top, thatched with prairie hay. The gables were built up with sod walls, and the only opening faced the river. Aside from the fact that the door was missing and the floor muddy, it made a good shelter from the deluge.

In the farthest corner, Philip found a dry spot where he spread the now wet Indian blanket. Jo dropped to the blanket beside him. She was warm, out of breath. "We do seem to have a penchant for getting wet, don't we?" She ruffled her short hair and the water flew.

277

"Hey, cut it out! You're worse than a dog," he teased.

She looked up at him and laughed. Just then a brilliant flash lit the interior of their shelter. His face was very close; his dark eyes gleamed, hot and eager. Then the flare was gone and his lips covered hers.

Jo's initial reaction was to stiffen and pull away—but his mustache tickled and his beard felt soft and warm against her wet cheek, like a fuzzy towel. His arms slipped easily around her, and she began to think kissing might be rather nice. There was none of the sweet awkwardness of Jeremy's first kiss, or the determination of his second. This was the practiced kiss of an older, experienced man.

She could hear Philip breathing now. She stirred uneasily and began belatedly to push him away. But he didn't move back this time the way he had out in the field. Instead, his arm tightened, and his hand slid up across her rib cage and closed over her breast.

Jo went hot and cold all at once. She pushed at his chest and twisted her face away. In the back of her head a little voice droned, *Don't make him mad, Jo. He could give you away to Drummond. Now don't make him mad.*

"Hold on, lieutenant," she gasped, "you're going a little fast for a poor country doctor."

His laugh was thick and thermal, his hands busy on her breast.

Jo wrestled against his bearlike arms, and her heart began to pound with the first real twinges of alarm. She tried to get at him with her knee but couldn't. Pa's lessons hadn't allowed for a situation like this. *Like Quimby*. The thought roared into her mind.

"Let go! Let me up!"

She elbowed Templeton's hand from her breast and felt her nails scrape his face. His body pressed her down. His breath rasped in her ear. His mouth chewed at her neck. Really frightened now, she thrashed from side to side, her fists pounding.

"No! Get off!"

Lightning flashed. She saw his face, eyes burning, mouth leering. Hot. Rutty. Ghoulish.

He seized her beating arms in one powerful hand while the other trapped her breast and began a savage massage. His fingers tugged cruelly at her nipple.

Fear ruptured her mind.

In a frantic spasm, she thrashed. Twisted. Fought. Shrieked at him, *Get off you bastard.*

His mouth smashed hers, and his tongue drove her screams deep into her throat.

On her back now. Clawing. Terror-crazed. She tried to knee him in the groin. His powerful legs trapped hers, ripped away her strength. His hard male organ strained erect against her hip.

*Oh God, not again, no, no God, not again.* Sheer panic turned Jo's flesh to fire. The man's hands were everywhere—forcing her down—debasing her body—

She heard the ripping of cloth and felt a cold wave of air wash over her hot breasts. Then his mouth curved over her fullness. Tore at her nipple with savage, sucking sounds. Her body burned and fear howled through her head.

She threw herself sideways. His mouth was a leech. One powerful hand chained her arms. Her nails clawed air. The weight of his body pinned her legs. His free hand tore at her belt.

Sheer terror exploded within her. A great roar ran amuck in her head. Her mind ceased to function. She fought silently, desperately—uselessly.

There was a huge clap of thunder. A blinding white flash. Jo saw his hairy mouth chew her breast, a predatory animal ravening its kill. Just inches away, his ear thrust through his dark hair.

She lifted her head, sank her teeth into his helix, and tasted blood.

He howled in pain.

She was free.

"Jesus Christ, you play rough!" he yelled.

Sobs tore her throat. In another flash, she saw him lean away to nurse his bleeding ear. She saw her doctor bag and coat. She made a grab for them, leaped to her feet, and ran for the door.

"Hey, hold on! I ain't hurt that bad. You don't need to run away."

Rain merged with Jo's hysterical weeping. She stopped just outside the hay tent, hunched over, unable to move, shattered in the aftermath of fear.

"Don't run off!" he called. "I'm sorry I rushed you. C'mon back, you little hellcat." He stood inside the doorway, wiping the blood from his ear. "I'll give you some warm-up time first. C'mon back, honey."

"You'll give me *nothing*," she grated at him, edging away into the rain.

"Aw, c'mon, honey. Ain't no use pretending you're a virgin. Sweet little gals from the country don't traipse around in men's breeches and pretend to be doctors."

She turned her back on him and stumbled down the hill.

"Joe! C'mon—I ain't complaining about what you did to my ear, am I? Come back, honey. I won't rush you this time. C'mon now. You can't walk all the way back to town in this storm."

She ignored him, slipping and sliding in the red Kansas mud. Tears and rain poured down her face. Her hands worked at the buttons of her coat to cover the torn shirt and the sore, reddened breasts.

"Oh, shit!"

She heard him jump into the wagon, heard the creak of wheels move close behind her. She ran.

280

"Come on—get in." He sounded resigned now. "What'd you expect anyhow? Any man's gonna think the same thing when he finds out there's a woman under them pants. For Chrissake, Joe, nice women don't go around dressed up like men and claiming to be doctors."

"And *nice men* aren't rapists!" she shouted at him.

"And ladies don't bite off ears either," he shouted back. "All right. Walk back for all I care," he yelled, suddenly bringing the whip down on the horse. "Go ahead and walk, you little bitch! Then next time you won't be so damn independent!"

It was miles back to town in the rain. Jo cringed at each clap of thunder and each flash of lightning.

But as she neared Leavenworth, another fear drummed in her heart. With each stumbling step, the realization grew that Templeton might give her away and wreck her chance to go to Oregon. Her future was locked in the hands of that dirty goat—and she didn't know what to do about it.

# 26

Gold-fevered miners plus battles between Border Ruffians and abolitionists had created a lawless frontier where even the most timid carried a brace of pistols and a bowie knife. Not comfortable on Leavenworth streets, even in pantaloons, Jo asked Mr. Brown to help her buy a gun.

"You not only got to tote one, Dr. Joe, you got to learn how to shoot it," he declared solemnly. "Greenhorns with shooting irons is worse than Injuns on the warpath."

A gun could be bought for less than a week's lodging so, much as she hated to part with the money, Jo followed his advice and bought not only a carbine, but a handgun as well. He taught her to shoot, but she snapped a firm "no!" when he suggested she join a wolf hunt the men were putting together.

She took his advice later concerning a horse though, and purchased a pretty two-year-old mare named Tess.

Once her trail clothes and medical supplies were purchased today, she knew she would have nothing left to do but sit back and wait for the grass to grow—and hope Templeton kept his mouth shut.

Crossing the public square now, she passed a store with a sign: Ready-Made Dresses. In the window was a pair of fine French calf boots priced at a dollar and a half. Peeking into the murky interior, Jo could make out a whole rack of colorful, ready-made gowns.

Oh, what she wouldn't give to put on a dress again. Being a man wasn't much fun. Even though she was looked upon as a beardless youth, Jo was still expected to participate in discussions about the size of a woman's breasts and hips and legs and buttocks. It was horrible. On one unforgettable occasion, the seemingly colorless Mr. Brown had even urged her to accompany him to the local sporting house. Her masquerade as a young man had been one long, revolting fiasco, perhaps with worse to come.

Jo eyed the dresses a long time before turning resolutely away. She had a "list of necessities" prepared by Mrs. Harrow's son and was determined to stick to it. No pretty, impractical gowns or French boots for Dr. Joe Gates.

Everything cost more than Jo anticipated, but the money Doc had sent lasted through a goodly supply of morphine and laudanum and dozens of delicate sponges for female caps. From here out she was on her own; she didn't have to answer to Doc anymore.

Following Mitch Harrow's list closely, Jo purchased a pair of dark-blue glasses as protection against the desert sun, some of the new fangled lucifers, a short wool coat, two blue flannel shirts, a woolen undershirt, one pair of thick woolen pants reinforced on the inside with soft buckskin to make horseback riding more comfortable, and one pair without the reinforcement, plus four pairs of woolen socks. Shoes, and stout boots large enough to tuck the pantlegs inside, completed the shopping spree.

It was late in the day when she pulled the rented buggy to a stop in front of the boardinghouse and discovered a hive of activity.

Mrs. Harrow hurried toward her, lifting her skirts

283

above the red Kansas mud. "Oh, Dr. Joe, I'm so glad you got back early. We've had word from Mr. Drummond—" Her voice ground to a halt and she turned away, but not before Jo had glimpsed her trembling lips.

Patience placed a comforting arm about the older woman's slumped shoulders. Above the bowed head, her eyes met Jo's. "We've just gotten word that the train is jumping off at dawn tomorrow morning."

Tomorrow! They were leaving a week early—and Mrs. Harrow's son not back. Right up until this morning, the older woman had fought against her dwindling hope. "When Mitch gets here—" she had begun at breakfast, then stopped abruptly.

Now Jo reached out to touch her. "Maybe he'll catch up on the trail," she said softly.

Trudy Harrow lifted bleak eyes. "I know he'll come," she said. "The only thing is, I'm afraid he's hurt somewhere and suffering—and no one there to help."

# 27

Drummond pushed back his broad-brimmed hat and raised his arms for silence. "This first day, things has been kinda kitch as kitch kin." He gazed around slowly, belligerently. "Now the time's come for you all to start pullin' your own weight. You had plenty time back at rendezvous to make friends, and you'll find that's gonna be right handy on the trail ahead. Tonight, after the meetin', I want you all to break into messes—team up with your friends. You'll camp together, stick together on the trail, cook together, and help each other out when they's trouble."

Already families were pairing off, calling to each other excitedly, trying to decide whether it was better to join up with the strongest, or the best cook, or with somebody you just plain liked.

Drummond called for silence again. "Them as has families and is drivin' one of my wagons—remember, I don't want no wagons lost and no ox neither. You got plenty o' grease in yer tar buckets. Use it. You keep yer axle greased and it ain't as likely to break." A harsh note had crept into the little man's booming voice.

He held his hands for quiet. "As soon as yer messes is formed, I'll come 'round and give each mess a number. In the mornin' you'll line up by number. Each mornin' you'll move up one in line, and the lead wagon'll move to the rear. That way nobody eats dust all the time. And you men'll stand watch one night a week, startin' with the men in mess one.

"They's lots of single men with the train. They gotta eat, too. So they'll join messes."

Mrs. Harrow leaned close to Jody and whispered, "We'd like you to eat with us, Dr. Joe."

Jo nodded and smiled her thanks.

"Now you wimmen—" Drummond pointed a blunt finger. "You gotta pull your share. You'll likely carry the water. You'll gather wood, when they is any, and build the fires. And later, when they ain't no woods, you'll gather prairie coal." There was a general shuffling and a murmur of protest. Drummond ignored it. "Foragin' for firewood and chips—that's where the youngens come in handy, too. You wimmen'll do the cookin' and the cleanin' up. And you'll do the laundry for yer own families and for the single men in yer mess. You'll find if you do your share without squabblin' and belly-achin', we'll all be a sight happier."

The choosing of messes gave the emigrants something to occupy themselves for the balance of the evening. There was much visiting back and forth, switching from one mess to another, happy laughter and friendly banter, and some indignation among the womenfolk over being expected to wash for strange men in addition to their own man and their brood of youngsters. But the biggest cries of outrage came when they understood exactly what prairie coal was, and that the women and children were actually expected to gather it for fuel.

"I'll not do it!" declared Agnes indignantly.

"I guess we'll all do what we have to do," said Mrs. Harrow, "no matter how distasteful. If that means gathering buffalo chips, we'll gather buffalo chips."

The day had turned cold and the sun was completely

286

obscured by heavy black clouds. They were in for another of those fierce Kansas thunderstorms they had come to know so well.

The rain struck at suppertime. Fires immediately hissed, spattered, and went out. Some of the hastily erected tents flattened with the first sturdy gust.

Drenched to the skin, Jo climbed under one of the Harrow wagons and rolled into her blanket. Her last thought, before she fell asleep, was of Philip Templeton. Where was he?

Don't let him be with this train, she prayed. Please don't let him be with this wagon train.

## 28

The morning air was clear and cold. A slick skin of ice skated across Jo's bucket of washwater. Since she came under the category labeled "men," she would draw guard duty, but was exempt from cooking. She sat on a camp chair and accepted her plate of bacon, eggs, and biscuits with averted eyes and a guilty, "thanks."

Someone came to sit beside her. She looked up.

"Morning, Joe," said Philip Templeton, his eyes busy, his smile more a leer than a smile.

Just then Agnes hurried up with a heaping plate of food. "And here's *your* breakfast, lieutenant." She spread her flirting glances equally between Jo and Philip. "Now I'll get you both some hot coffee."

Jo threw Templeton a sharp glare. "How did you wangle an invitation to this particular mess?" she asked, keeping her voice low.

"By charming the young Mrs. Harrow."

"Agnes?" Of course it would be Agnes. Even now she was fluttering about, preening herself like a mate-hungry peahen.

Jo made short work of breakfast and hurried to put space between them, but Templeton followed, his eyes busy as usual.

"Want me to saddle your mare?" he asked in a silky, tone.

Jo bit back a sharp retort. "No, thanks."

"If you change your mind, just holler. It's going to be a long trail, Joe. We might as well be friendly. I ain't holding any grudges long as you're willing to be nice."

She watched him mount and ride away, her heart still palpitating wildly.

It was to be a disastrous morning. Before they could get moving, one loudly bawling beast eluded the unfamiliar yoke and rampaged through the camp, upsetting cook pots and scattering greenhorns in all directions. Women screamed. Dogs barked. Men shouted and waved their arms in wild impotence.

Jo laughed so hard she almost fell off her horse.

"It is funny, isn't it?" smiled Trudy Harrow coming alongside.

Remembering that she was supposed to be a gentleman and a doctor, Jo wiped the tears from her cheeks. "I suppose it isn't funny to those poor men, but I can't help it." She burst into another peal of laughter, then sobered abruptly when she saw the strange look on Mrs. Harrow's face.

When Drummond rode along the wagons warning, "We roll in ten minutes," there were frantic efforts to extinguish fires, pull tent pegs and fold tents. There were loud wails of "My bread ain't done. What'll I do with my bread, Rafe?" Or, "Git Johnny off the pot. If he ain't done yet, he'll just have to hold it."

Astonishingly enough, when Drummond reached the head of the line and roared his mighty, "Roll out!" somehow Johnny was removed from the pot, the hot bread was stored in the wagon, the dog found, cows milked, fires extinguished, chickens tucked snugly into their coops beneath the wagon beds, and extra horses and cows tied to the back. The wagon train was on its way.

The second day, through lime-ridged hills abundant with oaks and hickory, was long and hard. It ended at dusk with the crossing of a swollen, angry creek.

"'Tain't high enough to be dangerous," Peavy said. This was the man Mitch Harrow had hired to see the ladies safely to Oregon in case Mitch did not return in time to join the train. Remembering Agnes's complaints, Jo looked him over carefully. He was gaunt and gimlet eyed with a perpetual squint, a sparse, tobacco-stained gray beard, wispy gray hair poking from a battered gray hat—a thoroughly ugly speciman—and somehow, completely trustworthy.

Riding behind as they approached the stream, Jo could see into the wagon where the three Harrow women huddled, and she noticed that Peavy had locked one wagon wheel.

They were about halfway across when a violent gust of wind rocked the wagon. The wide wheels slewed sideways in the mud. Agnes screamed. Mrs. Harrow reached out a consoling hand, but the meek little Patience suddenly whirled on the other girl. "Oh, do hush," she said. "You're not any more scared than the rest of us." Jo fought an almost uncontrollable urge to applaud.

At the far bank, brush had been thrown down to keep the heavy loads from sinking in the mud, but it made dangerous footing for the animals. The wagon tilted, then slowly mounted onto solid ground.

By now it was dark and raining.

That night Jo wrote in her new diary:

Friday, April 20th, 1860
    Made 13 miles yesterday and 14 today. I had no idea it would be so hard. Already we are passing

graves. Mrs. Harrow says not to look at them. But how can I not look?

One woman in the next mess is already big with child. How can she hope to survive the trip? And what of the baby, poor tyke?

Morning dawned dull, gray, and cold. The steady plop and suck of oxen hoofs was a chilling reminder of how far two thousand miles could be. One wagon had already turned back. Jo sympathized with them and was ashamed when a weak surge of desire to join the turnarounds rose sharply within her breast. Less than thirty miles and already she was beginning to realize how lonely the trail would be without Anne. They had been so good for each other.

Up ahead, someone swore heartily at his unbroken animals. Another greenhorn, thought Jo. At the slightest provocation, an unbroken ox would break into a wild run and turn the camp into a furious uproar. Mules, on the other hand, were fractious animals with big vicious teeth and a kick worse than a Colt revolver—as Jody's first patient discovered.

Clayborne Williams, in the mess just ahead, had a team of four young Spanish mules. Every morning they fought against the harness, kicked and bit at each other until Clay and his hired man were beside themselves with frustration. It was on the evening of the fourth day, after they had made fourteen miles over rough, broken terrain and Clay was bone tired, that he got too close to the bucking jacks.

Clay didn't see how it started, but the lead mules were trying to kick the wheelers out of harness. Determined to separate them, Clay grabbed a pole to beat them into submission. The wheelers bucked and plunged and bit the rumps of the leaders. And then it happened—so fast Clay couldn't say how. He didn't see the big yellow teeth, only felt the heat of sour breath. He leaped back as searing pain shot through his face. Blood spurted and a flap of skin and muscle swung where his cheek had been.

Jo was there, bag in hand, almost before Clay realized what had happened. His face was streaked with dirt. Sweat carried brown rivulets into the wound. Blood gushed between his fingers. His eyes were wide, staring.

"Get your hand off it and lie down," Jo ordered.

She knelt beside him in the mud and opened her bag. Swiftly she filled the syringe with morphine. "Somebody get water—hot if you have it." She cleansed the needle with whiskey and inserted it into the raw flesh. As she worked, her eyes studied the muscles, the curve of the white bone. She had never seen a face spread open like this before.

A pail of tepid water appeared at her elbow. From her bag, Jo pulled a cake of yellow soap. She washed her hands. Withdrawing a clean pad, she used it to cleanse Williams's face, then sloshed whiskey into the wound and slapped the torn muscle over the bone. Pressing it with another pad, her eyes raked the circle of staring emigrants.

"Clay! Clay!" Tears coursed down his wife's contorted cheeks.

People watched with twisted mouths and narrowed eyes—aghast, yet fascinated, as the man's lifeblood flowed into the rutted trail. One face, concerned but composed, stood out from all the others.

"Patience—come hold this in place."

The young woman stepped forward and knelt in the mud.

"Wash your hands and put your fingers here. Press hard. That's it. Good." Jo withdrew a threaded needle

292

and dunked it into the whiskey, catgut and all.

She looked up again. "You—and you." She pointed. "And you two. Hold him down. He won't feel anything, but we can't take a chance on his moving." Most people had never heard of the pain-killing morphine injections, and they sometimes fought against stitching even when there was no pain. Clay Williams's face was calm and sleepy now, but she wasn't taking a chance on his starting up suddenly and maybe taking a needle in his eye.

"All right, Patience. You'll have to let go while I sew." It was Jo's first experience with actual facial muscles. She pushed her mind to draw forth a picture of the maxillary region as it was illustrated in *Gray's Anatomy*: The *deep surface, superficial surface, Masseter, Zycomatic major*—

At last it was finished. Her stitches were neat, as her mother had taught her so long ago—neater than Doc Adams's stitches had ever been, she thought proudly.

Clay Williams was young—about twenty-five. If he didn't develop blood poisoning and die, he would have as clean a scar as she could make it.

As soon as he had been carried inside his wagon and settled on a pallet, Jo hurried to her beloved *Gray's Anatomy*. It was badly stained and wrinkled from its bath in the Missouri, but she had managed to get all the pages unstuck. Carefully she studied the drawings and descriptions of the muscles and fasciae of the cranium and face. Although she had never seen the real thing before—in the flesh, so to speak—she felt reasonably confident that she had at least sewn the right muscles together.

After supper that night, Jo scrambled over the Williams's tailgate. My first house call, she thought.

Clay was sleeping, his face waxen but his head cool. She hoped, first, that he would live, and second, that

293

she had sewn his muscles in such a way that he would be able to chew and speak. "He'll need his rest," she said to the young wife. "Can you hitch the team and drive?"

"We got us a hired hand. He's not much good but maybe he can manage. Is Mr. Williams going to be all right, Dr. Joe?"

"You see he stays in bed, takes the medicine I gave you, and drinks lots of coffee."

"Coffee?"

"You *boil* your coffee, don't you?"

"I sure do. Mr. Williams thinks I'm crazy, but I can't stand them little squiggleys swimming in the water."

Jo smiled. "That's the way most of the women feel about stream water. That's why I said coffee."

"Wait till I tell Mr. Williams what you said. That'll show him—laughing at me for boiling coffee. What—what do we owe you, Dr. Joe? We don't have much money."

Jo hesitated. "I understand there are lots of toll bridges and ferries between here and Oregon. Suppose you pay my toll the first time we come to one."

"Thanks, Dr. Joe. We can sure afford the price of an extra toll."

Wanting to be alone, Jo wandered through camp toward the line of trees that rimmed the open prairie. Everyone, it seemed, knew who she was.

"How's it going, Dr. Joe?"

"Dr. Gates! How's the patient?"

"Right fine job of sewing, Doc!"

A few stopped her to ask that she look at a child with a bad tooth or a belly-ache. When she was finished, they thanked her profusely and pressed a dime into her hand.

Jo finally escaped past the rim of the camp to lean against a gnarled tree. Before her lay the bluegrass belt with spring flowers beginning to dot the fields and new green grass just tall enough to show a faint ripple in the wind.

Her first case. She sank onto a fallen log and clasped her arms around one knee. Certificate or not, she was a doctor now. It bothered her just a little that what she was doing wasn't strictly honest, but after all, she wasn't hurting anybody. She was helping.

"Penny—" Philip Templeton's voice broke into her reverie.

She jumped up, staring at him. He must have followed her from camp. She backed away, her heart tripping in her breast.

"Come on, Joe, don't look like that. I won't touch you—word of honor."

"I was just going back anyhow—"

One eyebrow shot up. "You just got here."

"And now I'm going back."

"What were you thinking about anyway?"

She said the first thing that came to mind: "Oregon." She turned quickly to leave.

"You want me to tell you about Oregon?" he asked quickly.

"What do you know about it?"

"What do I know?" he hooted.

"You've been there?" In spite of herself, she was interested.

"I was up there near onto three years." He leaned against the tree and puffed on his cheroot. "I went up to Washington Territory back in '55 for a treaty with the Horse Injuns, and we like to of never got back. Somebody struck gold up around Colville, and the miners didn't wait for Congress to ratify the treaty. They poured into that territory like a spring flood, and Old Kamaikan—he went on the warpath.

"I was at Spokane Plains, too." Templeton's laugh wasn't nice. "We captured eight hundred of their

295

horses, and the colonel had 'em all shot. Sure took the heart outta them redskins."

"Tell me about Oregon," Jo said. "That's what I want to hear about—what it's really like."

He perched on the end of the log and crossed one leg over the other. "Well," he said, "this side of the Cascades has got right changeable weather. In the winter it's as cold as a married woman, and in the summer it's as hot as a—"

"The Cascades are mountains?" she interrupted.

He grinned again and nodded. "They run straight north-south and cut the state in half. On the east, on this side, the winter is one long snowstorm. And in the summer the whole eastern half sits and boils in the sun. But if you go through the Cascades, down the Columbia River along the Washington border, and then down into the Willamette Valley—you'll think you struck heaven. The valley just kinda sits in a mist between two mountain walls, with big fir trees all around."

Jo's heart beat strongly with longing. Could this be *her* valley? Caught up in the idea that her dream valley might really exist, she sank onto the log beside Templeton.

"The valley is long and broad," he continued, "with little streams kinda drifting down from the hills into the river."

"And are there fruit trees?" Jo's eyes shone eagerly. *Her* valley was fat with fruit.

Intent on her own thoughts, she didn't realize he was looking at her strangely until his arms suddenly shot out to envelop her, and his mouth grabbed hers with hungry purpose.

Jo jumped up, pushing him so hard and so abruptly that he fell backward off the log. "You could give rotten lessons, you know that," she shouted at him. "All you can think about is— Oh, you're disgusting!"

He picked himself up and dusted himself off. His laugh had a nasty sound in the surrounding quiet. "And I thought it was me brought that shine to your eyes." His face was hard, angry.

Just then something moved at the edge of the trees. Jo swung about in time to see the bushes tremble as someone rushed away. She peered through the waning light, but caught only brief flashes of quickly moving color. Whoever it was had fled back toward camp. Somebody sure got an eyeful, she thought—Dr. Joe Gates being kissed by Lt. Philip Templeton!

"Now you've done it," she raged at him. "Now you've really done it!"

# 29

Tomorrow was the Sabbath and the emigrants were eager for a day of rest and worship. There was no minister with the train this year, but a lay preacher had promised them a Sunday talk.

Anticipation was to be short-lived, however. Just after supper, Drummond called another meeting. "There'll be no rest day," he announced. "We roll tomorrow at seven, same as usual. We could get held up at the Big Blue—and even if we cross in one day, we won't make Fort Kearney under a week. So tomorrow's a travel day, same as always."

There were angry outcries and protests. "The Lord will send his wrath," called out one of the men. "If we don't observe the Sabbath, the Lord will not bless our train." Murmurs and shouts of approval greeted his words.

The women, particularly, were disappointed. They had looked forward to a day of rest, but even more, they anticipated Brother Matthews's message, for they were already in sore need of a bolstering of spirits.

But someone pulled out a banjo and began to pick out tunes. One after another, disgruntled emigrants extinguished their own fires and drifted toward the player's mess. Before long, one or two took up the tune with words of their own, and soon all joined in the singing:

"Oh, Susanna, don't you cry for me. For I'm on my way to Oregon, my seedlings on my knee. Oh, Susanna . . ."

When one buck grabbed a willing maid and swung her about in time to the music, an impromptu dance was born. Jo's feet itched to be out there in the moonlight, swinging and being swung.

Philip came to claim the bridling Agnes, and Jo watched with disillusioned cynicism as the young woman melted into the handsome officer's arms. In the flickering firelight, Agnes looked very pretty, a fact that didn't seem entirely lost on Templeton.

There weren't enough women to go around, and soon men began to grab other men and cavort to the rollicking tunes. Jo, laughing at their antics, was totally unprepared when a burly cowboy grabbed her with a wild "Ae-e-e-e!" and began to twirl her in time to the music. "We'll show 'em a thing or two, Doc," he yelled.

Philip grinned at her over Agnes's shoulder.

When the dance ended, the cowboy tipped his hat and bowed ceremoniously. "Damn!" he said. "Damn if you ain't a better dancer than the women, Doc!"

The merrymaking continued a long time. Philip Templeton claimed each dance with the starry-eyed Agnes while Jo sat on the grass watching, wishing she, too, could wear a dress and look pretty. She didn't want to dance with Philip, but she would have enjoyed dancing with some of the others. Being a man wasn't much fun.

That night Jo wrote in her diary:

April 21st, 1860
  Grass improving slowly. Everyone still buying grain from Drummond.
  Crossed the headwaters of the Grasshopper.

299

Saw five more graves in the past two days. Most of them small. Children.

Clay Williams, my first patient, has a slight fever tonight but is doing well, I think.


The next day's nooning held a special significance, for Brother Matthews based his message on Psalms 145:14. "The Lord upholds all who are falling, and raises up all those who are bowed down." The ladies declared themselves considerably uplifted, but another family turned back, announcing they would not go on with a Godless man who forced them to travel on the Sabbath.

They had been on the trail only five days. Already two families had left the train, and Jo had counted sixteen graves.

The caravan reached Nemaha Creek in mid-afternoon. The steep banks made for a hard crossing and slowed the train long enough for the women to do a bit of washing. The children fished, with no luck, and men swore as they labored with the guide ropes and chains. Jo sweated over the wagons with the men. She felt like swearing, too.

With the Nemaha behind them, the train swung north to avoid the Black Vermillion, and Jo spent one petrifying night on guard duty, riding the perimeter of grazing animals and shying from every sound. Guard duty was not for her. Yet, as a man, she had no alternative.

A growing circle of patients began to claim more of Jo's time. Her treatment of Clay Williams had gained Jo instant respect from the entire train. She was further elated when she finally reached an equitable fee for those with little or no money: one "house call" in exchange for half a night's guard duty—that was her

300

fee. Within two days, her next four weeks on guard were promised coverage by grateful patients. Jo thought she would never strike it rich, but she was getting lots of practice and, at the same time, neatly divesting herself of hated chores. She was more than pleased with the arrangement.

It was Wednesday afternoon when she was called to treat a man with another train. She went willingly, glad to escape Agnes's fluttering lashes and heaving breasts.

On the train behind them, a man had accidentally shot himself while cleaning his gun. "Won't nuthin' satisfy his wife 'ceptin' he have a real doctor," said the messenger as Jo rode back down the trail with him.

She felt guilty about that "real" part. "How did you know I was with the Drummond train?" she asked.

"It's posted on a dozen trees or more. See?" He pointed to a giant oak where two papers fluttered against the brown, ribbed bark.

Jo stopped to read and her eyes misted. *Mitch,* said the first note. *We're still looking for you.* She flattened the other paper and peered at the lettered message: *Drummond train passed April 26th. Have doctor and preacher with us and plenty grain stock and supplies.* Drummond didn't miss a trick, she thought. Well, she was glad he had advertised her presence. It meant she could get off on her own a bit, escape from Philip Templeton's growing persistence and Agnes's simpering smile.

The man's gunshot wound turned out to be superficial, and Jo spent the afternoon chatting with the injured man's wife. It was almost dusk when the man roused himself enough to suggest they had best catch up with their respective trains. Jo accepted her six bits' pay, helped the woman hitch the teams, and bade them good-bye. They had become friends in the last few hours—yet they would probably never meet again.

301

She wanted to urge Tess hard and fast, westward, straight into the setting sun, but for two days now the train had been traveling south again, heading for the Big Blue crossing at Marysville. Jody reflected that she had come a long way in just under two weeks' time—only a hundred miles in distance, but several hundred in the stretching of her capabilities, if they could be measured that way.

But it wasn't just Jo—everyone had changed. The hard trail life evoked a firmness, an acceptance, an erosion of timidity and fastidiousness. Johnny was never caught on the pot anymore. Now he, like all the other children, squatted anywhere, any time. Men stood behind the critters, and women—Jo felt sorriest for the women who had to go off in bunches and spread their skirts to shield each other from prying eyes. Snakes of St. Patrick, she thought, what would I do if I couldn't get away on Tess?

As she approached the circle of wagons, a guard called out a challenge, and she identified herself easily, for she was well known.

The camp squatted amid smoky cook fires and smelled of baked bread and coffee, sweat, and manure.

Mrs. Harrow had kept her supper hot. "You had best take supplies with you next time you have to leave the train," the old woman suggested. "Just in case you have to stay out a day or two." She frowned at Jo. "I don't like the idea of you being out there all by yourself. What with Indians and strange men . . ." Her voice trailed away.

Jo suspected that Trudy Harrow had furnished that streak of color in the woods a few days back. She obviously knew Jo wasn't a man. But somehow, Jo felt her secret was safe with the older woman.

Just after dinner a group of men on horseback, on their way to California and traveling fast, stopped long enough to announce that two cases of cholera had appeared in Leavenworth. There was quick concern and Jo sensed a contagion of fear, the need to be up and moving, the urge to flee before the cholera could somehow catch up with them.

There were no songs around the fires that night. Instead, Brother Matthews gave them a short talk before they turned in. "Only the wicked are struck by cholera," he shouted. "Cholera is a scourge, a rod in the hand of God, sent to sweep away the wicked because He can no longer bear to look at them. Only the wicked need fear."

Sorely troubled, the emigrants retired early and quietly. Jo, not believing in scourges from the hand of an angry God, burned her lantern late that night as she read notes and mulled over her sparse facts on the dreaded disease.

She was still puzzling over the cholera dilemma when they reached the crossing of the Big Blue near Marysville late the next afternoon. The river was up and they spent one whole day ferrying wagons across. Early the following afternoon, they headed north again, up the Valley of the Little Blue River.

Knowing it was a straight run now to Fort Kearny, the camp forgot the cholera scare in one great celebration that night. As soon as supper was finished, an accordion came out and dancing commenced.

It was toe-tapping music and Jo, young and naturally lighthearted, itched to join the gaiety, but her ability as an actress didn't stretch to taking the lead in a dance. And she had no desire to wear a red calico rag on her arm and pretend to be a man pretending to be a woman. Next time she danced, it would be in a dress, she vowed. Her heart was sore when she realized it might be a long time before that happened.

Patience stepped out shyly with a young lad from the

next mess, then shook her head and retired to sit with her mother-in-law when he requested a second dance. Agnes and Philip were nowhere in sight; surprising, thought Jo, since they were usually the first to begin to twirl when the music started.

Drummond set double guards that night, to prevent Indians stealing their stock, some said. Others talked excitedly about the numerous redskins they had seen the last few days, and how mean some of them looked. The animals were spooked tonight, they said, and it was the "smell of Injuns had spooked 'em!"

The talk was just talk though, not enough to upset the majority of the optimistic emigrants. Their cheerfulness carried them through breakfast into the nooning the following day when someone dug out an old fiddle and sawed out a few tunes. Usually the families spread out to rest in separate groups, but spirits were light today.

Jo sat by herself, the fiddle carrying her thoughts back to one day on the ship when they had been allowed topside, when Mama had laughed and tapped her foot in time to the music.

Above the rhythmic strains of "Lorena," a cry dragged Jo back to the present: "Halt! Who goes?"

Silence claimed the group. None had heard the approaching hoofbeats. Jo's heart tripped with a strange foreboding as she strained to hear the exchange between guard and strangers.

"Josh Hewet and Jesse Wade, bound for Oregon."

The listeners sighed deeply, tension easing. Although they rarely spoke of it, the fear of Indian attack was ever present. The fiddler took up the refrain, but softly now as all gave their attention to the newcomers, wondering if they brought news of cholera or of Indians. After a bit, the group opened to admit the two men.

The young, clean-shaven faces were lined with good humor and upholstered with trail dust. They accepted Canadian coffee with quick grins of thanks.

"Just passing through," said the taller of the two who identified himself as Josh Hewet. "Aim to make The Dallas by mid-July, set our claim, and get our land cleared before winter."

"Hooray for Oregon!" called out one of the youngsters. Everybody laughed.

"You come through Marysville?" asked Peavy.

"Yesterday."

"Hear talk of Injuns?"

Josh nodded soberly. "Heard there's a band of renegades—Pawnees they say—made some trouble down the other side of Alcove Springs. Might just be they're headed this way."

There was a general leaning forward to hear. "What makes you think that?"

The two men exchanged glances. "We found a man about fifteen miles this side of the crossing. He'd been ambushed, looked like. Robbed and left for dead. There was lots of horse prints around—unshod ponies—so we figured Indians."

The men pressed forward, intent on hearing all there was about the possibility of an attack, but Jo had something else on her mind.

"The man . . ." she began when the general hubbub had died. "Was he still alive?"

"He was as good as dead this morning."

"But he was still *alive* when you left him?"

"Yeah—but coffin meat for sure."

"He was out of his head with fever. We stayed with him all night." It was the stockier man speaking now. "He was in bad shape. No way he was going to last more'n a few hours."

"The Indians had stole everything but the clothes on

305

his back. We couldn't stay with him, but we wrapped him in a blanket and left him a tent. There wasn't nothing else we could do."

Jo was on her feet. "How far back is he?"

"About three hours on horseback. Maybe fifteen mile this side of where the trail hits the Little Blue."

Mrs. Harrow's eyes met Jo's. "You're going back?"

"I have to. I couldn't rest knowing there's a man suffering back there with no one to help."

"He'll be dead before you get there," said the man called Jesse.

"And he might not," Jo replied.

# 30

Her eyes raked the trail ahead, searching for the flutter of a tent. She had hailed a train an hour earlier and been told the tent was there when they passed by.

"'Tain't a doctor that man's needin'," a woman called after Jo as she rode on, "'tis a priest."

Jo hoped the woman was wrong.

She had been riding three hours now, having left the Drummond train as soon as Peavy had loaded a pack horse for her. He had begun to load a mule, but Jo balked at that. "No mule," she said. "And there's no time to find a spare horse. I don't need much anyhow. If the man's as bad off as they say, I'll probably be back for breakfast in the morning."

"Load Sissy with supplies, Peavy," ordered Mrs. Harrow. "Dr. Joe, I want you to take my horse—and I think Peavy should go with you, too."

"Thanks, but I'll be fine by myself."

"I don't think you should be riding out alone." Trudy Harrow's eyes held a pointed meaning.

Jo didn't pretend to misunderstand. "I have to learn to fend for myself, Mrs. Harrow. But thanks anyway."

The older woman had gone off then, to supervise the loading of her own mare, and Jo knew there would be provisions for a week or more. There was no doubt in the girl's mind that her secret had been uncovered—

307

and that it would not be revealed.

Now Jo's eyes searched the fields ahead. What would she find at the tent? If the man had a bullet festering in him for a week or more—

She reviewed in her mind what she might do for him. If nothing else, she could stop the pain and let him die in peace. Burning with fever, they had said. For a fever, most doctors bled, but it was plain to Jo that bleeding weakened the patient and left him vulnerable to even greater infection.

Uppermost in her mind, of course, was the removal of the bullet. She had never used a knife on anyone. That was one skill she had not acquired in her year and a half of study, yet Doc Adams had included surgical instruments in her bag, and they lay there now, wrapped in a clean towel, awaiting her hand.

She had read about surgery and watched some ten operations. She had studied until she knew all the procedures by heart, but she had never actually performed any, other than the repair on Clay Williams's face.

Suddenly Jo raised herself in the stirrups. Was that a flash of white in the sunlight ahead? There! There it was again. She dug her heels into Tess's sweaty flanks.

The tent was staked out at the side of the trail under a basswood tree, in a field of delicate blue and white violets. Inside, a man fought fitfully with a gray woolen blanket. He was too long for the tent and his feet, tangled in the blanket, struck restlessly at the confining canvas. His shirt was torn, and a filthy, blood-soaked rag covered his upper left arm.

He whipped his feet and flailed his arms. "Got to ride!" he shouted, suddenly bolting upright, his eyes wide and staring and very blue.

Jo knelt beside him, straightened the blanket, and eased him down again. "Shhhhh." She pushed his sun-streaked hair back and pressed her wrist to his forehead. Fiery hot.

Lifting the tent flap, she let sunlight pour over him. "Hold still for me now while I look at your arm," she whispered, more to herself than to him.

The man was clean shaven, but not for several days, and his square jaw was partly hidden by wiry bristles—dark, like the roots of his sun-streaked hair. Even in repose his face had character, a certain tightness about the firm lips that came not from pain but from an inner strength.

His entire shoulder and arm burned with fever.

Gently Jo unwound the bandage. Her heart banged against her ribs as the last strip fell away and the angry, pus-filled wound was exposed.

"Oh, dear Lord," she whispered, staring into the man's fever-ridden face. "Don't let me lose this one."

"Fort Kearny!" shouted the man with a violent jerk of his big frame. "Don't you speak English?"

"Shhhhh. Just hold still now. Everything's going to be all right. Shhhhh." She whispered softly and soothingly as she measured out a healthy dose of morphine and injected it into his arm. There was no one here to hold him down, and she knew instinctively that this one was a fighter.

Jo withdrew the bone-handled scalpel from the cloth and cleansed it with whiskey. Doc Adams had thought her crazy when she suggested cleaning surgical instruments, but she knew it couldn't hurt.

The man lay quietly now, his eyes closed, his mouth open. Sweat beaded his high forehead and glistened through the dark stubble of his unshaven upper lip. She lifted one lid and peered at his glassy eye. He was as ready as he would ever be.

But was *she* ready?

She dragged a shaky lungful of air and pressed the blade into the center of the swollen, sulphur-colored wound.

# 31

She came awake with a start of alarm. Beside her, the man was sitting up. Jo knuckled the sleep from her lids and slid from beneath the blanket.

As soon as she moved, his fever-bright eyes fastened on her face, glittering with appreciation. "There's my angel. And I thought I was dreaming." His voice scratched, his head bobbed weakly, and he squinted against the tent's muted sunlight.

"Lie down. You need your rest."

He stretched out and patted the blanket, his cracked lips split in a painful grin. "There's room for two."

He had drifted in and out of consciousness several times, but had never been coherent. Obviously he didn't realize she had been sleeping next to him for several days. And obviously, the breeches she wore had made no impression. Jo deepened her husky voice and tried to look stern and professional. "I am Dr. Jo Gates—" she began.

"Yeah, and I'm Paddy's pig."

"You need your rest."

"What in hell happened to me?"

"Somebody shot you."

He digested this in silence for a moment. His muscular chest rose and fell slowly. "Where am I?"

"On your way to Oregon or California, I guess."

"But where? How far did I get?" His voice was thick.

"We're in the Little Blue Valley—just up from Marysville, Kansas."

He shook his head slowly, as though to clear it, his eyes blinking. "What's the date?"

"Beginning of May, I think."

"Damn!" He licked his scored lips. "You with a train?"

"I was. Couple of men rode in last week and told us about you. I came back to see if I could help."

He blinked again. He was having trouble staying awake. "What train you with?"

"Angus Drummond out of Leavenworth."

"Well, what do you know about that," he muttered. His eyes drifted closed. "What do you know about that . . ."

She bent over him. His breathing was easier now, his head surely less hot than it had been these six long days and nights when he had alternated between a restless savagery and an almost deathlike coma. She smoothed his dark, sun-streaked hair with a gentle hand, as she had done a hundred times this past week. He sighed in his sleep, a soft moan of pleasure. A smile etched creases in the flat planes of his cheeks.

High on his right cheek, just under the eye, was a minute white scar she had not seen the afternoon she removed the bullet.

She knew his face so well now, the high forehead engraved with faint lines, the nose with a slight hump as though it had been broken sometime, the lips full but firm, and the strong square chin. It was an arresting face, even in repose. Yet he looked so defenseless in sleep. She let her fingers trail down his hollowed cheek. He frowned and pulled his head away. "Stop it Aggie! I told you it's no use."

Jo smiled. Twice now he had shoved her away and

311

called her Aggie. Apparently Aggie was not one of his favorite people.

Jo rolled to her knees and crawled past him. Grabbing the pail Mrs. Harrow had packed, she sang softly as she made for the river.

It was a bright morning with a slight nip in the air and the promise of rain later. She thought she had never been so happy. It was as though her whole life had suddenly been illuminated by a multitude of candles and a choir of thousands. Just to take a deep breath was an anthem to her senses.

The air was sweeter, the sky an endless arch above the jeweled plains, the river bluer, the clouds whiter, the flowers more brilliant, the world a golden miracle of creation she had never seen before. How could she never have noticed? Her eyes saw more; her ears were honed. Even the tips of her fingers, when they touched the man's hair, were so sensitive that something deep within her stirred with happiness. The sweetness, the aroma and newness of spring, swelled to a great, almost painful longing within her.

She hurriedly drew a pail of water. She couldn't leave him alone long and in her rush, she sloshed the cold wetness over her shirt and gasped as it soaked through to her bare skin. She whisked it with her free hand as she hurried back toward camp.

All was just as she had left it: camp smoke rising against pearly morning mist and the fresh, heady scent of dew on the grass.

With coffee set to boil, Jo carried the balance of the hot water into the tent. She would wash him first, then fix breakfast.

She worked a good suds into a rag and began to wash his chest, humming softly and carefully avoiding the bandaged arm, her eyes intent on the ripple of his muscles as he stirred slightly.

She washed only as far as the neat indentation of his

312

navel. Never again would she make the mistake of washing below his beltline. His body's reaction, that first time, had almost sent her screaming from the tent.

It was astonishing, she thought, how little you could know when you thought you knew it all. There were some things that could never be understood just by looking at drawings in a medical book or reading a text.

Tumescence, for example, was a new word few people had heard as yet, and Jo understood it to mean "to swell to readiness for copulation," but not until she had actually seen it happen had she understood the tremendous force behind the innocent-sounding word. Not until this man's male organ had risen beneath her softly washing hand, and she had experienced the body-rocking response in her own lower abdomen, had she ever suspected that perhaps the act that created babies might be more than she was ready to comprehend.

The memory of the man's tumescence had caused her several sleepless nights and many long hours of puzzlement as she sat beside him and watched shifting emotions cross his face even in sleep. The memory was with her while she scrubbed the rags torn from his extra shirt, while she cooked, and while she coaxed quinine and broth between his feverish lips.

The memory was even more deeply disturbing when she took hot water into the bushes and stopped to wash her own slender body. As she soaped her pointy young breasts, the memory rose up hot and strong, and her nipples swelled beneath the rough fabric of the cloth. She blushed, angry with herself, yet unable to keep her soapy fingers from sliding over the turgid nipples, unable to erase the memory of his tumescence, and unable to ignore her own swelling. Did that mean she, too, was "ready for copulation"?

Now, as she soaped the man's chest, she was careful

to stop at belt level, although it would have been easy to wash farther since he was still naked under the woolen blanket.

His chest was so brown, so broad, with a dark mat of hair that grew, as she had seen, in a narrow line down across his abdomen to spread in a wide dark vee. Averting her eyes from the beginning of that narrow band of dark ringlets, she rinsed the soap away and took the biggest piece of flannel to dry his chest. His skin glowed bronze in the half-light of the tent.

She had a sudden urge to *touch* him—to *feel* his flesh beneath her fingers without the cloth between. She laid her hand on his bare chest. It was warm, not hot.

She lifted her eyes to his face.

His eyes were open, electric blue, and very much aware.

Jo rocked back on her heels, her lips forming a round O of dismay.

"Somewhere, in the back of my head, I have a distinct impression that you told me you were a man. A doctor?"

She released her breath and swallowed. "I never said I was a man. I said I was a doctor." She could see him mulling this over in his mind. She was mulling it over, too. Until the words came out, she hadn't realized how important it was that this man know she was a woman.

"I admit to a certain haziness," he said finally, "But didn't you tell me your name was Joe? Dr. Joe something-or-other?"

"J-O. Short for Jody. Dr. Jo Gates." If he hadn't remembered, she wouldn't have lied about being a doctor. She was glad she didn't have to lie about being a woman. Then a startling thought struck. Snakes of St. Patrick, if he remembered this much, what else did the man remember? She felt her face grow hot.

His intense blue eyes swept across her shirt where her

314

breasts pushed against the fabric. In the wet shirt, without the protection of a coat, it was easy enough to see she was a woman. Jo blushed scarlet as his bemused gaze paused, then traveled on to her belt-cinched waist and her breeches that seemed to be tighter now than they had been when she bought them in Leavenworth.

"And you're wearing pantaloons because—"

"Because I had to ride three hours to get back here to save your life," she snapped. "And because sidesaddle isn't the easiest or fastest way to travel." Oh, Lord, she thought, here I am piling one lie on top of another. Why don't I just tell him the truth?

His hand touched hers lightly. She was astonished at her own swift, burning reaction.

"I'm glad you turned out to be a woman," he said, apparently unaware of her agitation. His blue eyes teased. "It would have been a terrible shock to find I'd been having such lovely fantasies about another man."

She pulled her hand away. "I'm glad you're feeling better, Mister—"

He dragged long fingers across the dark, heavy stubble on his chin. "How long have we been here anyway?" he asked.

"A week today, I think."

He sat up, leaning on his right arm, holding his left stiffly against his chest. "Whooo!" Suddenly dizzy, his right hand flew to his head and he blinked.

Jo rose quickly to her knees and caught him against her shoulder as he fell backward. "You're still weak from loss of blood."

He twisted to look at her. "And not enough to eat. How about some solid food, woman?"

"You lie down. I'll fix bacon and mush."

"No, I've got to get up. I've been lazy long enough."

With one quick motion of his hand he flung back the cover just as she yelled, "Wait!"

After one startled glance downward, he clutched the

315

blanket to him, his face breaking into a rueful grin. "Well now, did *you* remove my trousers or am I mistaken in assuming that there are just the two of us here?"

She could feel her face pink again. "I'll fix breakfast."

She let go of him, not caring much whether he fell back and bumped his head or not. Halfway out of the tent his taunting voice stopped her. "Would it be too much to ask what you've done with my money belt and my breeches, doctor?"

"You're using them for a pillow," she said, hurrying to escape the amused blue eyes.

She was stirring cornmeal mush when she heard him crawl from the tent. She kept her back turned. If he couldn't stand up without her help, he could damned well sit on the ground. She didn't know why she suddenly resented him so. As long as he had been helpless, in her care, she had felt nothing but tenderness and concern, but now he was up and speaking and walking—yes walking—she could hear him behind her—now she was on the defensive, as though he were a threat somehow.

His halting footsteps crossed behind her to where Tess and Sissy grazed. Jo's spoon churned at the mush as she fretted about what he was up to and why he was quiet so long.

Then he spoke and she looked up in shock.

"What the hell are you doing with Sissy?" he demanded. "What are you doing with my mother's mare?"

"Your mother's—" Jo stared at him, comprehension dawning. "Why, you're Mitch Harrow! Your mother's been frantic, waiting for you."

"She ought to know nothing could happen to a polecat like me." He grinned then, his teeth white and

316

even. "Are Mom and the girls all right?"

"Except for worrying over you. If I'd just known who you were, I'd have sent a message to them. Two trains and a group on horseback have passed us while you were delirious."

"We'll send word first chance we get." He studied her quizzically. "So you're a doctor. I never met a woman doctor before."

Jo's heart lurched drunkenly. It had finally happened. A man who accepted her at face value— none of that "you can't be a doctor, you're a woman" business. Oh, what a lovely man he was.

"What made you come back to help me anyhow? I wasn't anything to you. You didn't even know who I was."

"That didn't matter. I knew you'd been shot."

"Did you remove the bullet?"

"Yes."

"By yourself?" He didn't sound surprised, more that he was confirming an opinion.

"Yes."

"I owe you a vote of thanks." He was hanging onto Sissy now and looked about out on his feet.

"You better sit before you fall. I don't want to start treating a broken bone as soon as I get your shoulder patched up."

He perched obediently on a log, groaning slightly and holding his head. "Mmmmmm!"

"How does the shoulder feel?"

"I don't know. I'm too busy trying to keep my head attached."

"Here. Maybe this will help." She held out a tin of coffee and watched while he drank with greedy gulps. Over the rim of the cup, his eyes were the color of the sea.

317

# 32

Jo knew she and Mitch should take to the trail. She knew they had to start soon if they were to get to Oregon before first snow, but she kept postponing it by saying he wasn't well enough to travel. He didn't contradict her.

Then one day, after three weeks had gone by, she went to the river for water and saw him swimming strongly against the fast-moving current. She no longer had an excuse to keep him here in the Little Blue Valley.

"I think it's time to travel, Mitch. You're strong enough now." She hesitated. "We could take it easy— only do a few miles a day. It isn't like your mother is still worried about you. She should have gotten one of your letters by now."

"I'm sure she has."

Each time Mitch had written, Jo had peered anxiously over his shoulder, fearful that he would refer to her as "she" or "her," but so far he had written only of "Doc" and "Jo." Mrs. Harrow already knew Jo was a woman, but the rest of the train did not. Eventually, of course, she would have to explain her masquerade to Mitch—and possibly to the people on the Drummond train. But that would come later.

"Drummond's somewhere along the Platte River by

now," mused Mitch.

She couldn't look at him. "If we started tomorrow, how soon would we catch them?"

"A week maybe. But I don't think I'm ready to travel yet. I still get dizzy spells sometimes."

Her eyes flew toward his. "You didn't tell me that." She knelt in the grass beside him to feel his forehead with an urgent wrist. "No fever . . ."

"It's nothing, I'm sure. But I don't see any reason to hurry now that we have plenty of food and Mom knows we're both safe."

With gold from the money belt the Indians had overlooked, Mitch had bought food and clothing from a passing train. Yesterday he had taken her Green's carbine and gone hunting. Now they had deer meat drying in the sun, and if they tired of jerky there would always be a plump rabbit for the pot. Mitch was a good shot, even with his left arm in a sling.

The days flew by, bright as the hot Kansas sun. There was plenty of wood and game. The grass was soft, sweetly scented. The flatness of the valley unbound the sky, and playful wisps of clouds danced through an endless expanse of blue.

They swam in the cold river, she in one pool, he around the bend in the next—and called to each other as they splashed and gamboled.

They spread their blankets in flower-scented grass and lay side by side, sponging up the warm rays of the sun, talking—sharing—each exploring the mind of the other with a wonder that never ceased.

She talked first of her family, and of Ireland and Liverpool and the mill. When she told him of the trip across and her mother's death—her promise—he reached out and took her hand and held it while her words came haltingly—held her hand so hard it hurt. It was time for the truth, as her mother used to say. But the truth about her mother's death was painful, and Mitch's insistent pull on her hand dragged it back with a harsh reality that made it happen all over again. The memories tormented beyond belief, but he never let up on his hard grip and soon, for the first time, it became acceptable.

Talking with Mitch wasn't like confiding in Fabian or Anne, she quickly discovered. Anne had been a sounding block—toss your troubles against the block and back they bounced. "We'll take the first train out," she remembered saying to Anne when she was almost beside herself with fear of what lay ahead. "That sounds like fun," Anne had replied blithely. Fabian, on the other hand, had been a sponge, a place to park her woes. Though she always felt better after confiding in the priest, she knew that her problems had never touched the inner core of the man, and that he had never truly understood the woman in her—the needs, the wants, the fire.

Mitch was different. Mitch became involved. He seemed to feel with you, to be there for you with such fierceness, such strength, that any trouble could be faced and borne because he *was* there, a fighter, and on your side.

Sessions like this were so emotion packed that Jo could take them only in short spurts. It was only afterward, when she lay in the tent beside Mitch, her eyes staring into the darkness, that she knew the deep loss of her mother finally had been exorcised. Now Jo was free to remember all the wonderful things about her mother without having to deny the horror of her death.

Mitch talked of his childhood, too—in Bangor— where snow was sometimes so deep in winter that they were snowbound for a week at a time. His father had owned the local bank and had extended the fifteen-year-old Mitch his first loan. The young, would-be businessman had bought an axe, a saw, and twenty acres of timber, then set out to create a lumber kingdom. "I'd never have made it but for Paul Bunyan," he asserted. And then Mitch made her laugh with a tall tale about how he first met Paul Bunyan and Babe, the great Blue Ox.

"Sam and Willie came in with me after that first year," said Mitch, his jawline tightening with memories of early hardships. "We piled logs all winter, then drove them downriver to Bangor in the spring. We do white-water logging like that in Oregon, too, but out there we log year round. Sam's still my bull of the woods and Willie's still the mill boss."

"You haven't said what you do."

"I bounce around between the logging gangs and the mill. And I do the selling. And the hiring and firing. Timber beasts are a ready-fisted, hard-drinking lot, and it takes a bit of doing to keep a full crew."

"Why did you leave Maine?"

"Bangor's not the lumber capital of the world anymore. The Oregon Territory, that's where the real money is. It's taken two years, but we have a solid setup on the Thunder River now."

Jo loved the sound of his voice. She listened wide-eyed as he told her about buckers and peelers and river pigs, and how to clear a log jam by dislodging the key log, and of the typical Oregon problem in the building of better chutes and splash dams to get the logs down the mountains to the rivers.

"Now if I could have brought Paul Bunyan with me, there'd be no problems at all. Paul could lift a whole forest in one hand and set it down right at the mouth of the Thunder, ready to ship to San Francisco. The only reason I left Bunyan behind was because of Babe. That big Blue Ox would have drunk the Thunder dry in one day."

Jo began to look forward to Mitch's tall logging tales. He had a story to fit every occasion, and they never failed to make her laugh.

He told her about the saddle Paul Bunyan had made for Babe: "It was so heavy, the saddler who carried it sank knee-deep into solid rock every step he took." Mitch pulled a blade of grass, held it to his lips, and blew to make a shrill whistling sound. "You always use a western saddle?"

"I've ridden English, but I like western better."

"Ever ride sidesaddle?" His tone was casual, but she had the feeling he was getting at something.

"In St. Louie, I did. I haven't been wearing pantaloons all my life, you know." Her voice was indignant, but she avoided his eyes. "The first time I ever rode was with my father. He was a horse trainer near Liverpool, and I used to ride there sometimes. What made you ask about a sidesaddle?"

"Just curious."

The next day a wagon train stopped to noon just down the river from their tent. As soon as he spotted the campfires, Mitch disappeared on Sissy. He was gone three hours. When he returned, a package bulged above the mare's saddle.

Jo watched him jump down and fling the reins over a tree branch, his left arm moving easily. He was completely healed now, with full mobility, and she had a sneaking suspicion that his dizzy spells had been nonexistent for some time. Well, she didn't mind the delay in starting for Oregon. She had the rest of her life to be a doctor. For now, she was loving every minute of their idyll by the Little Blue.

"Where have you been off to all day?" she asked, eyeing the pale-green bundle with what looked suspiciously like white lace peeking forth here and there.

Mitch reached up to untie the roll of cloth, then paused to wave to the passing train. Several pioneers waved back.

"Maybe we'll see you in Oregon, Mitch," called out a pretty blonde.

"Could be, Mercy. If you ever get near the Thunder River, come look me up."

"We might just do that."

Now Jo knew where he had been. She stared resentfully after the disappearing wagons.

As the last of them rattled past, he turned. "Now," he said. "Now for your present."

"A present? For me?" Her husky voice cracked in a funny little squeal, resentment forgotten.

He laughed. "It doesn't take much to make you lose your dignity, does it?"

"Don't tease, Mitch. I haven't had so many presents in my life that I can act nonchalant about them."

"We're going to change all that when we get to Oregon, Jo."

Her heart began to pound. "Change what?"

He tucked the green bundle under his arm. "Come on, Miss Inquisitive, we're going swimming."

"But my present?"

"After we swim."

"You have a sadistic streak, Mitch Harrow, you know that." She tried to sneak a better look at the bundle, but he propelled her ahead of him toward the river, shooing her off to what had become *her* pool. He carried the present away, tantalizing white bits peekabooing from the green folds.

Jo shed her clothing and plunged quickly into the water. No matter how often she went swimming in the nude, daylight always made her self-conscious. At night, when there was no moon, she loved the velvety feel of the water against her body, no matter that it was

323

icy cold; but in the bright sun, she felt doubly naked, and she invariably hurried to hide her nakedness in the breeze-raked water.

She heard him dive in and saw ripples spread. Then she struck out, dog-paddling upriver, but she soon got cold and turned back.

Standing in her pool again, her shoulders scrunched against the chill breeze, she shook her head and knuckled the drops from her eyes.

"Mitch," she called. "Mitch!" There was no answer. She cocked her head. No sound of the usual splashing and playful sputterings. "Mitch?"

"Yes?" His voice was so near, she jumped.

He was sitting on the bank watching her. She sank deeper into the water, her heart pounding uneasily. Above his head, among green fronds of a weeping willow, two crows watched with beady eyes. Beside Mitch, in a field of golden buttercups, lay Jo's small stack of discarded clothing. Across his knees spread a soft green cotton dress with high puffed sleeves and a pert stand-up collar. The cuffs and collar were edged in delicate white lace, and there were three rows of lace around the bell-bottomed skirt. All this she saw in one startled glance.

Mitch was smiling at her, a soft, knowing smile. "Here's your present."

"Very funny."

He stood up, holding the pretty dress against himself and spreading the skirt. "Don't you like it? I'm sorry it hasn't any hoops."

"Mitch Harrow, don't you give me that innocent, butter-would-melt-in-your-mouth look! You get away from my clothes so I can get out of here. I'm freezing!"

He bent to gather her pantaloons and shirt. "I know you're used to these mangy old rags, but I'll like you better in a dress." He laughed softly as he draped the

324

dreamy green creation over a bush and sauntered off through the trees, carrying her breeches and shirt.

Damn his hide! She watched the treeline for a long time before she crept cautiously from the water, grabbed the garment, and dashed into the bushes. She was chilled through.

At first she was only grateful for the warmth of the dress, but gradually she began to notice the softness of it, molded to her curves as though it had been sewn just for her. Jo looked down at herself. Had she grown that much since New York? Nothing, not even the most expensive of those elegant dresses Quimby bought, had made her look and feel so completly feminine. "Oh, Dr. Gates!" she giggled. "How you have changed."

She knew the present was a success when she saw the glow in Mitch's eyes. She twirled for him, the turf soft and spongy beneath her bare feet.

"You like it?" he asked.

"Oh, I love it. Thank you." She might have stretched to kiss him, but the memory of the misplaced kiss she had once aimed at Fabian's cheek flipped into her mind. She pinked.

Mitch's eyes narrowed. "Who was he, Jo?"

"Who was who?"

"The man whose memory still turns you into a blushing rose."

"I don't know what you're talking about." She turned away stiffly. Was he going to spoil it now by going all he-man and domineering?

He grabbed her arm and spun her about. "Don't play Miss Innocent with me. Thinking about the first time you ate ice cream doesn't turn a woman pink as a rambling rose."

"What is this—the Spanish Inquisition? Let go my arm! You bought a dress, not the right to my life history!"

He stared at her, his face tightening into a knot of anger. "I didn't notice any reluctance to discuss your life history before."

The silence lengthened between them. A muscle pumped beside his mouth. Without another word, he leaped onto Sissy and rode away.

She wanted to shout after him: Mitch! Come back. But something inside whispered, This is the way it starts, Jo. This is what leads to male mastery. This soft, wonderful ache could lead you straight into the trap that makes you relinquish all rights and all peace of mind.

She watched Mitch's broad back grow smaller in the distance and wished she could cry.

# 33

It was almost midnight when Mitch came back. Jo had waited up, still wearing the green dress. It was her way of showing that she appreciated the gift and was sorry for her sharp words, but Mitch didn't even glance at her.

He was leading a rangy little burro with white markings on her muzzle. "We needed a way to carry our gear," he said. "Now we can hit the trail in the morning." He disappeared inside the tent.

Alternating between resentment and hurt, Jo scattered dirt on the fire, sprinkled it with water, and stared indecisively at the tent. She didn't feel right about sleeping in there next to him now that there was a rift between them—especially now that she was dressed as a woman. It seemed—suggestive somehow, improper.

She started forward, fully intending to pull her blanket from the tent and make her bed under the trees, but a sudden mulelike obstinacy rose within her. Why should she sleep out here in the wind when he was snug and warm inside? She had as much right to that tent as he did, and he was every bit as much to blame as she for the angry words that had passed between them.

Crawling over his long legs, she curled into a ball as far from him as possible and pulled her blanket tight around her shoulders.

It occurred to her, then, that he might think she had crawled in just to be near him, and that she was ready to apologize. The idea that he might be lying there grinning smugly about her capitulation grew in her mind until she couldn't sleep. "I have every bit as much right to be in this tent as you do," she burst out finally.

He snorted in disgust. "Just like a woman, always have to get in the last word." He turned his back.

Oooooh! How did you handle an accusation like that? If she responded now, if she said anything at all, she was getting in the last word, but proving his point. Yet if she said nothing, after his unfair and untrue accusation, *he* was getting the last word. She thrashed with frustration for well over an hour before falling into a fitful sleep.

It was raining steadily when she awoke, a gray drizzle that looked as though it would last for hours. Good, she thought sleepily, we won't be able to start today.

She was in for a large surprise. Mitch was already up and had begun to pack. He must have wangled a razor from one of those last wagons yesterday for he was clean shaven this morning for the first time. She caught a quick glimpse of his smooth, strong jaw as he thrust her worn buckskins through the tent flap.

"Get dressed," he said.

When he came back ten minutes later, bringing strips of jerky and a cup of mocha, she had already shrugged resentfully into her old clothes and curled the green dress neatly inside her blanket roll.

All day they rode, through rain that turned from a warm drizzle to a cold, needle-stinging gully-washer. This was the first rain since late April, and it was making up for lost time. They passed several farms where smoke curled cozily from stick and sod chimneys, but Mitch rode steadily northward.

At mid-morning they overtook the "Mercy" train, as Jo thought of it. When the pretty blonde called out to Mitch, he promptly left Jo sitting her horse in the downpour while he tied Sissy to the wagon and jumped inside.

Jo stared after him indignantly. If he thought she was going to sit here chomping at the bit while he cavorted about a dry wagon with some frowsy blonde, he had another think coming. Wheeling sharply, she dug in her heels and had to grab leather as Tess took off at a fast trot.

Jo followed the trail north, riding fast and hard, almost as angry with her own confused unhappiness as she was with Mitch's sudden desertion.

It was very evident to Jo that she had fallen in love. They were so well matched. He made her laugh; he stretched her mind with new ideas; he was thoughtful—at least he had been up until yesterday when he got jealous. Jo's heart leaped as she realized that his anger hadn't been directed at her at all, but at her supposedly lingering affection for Fabian. All this upset just because her expression had changed when she thought about kissing Mitch in thanks for the dress.

Love was so confusing. Being near Mitch made her senses sing. But at the same time, it brought on a jangle of confusion, a misery of mind that Jo found almost impossible to sort through. For one thing, she worried that love might not mix with being a doctor—that there was no way she could have both. She *had* to be a doctor, there was no doubt about that. Yet Mitch was a fever in her blood.

No one had ever told her that love made you unhappy. Only the loss of love should do that—like Pa when he lost Mama. It wasn't fair for love to make you so miserable when your love was with you.

Where *was* he anyhow? Why hadn't he caught up?

What was he doing back in the wagon with that friendly blonde?

Jo twisted in the saddle to peer through the slanting rain. No sign of him yet.

She was surprised to see the sad-faced little burro clipping along behind; she had forgotten his lead was attached to Tess. Poor animal. He looked so over-loaded—and probably every bit as chilled as she was.

Jo pulled Tess to a steady jog, ignored the McCanles Post Office station and the farmhouses in the distance, and tried to marshal her thoughts.

What would happen when they caught the Drummond train? Mitch hadn't shown the usual male prejudice when faced with a female physician, but that didn't mean he would continue to accept it when he found out about her masquerade. Then again, it was probable that without her breeches she wouldn't be accepted as a doctor by anyone *but* Mitch.

Jo rode for almost an hour before he overtook her. Preoccupied as she was with her thoughts, she didn't hear him until he suddenly loomed beside her.

She glanced at his face, expecting black clouded anger, but his brows were raised in silent amusement as if to say, Well, did you get it out of your system?

As she felt her lips twitch in response, he suddenly threw back his dark head and gave forth a loud guffaw of sheer animal pleasure.

Oh, damn him, she thought as laughter bubbled within her. Damn him, why did he make her feel so happy just by being there?

Mitch began to sing as though he, too, had need to express his happiness. His off-key rendition of "I Gave My Love A Gay Gold Ring" soon had her giggling helplessly. "Saying prize this thing above all things," he said, rain slithering across his open mouth and curling over his chin into his poncho. Poncho! Where did he

330

get a poncho?

He caught her sudden stare and grinned. "Here's yours." He rode close and handed her a large multicolored cloak. "She gave to me a gay gold watch, to count the hours while she's away," he sang happily.

It was late afternoon before the skies cleared and a low, orange-streaked sun peered from behind rapidly moving clouds. Within the hour they had left the storm behind and ridden into a fairyland of freshly washed prairie pinks on one side and graceful willows on the other.

Jo pushed her wide flopping hat back and let it hang, Spanish fashion, down her back. Her short red-gold curls blew in the evening air.

A damp mist rose and soon the breeze was a gentle sigh on moon-silvered grass, crowned by a band of glowing jewels. A waterfall of stars cascaded from the vast sky to the far, darkening horizon. Katydids and crickets and the cry of the whippoorwill filled the night air.

Far ahead, they could see a long line of wagons circled for the night. The full moon cast a pearly sheen over their billowing canvas tops and lent a romantic magic to the scene.

"You want to camp here tonight or ride on ahead and have some company for a change?" he asked.

She wasn't ready to be alone with him. "Let's have company."

"Good." It had been her choice, but she was immediately piqued that he had agreed so promptly. Maybe he didn't want to be alone with her at all anymore.

As soon as Mitch pitched the tent, she changed into her new green dress, giving only a passing thought to the serviceable brown boots that peeked incongruously from beneath three rows of delicate white lace.

331

There was dancing around the campfire that night, and for the first time Jo was one of the woman dancers. When Mitch led her into the circle of firelight, she might have stepped into a ballroom, floated to the strains of a full orchestra, and spun in satin slippers and a silk gown beneath a chandelier ablaze with candles.

They camped, the next might, with another train they had overtaken at dark. Mitch had bagged a wild turkey so they would have something to offer in exchange for corn pone and beans. Jo was discovering that folks—even strangers—couldn't do enough for her charming escort. He not only had quite a way with the ladies, he was a man's man as well. She could see why he did the selling for his lumber company, but she could also picture him with his sleeves rolled up, engaged in grueling physical labor. She had watched him swing an axe and been awed by the might of his blows, by the few strokes it took him to fell a thick-trunked tree—even with his recent injury. He did everything well, and Jo was beginning to see why he commanded such confidence from everyone who met him.

It was late that second night, after the dancing, when Jo smacked head on into prejudice against women in general and women doctors in particular.

To preserve her reputation, Mitch had opted for sleeping under a nearby wagon so Jo was alone in the tent that night when she was awakened by screams. She sat up, reaching for the green dress she had removed only two hours earlier. She knew that cry. It was a woman in labor.

Fumbling with the dress buttons, Jo snatched up her bag, not bothering with boots. She hurried toward the sound of the screams. The grass was wet and cold on her bare feet.

A middle-aged man and several children huddled

around a campfire. "Is that your wife in labor?" Jo asked.

The man looking up as another muffled scream split the night. "What's it to you?"

She stepped into the firelight. "I'm Dr. Gates. I'd like to help."

His lip curled as he caught sight of her dress. "We already got us a midwife," he said harshly.

Sharp words rose to her lips but she bit them back. "I'm a *doctor*," she said with all the dignity she could muster. "I can help your wife. There'd be no charge."

"I told ye, we got us a midwife."

"But I can give her something to stop the pain. She can have the child easily—with no pain at all."

"We don't need none of your mumbo jumbo. Women was meant to have pain; the Bible says so. We don't want none of your devil's concoctions."

One of the man's daughters stared up at him in anguish.

"It's called chloroform—it's perfectly safe," urged Jo. "It's what they gave Queen Victoria when her last child was born. You *must* have heard about it. Chloroform will make it easy for your wife—"

"Take your devil's brew and git out of here. What's the world comin' to—women talkin' about such things!"

Jo turned away reluctantly. From the wagon came a soul-searching shriek: "Oh, dear God in heaven—help meeeee . . ."

Jo was shivering uncontrollably by the time she reached the tent. She crept inside and curled into her blanket, too heartsick to even remove her dress. Scream after scream tore the night.

Jo didn't know how much time had elapsed when she felt Mitch crawl in beside her. Wordlessly, he gathered her in his arms and held her close. Finally the screams

333

stopped and Jo slept.

When she awoke in the morning, Mitch was already up and had coffee boiling and a pan of bacon set to fry. When she asked about the woman, he averted his face and said she had been delivered of a baby boy. Mitch was a poor liar. Jo knew they were both dead.

It was afternoon before she could force the screams from her mind and begin to appreciate the beauty of the serenading birds and the myriad of colorful wildflowers dotting the valley in bright-hued beauty. The grass was belly high on the horses now, and undulated softly in a warm breeze.

Low rolling sand hills spotted with cactus and thistle loomed on the far horizon. "The coast of Nebraska," said Mitch, pointing. "See the flag? That's Fort Kearny."

The fort was mean, set in the middle of a low flat bottom, about two miles from the Platte River, with no trees or high ground to alleviate the meanness. Unprotected from the elements, open to high winds and driving rains, the surrounding areas was a barren bog. This last oasis of civilization sported a few unpainted wooden houses and about two-dozen long, low buildings built around a central compound above which the stars and stripes fluttered in a stiff wind.

Mitch made at once for the post office where the genial Moses Sydenham presented him with a letter and a package.

*My dear Mitch,* Trudy Harrow had written. *I am still not over the miracle of you being safe. And that you, Dr. Gates, were there to pull him through—that's the second miracle. We feared the Indians had gotten you.*

*I want to pull out of the train to wait for you, but Peavy won't permit it. He says we must reach Oregon before snow flies, and since you're on horseback, you'll catch up with us soon.* Jo felt a twinge of guilt as she

334

remembered the carefree weeks they had lingered by the Little Blue.

*Peavy says to tell you Drummond has a shipment of horses for the army, so our train will go the old way, through Fort Laramie.*

*One thing I have decided, Peavy or no: If you have not caught up by the time we reach the last fort—Fort Boise, where Lieutenant Templeton is going—we'll wait for you there.*

*If I remember right, the men who told us about you said you had been robbed, so I am leaving this bag of gold to see you through.*

*Patience and Agnes are both well, as am I. The trip has agreed particularly with Agnes. She positively blooms these days.*

*We had an Indian scare at the headwater of the Little Blue a few nights back but Mr. Drummond gave the Indians two horses and told them that was all they would get. They must have believed him for they soon rode away.*

*Lieutenant Templeton shocked us all by pulling his rifle and trying to shoot one of the Indians in the back. Lucky for us, Mr. Peavy was able to deflect the gun. The bullet flew harmlessly into the air, but the cold fury in that Indian's eyes! We were glad to reach Fort Kearny safely, let me tell you.*

*We are fortunate to be traveling with a large train, but it has made me terribly concerned for your safety. I know you are aware of the dangers, Mitch, but since there are just two of you, I can't help but worry. Perhaps you could join a train? But then you'd travel too slowly and never catch us, would you? I know you will do whatever is best.*

*My dear boy, our prayers are with you. And with you, dear Dr. Gates—we can never repay you for what you have done.*

*Take care of each other.*
*Love, Mother.*

Mitch's jaw tightened. "We need to push on. You take this gold and buy yourself some clothes. I know you're sick of those breeches by now. I'll pick up another burrow and a sidesaddle for Tess. Then we'll stock up on supplies."

"Wait a minute—I don't want a sidesaddle. I'm very comfortable as I am. And furthermore, I can't let you buy clothes for me."

"I want to."

"That has nothing to do with it. I can't accept."

He grinned. "You already did. I bought the dress you wore last night."

"That's different. It's not like you bought that dress in a store and could return it. You got it from that blonde, so you can't very well get your money back. It *is* different."

"Then consider that my mother is buying the clothes." He tossed the package of gold to her.

"That's nothing but an easy way to get around something we both know is wrong." She tossed the gold back.

"You want to wear out what you have on and be naked as a jaybird by the time we get to Oregon?" His grin was devilish.

"Your exaggerating again, Mitch Harrow."

"I'm telling the truth. The trail's hard on clothes. You'll be in tatters long before we get there."

"The rest of my clothes are with the wagon train. I'll be fine as soon as we reach Fort Boise." *Men's* clothes, her conscience reminded her, but Mitch didn't know about that yet. "How far is Boise?"

"About twelve hundred miles."

She bit her lip. "But it isn't right for a lady to accept clothes from a man."

"You don't strike me as the prissy sort, Jo." His lips twitched. "But if you won't take them as a gift, then consider them payment for your medical services. After all, you did save my life."

"But it's too much. I wouldn't have charged anywhere near that."

His dark brows shot up. "My life isn't worth the price of a couple riding dresses and a pair of boots?"

"Stop twisting things. You know what I mean. I would have done what I did for nothing. I *wanted* to help you."

"And I want to buy you some clothes," he said simply. She didn't argue further when he tucked his hand under her elbow and guided her into the trading post.

Inside, they immediately locked horns again. He wanted to buy a new saddle for her. She objected, pointing out that it would slow them down for her to put on skirts and ride sidesaddle. Mitch relented at that and eventually settled for the purchase of one dress, one shirt, a soft, fringed doeskin jacket and breeches, and a pair of gloves. The gloves didn't fit, but Mitch insisted she would need them later.

She wore the delft blue dress to a cotillion on the post that night, and was miserable when Mitch proved too generous about sharing her dances with the officers.

One dashing young lieutenant claimed her again and again, and declared he had fallen in love at first sight.

"Miss Jody," he begged, "do stay over for a few more days so you can get to know me better. I know you would look kindly on my claim if you could just stay on a few days. There isn't much to do hereabouts, but we could go over to Grand Island for a picnic under the trees."

She laughed. "What is it with soldiers and picnics?"

"Has somebody already spoken to you of going on a

337

picnic?" the lieutenant asked anxiously.

"Not here. Mercy, no. But back in Leavenworth, I went picnicking with a Lieutenant Templeton. Maybe you know him? Philip Templeton? He passed through here a few weeks ago with the Drummond train—on his way to Fort Boise with a detachment of men."

"I know him." Lieutenant Larkin's face darkened.

"What is it?"

He looked annoyed, then angry. "What's a nice lady like you doing picnicking with a married man?" he burst out finally.

"Philip? Married?"

"Oh, Miss Jo, I'm sorry. I had no idea—I have a big mouth."

"It's all right, lieutenant," she assured him, laughing. "It never went beyond a picnic, believe me."

Mitch came to claim her then, announcing it was time to turn in. "We'll be leaving at dawn, Jo. Maybe we'd best get some sleep."

The lieutenant looked from one to the other, his mouth not quite closed. Obviously he was thinking that her relationship with Mitch Harrow *had* gone beyond a picnic or two.

She saw Mitch grin at the lieutenant—a knowing, infuriating grin followed by a broad wink. Oh, he was a devil, that Mitch!

# 34

The Platte Valley was immense, the prairie a rolling sea of tall grass. Golden coreopsis dotted the groves and clad them in the delicate hues of spring. The sky was endless and wonderfully clear, the river a silver strip bounded by low sandy hills. Before them stretched miles of waving grass and hundreds of wagons with ends like Shaker bonnets.

But all was not beauty in this broad valley, Jo soon discovered. The lush, spongy earth sprang from violent afternoon thunderstorms that struck without warning and almost drowned them as they slept in their blankets. Ribs of lightning mauled the big sky, rain fell in diagonal sheets, and mile-long fires often rimmed the horizon.

A tireless, lonely wind compounded the great empty globe of blue, and the land seemed like a woman after childbirth—open, vulnerable.

In the vast brooding solitude, Jo welcomed the merry ring of the little bell Mitch had tied to Tess's saddle. "She'll be our lead mare, our *Madrina,*" he had explained. The bell emitted a heartwarming tinkle and became a familiar, reassuring sound as they rode West.

There were signs of buffalo now: skulls whitening in the sun and circular wallows ground into the sandy soil. Jo's first glimpse of the big, shaggy-maned animals came when an enormous drove of them lumbered toward the river—an avalanche of sound and motion that continued nonstop for over an hour. It stampeded the horses of a train just ahead, and the emigrants were still rounding up strays when Jo and Mitch rode past the next day.

She immediately discovered why he had bought gloves for her and why the size had been of no importance. He expected *her* to gather buffalo chips for fuel.

She didn't even pause to consider the unfairness of it. After being forced to wear men's breeches so long, she knew that being a woman was something to be proud of, not something to hide behind an apronload of dried dung.

She created a bag of sorts by tying together the sleeves and tail of her old flannel shirt. Then she put on one glove, picked up one dried round disk and dropped it into the bag. Looking pointedly at Mitch, she silently extended the other glove.

His lips moved with suppressed laughter. "You've worn those buckskins too long," he said. "You think like a man."

"You want to share the fire? You share the fun."

"And I thought I was being kind to buy these for you." He tugged the work glove over his large knuckles, took the shirt-bag from her and bent good-naturedly to help.

The sun-dried chips, pulled loose, left a patch of whitened grass behind and little bugs scurrying to safety. Chips burned like Irish peat, and a buffalo steak, cooked over a chip fire, had no need for pepper, Jo discovered.

Since chips were plentiful, fuel was no problem. Water was.

The silt-clogged Platte was a shallow, turbid sheet,

two miles wide in places but not much over an inch deep, the bed a mass of rolling, boiling quicksand. The water grated the teeth. It wasn't a river, thought Jo; it wasn't even a good long drink.

They overtook the first cholera wagons early one morning. There were two of them, pulled off the trail, ostracized by the rest of their train and left behind. With Mitch at her side, Jo treated everyone with laudanum and water, but within three days, both women and all the children had succumbed to the dread disease.

As she and Mitch rode on, Jo looked over her shoulder at the two men, the only survivors, backs bent to the shovels, covering the mass grave. She felt drained, her throat constricted, her entire body sore as though it had been pushed beyond its endurance.

Mitch looked at her and sighed. "You can't take on the troubles of the world," he told her softly.

The valley shimmered with waves of heat and abounded with wildlife. Mitch killed two rattlesnakes, cooked them, and convinced Jo to try a few bites. The flavor was sweet, the flesh tender, but she settled for beans and biscuits. She couldn't eat the wild antelope he shot either, after seeing it bound free and beautiful across the ridge.

One source of amusement to both of them was the mile upon mile of prairie dog towns. When the funny little rodents got to barking, it sounded like a gigantic tea party, with all the guests chattering at once.

As usual, Mitch had a story to fit the occasion. "The Rocky Mountains used to be flat prairie land," he told her. "But when Paul Bunyan logged off all the trees in Kansas, folks back east got to complaining about the extra wind blowing through from the Pacific Ocean. Paul just plugged up the holes in a prairie dog town with his sourdough batter and that batter raised up pretty good and first thing he knew, it had raised up into a fine windbreaker. So, you see, the Rockies aren't mountains at all, just prairie dog holes filled with sourdough and hardened in the sun."

Another, not so amusing, animal dogged their tracks. At night, when hordes of lobos began to howl and snap their shearlike teeth, Jo often wished she could curl up close behind Mitch and draw reassurance from his broad, warm back.

It was about this time that she began to notice a strange contradiction in her own nature. Although she liked her independence and felt capable of taking care of herself under most circumstances, she also enjoyed handing the reins of command to Mitch. As long as he didn't actually order her around, she liked having him in charge and having him to turn to when she enountered small problems—like lighting a fire when there were no dry buffalo chips. It was reassuring to know he would wade across to an island, eventually return with a few dry leaves to start the fire, twigs to feed it, and bits of a stunted tree—green and smoky, but burnable.

He was also good when Indian braves became overly demanding—when those bent on thievery, or worse, sometimes followed Jo and Mitch for days.

Sioux and Cheyenne ranged the Platte. The eagle-beaked copper-colored braves often rode up in a wild flurry of dust to demand whiskey, corn, tobacco, or horses. Jo was only too ready to let Mitch handle the negotiations. He knew when to bestow gifts and when to run. Twice he had urged her up in the dark of night and they had ridden stealthily away.

Occasionally their hands touched and Jo's heart beat with anticipation, but other than a lifted eyebrow and a slight twitch of his firm lips, Mitch gave no sign that he was affected.

Now the prairie turned the color of hazelnuts—

endless waving sandhills, endless bobbing of canvas-topped wagons before and behind, endless drag of deep sand, endless monotony, and a dull river that stretched forever into the far horizon. The scorching sun was a hot iron, pressing, burning. Sand drifted in blinding swirls, and tall bluff formations frowned down on them.

Day after day they rode, stopping only to rest and eat, or while Jo set a broken leg, or Mitch helped hoist a water barrel back in place when it jolted loose from a wagon they were passing.

The approach to Ash Hollow crossed a chaotic jumble of rocks and gullies, then climbed steeply to a high tableland and the lip of a great basin. Scars of past caravans struggled toward the crest, then spilled over the deep edge in an abrupt, despairing drop. It was Jo's first glimpse of the rugged country yet to come, and it made her heart pound. It was beautiful, but it was frightening, too.

Just west of the ridge was the cemetery.

1849. Rachel. E. Pattison. Age 18, June 19th 1849

Unnamed Man, Found Shot. 1857

Jo shivered. That could have been Mitch.

B Kelly 1852

Unknown Emigrant's Graves

Jo turned away, reminded of her mother's dream of coming to America. Mama, too, had died before she reached her goal. "Oh, Mitch," whispered Jo. "So many graves."

"It's going to rain," he said. "We'd best lay by a load of wood." How could he be so thoughtful one minute, so uncaring the next? Jo didn't understand men, and that was no mistake.

The steep road down the face of the cliff was chopped and scarred, but at the bottom waited a fairyland—a dreamworld of fragrant wild roses, berries, dwarf cedars, and wildflowers of every description. Encircling the hollow, gnarled ash trees pirouetted, their lower limbs worn smooth where buffalo had rubbed. There was a scent of wild cherries in the air, the hum of insects, and the flash of goldfinches through the ash trees.

After lunch, Jo was very quiet. Her eyes rested on towering white cliffs, and her mind dragged back to all those left behind—especially to her loved ones—Mama and Pa and Anne. "What is it with you, Mitch?" she asked. "Don't you care about other people's suffering?" Her voice was a hoarse whisper, as though to ward off his answer.

"There's no use fretting about what you can't change, Jo." He looked at her, his blue eyes intent. "You know, in Paul Bunyan's camp there was a bird that always flew backwards. Because it flew backwards, it never saw all the wonderful things up ahead. We called it a dumbo bird, because all it ever saw was what had already happened—what could never be changed."

Jo stared at him and felt her cheeks grow wet. "Oh, Mitch, is that what I am? A dumbo bird?"

He wrapped his arm around her shoulder and she leaned against his chest.

"Tell me, Jo. Tell me what brings that haunted look to your eyes."

The tears burst forth in a great flood then, and the words.

The nightmares. Half forgotten pain and torment too painful to forget. She told it all: Ballareen and the blight; the mill in Liverpool; her mother's death aboard ship; the filth of Five Points, the riots and her father's death; Madame Restell and the house on Chambers

344

Street, the basket in the surgery, Kathie's baby; Anne and Quimby House, Quimby's death . . .

"Let it go," he whispered. "Let it all go, sweet. The past holds no mortgage on today."

She told him of their flight, of Meg, Doc Adams, and Sally—even the development of her female cap—there was nothing she couldn't tell this man.

But when she came to Anne's pregnancy and the plea for abortion, Jo saw Mitch frown and she stumbled. "I did what I had to do," she said, beating back the tears. "And then . . . when Anne found out that the baby might be deformed . . . she did . . . what she had to do. She killed herself."

Jo looked into his face and saw the pain in his eyes. Pain and something else—something unsaid but deeply felt.

Still his hand held hers. She dashed the tears with an angry hand and plotted doggedly on: Fabian, Marlene Schmidt, hiding in the trunk while the man with the hook tromped through Meg's house, searching.

Through it all wove the steely thread of Jo's thirst for knowledge—her drive to become a doctor—her resolve to keep her promise and lighten the load for women. Mitch listened in silence, his hand hard around hers, his face intent as he suffered with her.

When it was all told, she felt a great burden lift from her mind. Within her grew an acceptance, a knowledge that she was free of the past. It would never leave her, but she could live with it now. Even learn from it.

She was free. She should be happy.

But she knew there was something more.

With the past in the past, the future suddenly loomed with frightening imminence. What *was* her future? To be a physician—or to be with Mitch? Was there a way—any way—that she could have both?

Her heart was sore as they rode away from Ash Hollow.

## 35

They paused beside the prickly thornberries that edged Pumpkin Creek, and Jo was conscious only of the graves, thick near the trail, and of yet another burying taking place nearby. She swiped at tired eyes and dug her heels into Tess's flanks.

Never a mile passed without one or more crudely marked graves alongside the trail. Past Courthouse Rock, a towering sandstone spire, the crest guilded in the setting sun, pressed an accusing finger against the heavens.

Near Chimney Rock was a blacksmith shop and a small station where more mail awaited Mitch, again from his mother and his one sister-in-law.

"Agnes never writes, does she?" Jo asked as he handed her the letters to read.

His lips tightened. "Aggie never was much on penmanship," he replied shortly.

*Aggie?* A swift shock ran through Jo. She hadn't connected the "Aggie" of Mitch's delirium with Agnes Harrow, his brother's wife. Jo's mind raced back to those nights on the Little Blue when she had soothed his brow and he had pulled away and railed at her in his fever. What was it he had shouted? Something like, "Stop it Aggie! I told you it's over." What did Mitch have to do with that man-chasing baggage? Jo

346

wondered. Was he remembering episodes *before* Agnes had married his brother, or *after?*

Trying not to speculate, Jo lost herself in nature's astonishing display of rock formations. There were massive cones and squares and peaks now, whole cities of bewitched shapes, like an architect gone berserk with demented dreams. Awesome bluffs were neglected feudal castles, heaving violet shadows over the tawny plains and staring down at all the hours of the day and night.

There was a disturbing lack of privacy in this open land. Mitch had been most considerate, Jo would admit that. Nevertheless, it was embarrassing to have to say things like, "I see some wild onions over there. Would you mind turning your back while I pick a few?"

At Jo's insistence, wild onions and edible greens were a major part of their diet. She knew Mitch thought it just an excuse for her to answer nature's call, but it was more than that; it was her way of combatting the ever-present danger of scurvy. They had long since used up the desiccated vegetables Mrs. Harrow had packed so long ago, and now Jo wondered what she would do about scurvy, and about nature's calls, if wild onions and occasional greens disappeared somewhere between here and Fort Boise.

Scott's Bluffs formed a chaotic barricade of rocky peaks and beetle-browed cliffs where deep troughs marked the passage of thousands of wagons. Behind the intense blue of lofty hills, the sun sank in a red-gold splash of color, gilding the harsh cliffs with splatters of mauve and saffron.

They rode slowly through the Robidoux Pass, an enchanted valley where strange tangles of cedar driftwood were gray witch's fingers coiled in a carpet of apple-green. Each dell tugged at her heart with a quickening, a hoping—but lovely as they were, none approached the perfection of her own dream valley.

And even here, in these breathtaking settings, graveyards drew Jo's troubled gaze. So many dead. So much suffering. And Jo powerless to help because of men's stubborn refusal to accept her as a doctor.

Six times since Fort Kearny Jo had been called upon to use her doctoring skills. Four of those times she had been dressed for the trail in her fringed breeches and shirt. Twice it was evening and she had been wearing a dress. Four times the emigrants were pathetically grateful for her assistance and had willingly paid what they could afford. Twice her offers had been shunned and ridiculed.

Yet here before her, as it had been all along the trail, a pathetic scattering of markers screamed proof that her services had been needed—would be needed wherever she went.

"Why can't they see beyond the end of their noses?" she cried.

"It will come, Jo." The sun's final glory caught in her coppery hair and turned it to molten fire. He held her gently, and she leaned against his broad chest and heard his heart thud against her cheek. Her body felt like fluid, and she closed her eyes, and for a brief while her frustration was forgotten.

The following day, they topped the summit and Jo caught her first glimpse of Laramie Peak in the distance, towering over dismal desert. Her broodings were swept from her mind as she glanced at Mitch, his strong face as open as the land before them, his eyes gleaming with intense awareness. What did he think about as he studied the desolate desert and the far mountains? Was he afraid, too? No. The unknown would never frighten Mitch Harrow. Anticipation. That was what she read on his strong features.

Sensing her eyes, he turned and grinned. "You think that's high? You ought to see Pikes Peak. Pikes Peak is so high it takes thirty men, looking steadily for a week, just to see the top. Why, I had a camp about a third of the way up and I had to put hinges on my smokestack so the clouds could get by."

Jo was still smiling over his Bunyanesque tales when they overtook a small train. They stayed with it as far as Horse Creek, walking now to spare the horses. Sand and red dust. Scorching sun. Dead and dying animals. Children riding now, dull eyed. Men and women plodding through dragging sand. The sun a red ball of fire.

One hour tramped on the heels of another. Sand crept into her hair, gritted in her teeth, and ground in the folds of her clothes. She swam in sweat, her eyeballs burning in dry sockets, her legs driving with wooden determination, past knowing, but not yet past caring.

Now, when she wanted to look feminine and pretty for Mitch, the sand-rough wind chaffed her face and left it as coarsened as any man's. She wiped her face with her sleeve and pushed at her sweat-drenched hair. "I'm so thirsty I could suck a mop," she growled.

"You want to rest?" he asked with an impish smile. "We could take off our skin and sit in our bones awhile."

Had it not been for Mitch's unflagging good spirits, Jo thought she just might fold up and let the dust blow over her in a quiet quilt of peace.

Frequently they skipped the noonday rest but now, with the desert sun a trumpet blare of heat and unremitting glare, they shaded up like the other emigrants, to rest for several hours during the worst of the day.

It was a time to talk, and Jo was a willing listener

while Mitch regaled her with stories about logging and about the magic, the utter quiet, among the big trees in Oregon.

Hearing the yearning in his deep voice, she said, "It sounds like you're in the wrong end of the business. Sounds like you'd prefer logging to selling."

"I like it all. And I still get my hand in at the logging camp once in awhile." He laughed. "Something tells me I'll be spending even more time there when Sam has Patience waiting for him back at the house."

"She won't live at the camp with him?"

"A logging camp is no place for a lady. No, Patience will live in Glad Hand—where I live."

"Glad Hand?"

"Nice name, isn't it? It's named for the shape of the valley, but it describes the people, too."

Jo curled her head into the crook of her arm and closed her eyes. Glad Hand. It did have a nice sound. A welcoming sound. A happy ring, like the bell on Tess's saddle. Jo fell asleep thinking that she must ask Mitch more about his town on the Thunder River. But when she woke, and they set out across the desert furnace again, she forgot about it. Ahead of them lay Fort Laramie, its picketed ramparts a mere smudge atop the horizon.

They went immediately to the post office in the sutler's store where they waited their turn to paw through the bushel basket of general delivery mail. There was a letter from Mrs. Harrow, dated May 26th. *The desert has completely drained Patience,* she wrote, *but Agnes seems to thrive on all this heat. I don't know what's come over the girl, but after traveling all day, she still finds energy to go walking. Disappears for hours of an evening. She has positively bloomed since we started West.*

*Peavy has added extra teams for the hard pull into*

350

*the Black Hills. Our stock has stood the trip well,
Mitch. We have only lost one horse and three cows.*

   *The North Platte is on a rampage. Peavy says it is
even worse than the Laramie River. How I dread the
crossing tomorrow.*

   *I worry so about you. I do hope the river will have
settled down some before you and Dr. Gates get here.*

## 36

Jo eyed the raging North Platte River with alarm. An untamed force, it flashed in the sun, a gigantic, slashing, roaring, explosion of power. "You don't mean we have to swim that?" she demanded.

"Tess won't have any trouble."

"You're out of your mind! With me to carry, she'll never make it."

Mitch's strong white teeth gleamed in a quick grin. "Who said anything about you being carried?"

"Just how do you think I'm going to get on the other side?"

"Why don't you hush and listen?" He was busily tying a cord to the left side of Tess's bridle bit. Jo watched nervously. "You can't ride her across," he explained. "Your weight would only cramp her movements. She'll have to pull you over."

"Pull?" Jo's voice rose in alarm.

"Here, hold this cord—"

"But—"

"Listen to me, Jo. If you hang onto Tess's tail, she'll pull you across slick as bear grease. Use the cord to guide her—to keep her from turning back."

"Mitch—"

He took her by the shoulders and shook gently, his eyes intent. "Listen to me! Don't let the mare turn back,

352

Jo. Whatever you do, keep her headed toward the other shore. And hang on. Hang onto her tail. Whatever happens, don't let go of Tess's tail." He grinned encouragement.

"Snakes of St. Patrick."

"Don't stop to think about it. Just do as I say."

Jo's heart sat solidly in her throat. She tried to swallow but couldn't. Numb with fear, she grasped the mare's coarse tail. Mitch led Tess into the water. He handed Jo the cord, smiled encouragement, and swatted Tess on the rump.

The horse surged forward. Out of the corner of Jo's frightened eyes, she saw Mitch leap onto Sissy and race downstream, the burros trailing.

"Hang on," she heard him shout.

"Don't leave me," she yelled after him. "Mitch!" Then she was swept off her feet. Water slammed into her mouth, hammered at her body.

"Mitch!"

But there was only the pull of the water, the struggle to hang on.

Buffeted by the raging river, Jo soon lost her bearings. "Head for the other shore," he had said. Where was the other shore? She squinted. Water pounded into her eyes blinding her.

Left on her own, the mare tried to turn. Head up, eyes bulging, Tess went with the current and tried to make for the south shore. Almost too late, Jo realized what was happening. She yanked frantically on the cord, forcing Tess into the boiling cross flow.

The river was a convulsion of sound, an explosion of fury. They were in mid-river now. The roiling torrent thrust and tore. Jo threw her head to one side and gulped air. Water slashed at her hands, pounded her face, pushed into her mouth and up her nose. Her arms ached. Hands cramped. Lungs burned for air. How

353

much farther? She tried to breathe and gulped water. Gagged. She'd have to let go. Hang on, Mitch had said. Jo's fingers tightened.

She felt rocks scrape her knees and knew she had reached the other side of the North Platte. She lay for a moment, gasping. Mitch! Where was Mitch? She struggled to her feet, her legs buckling. Dashing the water from her eyes, she raked the river with a frantic gaze.

There he was! Downstream, hanging onto Sissy's tail, Sissy swimming strongly with the burros pumping along behind. Grateful tears mingled with the grit on Jo's cheeks.

Then he was beside her. "Are you all right?" His blue eyes probed hers.

"I'm fine. Why didn't you warn me?"

His laugh was shaky. "I was afraid you might not have the nerve to try."

"I thought you were leaving me—riding off like that."

"I had to be downstream in case you got scared and let go. I won't ever leave you, Jo. You know that." His arms went around her and his lips came down to meet hers. The last thing she saw before she closed her eyes was the tiny white scar beneath his right eye.

She gave herself to his questing mouth, an offering on the altar of their desire. His lips were wet with the gritty water of the North Platte; it was sweet, sweet nectar. She leaned against him.

He was shaking. Or was it she?

# 37

West of Laramie, black pines and scrawny cedars dotted the weathered white rock. Up the steep grades of the parched Black Hills, discarded articles littered the trail: a trunk, a chest of drawers, a broken churn, and the whitening bones of dead oxen.

Register Cliffs bore hundreds of laboriously carved names and dates. But Jo gazed at scars cut hub deep in rock and knew that *this* told the true story. *This* was the true record of the hardships of the trail.

At Warm Springs, Jo suggested a laundry day. Mitch spent the day hunting and brought back a pronghorn; she presented him with fresh-smelling shirts.

There was a soft closeness between them now that mushroomed with each passing day—the need to do for the other, the need to talk, to feel, to touch. He had not kissed her again, but their eyes met often. And when their hands met, Jo could feel the swell of longing start up within her. The urge was strong to clutch this happiness close, before it was too late. Happiness was such a transitory, intangible thing. She wanted to grab it with both hands and clutch it to her breast, protect and nourish it with the depth of her love for this man; but struggling to be heard was another small voice that spoke to her—spoke of her promise—her need to keep her word to her mother—and the growing fear that she could not have both Mitch and her chosen profession.

Very soon now, they would catch the Drummond train and Jo would be forced to choose: to be a woman and be with Mitch or pretend to be a man and a doctor. She hadn't told him yet that the people on the train thought she was a young man. It was the only thing she had held back.

One evening, after she had removed her buckskins and donned the new blue dress, they rode across to a small encampment, pulled well off the trail. Not until they had reached the first of the wagons did Jo see the red flag which indicated the presence of smallpox. Even here, with certain death facing the emigrants, she was turned away. Because she wore a dress, her claim to be a doctor was ridiculed—her services unwanted. As a nurse they would have welcomed her; as a doctor they made her an object of derision.

It was obvious to her now that there was no middle ground. As a woman, she would *never* be permitted to practice medicine. The very best she could hope for was to be a midwife.

And that wasn't enough.

But if she continued to wear trousers, she thought, she could never marry. Oh, dear God, what would she do? Could she give up Mitch? Could she sacrifice her love for the sake of her chosen profession? The argument raged within her. Her days with Mitch were stretched in happiness, her nights sleepless nightmares of vacillation.

They lay beside each other, yet apart. What would happen, she wondered, if she rolled those few separating feet and their bodies touched? Would he hold her close and rain her face with wild, disturbing kisses as he had done the day they crossed the Platte? Or would their touching loose his desires as hers were already loosened.

Her imagination would not let her rest, and after a long time, she said softly, "Mitch, are you asleep?"

In answer, his hand groped for hers and held it tightly. Her heart soared as she realized he had been thinking of her, too.

"Oh, Mitch," she whispered, "this is our world. I don't ever want it to end."

"It won't," he promised as he stroked her arm. "Trust me, Jo. I won't let it end."

From the upper crossing of the North Platte to the Sweetwater was a fifty-mile trek across chaotic, torturous mountain roads. Fifty miles of poisonous springs surrounded by strange reddish-yellow grass, alkali creeks, sage, and greasewood.

At the Sweetwater Crossing, the giant reddish-gray turtleback of Independence Rock reared above the river. In the shadow of the great outcropping, above a new grave, sat an old hickory rocking chair. On the high, scarred back of the chair, painted in black tar, the inscription read simply. *Grandma, 77 years, 3 days.* Jo rubbed her red-rimmed eyes and fought back tears that lay very close to the surface.

She began riding behind Mitch so that she could watch him without his knowledge. He sat straight and proud in the saddle, and her heart was sore with yearning.

Day followed scorching day, and night followed velvet night. Often now they lay close, arms touching, fingers entwined. Often, if she woke first to the bright, hot morning, she would study his face as he slept, imprinting it on her mind, wishing time would stand still for them, wanting to hold the days back so that they could be together always, so that their world would be forever.

They overtook a small procession of wagons from

357

Indiana and paused to pass the time of day with a young couple whose wagon proclaimed in optimistic red letters: California Here We Come.

The man was thin, stoop shouldered, and glum, a long stick of a man in sweat-stained homespun breeches and a tow linen shirt. A twig rode jerkily between his tight lips, and a flintlock was gripped in his nervous fingers. The woman, in faded calico and a pink sunbonnet, was heavy with child. She plodded beside her man, dull eyes fixed somewhere between the bobbing mule's ears. But she looked up as they neared, and her homely face brightened at the sight of company. "Howdy."

"Hello, there." Not much older than me, and well into her third trimester, thought Jo with a pang. If I keep up this masquerade as a man, I will never bear Mitch's children.

"Where you fellers bound?"

"Oregon." Jo's eyes flicked to the wagon. "You're for California, I see."

"Yup. I got kinfolk there—sort of." The girl sounded proud. "My maw's cousin's man. He sent fer us to come on West. Cousin Nettie died birthin' a youngen an' he sent mouthword fer us to come."

The man looked up then, eyes burning behind silver-rimmed spectacles. "We'd be going to Oregon, too, if it wasn't for Emmie's kin. I heard tell farmin's real fine in Oregon. Whereabouts you fellers headed? That Willamette River I heard so much about?"

"A town called Glad Hand," answered Mitch. "In the Thunder River Valley."

"Glad Hand." The girl seemed to roll the words in her mouth savoring the flavor. "I like that. It's a nice name."

\*     \*     \*

Mitch flung his bedroll beside Jo's and stretched out on his back, his head pillowed on his upraised arms. "The nice part about Glad Hand is, it lives up to its name," he told her. "We have sixty-one families—or will have when Mom and Patience get there. Glad Hand is this side of the white river section of the Thunder, near where Laughing Creek spills in. It's rugged country with mountains of fir and breathtaking canyons." His teeth flashed white in the darkness.

"Tell me, Mitch. I want to hear all about your town."

He told her, then, about the house Sam had built for Patience, a tall white box of a house with a red roof, a replica of the one they'd had in Maine. "He's planted pear trees and apple trees and strawberries and flowers—you wouldn't believe the pretties my brother has put in for his bride."

"It sounds like he's as much in love with her as she is with him."

"No doubt about that." Mitch stretched out his hand and idly curled Jo's hair around his finger. "Willie and Aggie will live down in Milltown."

"Not in Glad Hand?" Jo felt a weak surge of relief to know that Agnes wouldn't live in Mitch's valley.

"Milltown's on the coast, in a dog-hole harbor near the mouth of the river. That's where they'll live—in a big, fancy house—very proper." Mitch rolled on his side suddenly and lifted Jo's hand. His voice softened, a velvet kiss in the warm silence of the night. "Now my home is different. It sits on the side of Glad Hand Mountain and looks out over Thunder River Valley and down into the lake. It's a big, sprawling log place with a wide porch that runs the whole length of it. On a calm day, you can sit on that porch, of a morning, and see the rocks on the bottom of the lake. And if the sun strikes them just right, they'll wink at you."

Jo's heart lurched against her ribs. *Her* valley?

"At night when the sun goes down, it turns the whole valley red, and the lake is liquid gold rippled with fire. There's a cleanness in the air, Jo, that brings an ache to your lungs." His fingers made gentle rings on her wrist. "You *are* coming to Glad Hand with me, aren't you." It wasn't a question.

Her heart pounded. Here it was. He was asking her to come with him. But he didn't realize what he was asking her to give up.

He raised on his elbow and stared down at her. "Aren't you?" he demanded. He sounded more astonished than angry.

"I. . . I haven't thought about where I'll settle."

"Well, you better think about it before we get there."

"I have lots of time," she said, defensive now. "We're only halfway."

"We'll be catching the train soon now."

"We will? I thought we wouldn't catch up until Fort Boise." She couldn't keep the consternation from her voice.

"That was Mom's idea. Peavy knows I planned to go by way of the Applegate Trail. It's shorter than through The Dallas. Only trouble is, if we don't catch them by South Pass, they'll *have* to go the long way with Drummond."

He looked at her again, his blue eyes intent, the muscle in his cheek jumping ever so slightly. "You haven't said you'd marry me yet."

"Oh!" He wants to marry me, cried her reeling senses. Her heart was an animal tearing frantically at the cage of her ribs. She would die of happiness. Or she could die of misery.

"Why the stunned look? It must be pretty obvious you've got me spinning like a log in white water. I'm in love with you, Jo—right down to those three freckles on the bridge of your nose."

360

"I don't have freckles."

"You do now. And you'll have more before we get to Oregon." He pulled her to him and wrapped his hard arms around her. His lips on hers were hot and insistent. "Say you'll marry me, Jo," he whispered against her mouth. "Say it!"

She could feel her heartbeat melt into the hard pounding of his own. She wanted to drown in the rush of her love. She wanted to cry at the futility of it. She turned her head aside to avoid his questing lips. "Stop it, Mitch. Stop. There's something I haven't told you."

A stillness settled over him. He drew a rattling breath deep into his lungs. By some powerful effort of self-control, his heartbeat slowed and he moved away, eyes hooded. "I thought you pretty well spilled your guts that morning in Ash Hollow."

She sat up. "Mitch . . . it isn't what you think."

"How the hell do you know what I think?" He stood, his face averted.

"I *want* to marry you, Mitch. You know I do."

"Then what's to stop you?"

"If I marry you, I can't be a doctor!" The words burst from her.

"Why not?"

"As a doctor—if I wear breeches—I'm a king among men. As a woman, I'll never be accepted. You've seen what happens. In a skirt, I might as well be a leper."

"That's nonsense. You're only saying that because of a few stupid bigots we've run into. We're not prejudiced in the West the way folks are in the East, Jo. In the West, you can be anything you want." His eyes gleamed at her in the moonlight. "I don't object to your being a doctor, do I?"

She wanted to believe, but all the evidence had been otherwise.

"I'm proud of you, Jo. Proud of what you do and

361

how well you do it. And the people on Drummond's train—they didn't object, did they? Well, did they?"

"They think I'm a man." The confession hung on the air between them. "I signed on Drummond's train as a man."

"Oh, Christ!" He jumped to his feet, paced down to the river and back. "Good Lord, Jo, you aren't suggesting that you might go on pretending to be a man?"

"Don't you see, Mitch—all my life I've wanted to help other people. I can't throw it all aside now just because society refuses to recognize that a woman is as capable as a man. Being a doctor is my *life,* Mitch. It's too important . . ."

"More important than me?" His voice cracked. "More important than becoming my wife?"

"Mitch, I *have* to be a doctor. I just *have* to!" She stood and turned her back.

"You can be a doctor and still be my wife."

"I can't." She swung to face him. "Don't you see? They won't let me. And it would kill me, now, to see people suffer, and me not able to help. I'm *good,* Mitch. Oh, why won't you understand?"

"You aren't even a real doctor, Jo—you told me that yourself. You have no degree. You haven't ever been inside a schoolhouse, much less a university."

"I don't care. I'm still better than half the others. All that's missing is that one miserable piece of paper. Why can't I make you understand?" Her voice rose. "My female cap, Mitch—it can save so many lives. Don't you see?"

"All I see is a blind spot in you as big as a redwood tree. There's no conflict here—you don't have to choose. You can marry me and still be a doctor. But as far as your female caps are concerned—even a midwife could hand them out."

362

She shook her head impatiently. "No. They work but they . . . they need improvement. They're not perfect. They may not even be the full answer." She searched for words to break the crust to his understanding. "There's so little known about the human body—but already I'm miles ahead." She rubbed her smoke-rimmed eyes. "Oh, how can I make you understand? In some ways I'm already a better doctor than a man can ever be. Why, most men are so hell-fired stubborn they can't even see what dirt and germs are doing to their patients. They won't even open their eyes to see what's plain as the nose on their faces—that things like whiskey to wash wounds—and soap and water—will save lives."

"Get off your stump, Jo. You don't have to preach to me. I'm on your side."

He came to her then, pulling her into his arms with urgent need. "All my life I've been alone, Jo. I wanted it that way. But when I looked up and saw your face that first time, I knew I never wanted to be alone again. Be my wife, Jo. Say you'll marry me." His kisses rippled over her cheeks and pressed her eyes closed. "Say it, Jo. Say it!"

She groaned. "I can't. Don't you understand? I can't."

She pushed him away and sat abruptly on her bedroll. Curling into a ball, she stared into the smoke-misted sky, her eyes dry, her heart empty.

Behind her, she heard Mitch walk slowly into the night.

It was almost morning when he came back and dropped restlessly to his blanket. Half an hour later, he was up again, unable to lie still.

He made coffee and brought it to her. "Have you changed your mind?"

She met his eyes squarely. "No," she said.

363

He did not speak again. If he looked at her, she did not know. They packed the burros and headed down the trail.

At noon, they reached the Continental Divide and crossed the Rockies through South Pass. It was here they found the Drummond train.

# 38

The dance was in full swing, but Jo's heart hung still and dead within her breast. Tomorrow Mitch, Peavy, and the Harrow women would leave the train. They would take the Applegate Trail for *Thunder River,* and she would stay with Drummond, go through The Dallas and down into the Willamette Valley. She would never see Mitch again.

Unable to watch the dancing, she wandered through the moonlight, wanting to escape the music and the laughter. She slowed at the rim of the encampment, the merriment now a distant backdrop to the night call of the Rockies.

"Joe!" The voice came from behind one of the empty wagons. "You're just the one I need."

"Who is it?" she asked, peering through the darkness.

"Me. Philip."

"Oh." She walked on.

"Wait. I need you. Joe! I'm hurt. I've cut myself." She stopped.

"You got your doctor bag, ain't you? You always got your doctor bag. It's a bad cut, Joe. Honest it is."

His voice did sound strange.

She turned back reluctantly and frowned into the darkness behind the wagon. "Come out where I can see you."

"I can't. It's my leg." His voice wore a strangled sound. "Help me."

She moved cautiously into the black shadow of the wagon. He was crouched on the ground, hunched over, holding his thigh. She bent quickly. "What happened?"

He raised his head and his teeth gleamed in the darkness. "I've missed you, Joe." His leering mouth reeked of cheap whiskey.

She pulled away, but his hand was a sudden vise on her arm.

"Let go of me, you worm! I should have known you didn't need help."

"So I lied." His other hand whipped out to grab her waist. It caught her off balance and pulled her to her knees. "Jesus, you smell good," he whispered hoarsely. "Even in buckskins, you smell good."

"Take your filthy hands off me," she gritted. "Or so help me, I'll scream. We're not off alone in the woods this time—I'm not afraid of you now."

His voice rose mockingly. "Dr. Gates—the well-known *male* physician is going to scream? I don't think so."

His wet mouth nuzzled her ear, and his tongue flicked along the pulse in her neck. His free hand snaked inside her coat and roughly massaged her breast.

Jo's body went hot with a sudden spurt of adrenaline. But the trail had hardened her; she wasn't afraid of him any longer. Her mind turned cold and logical. She couldn't knee him. Again he had her down so that she couldn't give him a knee to the groin.

She stopped struggling, leaned away, and a small sadistic smile touched her lips. She stretched her left arm languorously around his shoulder. "Then let's see how the well-known male *lieutenant* screams," she said softly, sweetly.

There wasn't much space for leverage, but crouched as he was with his legs spraddled, he was a wide-open target for the hard edge of her doctor bag.

He gave a sharp grunt and crumbled into a gasping ball. Jo stood and straightened her shirt. "*Now* you might want to call for help, lieutenant," she said, staring down at him.

As she made her way back toward the campfire, she saw a woman coming toward her. Agnes Harrow. Even in the moonlight, Jo could see that the girl's face was swollen and streaked with tears. "Have you seen Philip?" demanded Agnes.

Jo hesitated, thinking sourly that Agnes probably deserved whatever might happen to her back there with Templeton; they probably deserved each other. "No," she said. "I haven't seen him."

As she moved on toward the sounds of the dance, she could hear Agnes calling softly behind her, "Philip? Philip?" Then a sharp intake of breath. "Oh, Phil! Darling, what is it? What's wrong?"


Jo stared toward the mountains where the Harrow wagons had disappeared. They had pulled out before dawn this morning, heading for the Applegate Trail. Trudy Harrow and Patience had pleaded with Jo to join them instead of going on with Drummond. Even Peavy had come to say good-bye and that he hoped to see her again someday—but not Mitch. She hadn't seen Mitch since they rode into camp at noon yesterday.

Jo's heart was shattered. She couldn't believe it had ended this way—yet it had to end this way. She had no room in her life for romance; she had realized that long ago in St. Louis. How had she forgotten so quickly?

She told herself it was for the best—that she was free now—free to settle in the Willamette Valley and open an office. Free to keep her promise to her mother and forget all about Mr. Mitchell Harrow. Over and over she told herself these things. It didn't help. Mitch was gone and her life was suddenly dull and drab.

Mounted, ready to roll, she frowned as a rider approached from the hills. He seemed familiar and Jo's heart pounded as she stood in her stirrups for a better look.

It was! It was Mitch! He had come back for her!

Jo rode eagerly to meet him, sudden confusion biting holes in her careful composure.

He reined his black stallion and his face was stern. Her welcoming smile died on her lips. He hadn't come back for her at all, she realized with sinking heart.

"What is it?" she asked, meeting his eyes. "Is someone hurt?"

"No. Nobody's hurt." He pushed his hat onto the back of his head. "It's Agnes. She's taken a fit of some kind, and nobody can do anything with her. Mom says will you please come."

"What does she think I can do?"

"I don't know. But Aggie's threatening to kill herself."

"Oh! What do you think?"

"I think she needs a good spanking."

"Then I'm really not needed?"

"I've no tolerance for Agnes's tantrums—"

"Is that all it is? A tantrum?"

"I don't know," said Mitch, a muscle jumping at the side of his mouth. "All I can tell you is that Mom's really worried. She'd like you to leave Drummond and come with us." His eyes were very blue. "I know it's an imposition, Jo, but I'd appreciate it if you could set our personal problems aside and do this for Mom."

Drummond had moved to the head of the train now. He raised his arm and his voice was deep and commanding. "Roll out!" he called.

"Mom needs you, Jo," Mitch said with simple honesty.

She sat there, knowing she should go on with the Drummond train—knowing she should let Mitch Harrow ride out of her life and never see him again. She was just asking for trouble if she went with him to Glad Hand.

She was still sitting there, fighting her battle, when the wagon train wound into the distance.

Slowly she turned her horse and followed Mitch toward the mountains.

# PART IV

# GLAD HAND, OREGON

## 39

*August 23, 1860*

"I don't understand it," Mrs. Harrow said distractedly. "Agnes has been so sweet these past months. I know she didn't like the idea of our leaving the Drummond train and going off on our own, but you'd think she'd be over that by now."

It was the lieutenant Agnes hadn't wanted to see ride off toward Fort Boise, thought Jo sourly, not the Drummond train.

It was not to be Jo's only sour thought. Through the final soul-drudging weeks on the trail, she and Mitch were like strangers, yet not strangers, for strangers had no need to avoid each other. She told herself fiercely that when they reached the Thunder she would just pass on through. She wouldn't spend one night in Mitch's valley. Not one.

From Gilbert's Trading Post at South Pass, they took Lander's Cut-off, a new military road constructed two years before. Jo wrote faithfully in her diary, describing the landmarks, the hardships, the graves they passed. Somewhere along the Humboldt River they parted from the California trail and headed northwest along the rugged Applegate Road. Around Black Rock Desert and Massacre Lakes. Through

Fandango Pass and Sunrise Valley.

Agnes continued to alternate between tears and surly brooding. Mitch, acting as scout now, was never seen except occasionally at mealtime.

Then, on the morning of August 29th, over four months from the day they had started, Jo rode through the cleft in Glad Hand Mountain and stared into the valley. Below her lay the Thunder River, widened here into a breathtaking lovely lake, a dazzling gem set between rugged peaks and fringed with rough cottages. She couldn't believe what she was seeing: *Her valley*— right down to the rumble of rapids downriver, the hum of the bees among the tumble of flowers, and the happy stream singing off the mountain, dancing over a pebbly beach, and skipping into the sun-dappled lake.

Her valley. It was her valley. The sky was a deep blue—almost purple—the color of violets in the sun, and on the hillside across an incredibly blue lake, a field of bottle gentian winked sleepily in the bright afternoon sunlight. There—nestled beside a stand of dogwoods with another mountain peak at its back— there was the very spot she had seen so often in her dreams. She had seen it a hundred times or more—her office—with the white shingle and the bold black letters: Dr. Jo Gates.

She looked up to find Mitch beside her, a strange light in his blue eyes, a slight smile curving his lips. Damn him, she thought, turning away angrily. He knew it was my valley. He had known all along.

She told herself she wouldn't stay. Told herself there was nothing for her here. Sixty-four families wouldn't even support a doctor. She couldn't even make a living in this place. She told herself she would move on in the morning. She told herself all these things, over and over, for two weeks.

Unfortunately, she had fallen in love with "her"

374

stretch of land on the west side of the river. It stood alone on the upper edge of the lake, near the bridge—began on the slope of the mountain and ran through a lush meadow to the water's edge. Across the way from her dream site stood Mitch's beautiful log home. Further along was Patience and Sam's square white two-story box. Below them, on First Street, was the Harrow Company General Store and the livery stable and the footbridge. Down the river, the valley was dotted with cabins—all on the east side of the lake where the ground was high.

Jo liked the town. She liked the people. Several of them had already expressed the hope that she would stay. Yet she knew she must move on. They wouldn't want her anyway if they knew—if she suddenly sprouted skirts and breasts. Did people think breasts sapped your brainpower? Or that a male organ automatically spelled brains as well as brawn? What was wrong with people that they couldn't see that women were equal and should be treated that way?

She sat in her own secret bower one afternoon, hidden in the grove of dogwoods, telling herself she must call an end to all this shilly-shallying. Behind her the setting sun threw violet shadows across the lightly rippled surface of the water. It was time to stop playing the sentimental fool and get on with her life. She had set out to be a doctor—she'd damn well better get on with it.

A crackling of twigs made her turn. Mitch came striding down the path from the bridge, a sheaf of papers in one hand, the other arm bent, with his jacket crooked over one finger and hanging down his back.

He must have seen her from across the lake and followed her. She wanted to run. There was nowhere to go. "Hello, Mitch."

"I knew I'd find you here."

"I came to say good-bye to my favorite retreat."

"You're leaving?"

She nodded. "I have to find a place to settle before winter sets in."

"What's wrong with staying in Glad Hand?"

She swallowed. "It's not big enough to support a doctor."

"Is that the only reason?" His eyes were hard, intent.

"Of course. What other reason could there be?" It was only partly a lie. She couldn't stay because of Mitch either, but she couldn't say that. "It's lovely here. Obviously, I'd like to stay."

He came to sit on the other end of the log. "What if Glad Hand could support a doctor?" he asked casually. "Then would you stay?"

"It can't and it won't—at least not for years yet. So there's no use supposing."

"You are one stubborn woman, Jo Gates. If it's an impossibility for Glad Hand to support a doctor, then you shouldn't mind answering a hypothetical question. What about it—if you could make a living here as a doctor, would you stay?"

"Of course I would." Another lie.

"I'm happy you said that because Glad Hand needs a doctor."

"What are you talking about?"

"On that mountain behind you, Sam has two logging crews. On Laughing Creek, he has another. By this time next year we'll have at least a hundred men logging these mountains, maybe even more. Next spring we'll be building a new barrack, maybe two. And I've got sixteen married couples on their way from Maine right now. Coming by boat. They'll build here in Glad Hand. Now, I've explained logging enough so that you know how dangerous it is. Accidents are everyday occurrences—many of them serious. It should be pretty obvious to you that we need good medical care. I'm prepared to offer you a contract as our company doctor, Jo. It'll leave you plenty of time to handle a private practice as well. It won't make you rich, but it will put a roof over your head and bread on the table. I've got the contract right here." He held out the sheaf of papers. "You read it over and see if it meets with your approval."

She thought she must look pretty stupid, sitting here with her mouth hanging open. She shut it abruptly but made no move to take the contract. "I can't accept that."

"Why not?"

"You're creating a job just to get me to stay in the valley."

"Don't flatter yourself." She flushed, but he appeared not to notice. "Harrow Lumber needs a doctor, Jo. Glad Hand needs a doctor. And you need a place to set up shop. It's as simple as that."

"It's not simple and you know it." She jumped to her feet.

He was beside her in an instant, his eyes black with sudden anger—an anger that wanted to hurt. His arms went hard around her. His chest crushed her breasts. His mouth on hers was harsh, demeaning, his tongue a predator. His teeth ground against hers.

She stopped struggling and forced herself to stand stiffly, waiting for him to let go.

A long time passed before he released her. "Make up your mind, Jo." His voice was as steely as his arms had been. "You want to be a man or a woman?"

She wiped her mouth with the back of her hand and spat her answer at him: "I want to be a doctor."

"Then here's your chance." Bending, he retrieved the dropped contract.

He had trapped her. Either way, as man or woman,

377

Glad Hand was the place for her. This was her opportunity—her chance to be accepted as a doctor. If she worked for Harrow Lumber, no one would question her lack of a certificate—or her lack of a beard. But she struck the thought aside. "You're asking me to be a doctor for a bunch of men," she lashed out. "You're out of your mind. What do I know about men? I'm a woman's doctor."

"I seem to remember that you were—how did you put it—a better doctor than half the men? I didn't know you were qualifying that statement. I don't see any men doctors claiming they're interested in healing just one sex."

"You know very well what I mean. I can't handle men's . . . uh . . . men's . . ."

Her voice trailed away and his eyes gleamed with amusement. "I don't seem to recall you had any compunction about handling *my* . . . uh . . . uh . . . when you thought I was unconscious back in the Little Blue Valley."

His voice teased, but she had the light of battle in her eyes. "Damn you, Mitch Harrow!" she burst out. "You're no gentleman."

"I didn't claim to be," he replied calmly.

"You're deliberately putting me in an impossible situation. I can't handle a bunch of naked men and you know it."

"I see. You like to handle your naked men one at a time." His lips twitched.

She pulled her arm away. "I'm a *good* woman's doctor. I don't want to treat your blasted logging crews."

"In that case, you're no doctor at all, Jo. You're not even half a doctor." His eyes mirrored the derision in his voice. "You want to treat just a portion of the population."

She wanted to scream at him, *I'm in love with you. I can't stay here where I'll have to see you every day and not be able to be with you.* She bit her lip.

"There's something else you need to consider, Dr. Gates. There probably aren't enough women and children in the whole state of Oregon yet to keep you busy full time. If you won't treat men, you won't *have* a practice."

She chewed her lip. He was probably right, as usual. This wasn't the time to go weak and feminine. But how could she stay here, where she would have to see Mitch day in and day out? She reached for the contract. "It's getting too dark to read," she said after a cursory glance through tear-blurred eyes. "I'll look at it later and let you know in the morning." She started up the trail.

His voice, very low, stopped her. "Jo . . . there's one more thing . . . if you do decide to stay. I won't bother you again."

She wiped angrily at her eyes, her back still turned.

"If you ever change your mind," he said softly. "If you decide to be a doctor *and* a woman, I'll be waiting." There was another long silence. "But I won't force myself on you again," he said finally.

Oh, Mitch, whispered her heart.

"I don't think . . . I don't think I . . . can stay here," she said, trying to steady her voice. "Not with you waiting . . . expecting me to change my mind . . ."

He was close behind her now, his warm breath caressing the curve of her cheek. "I'll wait whether you're in Glad Hand or Walla Walla, Jo. Your going away won't change that. I'm a one woman man, and you're my woman. Someday you'll realize that." His fingers touched her bright hair in a feathery caress. "And someday you'll get tired of playacting. Meanwhile . . . I'll wait."

379

He pushed past her and disappeared into the woods.

Jo sank onto the log. The papers gave off a harsh, rasping sound as she snapped them open.

The contract was a generous one, providing a four-room house and office to be built on—she squinted at the land description again—yes, a house and office to be built on the very spot where she was sitting. Her heart turned over. Mitch knew her so well. He was offering her what she had wanted since childhood: the chance to keep her promise to her mother; the opportunity to practice medicine, and the dream house in her very own dream valley, all come true.

And a family? her heart reminded. She thrust that thought ruthlessly aside. A family would have to come later.

Mitch was right about there not being very many women in Oregon yet. No matter where she went—in Oregon, Washington, or even California—she would have to treat men as well as women. Someday there would be enough women to support a woman's doctor, but not yet. That being the case, she might as well stay here and become the logging crew doctor. At least here she would start out already accepted as a man and a doctor.

I can't afford to pass up this opportunity, she thought miserably. There have been other disappointments in my life—Mitch will be just one more. To keep her promise and be a doctor—to help women like Mama—that is all that matters.

A light, misty rain had begun to fall. Jo felt its warm fingers on her face, not knowing where the raindrops ended and the silent tears began.

# 40

"How would tomorrow do for your first tour of the camps, Jo? Say in the morning about eight?"

"Fine," she replied, squirming uncomfortably on the petit point chair. She would never be comfortable in the same room with Mitch—probably not even in the same world, Jo thought. Yet here she was, bound by a contract and agreeing to spend the day with him.

"Why don't I take Joe up with me, Mitch?" offered Sam who was home for the weekend. "Polsky, up at Creek Camp, has another cut that needs looking at. That man is a walking disaster. I could show Joe around, then run him back down here in the afternoon." Sam winked at Patience. "It'd save you a trip, Mitch, and I could be home again for supper."

"That sounds fine to me," said Jo quickly.

"Don't do me any favors," said Mitch as if she hadn't spoken. "Jo can go up to Creek Camp with you to look at Polsky's cut, but you wait there until I come along. I've told Jo about the camps; I'll do the escorting."

"All right," said Sam. "All right. No need to get touchy about it."

"You two stop sniping at each other." Patience playfully tapped her husband's hand with her fan. She had bloomed like a prairie pink since being reunited with her husband. He, in turn, couldn't keep from touching her whenever she was within touching range, as though to reassure himself that she was actually there. The one flaw in their happiness was the time Sam was forced to spend in the woods.

"If I didn't have to earn a living, life would sure be beautiful," he told Jo now. He was laughing, but his bright blue eyes followed his young wife's every move.

Jo liked Mitch's brother, but found him too intense. He was like an overstretched circus wire: pulled taut and threatening to snap. Everything was too important to him, and he was too precise, too unbending. She didn't envy Patience, having to live with such fierce intensity day in and day out.

Dinner over, the women retired to the parlor, leaving the men, Jo included, to their cigars and brandy. Over the rim of his snifter, Mitch's eyes laughed at her as she refused the proffered cigar and held her hand over her glass.

It was only a few minutes later that Jo received an urgent summons from the Cruikshanks, down the road. Mitch and Sam were discussing a new stumpage contract when Jo rose from the table.

"See you at seven in the morning," said Sam.

Jo nodded, glad to escape.

She tossed restlessly that night and was up early, while the morning mist still curled above the lake.

Nervous about the day ahead, Jo tucked her trousers inside her boots and slipped into a blue plaid shirt. If she wore a coat, she could leave her breasts unbound, but already the day was hot. She studied her shirt front. It was a large shirt; she decided she could go without a coat today and still not wear that miserably uncomfortable breast binding.

She was ready by six, and waiting for Sam, when a frantic Trevor Mellott came pounding across her porch. "It's Johnny," he panted. "Pulled the coffee off the stove and burned himself something fierce. "It went all over his face and chest. Hurry, Doc."

It was eleven o'clock before Johnny was treated, sedated, and comfortable enough to leave in his mother's care. By then, Sam had been gone for hours, and it was Mitch who waited at the dock.

"I'm sorry I'm so late," she said, stepping carefully into the canoe."

"It's all right. How's Johnny?"

"Not as bad as we feared. He'll have scars on his chest, but his face escaped the worst of it. Bless his heart, he tried so hard not to cry."

Mitch picked up the paddle. "That's one thing we boys learn early."

"I'm really sorry I couldn't make it in time to go with Sam," Jo said, determined to start off on the right foot.

"They've been keeping you pretty busy, haven't they? I hear you've been called all the way up to Canyonville."

"And down to Kirbyville." She leaned back in the canoe, pulled off her hat, and let her fingers trail in the water. From here she could see where the valley got its name. It lay like a great open palm—the five ridges of Glad Hand Mountain rising like fingers on one side, Welcome Peak forming the thumb on the other.

"Enjoying yourself?" asked Mitch.

"You know I am."

His smile flashed, wide and easy. "Me, too. You know, Paul Bunyan had a canoe once. His canoe was *so long* that he could step into one end of it in St. Louis and out the other end in New Orleans without ever leaving the dock."

She laughed. Mitch was such fun to be with.

He kept up his nonsensical tales all the way down the river, and she soon forgot she had ever felt ill at ease with him. All she had to worry about now was how vile the logger's language might become, and how red she would get with Mitch standing there beside her. She wished it were Sam who would show her around. At least he didn't know she was a lady.

The current picked up as they passed the ferry and waved to Ed King. Jo could hear the roar of white water where the Thunder rushed between high canyon walls and sped on its way to the Pacific. Mitch paddled hard for the mouth of Welcome Creek. She sat up to wield the other paddle.

Soon the quiet banks of the small stream closed about them, massive firs forming a wide, deep canopy overhead. Huge logs began to appear on the banks with great regularity. Jo jumped as a distant cry of "timber-r-r-r!" was followed by a great crash that reverberated through the forest.

"The camp we'll visit first is right down on the water," said Mitch. "We have two mountain camps up the side of Welcome Peak, and there's a trail over the mountain from right behind your place—comes out about midpoint between the two camps. Laughing Creek is the gathering point where we rough cut most of the logs and chain them into booms to float down to the mill."

By the time they pulled to shore it was noon, and the crew was coming in for lunch. They wore floppy hats, gallusses, and calked boots.

Staring doubtfully at the rough men and praying she could get through the day without dying of embarrassment, Jo rose to step from the canoe. She caught her boot heel on a rib in the bottom, teetered for a moment, and went flying into the water.

Sputtering to the surface, she found Mitch grinning down at her, backed by at least twenty bearded men in various body contortions of what passed for belly laughter. Blast their ugly hides! She wished their galluses would snap—every last one of them. Then let's see who'd laugh.

She reached for Mitch's proffered hand and allowed herself to be dragged awkwardly ashore. On her stomach, gasping for breath, she wiped her face with the back of her hand. A solid wall of laughter surrounded her. Worst of all was the low, dirty-sounding chuckle from right beside her. Mitch was having a field day.

She rolled onto her back and stared up at him balefully.

His laugh coagulated. Consternation and something like shock swept across his face.

Now what? she wondered. Quickly, he bent over her and flopped her unceremoniously onto her stomach.

"The doc's been suffering from a bad cold," he said in a loud, false voice. Something dropped over her shoulders. "For God's sake," he hissed in her ear, "cover yourself with my coat."

What in heaven's name was he up to now? She grasped the edges of the coat and pulled it close about her throat. Cautiously, half expecting another attack, she sat up.

"I'll have to take Doc right back to Glad Hand," said Mitch in that strangled voice laced with poorly concealed laughter. "We'll be back up tomorrow if his cold isn't worse." Mitch grabbed her arm to help her into the canoe. "Hold that coat, Doc," he said loudly. "You don't want to get pneumonia. See you tomorrow, Sam."

They were in mid-creek by now, Mitch paddling a great deal faster downstream than he had up.

Jo took a deep breath. "What was that all about? I thought I'd done a pretty good job of making a fool of myself when I fell into the creek, but you sure topped it off great."

"Lady, I didn't even begin to make a fool of yourself like you'd have done if you'd stood up."

"What are you talking about?"

"Why don't you drop the coat and see if you can figure it out."

She threw off the coat angrily and looked down. Two things had happened when she fell overboard. The top three buttons of her plaid shirt had come undone, exposing the upper curves of her breasts, and the wet flannel had become so attracted to the lower curves that it clung like a second skin. Blushing furiously, Jo made a grab for the discarded coat.

He was chuckling again, that low, disgusting sound that made her absolutely livid. Then the humor of it struck her, and her own lips began to twitch and her shoulders to shake.

"Isn't this nice," said Mitch in a conversational tone. "Now you don't have to worry at all about meeting the timber beasts. Nothing could be worse than this first time."

She didn't ask how he knew she was worried. She simply rolled into the bottom of the canoe and gave herself up to the laughter bubbling within her.


As far as Jo was concerned, her second trip to the logging camp, two days later, was a greater disaster than the first, for it marked an almost total break in her relationship with Mitch.

Instead of coming by river, they rode over the mountain this time, with Mitch guiding her through miles of timberland to point out company boundaries. The forest was alive with the thwack of axes, the cry of "timber-r-r-r," and the earth-shaking crash of giant Douglas firs.

"We own all of Welcome Peak," he said, pointing.

"Everything in the triangle between this camp and your office on the Thunder River plus some over on Glad Hand Mountain, but we don't plan to cut over there."

"That's good. I'd hate to see the valley spoiled." Although Mitch had explained that they always left a good stand of trees for later cutting and would never leave the mountains bald as other companies did, Jo still was aghast at the devastation.

"We're negotiating a lease on a stretch up through there, on the west side of the creek," said Mitch, pointing. "And I've got a new contract for stumpage farther up." He grinned at her as they approached Creek Camp. "Incidentally, I suggest you stay away from the water this time."

Set well back from where the streams widened into a large pond, Laughing Creek Camp was a sorry-looking camp with a log bunkhouse, a cook's cabin, a small sawmill, and an open-sided shed for oxen. Winding down from Welcome Peak and ending at the pond, a wooden chute slashed a white scar into the timber-strewn mountainside.

The bunkhouse, a year-round log-built home for twenty timber beasts, as the men were called, was about thirty feet long and raised two feet off the ground, like some of the Indian huts Jo had seen on the Oregon Trail. Inside, the rough hut was divided into two rooms: the kitchen in one end, the bunks in the other.

Jo looked around, struggling to hide her repulsion. Rain-soaked workclothes dried on a line. In one corner, hung on pegs by their suspenders, were several pairs of short, stiff-looking breeches.

"Now you see why we need a new barracks," said Mitch, his voice rueful. "This camp's the oldest and the worst of the three. It's a real muzzle loader."

"What's a muzzle loader?"

He pointed at two tiers of straw-covered planks

387

lining the walls. "The bunks are so crowded, the only way anyone can go to bed is to climb in from the end of the bunk—down the muzzle, so to speak." Mitch was obviously enjoying his role as guide. He grinned. "They're so crowded, when one man turns, they all have to turn."

The smell of the place was nauseating. Smoke, wet wool, sweat, kerosene, and stale tobacco juice blended with the aromatic evergreens of the roof to form a nostril-dredging concoction. In the center of the room was a mud and stone fireplace, which obviously doubled as a spitoon. Above the fireplace, a crude chimney was suspended from the ridgepole to let the smoke escape. It wasn't too efficient, she noticed.

"That's another reason we need a new bunkhouse," Mitch said, grinning at her wrinkled nose.

"What you need is a crew with manners," she exclaimed as she eyed the tobacco-stained fireplace.

He laughed outright at that. "One thing I will say— Sam's got rid of their lice."

"How'd he do that?" she asked, remembering her own lice and bedbugs battle in Five Points.

"He seals the bunkhouse up tight, runs in the steam pipe from the saw, and pumps the place full of steam. Then if the little buggers have set up any *personal* camps, Sam makes the men douse their heads in kerosene. Every time we get a new timber beast, Sam's got to delouse the place."

The camp kitchen was ruled with an iron skillet by the cook, Lily. She was a big, uncorseted woman in her mid-fifties. Cook's helper was named Irene. She was older yet, thin and scrawny, with straggly gray hair and a slight limp. The kitchen end of the log house contained a well-stocked pantry, a stove, two rough plank tables with twenty chairs, a water barrel, wash bucket, and a large grindstone where the men sharpened their axes.

Polsky, the "bucker" with the infected cut, suffered stoically while Jo dressed the wound and issued strict instructions on keeping it clean. She worked quickly, wanting to leave the smelly barrack.

Outside again, she sucked gratefully at the sweet, pine-scented air and listened to the sounds of the lumber camp: the scream of the circular saw, the pound of giant planks as they hurtled down the chute, hot with friction from rubbing against the peeled tree-trunk sides, and finally burst into the open to be flung into the pond with an electrifying sizzle.

"We use teams and a skid road from Mountain Camp One," explained Mitch, "and the chute from Camp Two. Down here all we need are wagons."

That accounted for the clanking chains, Jo realized as she watched the Durham oxen haul a loaded wagon toward the sawmill. Chained to the top of the wagon were three massive tree trunks. Thick tree slices rimmed with heavy metal formed the wagon wheels. The din, the clanking, and the cursing of the bull whackers was a disturbing jolt to what should have been the peace of deep woods.

At the cutting area, two fallers stood on scaffolding, about twelve feet in the air, facing each other. Their long-handled axes had just begun to bite into a tremendous Douglas fir that towered two hundred feet above their heads. The men were midgets against the massive trunk.

"Why are they up on that platform?" Jo asked.

"The base of the tree is too fat. And they run into too many problems."

"Hey, Mitch! You wanta get in a few licks?" called the head faller.

"Why not?" Mitch shucked his coat and climbed onto the platform the faller quickly vacated.

"See you don't take the edge off my blade."

"Don't worry about your blade," replied Mitch happily. "You just tell me where to drop 'er."

"Right here," said the burly logger. He picked up a stake. "You want to try to thread the needle?"

"Whatta you mean, try?" demanded Mitch.

The faller laughed good-naturedly as he strode off to plant a stake in the forest floor.

"What's that for?" asked Jo when the man came back.

"That's to show him where to drop the fucker." He pushed back his floppy hat and raised his voice. "Month's pay?"

"You're on," Mitch shouted back. "Double if it don't go all the way."

"What are you betting?" asked Jo, hoping her blush would be mistaken for sunburn.

"I'm bettin' the boss ain't so good as he used to be. I say he'll miss the stake. He's bettin' he can make the tree trunk drive that fucker right into the ground."

Jo ducked her head, hiding another quick flush.

On the platform, Mitch laughed a happy laugh.

Jo turned to look at the little stake about a hundred fifty feet away, then back at the Douglas fir. The tree was a good five feet across and two hundred feet high. They couldn't be serious, she thought.

Long-handled steel axes swung in rhythmic grace, biting into the wood and sailing fat chips into the air. There was a hypnotic beauty to Mitch's powerful swing. Aside from the scar on one muscular arm, he might never have been injured.

Jo sank into the soft carpet of needles and leaned against a rough tree trunk. From somewhere behind her came the steady click of a woodpecker at work. A delicious green aroma, the scent of fir, was thick in the air. From the platforms came the steady whop of the men at work.

Swinging his axe with powerful strokes, Mitch was a god of grace and symmetry, a Greek sculpture come to life. Jo's eyes were riveted to his sheer maleness, the clean beauty of his muscular frame in motion. *Oh, Mitch.*

An hour passed. She could see the shape of the undercut now, smoothly carved, flat on the bottom and angled on top. Mitch had told her that for a big, three-hundred footer, fallers actually had to stand inside the undercut to reach the middle of the tree. She shivered.

Another hour. The undercut, reaching over halfway through the trunk, was finished. Now Mitch and the other faller moved the platform and began a second cut on the other side. This was a flat cut, a horizontal cut, not too deep.

Half an hour went by. Then Mitch's shout rang out: "Timber-r-r-r!"

He tossed his axe into the brush and came hurtling from the platform.

The crack of the massive fir splintered the air, and the swoosh of its branches was a percussion roll. The ground heaved as the fifty-ton monster thundered down, bounced, and lay still.

"Shit!" said the logger standing beside Jo. "It fell true." He made his way to the upper end of the trunk and clambered among the branches.

"How'd we do?" called Mitch.

"Nailed it slick as shit," replied the faller in disgust.

Mitch grinned. "Don't worry. I'll come back next week and watch you drop one so you can win your money back."

His eyes flicked at Jo, then away, as he grabbed his coat and started toward the horses. "First chance you get, Jo, I want you to come up and examine all the camp women. You'll have to come early, right after breakfast, to catch the cook-house ladies with a few spare minutes. What with new timber beasts hiring on all the time, the women will have to be examined every month now."

"What do new loggers have to do with examining the cook-house ladies?"

He held his hands for her to mount. "New timber beasts might have . . . well, they might have . . . varmints," he said, swinging easily into his saddle.

"Lice?" Already he was riding off. She kicked Tess to catch up with him. "I thought kerosene shampoos and bunkhouse steambaths took care of the lice," she protested.

He looked uncomfortable. "That's not exactly the kind of varmints I had in mind. These bugs are the kind the men might . . . might pass on to the ladies."

Snakes of St. Patrick! He was talking about the crab louse! Jo had learned about those from the girls at Claire's Sporting House in St. Louis. Was Mitch saying that the men would pass on crabs to the lady cooks? Jo's mouth dropped open. "Are you saying the cook-house women are prostitutes?" she demanded.

"No, they're cooks. But if they happen to make a little money on the side, we don't want them spreading the French disease or infecting the whole camp with . . . bugs."

"Then they *are* prostitutes."

"Of course not. Lily's still married. Her husband logs somewhere up around Coos Bay. Irene's a widow lady. The girls aren't any better than they should be, maybe, but they're not whores. Manda's the whore."

"Who's Manda?" Jo couldn't believe she was having this conversation. Later, she knew she would look back and die of embarrassment. Right now she was too angry to be niggled by modesty. "Who's Manda?" she demanded again.

"The half-breed up at Camp Number One, in that shack next to Sam's"

"And she's a prostitute?" Jo slapped a branch away, unable to believe he had actually said what she heard.

"A good one, so they say." His grin was positively wicked.

"And you let her live right there on your land?"

"Let her? No, we pay her to live there." Mitch's mouth curved with devilment. "I didn't think a doctor would need to have the facts of life explained. I can see I was wrong."

"Don't you talk down to me!"

They had reached Creek Camp. Mitch jumped down and waited for her to join him. "Listen, Jo—loggers are the biggest womanizers, the hardest drinkers, the roughest bruisers, and the worst drifters God ever set on this earth. And what's more, they're proud of it. It isn't easy to hang onto good loggers. They'll work six months to save up a hundred dollars, then head for the nearest skid road and blow it in by noon the first day. Then they'll sign on with some other company, and I'll never see them again. That's why it's so hard to keep a full crew. Bawds, booze, and brawls. That's all most of them live for."

"And you cater to those low instincts by providing the bawds."

"And the booze." He grinned, clearly enjoying her discomfiture.

The circular saw had started up again, screaming as it chewed its way through the fir trunks and spat out thick rough planks. Mitch took Jo's arm and led her off into the woods where they could talk.

"Now, suppose you park on that windfall while I acquaint you with the facts of life—doctor."

Jo sat on the fallen tree. She couldn't bear to look at

393

him. How could he be so crude, so low? She stared up at the forest giant where patches of blue sky winked through wind-riffled branches. Under her feet, fir needles were deep and soft. Under her hand, the rough tree trunk scraped her palm. She didn't want to hear his excuses.

"Harrow Lumber isn't out to make a million in a couple years like the big coast operations," he began. "You thought it was great when I explained our policy of leaving some of the trees growing instead of stripping the woods as most operators do. Right?"

"What does that have to do with prostitutes?" she challenged.

"Just wait—I'll get there." His tone was infuriatingly calm. "You liked the idea of our holding the logger's pay back so they could save up a nest egg and not have it gobbled up on foolishness. That's another policy I started in Maine and intend to hold to here in Oregon. One of our men from the Penobscot camp let his wages lay and had enough saved to buy up stumpage on a hundred acres when we came West."

Jo was looking at him now.

"Then there's the company store in Glad Hand—you probably don't know that most companies pay in scrip and set their store prices so high it keeps the loggers deep in debt. Loggers can work for one company for years and never have anything more to show for it than an extra pair of galluses. That doesn't happen with Harrow Lumber."

She was listening in spite of herself. "Get to the point, will you."

"The point is that we're the only company around who's trying to upgrade the timber beast's life. When the weather's so bad they can't work, we don't charge for the first three days' bed and board. Other companies charge bed and board no matter what.

"We charge for liquor. Most companies won't allow liquor in camp, but we sell one pint per man per weekend. It keeps him in camp instead of running off to the nightlights in the city. If he has any booze left—which he doesn't—it's tagged with his name and locked up until the next weekend. Any man caught drinking during the week is paid off and sent on his way. That, incidentally, helps keep the accident rate down."

Mitch paused for a deep breath, and Jo knew he was finally getting to the prostitute.

"We use women cooks instead of men because a man likes to have a woman around. If the cooks choose to make the men even happier, that's not our concern.

"Now Manda is something else again. She sets her own rate and she's available any night of the week. And she's clean. We give her a shack, food, clothes, and now—a doctor." He grinned audaciously. "You said you were all for treating women, Jo. Here's your chance. That is, unless you've got something against treating these particular women?"

Jo stared at him. He stood there, staring back, daring her to object, and a picture of Nicholas Quimby rose like a black specter in her mind. She blurted out her first thought: "Was Manda a virgin when you recruited her, Mitch? Did you find your beasts a nice clean virgin?"

His eyes narrowed. "In case you haven't noticed, Jo, virtue is acquired."

"Virtue is God-given," she replied hotly.

"All right. Virtue is God-given. *Virtuousness* is acquired."

She rolled her eyes mockingly. "Oh, heaven protect us—an intelligent man. That makes what you're doing even worse." Her eyes flashed fire. "You didn't answer my question—was she a virgin?"

"Manda was *not* in possession of her God-given

virtue when we hired her. She was working the streets up in Portland." He bit the words off and spat them at her.

"Are you trying to say you brought her down here to make her life better? And that makes what you're doing all right?"

"I'm answering your damn question, that's all."

"You're trying to justify prejudice instead of doing away with it," she yelled at him. "You think of this Manda as a woman—put here just to satisfy a man's rutting instincts. You don't think of her as a human being at all. You think of her as a subordinate, not an equal."

"Everyone who works for me is a subordinate. Why should Manda be any different?"

How could she explain to him—make him understand that by using a woman as a vessel for the base side of a man's nature, he was destroying the best in both men and women? "The sexual part of a man shouldn't destroy the human part, Mitch."

He sat beside her, his voice softening. "The sexual part *is* human, Jo. You ought to know that much."

"But it shouldn't be so damned important it overshadows everything else a woman has to offer." She turned her back, unable to look at him. How could he? How *could* he? From the far reaches of the forest came the muffled cry, "timber-r-r-r!" followed by a resounding crash.

Quimby had told Anne that women were made to be toys for men. Was that what Mitch thought, too? Was Quimby and his string of whorehouses any worse than Mitch and Manda? A picture of the little maid, Tina, flashed behind Jo's disillusioned eyes. She swung back to stare resentfully at Mitch. "Why are you forcing that poor woman to give her body to those animals?" she burst out.

"Forcing? What kind of a warped idea do you have about whores? Listen, I'm no pimp!"

"No? What would you call it?"

Now he was angry, his eyes blue caverns of fury. "You get this straight, Jo Gates: We supply a clean woman so our men aren't tempted to roar off to some skid road in the city and blow in a month's work in half a day. Forcing Manda? Christ, when Manda was in Portland, she took on more men in one night than she does here in a month. And she was nothing but a two-bit hooker, so she had less to show for the time spent on her back. She's nothing but a kid, but she had a hell of a life in Portland. And let me tell you something else. There are only two groups of working women in the West. First is the domestic and second is the prostitute. It may not be right, but that's the way it is."

"If you don't mind, I'd like to go home now."

"That's all you've got to say?"

She laughed an ugly laugh. "I think you said it very well—you're a pimp! Now I'm going home." She jumped up and plunged through the woods.

Sam was just coming out of the kitchen, his big open face glowing with color from the scrubbing he had given it. He stopped in his tracks and frowned as Jo brushed past him. "What's wrong?"

"The good doctor thinks we're a couple of pimps, that's all." Mitch left Sam staring after them and tromped across the camp in Jo's wake.

# 41

Two months had passed since Jo's morality brushed against what she considered Mitch's lack of it. During that time, she had settled into a reasonably workable routine with the loggers, the cooks, and Manda, the prostitute. The townspeople, cautious at first because of Jo's youth, now accepted her as a competent doctor. Aside from an angry stab of pain when she bumped into Mitch, and an inescapable prickle of conscience over her masquerade, Jo began to fit comfortably into the Glad Hand scene.

In late November Agnes and Willie came to spend the weekend with Mitch and his mother. Willie was thirty-two, tall, stolid, opinionated, and gossipy, with a paunch, a heavy gait, and a nervous tic in his left eye.

Jo had reluctantly accepted an invitation to Sunday dinner with the Harrow clan and now was seated uncomfortably beside Agnes. The other girl had put on weight, Jo noticed; she was wearing her hoops high, and her once trim ankles looked swollen. Jo had the passing thought that Agnes might be pregnant, yet knew she hadn't been reunited with her husband long enough to be showing. Her eyes were puffy, too. Remembering the tantrums and threats of suicide when they parted from Lieutenant Templeton, Jo wondered if the pale-lashed, plump-bosomed girl was still mooning over her lost admirer.

Agnes's chatter was light and innocuous, but Jo could feel her eyes, calculating, searching. She wants something from me, thought Jo. What does she want?

Willie, who had been regaling them with choice Milltown gossip, had now turned to politics and launched into a vituperative attack on "that backwoods lawyer from Illinois" who had no right messing into the South's need to keep slaves. "They need slaves same as we need millhands," declared Willie. "Where'd we be without loggers and millhands? You tell me that."

A pall of silence gripped the room. Everyone knew of Sam's steely belief in the preservation of the Union and his avid support of Lincoln. Patience went white as a muscle jumped in her husband's jaw.

"Willie," said his mother gently, "why don't you save that discussion for after dinner, over cigars and brandy?"

"I brought back some new Havanas you may want to try," offered Mitch smoothly.

Patience cast a worried glance at Sam's set face. "Have you all seen the message somebody carved up on Glad Hand Mountain?" she asked in a bright voice.

Jo's heart knocked against her ribs.

"The one that says J—I'm Waiting?" Malice laced Agnes's voice and tatted a pursed edge to her thin lips. "We saw the simple thing. It's the first thing we saw when we rode into town."

"I think it's a lovely carving." Mrs. Harrow's serene face held a trace of a smile. "It must mean a great deal to J, whoever she is."

The message, carved at the peak of the mountain where the sun struck it in the early morning, was the first thing Jo saw from her new house-office these days. She ducked her head and studied her mashed potatoes.

"And there's something else new in town that

warrants comment," Mitch said, his voice tinged with teasing laughter. "That's a mighty fine sign went up in front of your new office, Jo."

How could he tease about it? The sign had arrived the day the cabin was completed. Mitch had sent a logging crew to build her cabin, and it was no sooner finished than the Cameron boy, bearing a package, knocked on the new door. There was no note, but Jo knew Mitch had sent it: a neat white sign with bold, black lettering, Dr. J. Gates. It was beautiful, and she thought her heart would burst with love and frustration.

And it was then, standing there with the sign in her hand, that she had raised her eyes to the mountain across the lake and seen the carving for the first time.

She looked across the table now, directly at Mitch. "Thank you," she said. "I think the sign is beautiful, too."

He inclined his head, a small smile touching his eyes.

She carried Mitch's smile in her heart when she left the Harrows' that evening, and it was still there when she stopped to make sure old Mrs. Cameron was still holding her own after a long bout with pneumonia; and still there while she changed the dressing on the Mellott boy's slowly healing burns.

It was late that night, the moon drifting high overhead, before Jo completed her house calls, wearily climbed the steps, and crossed the porch to her own front door. It always depleted her energies to treat a suffering child, left her drained and strangely vulnerable.

The moon skimmed the lake with white purity, and she paused to let peace seep into her soul and settle her aching heart. Every time she came home, Jo marveled at how good Mitch had been to her—despite her stubborn clinging to her breeches and doctor bag. The house was compact and efficient, containing her office with a separate door on one end, a parlor, kitchen, and bedrooms to the rear for Jo and Peavy. At Mitch's insistence, Peavy had stayed to work for her, and she was grateful for that, too. As her mother had often commented, a house without a man wasn't a home. Although Peavy wasn't what Mama had in mind, he was a wonderful help.

The sign Mitch had sent was a symbol of her success as a physician, but his carving on the mountain—J— I'm Waiting—was at once a comfort and a mocking reminder of what could be and was not.

Standing on the porch now, staring into the moonlight, Jo wondered if she would ever get used to wearing breeches and pretending to be a man. Still, it wasn't being a man that bothered her, it was *not being a woman*—not being able to be with Mitch, feel his arms hard around her and his lips on hers. Hopefully, she lifted her face toward the mountain, but the carving hid in the shifting shadows of the night.

From the far end of the porch, a dark shape detached itself from the blackness and slipped toward her.

"Who is it?"

"Shhh! It's me. Agnes Harrow."

"Agnes? What on earth are you doing out here in the dark? Why didn't you go inside to wait?" Jo led the way into the parlor and turned up the wick.

Agnes was heavily cloaked, a hood pulled close over her pale hair. She reminded Jo of the women who had come late at night to seek help from Madame Restell. "Where's your husband?"

"Willie's asleep. He doesn't know I'm here." Agnes threw back her hood and adjusted it nervously.

"Are you sick? Do you want to go into the office?"

"Couldn't we just sit here in the parlor and talk a few minutes?"

"Of course. Take off your cloak. I'll stir up the fire." As Jo bent to the fireplace, she could hear the quick, agitated movements of the other woman removing her wrap, settling in a chair, smoothing her skirt.

The fire flared into cheery brightness. Jo turned uneasily. She was settled in her role as a man now, but Agnes still had the capacity to make her uncomfortable.

"That Peavy character won't come in, will he? I don't want anybody to know I'm here."

"He won't bother us." Jo seated herself opposite Agnes. "Now, tell me what's wrong."

The girl opened her pink mouth, but no words came. Her fingers rubbed her ear, tugged at the sleeves of her red silk gown, and smoothed restlessly over her pale face and hair.

"What is it, Agnes? I'm a doctor—you can tell me anything."

"It's . . . my monthlies. They've . . . they've stopped," she said finally.

"When was the last one?"

"On the trail somewhere. Fort Kearny, I think. Yes. It was Fort Kearny. I remember because there was a dance, and I couldn't go because I was unwell."

"But that's six months ago." Agnes had been reunited with her husband for only three months. Philip Templeton's leering face popped into Jo's head. She tried to see what the wide hoops hid, but it was hard to tell. "Were your monthly periods regular before that?" she asked.

"Like clockwork. Oh, Joe, I just know I'm that way. Whatever am I going to do?" Agnes's pale eyes darted around the room, never landing squarely on anything, least of all Jo.

"Let's find out if you're really pregnant first. Let me ask you a few questions . . ."

Ten minutes later, Jo had the whole sorry story, at least from Agnes's warped viewpoint. The handsome lieutenant had fallen in love with her and pleaded his case with such eloquence. Of course, the virtuous young woman had resisted his advances. After all, she was married. Then one night he had begged her to meet him after the others were asleep. She had gone, only to tell him, of course, that his hopes could never be fulfilled. But when he got her alone, at his mercy, he had forced himself on her. And now this! "Oh, Dr. Joe, what am I going to do now?" she finished.

The question hung on the air between them. To Jo, the question was a living, breathing thing. The memory of Anne, always there, always waiting, was a sudden wall of pain. "Help me," Anne had cried.

Jo squared her shoulders and thrust the memory ruthlessly aside.

Of course, it was Agnes who had initiated the affair, who had flirted outrageously with Philip from the moment they met—not that Jo imagined the lieutenant had been all that reluctant. She remembered Trudy Harrow's letters about how Agnes had changed so on the trail—begun going off by herself at night for long walks in the desert. And the concern in Agnes's voice when she had cried out: "Oh, Phil, darling, what's happened to you?" The tantrums when she was separated from him. The suicide threats.

But most of all, Jo remembered Mitch's feverish cry: "Stop it, Aggie! I told you it was over." Why did that stick in her head?

"Does Willie know you're pregnant?"

"Of course." Her mouth pursed spitefully. "That's the only way I can make him leave me alone. Of course, he thinks it's his. But even Willie'll know different when the baby comes four or five months early." She looked straight at Jo then, her eyes taking on a speculative

403

gleam. "You got to help me, Joe. I *can't* have this baby. You got to help me."

"No!" Jo backed away, shaking her head. It was Anne all over again. She wanted to bolt and run.

"Joe—you could fix it, I know you could."

Jo forced her words through tight lips. "You're too far along for me to do anything, Agnes. In your first trimester, I could have given you ergot, but not now. There's nothing I can do now."

Agnes's violet eyes gleamed red in the firelight. "I couldn't come see you sooner. By the time I realized, we were already in Oregon. I was in Milltown and you were up here, and I couldn't get Willie to come up until now. I don't want to have this baby, Joe! I'm too young to start in with a passel of brats like my mother did. Besides—everyone will know it's not Willie's. There are things you can do—I know there are. There was a doctor in Portland used to take care of women who didn't want kids. I know you can help me." She leaned forward. "Please, I'll do anything to get rid of this kid, Joe. Anything."

"I can't help you, Agnes. I'm sorry."

Agnes rose and moved gracefully across the room, her hoops swaying. "I'd be nice to you, Joe. I'm not all that big yet. I still have a good figure." Jo froze as Agnes slipped to her knees. Her eyes gleamed in the firelight; her pale lashes fluttered. She placed her hand on Jo's leg. Her hand was hot. It burned through the cloth of Jo's breeches.

Jo stared. Aghast. Unable to move.

"Paw used to say I had a better breastwork on me than the town fort."

Gazing into the other girl's eyes, half hypnotized by their intensity and the play of firelight in their pale violet depths, Jo was rooted to the chair.

"I could make you happy." The whisper slid into the silence between them. "I made Philip happy. I could make you happy, too."

Jo's mind said, *Get away from her,* but her body refused to move. This wasn't happening. It couldn't be happening. It was ludicrous. It was impossible.

Agnes lifted Jo's hand and started to guide it to her lush breast. Jo sprang to her feet and sprawled Agnes backward onto the floor.

Somehow, the girl had gotten her bodice open all the way to the waist. Her full breasts spilled out, pink and lush in the firelight. Around her slender neck, a garnet necklace winked with blood-red fire.

"Get up!" Jo turned her back.

"Please, don't run away. I'll do anything. Anything." She pulled herself tight against Jo's leg and one hot, hardened nipple pressed Jo's thigh. "I'll do things for you that will drive you wild with pleasure," she whispered as her hand crept slowly upward. "Let me show you."

"Snakes of St. Patrick! You let go of me!" Jo struck at the leechlike hand. Oh, Lord, were there many women around like this? Did men have to go through this often? "Agnes Harrow, you get off your knees and button your dress before I call Peavy to bundle you up and take you home."

"You wouldn't dare."

"Try me."

"Wait." Agnes scrambled to her feet. "Don't you dare call him." She stared at Jo, her eyes flinging fire. "You're no man! You're not half the man my Willie is! You can't even grow a beard," she spat with contempt. "Maybe you never grew any balls either!" Buttoning her dress with quick, angry fingers, she reached for her cloak.

In the doorway, she stopped, her eyes glowing coals of venom. "You wait, Joe Gates! You just wait! I'll pay you back for tonight. You wait and see if I don't!"

## 42

Jo enjoyed her visits with Manda each month. The Indian girl was younger than Jo's eighteen years, a lighthearted, breezy child, yet old in the ways of the world. "One day Manda marry," she told Jo today, her sloe eyes gleaming. "Marry rich timmer beast. Go back home. Make babies."

Jo was chuckling as she closed the door to Manda's one-room hut and ran smack into Mitch who was just tying his horse at Sam's cabin.

Mitch's eyebrows shot up in amusement, and Jo's laugh froze on her face.

"Good morning," he said smoothly. "You look like you're enjoying yourself."

"Morning." She tucked her head and strode toward her horse. She didn't want to talk to him, didn't even want to look at him. Why didn't he just leave her alone? she thought miserably. It tore her apart to be near him, left her weak when he accidentally touched her. It was that weakness that made her turn on him with angry words whenever he came near.

She heard his quick step behind her.

He grasped her arm and swung her about. "What in hell's wrong with you?" he grated. "You've been avoiding me like a poison spring."

"Let go. I don't have to be nice to you. I work for

you, but there's nothing in my contract that says I have to be pleasant." She pulled away and marched stiff legged to the waiting mare. She could feel Mitch's eyes follow her as she mounted Tess and headed up the mountain trail.

For a moment she thought he was going to let her go, but she was just into the treeline when she heard him come after her.

"Get up, Tess!" Jo leaned low and clapped spurs to the mare. She could hear Mitch's sorrel behind her, pounding over the mountain.

As she broke through the treeline behind her house and raced across the meadow, Mitch rode alongside. She didn't even glance at him.

He had the nerve to ask what was wrong? He apparently didn't see anything wrong in employing a woman just for the pleasure of those foul-mouthed brutes! Jo liked the merry little Indian girl. Manda hadn't much of a vocabulary, but they had established an early rapport and Jo felt protective toward her. Why couldn't Mitch see the girl as a human being?

Reining the mare, Jo slid from the saddle and dashed across her front porch.

Mitch was beside her before she reached the door.

"Leave me alone," she railed, trying to shake off his hand.

"You're not getting off so easy this time," he said with maddening calmness. "We're going to settle this here and now. Every time I get within speaking distance of you, you lash out. I'm not asking much, Jo, just that you stop treating me like a leper."

She bowed her head as the anger drained away. She had been a bitch; she knew it. And not because of Manda or the cook-house ladies. No, in the past two months, she had come to understand the logger's nature and Mitch's unique problems in keeping a full

407

crew. She had met some of the other lumber barons and found them sanctimonious hypocrites who milked the men of their wages and closed their eyes to the hideous skid roads that had sprouted all over the Northwest. The big lumber men were great church-goers who conveniently ignored the unbelievably vile areas where the timber beasts blew in their earnings, fought, caroused, and picked up all the social diseases from the low whores who operated there.

As Mitch said, Manda was better off here than she would have been in one of the cities. Were there gradations of whoring? Jo wondered. Was this a case of two wrongs making a right? Or of one wrong being right simply by virtue of its not being quite so wrong as the other?

Hard as these questions plagued her, they were no longer as important as they had once been. Now it was her own wayward body that drove her insane with longing.

It wasn't Mitch's morals that made her fly at him whenever they met; it was her own desires, her own weakness.

She dragged her eyes from her boot tips and looked up at him. "I'm sorry, Mitch," she said softly. "Really I am. I don't know what's gotten into me lately." Tears glittered on her dark lashes.

"Jo . . ."

She swiped impatiently at her eyes and gave a rue-ful laugh. "You told me once that boys learn early not to cry. I guess I'm not very good masculine material after all."

Before he could form a reply, the door behind her opened and Peavy's whiskey-hoarse voice sounded: "Mr. Willie was here lookin' for you, Mr. Harrow."

Mitch frowned. "Willie up from Milltown? What did he want?"

408

"I don't know, but he looked mighty upset. He's waitin' for you over to your office."

"Thanks, Peavy."

The door closed.

Mitch stared at Jo, his jaw tightening. "We can't talk here. Come back with me to the office."

"Oh, Mitch, what's the use? Besides, Willie's waiting for you."

"Damn Willie and his imaginary problems. We've got to talk, Jo. You know as well as I do we can't go on like this. Whatever's on Willie's mind, his few worms in the woodwork won't take more than a minute or two."

She sighed. Maybe he was right. Maybe it was time they stopped pretending that they could live in the same town and not be together. Silently, she followed him down the steps.

They crossed the upper bridge and cantered down the lake road, Jo's mind racing ahead of her horse's gait. Was Mitch going to ask her again to be his wife? What would she say this time? Doctoring was still top priority with her, but now she knew it wasn't enough. Without Mitch, she was only half a person—had only half a life. Jo's heart began to pound with expectation and indecision.

They crossed the wide veranda. Trudy had already begun to string Christmas decorations, Jo saw.

Mitch flung open the door.

Willie was pacing the office, his gait uneven, as though he'd had one too many. His normally prim appearance had undergone a shocking alteration. His face was a mottled gray and red. The tic in his eye had spread until it twisted the entire left side of his face. His eyes were bloodshot; his hair stood in tufts where distracted fingers had torn. His cravat was askew, his clothes rumpled.

He grabbed Mitch's arm as a drowning man will

409

grab at a twig. "Mom's getting packed to go back with me. You better come too," he babbled. "The bleeding's stopped and the doctor says she'll be all right, but she's like a ghost there on the sheet, and she won't even talk to me anymore. Just lays there and stares at the ceiling."

Jo stepped inside and quietly closed the door.

"Easy, man, easy," urged Mitch. "Who's hurt?"

"Aggie. My Aggie. She just lays there. Mom's packing now. She's going back with me. You come, too."

Mitch's eyes questioned Jo. She nodded. "Dr. Jo can be more help than I can. Jo will go back with you."

She stepped away from the door then and into the room. "What happened to Agnes, Willie?" She was sure she knew, but she had to ask.

Willie swung on her then, eyes bulging, face twitching, lips contorted. "You know goddamn well what happened to her, you son of a bitch! You did it!"

Before Jo realized what was happening, the big man hurtled across the desk. His fingers found her throat. His weight threw her backward and she fell heavily to the floor.

"Willie! Have you lost your mind!" Mitch hauled the big man off like a sack of meal. He shoved Willie aside and knelt over Jo. "Are you all right?"

She nodded, holding her throat and trying to swallow.

Mitch swung on his brother. "What in hell's got into you?"

"You son of a bitch!" screamed Willie, his bloodshot eyes pinning Jo to the wall. "Innocent lookin' son of a bitch!"

"That's enough, Willie." Mitch helped Jo to her feet and stood protectively in front of her.

Her hazel eyes were beginning to snap with anger.

Agnes had sworn she would get even. Apparently she'd kept her vow. Obviously, Agnes had tried to abort her own baby, then blamed Jo. Well, I'm not taking the blame for any abortions, she thought. I didn't perform any and I'm not being blamed for any. "You listen to me, Willie Harrow—"

"Let me handle this," interrupted Mitch.

"It doesn't concern you. If Willie's wife is spreading lies about me, then I'm the one—"

"Lies!" The vein in Willie's thick neck threatened to pop. A harsh shade of puce belched into his face. "My wife's no liar," he screamed. "She says you're the one and she don't lie." His face crumpled suddenly, splintered as if he were about to cry. "What's she see in you anyhow?" he whimpered. "You're the biggest goddamn nothing of a man ever was. Sissy britches— can't even grow a beard, for chrissake. What the fucking hell does she *see* in you?"

Jo's mind was like a bad dress rehearsal—ideas tearing dramatically on and off stage, none of them staying long enough to complete their lines: Willie found out the baby wasn't his—Agnes aborted her own—then she got even with Jo—saying Jo had done it? No. There was more to it than that. Agnes told Willie— What *had* she told him? What made a grown man cry? Agnes said *Jo did it*— Agnes had told her husband that— She told him—

It was Mitch's incredulous voice that completed the line. "You think *Jo* is the father of Aggie's kid?"

That was it, thought Jo, fighting the hysterical giggle that caught her aching throat. That was the line that refused to form.

"Aggie said *Jo* got her pregnant?" Mitch's hoot of laughter boomed across his brother's sputtering accusations. "Oh, my God, has your wife got an imagination!" He stepped toward Jo, still laughing,

411

his hand outstretched.

"You want proof your wife's a liar?" cried Mitch. "Well, here's your proof—" Before Jo knew what was happening, his hand had flicked her coat back, grasped the neck of her plaid shirt and torn it open.

She grabbed frantically, but not in time to hide the soft swell of her upper breasts.

Willie's eyes bulged.

"Now you see why our good doctor has no beard," Mitch laughed. "And why you'll have to look elsewhere for the man who put the horns on you." When his eyes met Jo's, he was still laughing.

She wasn't. With that one quick gesture he had stripped away her professional credibility. In Jo's hazel eyes smoldered anger and frustration and something very akin to hatred.

# 43

Mitch went outside to say good-bye to his mother and brother. "You don't want Jo and you don't need me," he said. "I'm not one of Aggie's favorite people. I'd only be in the way."

Jo stood at the office window, staring into the thin December sunshine, her back to the departure scene, her foot tapping angrily. She couldn't wait for them to leave so she could tell Mitch Harrow exactly what she thought of him.

How dare he expose her like that? What gave him the right to tear down all she had built up these many months? How had she ever thought him understanding? He could go straight to Halifax, is what he could do! How had she ever considered marrying him?

The door closed. Willie and his mother were gone. Jo spun about. Her cat's eyes glittered. "You think you're God?" she raged at Mitch. "You think it's your place to arrange *my* destiny to suit *you?*

"I'm sorry I tore your shirt, Jo. It was just so damned ridiculous."

His even-tempered response inflamed her further. "You saw your chance to expose me as a woman and you grabbed it, that's all. Now you think you've got me where you want me? You think now I'll marry you?"

Her eyes burned hot and her mouth twisted in an ugly sneer. "No way, buster. I wouldn't marry you now if you were the last man on earth."

"What are you talking about? You think I planned that show? My God, Jo, you know me better than that." He raked annoyed fingers through sun-streaked hair. "I'm sorry I exposed your secret, but it struck me so funny—I did it before I thought." A smile tugged the corners of his mouth. "You'll have to admit it *was* funny, Aggie accusing you of being the father of her baby."

"Ohhhhh!"

His smile vanished. "I *am* sorry, Jo. I wouldn't deliberately hurt you for anything. You know that."

He stepped toward her then but she backed away. "Don't you touch me. Don't you ever touch me again."

"Jo—"

"Your brother's not the type to keep secrets. He'll spread gossip all over town—all over Oregon. My days as a doctor are finished. You saw to that!"

"Jo, believe me—"

"You deliberately exposed me so I couldn't pretend to be a man anymore. Then you thought I'd have to marry you!" Her voice rose shrewishly. "Well, there's one thing you forgot—you forgot *me*. You've neatly arranged my life? Oh, no—I may have to put on a dress because of your brother's big mouth, but I'm still in control of my own life, thank you. If I can't practice medicine in Glad Hand, I'll go somewhere else. But I'll be a doctor. And I'll be damned in hell before I'll be your wife!"

Mitch's eyes darkened dangerously, and a muscle jumped at the edge of his hard mouth. "If Willie's talking is what you're worried about—don't. I'll take care of Willie. You can go right on parading around in breeches if that's what you want." His voice was a fuse—a bomb waiting to explode. "As far as marriage is concerned—I suggest you wait until I ask before you turn me down."

He spun on his heel. The door closed firmly and finally behind him.

# 44

News of the fall of Fort Sumpter reached Oregon at the end of April, 1861, two weeks after it happened. By this time the entire state was engorged with rage, having discovered that their beloved territorial governor, Joseph Lane, was a secessionist. At The Dallas, he was hanged in effigy when he was caught trying to smuggle arms out to equip an Army of the Pacific Republic.

The first war dispatches by telegraph shocked the Pacific Coast with the message that Oregon's republican senator, Edward Baker, had been killed at the battle of Ball's Bluff.

Sam immediately packed up and headed back East to fight for the preservation of the Union. He and Willie were not speaking when Sam boarded the ship at Port Orford. Patience was devastated. She faded, pale and silent, living only for Sam's letters and the day he would come home.

Indians began to harangue the immigrant wagons again, and a train of fifty-four people in eight wagons was attacked on the Snake River plains near Fort Boise. Several pioneers were killed. The remainder lost their way, fled across the Snake, then made camp on Owyhee River. It was here that the same desperate circumstances as the ill-fated Donner party overtook them. When they were rescued forty-five days later, they had already eaten the bodies of four children and exhumed Mr. Chase in preparation for further meals. The decision of the living to eat the dead, brought upon by their awful extremity, was unanimous, they said. It was reached "after hours of consultation and prayer." Only fifteen of the fifty-four survived.

The people of Oregon were more frightened by the resumption of Indian attacks than by the cannibalism, however. Having just gone through an Indian war, they hastened to build temporary forts: one at Grand Rond, one on Burnt River, plus permanent posts at Boise and Great Falls on the Snake.

Volunteers were called out, and Mitch served a brief spell at Fort Umpqua. His going brought the war home to Jo for the first time, but when he returned after his short stint, she immediately settled back into her familiar niche. The fighting was back East—so far away. The Thunder River Valley was still her lifeline to peace and contentment, no matter what happened in the outside world.

By this time she and Mitch had reached an uneasy truce—a kind of status quo that enabled them to live in the same town and be polite when their paths crossed. It wasn't a happy arrangement, but it was the best Jo could manage. She knew, now, that his exposure of her masquerade had been, as he said, a thoughtless act; and he had kept his promise to stop Willie's wagging tongue. She was still Dr. Joe, not one hint of scandal about her having reached Glad Hand.

In June, 1861, another Harrow crisis occurred when Agnes suddenly ran off with a ship's captain. Willie surprised everyone by accepting her departure with equanimity. He lost weight, divorced his errant wife, and within three months had found himself a new one. It was a different man who married pretty Eileen

Magillicutty one Sunday in July. She was a widow lady, a church organist from somewhere upstate, with two small children of her own.

With a new wife, Willie was suddenly spurred to greater interest in the business, even to enthusiasm over the new bunkhouse under construction on Welcome Mountain.

Unfortunately, all Mitch's expansion plans collapsed when gold was discovered in the eastern Cascades. Instead of production doubling as he had predicted, half the crew deserted logging for mining.

The gold petered out and the men drifted back, but there were new gold flurries with discoveries on John Day and Powder Rivers. Things were temporarily on hold now at the logging camps with mill production cut more than half.

After six months, Mountain Camp Number Three still sat empty. Now Mitch often worked as a faller to help the depleted logging crews. Even Willie rolled up his sleeves occasionally and pitched in at the mill. Peavy had left Jo to become a bull whacker at Creek Camp. Sam's cabin and Manda's shack stood empty.

Jo could smile now when she thought of the young half-breed prostitute with the coarse, glossy black hair, the shoe-button eyes, and flat cheekbones. Manda had gone back to her mother's people on the reservation at Grand Rond, a rich woman in their view—with lots of money and a new white husband.

Thinking of Manda reminded Jo of one evening when she had been kept late at Number One to treat a deep abrasion on Polsky's right cheek.

Accidents were frequent among timber beasts, but Polsky suffered more than his share. The trim little man with the handlebar mustache was forever cutting himself or dropping a sledge on his foot.

Jo had just begun to caution him that in the future he

418

must be more careful when the bunkhouse door opened and Mitch sauntered in, followed closely by Manda.

Jo looked up, surprised to see Mitch who had been away on a trip. Her heart began an irregular tapping against her ribs. "Hello," she said, trying to hold her voice level. "What are you doing here with the working people?"

"Checking up on you. It was dark at your place, and I thought you might want an escort back over the mountain." His eyes met hers briefly, then turned to the injured man. "What happened, Polsky?"

"The goddamn saw, he stuck in the pitch," said Polsky in disgust. "I throwed on kerosene and you know what that fucker did? Instead of slicin' through, he bucked back at me and like to took my head off."

Mitch's eyes flicked at Jo and away again. "Manda, here, was worried about you."

The little Indian girl peered past Mitch's shoulder, her black eyes gleaming. "Polsky prick no hurt?" she asked anxiously.

"He a good customer, is he?" Jo could hear Mitch's suppressed laughter.

Manda's guttural voice was almost shy. "Polsky heap big. Stuff Manda good."

From the corner of her eye, Jo could see the movement of the girl's hands as she held them apart to show just how big Polsky was.

Polsky was married to Manda now, and they had gone back to the Grand Rond Reservation to live with her and her people. Jo hoped the little Indian girl would have the many children she wanted.

A falling branch struck the roof with a loud thud. Jo jumped.

Setting her mug on the sill, she leaned her forehead against the window. Glad Hand Mountain was completely obliterated by the driving rain. She hadn't been able to see across the river for several days now, and she missed the view. Usually, when she raised her eyes to the far side of the lake, the first thing she saw was Mitch's huge log house, blending into the dark stand of Douglas fir as though it had grown there. Then, looking higher still, to the peak of the mountain, his message would stand out white and clarion clear. *J*—proclaimed the large bold letters, *I'm Waiting*.

The message put heart into Jo whenever she became discouraged. Like now, with this infernal rain.

If possible, the storm had worsened during the night. Rain lashed the house, vicious, driving. It had been raining for two weeks now. Jo hadn't seen a patient in six days. For that matter, from her window, she hadn't seen a living soul in over three days. Nothing moved in the valley except the swollen river, the driving rain, and the sodden firs slanting before the wind.

She peered through the gray-fingered storm. The river was higher than she had ever seen it. Dangerously high and rising every hour.

Just yesterday she had thought it couldn't come any farther up the slope toward her cabin, but now it looked as though it had risen a good six inches during the night. She strained to see the far side of the lake, but not even Patience's white house shone through the solid gray wall.

Patience would be with Trudy at the big house anyway, Jo thought. Now that Sam was gone, when Mitch was away on a prolonged business trip as he was this month, the two women always stayed together.

An uneasy feeling stirred in Jo. All the houses in Glad Hand were built on high ground on the west side of the river—all but hers. Her house stood at the upper end of the lake on a little bluff only four feet above the lake edge. If the water continued to rise at this rate—

From a hook on the back of the office door, Jo grabbed the poncho Mitch had given her so long ago.

Outside, wind-shredded clouds drove across the leaden sky. Laced with pitching rain, the wind was a savage force that strained and battered. She bent into it.

Tess, in the lean-to at the side of the cabin, whinnied hopefully. "I'll get to you in a minute, girl." The wind tore the words from Jo's mouth. She struggled toward the lake and was astonished when she stepped into swirling water—within two feet of her front porch.

Normally this stretch of the Thunder, widening into Glad Hand Lake, was placid with a steady pulsing flow toward the Pacific. Now it raged, a maddened bull with horns down and hoofs pawing, a brutish beast unleashed to pillage and destroy.

The din was deafening. Frigid wind from the northeast roared through the valley. The giants of the forest trembled, cowed by its hoary breath.

Before Jo's horrified eyes, a house swept past. Even as she watched, a huge uprooted fir rammed the pitching house. Planks and joists and logs exploded into bits of kindling and rolled on their way to the ocean. A great saw, its blade chewing angrily at air and water, tumbled jerkily through the raging river.

Jo didn't wait to see more. Her mind churned into high gear. There was no way to get across the lake to join Trudy and Patience. She had waited too long. The bridge would be down, the ferry closed—maybe even swept away during the night. If the water continued to rise, at this rate it would be swirling through her cabin within the hour.

Inside, her poncho hung to drip, Jo systematically gathered warm clothing, food, and all the drugs she could carry. Her only hope was to head back over Welcome Peak and make for one of the camps.

Laughing Creek Camp was on low ground, but all three mountain camps sat empty now. They would be high, safe from the rampaging river.

She cast a regretful look about her office. Oh, please, God, don't let anything happen to it. Immediately she was ashamed for the selfish thought. Hundreds of people along the Thunder must be suffering—maybe even dying as their houses were being swept away. At least she had a safe place to go.

She turned to leave, but a thought struck her and she crossed quickly to the desk, grabbed a piece of stationery and wrote hastily: *Have gone across the mountain to the new barrack*. Until she wrote the words, she hadn't decided which camp she would head for, but having written, she knew it was right. Number Three, in a virgin stand of ponderosa pine, was the farthest away, but it was new and clean.

With saddlebags packed and her doctor bag securely tied to the horn, she made one last trip inside to lift the always loaded Green's carbine from the peg on the parlor wall.

The road over Welcome Peak was a sea of slithery mud capped by sodden pine needles. The wind slashed at her poncho. Jo hunched and let the mare feel her own way. They plodded steadily up the steep trail into the screaming green timberland. Branches whipped Jo's face. Tess stumbled, then trudged onward. Wind wailed through the towering trees. The din was frightful. Nearby, a widow-maker limb plummeted to the ground in an explosive crash. Tess snorted and reared.

"Easy, girl. Easy." Jo's words were ripped away, lost in the howling forest.

The rim of the mountain was a nightmare of savage rain and piercing wind, a thick gray nightmare. Tess slid over the edge of the ridge and wallowed down the muddy trail.

Soaked and exhausted, Jo guided the horse into the virgin stand of ponderosa. Through bowing trees and slanting rain, the new log bunkhouse loomed, long and squat. She pulled the mare up just short of the kitchen door and stared.

A horse was tethered to the hitching post.

A pale light flickered through the windowpane. Someone was in there. An Indian?

A lump of fear rose in her throat. Earlier this year, the abandoned Fort Umpqua had been captured by renegades, and several people had been murdered by wandering bands of Modocs.

Heart in mouth, Jo slid from the mare and reached for her breechloader.

## 45

Jo peered cautiously through the window. From a candle beyond her line of vision, light flickered against the gray wall, but nothing else moved in the dimly lit interior. One of the loggers from the creek camp? Oh, let it be one of the timber beasts, she prayed silently. Not an Indian. Please not an Indian.

She approached the door, raised rifle cradled in one arm. Her finger hovered on the trigger. Her heart bruised her ribs with its pounding.

She lifted the latch and pushed the door inward with one foot.

A tall, rangy man was bent at the kitchen table, writing. He straightened and turned, his gaunt face lighting with love and relief.

"Mitch! Oh, Mitch!" The gun almost slipped from her fingers. She laid it on the table and flew across the room into his waiting arms. She clutched him tightly. "Oh, Mitch. Mitch."

"My Jo." He rained kisses over her wet face and bedraggled hair. "Are you all right, darling?"

"I'm fine. Oh, now I'm fine." Shaking with cold and weak with happiness, she looked down at the note he had been writing. *Jo*, it said. *I'm on my way over the mountain to your place. If we miss each other in the storm, wait here for me. I'll be back.*

424

"I've been looking for you at each of the camps, leaving notes everywhere." His lips touched hers, his arms folding her close. "I was so worried about you."

She fitted into his embrace with a gentle sigh and a sense of forever. She had come home.

"Is Mom all right? And Patience?" he asked, his mouth trailing across her wet cheeks.

"I couldn't see across the lake, but I'm sure they are. The water was just up to my place when I left. How did you know the Thunder was flooding? Weren't you up in The Dallas?"

"It isn't just the Thunder, darling. I don't know about the eastern part of the state, but every river this side of the Cascades is on the rampage." He held her away and looked at her then. There was tenderness and love in his gaze—and a lively tingle in the pit of her stomach.

He brought his fingers up to her face and stroked her cheek, tracing her lower jaw and the tender flesh beneath her ear. The past year of recriminations and accusations fell away.

"You're shaking," he said. "Get out of those wet things while I lay a fire."

"I'll get my saddlebags."

"You get out of that wet poncho. *I'll* get our saddlebags."

When he came back, Jo had removed the poncho, found some clean flour sacks and was drying her hair. "Is there wood?"

"There's everything we could want, unless you're expecting a feather mattress. If you remember, this bunkhouse was ready to be occupied when news of the gold strike blew all our expansion plans. I'll start the fire in the bunkroom first. We'll think about hot food later."

"Have you had breakfast?"

"I haven't had anything but jerky for over a week."

She saw the dark rings under his eyes and knew he was about to drop from fatigue. "Here, let me do it." She knelt beside him to lay kindling.

With the fire flaring brightly, she turned to his saddlebags and quickly found a dry shirt and pants. "Here. Put these on. I'll go into the kitchen to change. There are flour sacks on the end bunk." She grabbed her own saddlebags and left the room.

Ten minutes later, toweled and dressed, her wet clothes draped over chairs, she rapped on the bunk-room door. "You decent?"

There was no answer.

She opened the door and peeked inside. Mitch was stretched out in front of the fire, still in his dripping clothes, sound asleep. He looked so vulnerable. She hadn't the heart to wake him, yet she knew those wet clothes had to come off.

"Mitch. Mitch." She shook him gently.

He gave a soft sigh and smiled in his sleep.

Well, she had undressed him before.

Her fingers worked at the buttons of his shirt and touched the mat of dark hair on his chest. He muttered something—faint, inaudible.

She eased the coat from his shoulders and unbuttoned his breeches. She rolled him onto his stomach. He was limp, giving no resistance, but not helping either.

The coat came off, the breeches down as far as she could get them. She needed something dry to put under him. She looked around. How different this new camp. Plenty of room between bunks—not like the old barracks where Mitch said whenever a man wanted to turn during the night, he had to yell, "spoon!" and the whole row would turn.

Each of the bunks held a soft new buffalo robe.

426

Grabbing the two nearest, Jo spread one on the floor and rolled Mitch onto it.

She panted from her efforts to undress him. It took two more rolls and a lot of tugging before his clothes were off. His long, rangy body gleamed in the firelight. She rubbed him gently with the split flour-sack towels.

He sighed and reached for her, his eyes still closed, mouth curving. "My Jo," he murmured.

She pulled the second robe over them and settled into his arms. Her red-gold curls mingling with the dark ringlets on his broad chest. "My Jo," he whispered contentedly.

All day he slept. She climbed once from the warm covers to lay more wood, feed the animals Mitch had led into the shed, hang his clothes to dry, start a fire in the kitchen, and open a few cans for a hurried meal. Then she curled beside him again, her cheek against his shoulder.

Outside, the storm raged. Occasionally she would hear a sharp snap and crack, and a muffled roar as a tree gave way to the howling wind.

Mitch slept all day and never moved. She would have worried, but his head was cool. He was simply sleeping off utter physical exhaustion. He must have been riding through the storm day and night to get here.

Her heart overflowed with love. If only she could tell him how much he meant to her.

She raised her face to his and kissed him gently. Eyes still closed, he rolled onto his side suddenly and wrapped her in his strong arms. Beneath the surface of her skin a slight tremor began. His lips were warm, demanding. With a little cry of surprise and pleasure, she pressed herself against him, surrendering to the flames of love that filled her.

Her lips opened beneath his gentle probing. It

427

shattered all her conceptions of what a kiss could be: passionate yet tender, violent yet gentle. She was unprepared for the hot leap of desire in her loins, the sudden tightening of her—Jo had a fleeting thought that this was no time to be putting medical names to body parts. A drift of dizziness engulfed her. Her slim curves fit to his lean frame as delicious sensations flamed her veins and exploded at her nerve endings.

His breath came faster, hot and sweet against her cheek. Her heart stirred uneasily. She knew that sound. Then his mouth claimed hers again, and she gave herself to the wonder of their love. This was Mitch. She loved and wanted him as much as he loved and wanted her.

When his fingers worked at the buttons of her shirt, hers moved swiftly to help. When his mouth possessed the bare flesh of her breast, her nipples rose and rasped his palm. And when she felt his male hardness demanding entry, her fingers guided him.

She leaned back, filled with a lovely languor. *Why did no one ever tell me?* It was no wonder women were always pregnant. How could they possibly say no to something so deliciously magnificent?

"Mitch . . ." Her voice was dreamy. "Is it like this for everyone? Is it always like this?"

His smile was broad and very male, but she didn't seem to mind.

"I didn't hurt you?" he asked.

"I don't want to get clinical about it, but my hymen seemed nonexistent. Were you terribly disappointed?"

His body shook with silent laughter.

"It isn't funny. Men expect the breaking of the membrane. I had one young woman ask if I couldn't give her a vial of blood to break on the sheets. If it doesn't happen, a man thinks—"

At that, his laugh burst out, deep and thoroughly delighted. "I have no complaints," he said when he could talk again. He took her chin between his fingers and tilted her face to his. "What about you? Was it good for you?"

Jo stretched voluptuously. A smile played across her kiss-swollen lips. "Harrow heap big," she said in Manda's gutteral tones. "Stuff Jo good."

With a throaty chuckle, he gathered her close. His lips were hot but gentle.

This time, it was long, and slow, and very tender.

When she awoke, she was alone. She could hear Mitch in the kitchen, building a fire. She supposed she should go fix breakfast, but she needed time to sort things out.

She blushed poppy red as memories of the night of love flooded her mind. The things she had let him do. The things she had done. How could she ever look him in the face again?

Then sudden fright caught her breath and brought her bolt upright. She was a fallen woman! The buffalo robe settled in her lap as she looked down at herself. Firelight danced across breasts still full and swollen from Mitch's hungry kisses. Jo jerked the robe to her, covering her nakedness. I'm just like Agnes, she thought in sudden shock.

She'd had no sympathy for Agnes—the other girl had gone looking for trouble. Yet how am I different? agonized Jo. I've fallen from virtue just like Agnes. And Agnes was married and *knew* what she was missing when she took up with Templeton. I have no excuse at all. I had no conception until it happened. Oh, I've been so full of talk, she thought. So full of ideas—without the faintest notion of what it was all about. When will I ever learn?

By the time she heard Mitch returning, Jo had herself well in hand. For as long as the storm lasted, Mitch was hers and she was his. This brief time might have to last them the rest of their lives, and she was determined to cram every moment with happiness. She wouldn't tell Mitch yet, but she knew that nothing had changed—nothing except that now she was chained to him for life. She still couldn't give up her medical practice, yet in every way but name, she belonged to Mitch—and he to her. With the knowledge that she must give him up, Jo knew real pain. Worse than a physical pain, it transcended the physical and attacked the very essence of her being.

He was coming back. She brushed a telltale tear aside and donned a soft smile.

"Tell me how bad the floods were," she said when they had finished eating and she was snuggled in his arms again.

"Everything's been swept away. The Willamette Valley is covered with water and wreckage. Houses, mills, cattle. All gone. The streets of Salem had water four feet deep and a quarter of a mile wide when I came through.

"The Umpqua carried away all of lower Scotts-burg—all the mills—everything along the river. The military road's completely washed out. I'm glad Mom and Patience are safe on high ground. I only hope Willie and Eileen are all right down in Milltown."

"It must be bad down river—and Eileen's pregnant."

"Willie will take care of her and the children. But I'm sure the mill is gone. We'll have to start all over again, Jo."

"Oh, Mitch . . ."

"I came through Laughing Creek Camp. It's gone."

"Gone? What about Peavy and the others?"

"They're over at Mountain Number One. Peavy drove all the oxen up, even hauled the saw up there. If it wasn't for Peavy, I wouldn't have anything left." He rubbed his knuckles gently over her cheek. "Except you. Jo, if anything happened to you, my world would end."

She was silent, unable to meet his eyes.

"Look at me, Jo." He studied her face a long time before he spoke again: "Don't start comparing yourself to Agnes, darling. Agnes was no good. You're not even on the same river with her, much less in the same boat."

"What makes you think I'm comparing myself with Agnes?"

"I know you—right down to your determined bones and your hard, stubborn head. I know you better than you know yourself. I'm not going to let you castigate yourself for what happened last night. You're no Aggie, darlin'."

She looked up sharply. "You ought to know," she said, unable to hide the long-buried rancor.

Mitch's startled look turned to a quick grin. "How'd you find out about Aggie and me?" he demanded.

"You talked when you had a fever."

"Back on the Little Blue? Well, I'll be damned. And I suppose all this time, you thought I'd been messing around with my brother's wife? What happened between Aggie and me was *before* she took up with Willie. I kissed her a few times, that's all. After that, she was flypaper."

"I believe you. But did Willie?"

"Not for a long time. And of course, she spilled her guts before she took off with the captain of the *Musquash*. She really cut old Willie down to size. Sank the axe in good and deep. Told him all about the

431

handsome Lieutenant Templeton and the boys in Bangor." Mitch's laugh was bitter. "Oh, yes, she tarred me with the same brush. Thank God that's past history now that he has Eileen."

Jo levered herself up on one elbow and gazed at him earnestly. "I want to thank you for keeping Willie from talking about me. I should have thanked you a long time ago."

"You know I didn't mean to hurt you when I tore your shirt, don't you?"

"I've known it for a long time." She gave a rueful little laugh. "I guess I've been pretty stubborn."

He grinned at her. "How'd you get so opinionated so young?"

"I had to grow up in a hurry."

"Are you sure you're all grown up now?"

She ignored his devilish eyes. "I've been thinking, Mitch. It seems to me that there are two things that build walls between men and women: *her* sex and *his* authority."

"Let's hear three cheers for her sex." He was teasing again, but somehow she didn't mind.

They were quiet, her head resting on his broad chest, his fingers curling in her red-gold hair.

And then—right then—when she was happier than she had any right to be, a thought fell upon her like a giant fir and pinned her to the bunkroom floor. *Suppose she got pregnant.* Snakes of St. Patrick, what if she were to have a baby? She lay very still, counting the days since her last period. It would be close, but if her theory was right, she was safe.

But what if she were wrong? What if she *were* pregnant? She got a mental picture of herself making rounds—waddling about in breeches—with a distended stomach—trying to explain the medical phenomena that permitted a male physician to bear a

432

child. Suddenly she began to giggle, hiccoughy little giggles that swelled and swelled until she was unable to stop.

He shook her gently. "Shhh, darling. It's all right. It's all right."

"Oh, Mitch," she gasped at last. "How would it look for Dr. Joe Gates to come up pregnant?" Her hysterical laughter dissolved into a flood of sobs.

## 46

The deluge of rain had begun in late November. In mid-December, Jo had fled from the rising river. It was toward Christmas when the rains turned to snow as a paralyzing cold gripped the Northwest.

In Mountain Camp Three, Jo and Mitch, snow-bound now, were two children playing house. They surrendered to the winter wonderland—the stillness of the forest under tons of white fluff, branches bending beneath fairy fingers of ice, the beauty of frosty tracings on windowpanes, shadows on the snow, shifting shades of blue and gray, with light spreading slowly, riding the swells of the mountain and sifting into the hollows.

Jo yielded to physical love with all the youthful ardor of her nature. Mitch was tender and passionate by turns as he came to know each sweet curve of her body, as she had known his since those first, long-ago days on the Little Blue.

One morning, after a delightful night of love, she stood at the window, shivering. Snow-weighted branches hugged the giant trees like birds with their wings folded against the cold.

Mitch finished rebuilding the fire and came to warm her with his arms. "If you think this is cold," he said, "you should have been in Paul Bunyan's camp one year. It was so cold that when Paul poured a cup of boiling coffee it froze so fast the ice was too hot to hold."

"You're an idiot," she said, twisting to kiss the tip of his nose. "Mitch, when there was so much snow in Maine, why did you log in the winter?"

"We had to get the logs out of the woods to the river. We could do that easier in the snow. We sprinkled water on the trails until they were solid ice, then put skids under the logs and pulled them to the river with a team of horses. Then in the spring, we moved them down the river to the mill."

Mitch brushed his lips across her hair as he stared thoughtfully out the window at the world of white. "Even the Thunder will be iced solid now. I've never seen it like this in Oregon."

"Do you think Trudy and Patience are all right?"

"They're fine, worry wart!" He slapped her bare bottom. "I never saw anybody so anxious to take on the troubles of the world."

They marked the passing days on the cook-house wall, and when Christmas came, they cut a small fir and decorated it with bits of tin snipped from empty food cans. The dangling silver shapes glinted rosy red in the firelight and sent pearly flickers pirouetting across gray bunkhouse walls.

They dug their way out and cavorted in the snow, pelted each other with snowballs, and fell laughing into a snowbank where she rubbed his face with cold white fluff and he licked the flakes from her lips.

They gathered armloads of greenery to pile in the empty bunks. The room was festive with the sight and scent of fresh fir.

Mitch bagged a fat buck and they feasted on steaks and canned oysters and sauerkraut. He balked at the sauerkraut but she remained firm. "I'll not have you

435

coming down with scurvy," she said primly.

In mid-January, the snow began to melt. The cold snap dissipated as the warm, moist, ocean breezes returned and patches of brown earth winked through the yellowing snow.

Jo was pouring coffee when a distant roar brought her head up with a snap.

There it was again. A tremendous cracking boom that echoed through the forest. "What is it?"

Mitch's voice held a deep regret. "The ice is breaking on the river."

"Oh."

"When the ice begins to move, things will get worse," said Mitch. Her heart turned over as his bleak blue eyes met her. "We have to go back, Jo. They'll need us—especially you."

She nodded, unable to speak.

They cleaned the bunkroom and cook house, obliterating all signs of their brief idyll.

Then they made love one last time before the fire.

"You aren't going to marry me, are you, Jo?" His deep voice was laced with sad resignation. "You still aren't ready to accept the fact that you're a woman."

She shook her bright head and her lips quivered. "You said it yourself: There'll be injured people down there who need me. And there's Nettie Hall's baby due in a few weeks. And Winlon Hogue—and the Cruikshank twins. I can't turn my back on them."

"How does your being a woman affect your patients?"

"If I went back in a dress, there's no way they would accept me now. You know that, Mitch. They'd laugh me out of town."

"There are some things you can change, Jo, and some you can't. You've got to distinguish between the two. You'll never be happy if you keep on knocking

436

your head against things you can't change."

Frustration dredged a well of anger. "Then stop trying to change my mind!" she snapped at him. She couldn't do what he wanted. Why didn't he see that?

"Your mind *is* changeable, Jo. Your sex *isn't*. That's what you've got to realize. You're a woman. *That's* what can't be changed."

"I'm only trying to help people, Mitch. I'm not trying to alter my sex."

"The hell you're not! Parading around in breeches and pulling your voice down to your belly won't make a man out of you. You're all woman, Jo, and the sooner you face that fact, the sooner we can get on with our lives."

"If I tried to live the way you want me to, pretty soon I wouldn't suit you at all. Don't you see, Mitch, you're in love with me because of what I am. Just as I love you for what you are. If I change into what you think you want, you won't want me any longer."

Their eyes locked, soft misery in hers, sudden hard enmity in his.

"I can't help it," she cried. "As long as women doctors aren't accepted, I'll have to be a man and that's that. I'm sorry, Mitch, but I'm a doctor. First, last, and always, I'm a doctor."

# 47

It was January 20th, 1862, when the ice began to break. It went on for days. By then, Glad Hand had been without mail, without communication with the outside world, for over seven weeks.

Jo's cabin was gone, the grove of trees that had surrounded it washed away. She based herself with Trudy and Mitch, but was seldom at home. Pneumonia, pleurisy, and flu rode the valley, and Jo rode with them.

Waste lay like the sentence of God on the land. From the sparsely settled upper reaches of the Thunder came dozens of dead men and hundreds of cattle, washed down by the spring floods.

Mitch came home from Milltown with news that would have been disastrous at any other time, but which was miraculous in the midst of such total destruction: Willie and his new family were fine; Willie had managed to haul one of the circular saws and other equipment to safety before the floods struck. Thanks to Willie and Peavy, Harrow Lumber was not completely wiped out as were many other firms.

At Oregon City, Milling and Lumber Company had lost their hoisting works and the mills. The foundry had washed away, Linn City was swept clean, Canemah laid waste. There were no homes left in Champoeg.

On and on went the recital of disaster and devastation. Miners, camping at the base of the Blue Mountains and waiting for the spring opening of the John Day Mines, had been murdered and eaten by Snake Indians.

Portland was flooded and several feet of water flowed through the streets of The Dallas.

Mitch was everywhere that spring, trying to hire timber beasts, overseeing reconstruction of Laughing Creek Camp, ordering new machinery. Because of the war back East, it wasn't easy to get equipment or supplies these days. Often, when Jo came home late from a call, Mitch's office lamp cast a yellow glow onto the wide porch, and she could see his dark head bent over his desk. Working—always working.

He grew thin and pale and irritable. Sometimes she would hear his voice raised in anger—at his mother— at the half-breed servants. It was so out of character. Jo ached to comfort him, smooth his furrowed brow and see his tense muscles relax, but she daren't approach him lest she give in and say she would marry him. Or worse still—lest he turn on her as well.

One night, very late, when blackness claimed the house, she climbed the front steps to find him waiting on the porch.

"Mitch?" She couldn't hide the pleasure in her voice.

His arms enfolded her with the softness of a spring breeze. "Just let me hold you a moment, Jo. Just let me hold you." His tall frame trembled, then relaxed as the tension drained from him. He took her chin in his fingers and tilted her face to his. His mouth came hungry on hers, a swift kiss that swept the depths of her being. Then he groaned and pulled away. Before she could stop him, he was gone.

She stood alone on the porch for a long time, wishing, wanting, willing him to come back. But he did not.

In June, 1862, three companies from southern Oregon reported to the First Cavalry at Fort Walla Walla. Mitch went with them. He called Jo into his office before he left and handed her a package. "I hope you'll be wearing this when I come back," he said. Then he was gone for good, and Jo's heart with him.

Folding back the tissue, she lifted out a pale-green dress and matching slippers.

With the war, new clothes were almost impossible to obtain. She wondered how long ago Mitch had purchased this sweet cotton gown and whether she would ever be able to wear it for him.

Trudy took over the Harrow Company ledgers. She and Willie tried to keep the lumber business afloat, but neither was particularly good at the job. The source of their lumber began to dry up when Trudy was unable to contract for more stumpage. Willie urged that they cut their strip of timber on Glad Hand Mountain, but Trudy refused. "Mitch wouldn't like it if he came back to a bare mountain," she said firmly.

Jo dragged herself through busy days, wondering how she could live until Mitch came home—and how she could live after he came home.

Her house, swept away in the flood, was not rebuilt. Instead, she had moved into the big Harrow house on Glad Hand Mountain with Trudy and Patience, and they waited out the war together. Fond as she was of the other women, Jo hated not having an office of her own. Somehow, not having an office was a constant reminder that she was not a real doctor—but there was nothing she could do to alter the situation.

Living in such close proximity, it was not long before Patience discovered Jo's secret identity. She accepted Jo's being a woman with no show of surprise and very little interest. Patience wasn't interested in much these days—only in letters from Sam who was with the Army at the Potomac somewhere in Virginia. She wrote him everyday.

Jo had no letters from Mitch. All she had were memories.

Thinking back over their all too brief time in Mountain Camp Three, Jo carried her morning coffee into Mitch's office one winter morning and closed the door behind her.

She lifted her watch from her vest pocket—almost an hour until time to open the office.

She sipped her coffee thoughtfully, wishing she could write Mitch, but fearing it would make matters worse. What could she say that hadn't already been said?

The Harrow Lumber calendar on the wall said December 13, 1862—just one year from that long-ago morning when she had opened the barracks door and found him writing a note.

Standing at the office window, she gazed across the lake. It was a bright, crisp day, nothing like that day a year ago when the river had rampaged, wild and out of control.

Glad Hand, on high ground, had largely escaped the destruction that had occurred throughout the state. Now it nodded sleepily in the sun. Jo couldn't see the carving from this side of the lake, but she knew the message on Glad Hand Mountain, behind the house, was still there. J—I'm Waiting.

Only Mitch wasn't waiting anymore. Now she was waiting—like most of the other women in the valley. The only difference was, no one knew that she was a woman, concerned with a handsome cavalry captain off guarding roads, escorting trains, and fighting Indians—no one except Trudy, and now Patience. It was a steady ache in Jo's heart that she couldn't be a woman and be proud of it.

She turned from the window, annoyed with her brief

441

relapse into regret. It wasn't like her to get all mushy and start remembering the past.

But how did you hide from memories so real that they were the very beat of your heart, the very breath in your breast? Painful as her memories were, they were all she had left.

She was nineteen, an old maid, with an ache in her that refused to go away. Doctoring, which she had been certain would fill her life and fulfill her dreams, was not all it had promised. Somehow, it wasn't enough. There was a hole in her life now where femininity ought to be. Swaggering about like a man had worn more than thin, and she couldn't help but wonder how long she could expect to be looked upon as the beardless boy wonder.

Once, in St. Louis, she had worn a false beard in a play, but she wasn't about to add a beard to her bag of tricks here in Oregon. To tell the truth, she was fed up with the whole masquerade. She wanted to marry Mitch and bear his children.

Manda was probably a mother by now. Even Anne, poor sweet, had known the brief joy of carrying a child within her. Was Jo never to know that joy? Never to bear Mitch's children?

In sudden rebellion, she plunked her cup on the edge of the desk and ran from the office.

In her room at the back of the sprawling log house, Jo pulled out the green dress Mitch had given her when he went away. Her fingers tore impatiently at the buttons of her shirt and pantaloons, and fumbled in her rush to remove the gauze binding she was now forced to wear all the time.

Her breasts sprang free, full and firm above a narrow waist and rounded hips. Hips made for childbearing, Jo thought proudly. Breasts made for nursing—not for hiding behind the trappings of a man's garb.

The dress fit as though it had been made especially

for her. How was Mitch so unerringly right about everything? "Oh, darling," sang her heart as she buttoned the bodice across her unbound breasts. "Come home to me soon. Come home to me soon."

It wouldn't be easy, facing her patients as a woman— not after their thinking she was a man for two years— but she cast that worry aside. It wouldn't be easy, but it was right.

She coaxed her hair into a soft feminine frame. Now that I'm a woman, she thought happily, I can have my ears pierced like Mama. She looked in the mirror. A steady-eyed woman looked back: an oval-faced woman with full, tremulous lips, a pugnacious chin, and apricot-pink cheeks. How had anybody ever believed she was a man?

Her dress swished softly as she walked down the hall. With her hand on the office doorknob, she heard footsteps and paused.

"I believe you're a little early," said Mrs. Harrow coming up behind her. "Doctor's office hours don't start until eight."

Jo turned.

The older woman started in surprise. Her mouth dropped. "Jo?" A slow, disbelieving smile suffused her face. "Jo? Oh, my dear!" She came forward then, tears in her eyes, her arms outstretched. "You don't know how I've prayed for this day!"

Jo returned her hug, then backed away to pirouette. "How do I look?"

"Beautiful. Oh, my dear, you are beautiful. Oh, Mitch will be so happy—" She broke off abruptly and the color drained from her face. "But what about your patients? What will they say? Merciful heavens, you're going to be the scandal of all time!"

\*　　　\*　　　\*

443

Trudy Harrow's prediction was not far wrong.

There were snickers behind Jo's back, and even some to her face. The men of the town chose to look upon her as a loose woman who had been getting her perverted kicks at their expense.

Zeke Redfield summed up their feelings pretty well when he said, "She's seen all there is to see—ain't no point in treatin' *her* like a lady."

The women of the town, however—with the exception of one or two—rallied around her with the determination of salmon fighting their way upstream to lay eggs.

"If my Ken says one word about you," declared Mabel Cutter who, thanks to Jo's female cap, had not been pregnant for almost three years, "I'll lock him out of the house."

"I been uneasy all this time," Ida Cruikshank confided, "lettin' a strange man in my bedroom even though you were a doctor. I'm right pleased I don't have to worry about that no more."

The biggest bonus of Jo's new status came from three of the ladies who had refused to even discuss a female cap when they thought Jo was a man. Now they came to her asking to be fitted. She floated on a cloud of happiness and wondered why she had masqueraded so long.

The biggest surprise came from the least expected quarter. After the harsh reception she had received from the men of Glad Hand, Jo had postponed a trip to Creek Camp, thinking the loggers' crude ridicule might be more than she could take. Then, in the company store one day, while Jo was picking over a few new calicos, Peavy trudged up behind her.

"That you, Dr. Jo?" he asked.

She turned. He looked at her dress and his red-rimmed eyes beamed approval, but no surprise.

She laughed into his weather-beaten face. "So you knew all along."

He turned his head and spat a long brown stream onto the planked floor. "Pshaw," he said, "ain't no man on earth would make such a to-do over soap and water as you do. You *had* to be a woman."

She asked Peavy to break the news to the loggers, and waited another week before venturing into their camp.

Then came the surprise of Jo's young life. The timber beasts, the roughest, toughest hell-raisers around, had turned into shy pussycats. In the face of the slim young woman who rode sidesaddle over the mountain with her doctor bag tied to Tess's horn, they turned red, scuffed their feet in the dust, and said, "yes, ma'am" and "no, ma'am," like polite little boys meeting the schoolmarm for the first time.

They were so shy, it embarrassed Jo more to treat them now than it had when they were so outspokenly crude; but she was touched by their acceptance and felt she had finally arrived.

## 48

Mitch didn't come home that Christmas, but he wrote. It was the first letter she had ever received from him. She took it to her room where she could be alone to read it.

"My Jo—I know last Christmas is as fresh in your memory as it is in mine. Without you, my days are empty, my nights a living hell. Dammit, woman, a man can't wait forever. My only solace is the certainty that your days and nights are almost as miserable." He had made no reference to the fact that she was wearing dresses these days. Perhaps Trudy hadn't written him about that? Jo smiled as she folded the note between the pages of the *Deerslayer* and placed it on her bedside table. She was glad Trudy hadn't told him. What a surprise when he came home and found her wearing the pretty dress he had bought.

She wrote a brief answer, giving the local news and cautioning him to be careful. Her heart overflowed with unexpressed love and the delicious knowledge of how her surprise would delight him when he came home.

There was no Christmas letter from Sam. There had been no letter for three weeks now. Patience crept about the house, a small self-effacing ghost.

News of the disastrous battle at Fredricksburg

reached them two days after Christmas. Eleven hundred Union soldiers dead, over nine thousand wounded, and more than three thousand missing. The *Statesman* printed the names of the Oregon men. Sam was among the dead. Jo expected Patience to sink even deeper into white-faced apathy, but she surprised them by reading the list with quiet acceptance. It was as though she had known it was coming and had lived in dread; now it was here, and it was almost a relief.

Despite Trudy's pleas, the raven-haired girl packed to move back into her own white clapboard house. "Sam built it for me. It's where I belong," she said.

Trudy retired quietly to her room and was not seen for several hours.

Eighteen sixty-three began with the usual foggy mists and mild ocean breezes. A small crew worked Laughing Creek Camp again, and Willie had one circular saw back in operation at the rebuilt mill. On February 4th Eileen gave birth to a fine bouncing boy. Having miscarried their first child during the flood, she was slow to recover after Ollie's birth. Willie dropped twenty pounds worrying about her.

A week later a note arrived from Mitch. "I've had the flu," he wrote, "but am fine now, so don't believe any rumors you may hear. I'm as mean as ever—and as lonely."

Jo knitted him a muffler and begged him to take care of himself.

She was still boarding with Trudy Harrow. With valley population tripled, her practice had grown until she spent most of her time riding from one house call to another. Without an office, she worried about her standing in the community and began, again, to feel as if she weren't a real doctor—which she wasn't.

447

The only improvement over her former status was that now she had a choice of clothing. Having masqueraded so long as a man, it was natural for her to tie back her hair and wear fringed buckskins when she rode into the country on a house call. Dresses and flowing curls were reserved for town and evenings. Now that she was recognized as a woman, she enjoyed the freedom of men's attire whenever it suited her—and even the men of the town were beginning to accept her in her changeable garb.

Harrow Lumber was barely hanging on, Trudy and Willie managing the best they could until Mitch came home again. With all the rebuilding after the floods, the company should have been booming, but Trudy couldn't buy stumpage, couldn't hire men nor keep those they had. Jo could tell that the older woman was more worried about the family business than she admitted.

Jo had not signed a new contract with Harrow Lumber because she knew they couldn't afford it. Trudy would have ordered Jo's office rebuilt despite their money shortage, but Jo couldn't allow that. She continued to treat the loggers, but on individual terms rather than contractual.

Sam's last letter, written just before his death, arrived in late February. It had been mailed by an unknown soldier who had been with him at the Battle of Fredricksburg. The soldier had inserted a note of his own. Patience read both letters silently, then passed one over to be read by the waiting women.

*Mam,* the soldier had written. *The lootenant dide at Frederksberg. he saved me life and ast me to male this to ye. he was a brav man. he talked abot ye afor he dide and sed he was sory he left ye. he dint sufer none.* The note was unsigned.

Patience folded the two letters and left the room. As

they heard the front door close behind her, Jo began to rise, but Trudy shook her head. "She needs to be alone. I'll go to her later." Then Trudy buried her head in her arms and gave vent to her own grief. Jo's heart ached.

What if Mitch didn't come home, she thought. Then she was aghast at her own selfishness in light of Sam's death, but she couldn't help herself. Oh, God, don't let anything happen to Mitch, she prayed.

Absorbed with her own worries, several weeks passed before Jo realized how often she was running into Patience these days. When Jo stopped at the company store, there was Patience, deep in conversation with Tadlock, the manager. When Jo made a house call at Gall's, there was Patience's buggy just coming down the lane.

Mr. Gall, who owned the dry goods store in Glad Hand, had suffered a mild heart attack. Jo left a bottle of tincture of foxglove leaves, with instructions, and told Mrs. Gall to keep her husband in bed. Under no circumstances was he to go down to the store to work. Mrs. Gall assured her he wouldn't.

That afternoon, when Jo was summoned to set a broken arm for the Yarnel girl, she noticed Patience sitting on the front porch next door, talking with Mr. Birdseye, the chairman of the new schoolboard.

The following Sunday Patience invited Jo to dinner. The meal was almost finished when Jo remembered the other woman's strange excursions. "I'm beginning to think you're running for political office," she teased. "Everywhere I go these days, there you are."

"I'm hunting for work," said Patience simply.

"Work? Why on earth do you want to do that?"

"I'm nothing but a drain on the company, Jo. It wasn't so bad before I knew for sure about Sam, but it's inexcusable for me to sit here and do nothing when the company's in such bad financial shape."

"Mitch wouldn't want you to go to work, you know that."

"Willie and Mother Harrow are barely making ends meet, Jo. They don't need me and my house to keep up, too." She looked around the tastefully furnished room and her eyes were bleak. "If I don't find work soon, I'll have to sell this house."

"Oh, Patience, you can't give up your house."

"I don't want to, but I've no choice. I've scoured the valley, looking for work. I thought Mrs. Gall would hire me after her husband had a heart attack, but she's just been waiting for a chance to get her brother in there. Then Mr. Birdseye said if I had just come sooner, they could have hired me as the new schoolteacher, but they'd already accepted a widow lady from down San Francisco way."

Her heart aching for her friend, Jo gazed around the tastefully furnished room. It was really a lovely house—big and light, with two stories in the front, sloping to one story in the back. Downstairs were parlor, dining room, kitchen, and a large back porch. Upstairs were three good-sized bedrooms. Oh, what she wouldn't give for a house like this. This—the dining room—this could be the office, she thought.

Her heart gave a sudden jump. Why, it could—it really could—

"Patience—Patience, why don't we join forces? I need an office of my own and you need to put food on your table. If there's one thing I have to offer, it's food," Jo said eagerly, remembering the moist yellow cake and the sack of potatoes she had received in payment just yesterday.

Patience's eyes lighted with sudden hope. "You mean—make your office in my house instead of over at Mother Harrow's? And you'd pay rent? Jo, that sounds like heaven. We could turn the parlor into a waiting

450

room and make the dining room into the office. You could move into one of the bedrooms upstairs. And I could be your nurse." Patience looked alert and interested for the first time since Sam had gone off to war.

Jo was astonished. That last part had never occurred to her. But she remembered how steady Patience had been when she helped with Clay Williams back on the trail. Why not try her as a nurse? Hadn't Mama always said not to get hemmed in by set ways of doing things just because that's the way they'd always been done?

Jo studied the other girl closely. "Are you sure? Are you ready to make such a big decision?"

"I'm ready. I've cried for almost two years now, waiting for this news about Sam, knowing it was coming. Now he's gone and I've got to earn a living, that's all. Harrow Lumber is struggling just to stay alive. It doesn't need me hanging onto it." Her gray eyes were steady. "I think we could really do it, Jo."

"I don't get much in cash, you know. I'll have to pay you with whatever I have. Will it bother you to be paid with a chicken or a basket of pears?"

Patience laughed. "Not if it won't bother you to have a piano in the kitchen. There isn't space for it anywhere but the parlor or the kitchen, and if the parlor becomes a waiting room . . ."

"I can't think of anything I'd like better. We'll have to eat in the kitchen, too—we can have music with our meals." Jo laughed a happy laugh. "Oh, Patience, I don't want to take advantage of you at a weak moment, but it sounds wonderful to me."

"Don't worry about taking advantage. My weak moments are all behind me."

There being no men available, Jo and Patience moved the furniture. Trudy was pressed into service to do a bit of sewing, and came up with a fine pad for the dining room table. The pad, stuffed with straw and covered with oilcloth, turned the long pine trestle into a very credible examination table. A rosewood desk came from the spare bedroom upstairs. A corner cupboard easily converted to a medicine cabinet. A small washstand with bowl and pitcher, plus two dining room chairs, completed the office furnishings. Jo thought it was beautiful.

The parlor, with the piano removed, made an excellent waiting room—and Patience, Jo soon discovered, an excellent nurse. She lived up to her name, quickly shed her gloomy quiet and reverted to the cheerful, accommodating girl Jo had first met in Leavenworth.

The white clapboard house soon came to be known as Dr. Jo's, and Patience became Nurse Harrow.

The war news, meanwhile, was not good. Lee had carried the war North. In mid-June, he crossed the Potomac and neared Chambersburg, Pennsylvania.

Lincoln sent out a frantic call for 100,000 volunteers for six months' service. While Vicksburg was surrendering, the bloody Battle of Gettysburg was drawing to a close. Jo thought she couldn't stand to hear of more deaths, more killing, more maiming of strong young men. When would it ever end?

She tried to bury herself in her work and ignore the war, but it intruded despite her good intentions. Chickamauga. Lookout Mountain. Missionary Ridge. The names sounded in her sleep with the finality of a church bell tolling a funeral. Battle of the Wilderness. Cold Harbor. Petersburg.

In the summer of '64, men who had gone East to fight began to straggle home again. Sherman was camped outside Atlanta, and it looked as if the war would soon be over.

Ed King wore a patch over his left eye socket when he

came riding home to Glad Hand; Tom Gall had lost an ear; Mr. Cruikshank, the carpenter, was missing two fingers on his right hand; Orville, one of the Yarnel boys, cried all the time. Tom's ear was infected. For him, Jo concocted a formula of enchinacea, capsicum, and the roots of pokeweed and goldenseal buttercups. Ed had dysentery, which she dosed with small amounts of Dover's Powders. To all their wives and mothers, Dr. Jo issued strict delousing instructions.

But a new illness came with the returning warriors: the soldiers' disease. Overuse of painkilling morphine by army doctors had left the men with a heartbreaking dependency on the drug. Jo put a lock on her own drug cabinet. She had no cure for the soldiers' disease except a prompt withdrawal.

It was a Sunday afternoon in late July. Mitch had been gone for over two years now, and for a year and a half Jo had been wearing women's clothing. The townsmen had long ago ceased to resent her masquerade. She wondered if even Mitch would care now. He had been home only once during the past two years, when she was upriver on a breech-birth delivery, and she had not seen him at all. Trudy told her he had aged and looked very tired. "Did you tell him I'm wearing dresses now?" Jo asked.

The older woman smiled. "No, my dear, I left that to be your surprise."

"He's probably heard about it anyhow, don't you think? News like that always spreads like a prairie fire. He's sure to know before he comes home."

"Maybe not," Trudy replied slowly. "That was about the time he had the flu, remember? The winter of '63. If he didn't hear it then, he probably won't. The gossip has all died down now—and he's too proud to ask for news of you."

"Oh, Trudy, I do hope you're right." Jo flushed. "I want to watch his face when he sees me in a dress."

But lately Mitch's brief notes had changed. He no longer mentioned his emotions, but gave impersonal camp news, spoke of the winding down of the war, of his need to see the valley again.

*Oh, Mitch,* Joe wrote in her journal, *was I wrong not to tell you that I am waiting? Was I selfish to want to surprise you?* But in her heart, she knew he hadn't really changed. After all, he had promised.

Closing her journal, she leaned back and looked around proudly. She had so much to show him now. They had come a long way, she and Patience. The office looked much the same as it had that first day, but Jo's practice had grown steadily this past year.

Patience was even talking about enclosing the back porch to make a hospital ward, and had already given Jo orders that if Mr. Cruikshank's family got sick again, under no circumstances was Jo to accept another six jars of Ida Cruikshank's apple jelly as payment. "This time, we need her husband's carpentry services," Patience had said.

Now Jo crossed to the window and looked out. The curling mist had burned off early, and it was a fine summer day. She glanced across the lake to the knoll where her log cabin had once stood. It was there that Mitch had offered her a contract—there that he had held her and kissed her and told her she had to choose between being a woman or a fake. Now she had chosen—she had chosen to be a woman, but he wasn't here to see.

The unfulfilled holes in her life were immense these days. She longed for Mitch. And she longed for a diploma to hang on her wall—a piece of paper that proclaimed her a bona fide physician. Sooner or later someone was going to question her—demand to know why Doc Adams hadn't ever sent her another certificate. If hers had been lost on the *Tropic* as she claimed, it would have been a simple matter for him to send her another. Sooner or later, one of the town's scoffing men would begin to ask questions.

Another nagging emptiness in Jo's life was the fact that she couldn't see Mitch's carving from this side of the lake. She needed the reassurance of that message. Often she rode down River Road just so she could look up at the carving and be comforted.

A knock at the door roused her from her reverie. "Come," she called.

Peavy's spare frame filled the doorway. She hadn't seen him in weeks. "I heerd tell you're thinkin' of openin' a hospital," he said without preamble. "So I'm movin' back to town. Ain't no sense in two females trying to run a hospital alone. I'll bunk out in the barn." He punctuated his edict with a strong stream of tobacco juice that hit the hall spitoon with unerring accuracy. "They ain't enough work at camp to warrant a bull whacker now anyhow. No need for a bull whacker when they ain't no fallers."

Jo never would have believed how much she had missed having a man around the house. Within the next few weeks, a late garden was planted in the backyard, the bushes were trimmed, the back porch cleared, and Willie had sent a small load of finished lumber up from the mill so the back porch could be enclosed to build a ward.

The new ward filled rapidly, and Jo soon realized that if they could enlarge even more, they would have a real hospital and could draw patients from miles around. What they needed was a whole new wing!

Nights, when there were no emergencies, Jo and Patience sat around the kitchen table, discussing

455

further expansion, pouring over supply-house catalogs, choosing what they would like to have and what they could afford—and wondering if they would be able to get even half of what they needed before the war ended.

"A water closet for each ward," suggested Jo, remembering the opulence of Quimby House. "And lots of windows. We're going to have bushels of fresh air and sunshine in our little hospital."

"You'll make it so nice people will be coming for vacations instead of treatment," laughed Patience.

"Rationing fresh air in a hospital would be like Noah rationing water," declared Jo. "We're not going to be that foolish."

Through the early fall, the new twenty-bed wing took shape. With the war grinding to a halt, the North was eager to get back to business as usual, and Jo found it surprisingly easy to obtain the necessary supplies.

At Trudy's suggestion, Jo had officially purchased Patience's house. The payments were small and erratic, but the white clapboard house now wore an official sign proclaiming it Glad Hand Hospital. The big, official opening was only a month away.

One drawback to the new venture now loomed large in Jo's mind: Everything was "official" but her. She had no claim to the title of doctor. It was a steady worry now, a cloud she carried with her wherever she went. Every other drawback had been met and conquered—but not this one. How could she hope to own and run a hospital when she didn't even have a medical license? A slow resentment toward Doc Adams grew within her. He could have given her a certificate attesting to her apprenticeship. If he had wanted to, he would have.

Jo knew that medical schools would be springing up everywhere as soon as the war was over. Meantime, a man could still earn his certificate by reading with an established doctor. A man could—but not a woman.

"I did everything they do," she raged at her bedroom walls. "I did every bit as much as Doc Adams did to earn his certificate. The only reason I don't have one is because I'm a woman."

The more she thought about it, the more certain she became that if she hadn't gotten into trouble with Karl Schmidt and been forced to run away in the middle of the night, Doc eventually would have given her a certificate.

In a fit of unreasoning frustration, she sat down one afternoon and opened her heart in a long letter to Meg.

*I feel cheated,* she wrote. *Stripped of my natural pride in my accomplishments. Here we are, about to open our new twenty-bed wing, and the doctor doesn't even have a certificate.*

As the new ward took shape, Jo became almost frantic over her lack of a license. Her only hope had rested with Doc Adams, and she had blown that when she fitted Karl Schmidt's wife with a female cap. She had condemned herself to practice without certification—and now her conscience bothered her until she knew no peace. It was as if she had besmirched her promise with mud.

"How come you ain't got a degree hangin' on the wall like other doctors?" Zeke Redfield demanded one day.

Here it comes, she thought. The questions have finally begun. She had always known it would happen sooner or later. "My certificate went down with my luggage on the Missouri River," she replied, her heart drumming wildly.

"That so? Where'd you go to school anyhow, Doc?"

"I apprenticed under Dr. Archibald Adams in St. Louis."

"That so? He know you were a woman or were you paradin' around in pants in them days, too?"

457

"He knew I was a woman. Open your mouth, Zeke, and say 'Aaaah.'"

After he left, Jo sat for a long time, staring at the banjo clock on the wall where her certificate should be. This was the beginning of the end, she thought.

With bottomless regret, Jo accepted defeat. Her heart broke with the realization that she must not only give up her dream, she must give up the entire hospital. She couldn't open the hospital now—not without that one all-important piece of parchment.

She had trouble gathering nerve to tell Patience of her decision. It had to be done, but she kept postponing it.

The longer she hedged, the closer it came to opening day.

It was while she was in such a furor that Meg's reply to Jo's letter arrived. It was a large brown envelope, and the first thing that fell out was a beautifully hand-lettered medical certificate made out in the name of Dr. Jody Gates. What on earth?

Jo's fingers trembled as she picked it up. It was so beautiful! *Kansas Medical Society—Dr. Jody Gates—* She unfolded Meg's letter and read quickly, phrases jumping at her like magic lanterns of hope: . . . *couldn't manage a Missouri license for you . . . old friend in Kansas . . . you're capable . . . you deserve . . . no one will ever know . . . it won't hurt anyone and that's all that matters.*

Jo's heart lurched drunkenly as she stared at the parchment—so professional!

Oh, Meg, wonderful Meg. And she was right. It wouldn't hurt anyone. It would help.

All Jo had to do was hang this certificate on the wall and Zeke Redfield's questions would be silenced forever.

It was an omen. Like God speaking to her, telling her

458

this was the right thing to do.

Then the unwelcome, niggling voice began in her ear. "Two wrongs make a right?" it asked. "That's not a very Godlike message."

Jo ignored the pesky voice. As Meg said, as long as Jo wasn't hurting anyone, how could it be wrong?

Of course, it would be better if Doc Adams would send her the certificate she had earned. "And I did earn it," she muttered rebelliously. "I worked myself bowlegged for almost two years!"

She looked longingly at Meg's parchment. Beautiful as it was, it was still a phony.

I'll give Doc Adams one more chance to send me a certificate, she thought. He can still do it if he wants. Tonight I'll write Doc and explain that in spite of his prejudice against women doctors, I *deserve* a certificate. Then, if he still won't send me one—then I'll hang Meg's certificate and open the hospital with a clear conscience. As Meg says, I earned it.

Between patients, that day, Jo pulled the certificate out of the drawer and ran her fingers over the lettering. Dr. Jody Gates. Oh, wasn't it grand looking! Wouldn't she be proud to hang it on the hospital wall!

Eager to write Doc's letter, she bade Patience good night immediately after dinner.

She donned her prettiest frilly nightgown. It helped remind her that she was a woman and made her feel closer to Mitch. Oh, wouldn't he be proud when he came home and found her wearing dresses, with a real license on the wall, in charge of a beautiful hospital. He had always said she could be a woman and a doctor at the same time. Why hadn't she listened?

As she sat at the desk, pen in hand, a picture of Doc flitted through her mind—Doc as she had seen him that first time, when he thought she was a hard little hooker who had gotten herself pregnant—the way he had

459

laughed when he found out she was just a stand-in for Anne.

Anne.

Jo leaned back in her chair and let memories wash over her. For years she had closed those memories—believing, as Mitch had said, that "yesterday held no mortgage on today." Now she took her dear friend from the niche in her mind and examined that long-ago night when Anne had pleaded with her to abort the baby.

If I had done as she asked, thought Jo, she'd be alive today. I was wrong. Wrong to refuse. Wrong to set myself up as the final arbitrator over what should have been Anne's decision.

But you didn't do *that,* her other voice intruded. You set what was right and wrong for you, not for Anne.

"But Anne was raped," Jo cried aloud. "Anne was raped and she came to me for help—pleaded with me to help her. And I turned her down."

What was it Jo had whispered as her mother lay dying that day so long ago? "I'm going to look for a way so that women don't have to accept all the babies God sends," she had promised. "And if I find a way, that will mean He's put it there for me to find, won't it?"

God had provided the means to procreate, Jo thought, but He had left the final decision to the individual. A woman might not have the right in today's society to refuse her husband's demands, but she still had a choice. A woman could defy her father and not marry. All over the West, women were beginning to make their own living, without husbands, on their own. So a woman didn't *have* to marry. She didn't *have* to copulate. And if she chose to marry and to copulate, Jo reasoned, then she still should have the right to choose whether or not to produce children. If a man could refuse to use a condom, a woman had the

460

right to use a female cap, whether her husband approved or not. After all, it was *her* body.

Jo believed, with all her being, in family limitation. Now she faced the question that she had thrust aside so many years before. *Was abortion an acceptable form of family limitation?* It was. At least in Anne's case it was. Jo knew that now. She could hear her mother's voice: "Just because something has always been done a certain way, darling, that doesn't necessarily make it the right way."

Anne's freedom to choose had been violated. With sudden pain, Jo realized that it had been within her province to restore Anne's freedom of choice—and she had refused. She wouldn't have compromised her own position to have performed that one abortion. Saving Anne from an unwanted child and the possibility of its being deformed—that wouldn't have set a precedent and forced Jo into the abortionist mold.

I was wrong. In my stubborn certainty, I could not see—

Jo did not cry. She accepted her guilt, but she did not cry. As Mitch said, she couldn't change what she had done.

"Anne, my friend," whispered Jo, "wherever you are—forgive me."

It was a long time before she picked up her pen once more.

*Dear Doc*— Again her mind flooded with memories: how Doc had sometimes flared with anger because she insisted on washing her hands and taking his coats home to launder. Recently, since Sally's death, he and Jo were corresponding again, and Doc had written to say that he was coming around to her way of thinking. *I used to think you were crazy,* he had written. *Now I'm not so sure.*

She remembered the first time she had watched him

461

set a compound fracture. She had been so fascinated by the bone sticking through the flesh, and by the efficiency of his big hands, that she forgot to hold the flailing patient until his good leg had flung up and kicked her in the stomach.

*Dear Doc—*

How forbearing he had been. Especially when he found out she had been preaching abstinence and onanism to his patients. Oh, he had roared and carried on, but nothing like he might have done if he had ever found out about the female cap.

Now, since Sally's death, he had mellowed. Now she could tell him about the cap. And she would, right now, tonight.

*Dear Doc—I have been thinking long and hard about the fact that, after all these years, I still have no certificate to show that I ever studied medicine under a competent doctor. I realize that you teach at Dutton and that, as such, you must uphold the conception of university diplomas. However—* On and on she wrote, explaining her beliefs, telling him of her medical victories—and her failures—confessing about the female cap and giving brief facts on its success in family limitation.

*The cap isn't the final answer, of course,* she wrote. *It has even failed on three occasions that I know of, but it's better than nothing, and I'm sure I'm on the right track. I am beginning now to think that the ultimate answer may lie in the chemicals themselves.*

Most of all, through the whole letter, Jo set forth her claim to a medical certificate that would enable her to open the hospital without a cloud of incompleteness and dishonesty hanging over her.

At last it was done. If he didn't send a certificate now, it wouldn't be for lack of effort on her part. If he didn't send it, she could hang Meg's beautiful parchment with a clear conscience.

Jo sat back in her chair and stared at the ceiling. She lifted her hand to massage the back of her neck. It had been a long day.

Her hand slid along the front of her nightgown, and her elbow rested on the desk. Out of nowhere, Mitch's eyes appeared before her, so blue, so clear, so penetrating. "If you're true to yourself, Jo, that's all that matters," he had told her once. Suddenly she was caught in an emotion she could not name.

She stared at the letter she had just written, and her eyes lifted to Meg's elaborately scrolled certificate. *Meg's* certificate, she thought. Not *my* certificate. Nothing *I* earned through my own efforts.

She couldn't believe she had actually considered hanging that fake on her office wall. She had set out to be a proper physician, not some quack with a ten-dollar degree by mail.

She couldn't do it. No matter how much she wanted to, she couldn't hang Meg's phony piece of parchment.

Jo rubbed her fingertips across the lovely script. Then tore it in half. Then in half again. And again and again until it was reduced to shreds to match her fractured dreams.

Finally she picked up the letter she had written Doc. Tossing it into the wastebasket with the torn certificate, she once more took up her pen.

*Dear Doc,* she wrote. *I am giving up medicine temporarily and going back East in the hope of finding some way to obtain a real diploma. It will be a long haul, but apparently it's the only way I can fulfill my life's dream. By the time I have enough education to qualify for medical school, perhaps they will have relaxed their prejudices against women. It is the only solution I can see, and it will make me sleep better at night.*

*Now, about my situation here— As you know, we are preparing to open a small hospital. I remember that you dreamed of having a hospital of your own someday, and since I will not be here . . .*

With breaking heart, she wrote, in depth, about their plans. In every line, her love for the new hospital shone through.

There was no doubt in her mind that Doc would accept what she offered him—too frequently he had talked of his own buried desires, Jo's little hospital filled his dreams to the last crossed t and dotted i. Her one stipulation was that as long as Patience wanted to remain as head nurse, her position be secure.

Signing the letter that disposed of her practice and her hospital, Jo sealed it and put it on the table by the front door so Patience would take it with the other mail early in the morning.

She would leave Glad Hand and go back East to study.

She stepped onto the porch and looked up. The stars were icy tears in the night sky. Oh, Mitch, cried her heart.

She had burned her bridges. She had done what was right, but somehow, there was no solace in being right. She had faced the truth squarely. But it was no comfort.

Jo crept into bed and pulled the covers over her bright hair. Hiding her head hadn't helped in Liverpool; it didn't help now.

She cried.

## 49

"Lots of fluids, bed rest, and keep him warm—" The same old panacea. What else was there? Jo had discovered that many of the accepted cures were as foolish as the handwritten Irish remedies her mother had marked with a question mark. Sometimes Jo thought her war on dirt did more for her patients than any of the herbs and patent medicines in the office hutch—that, and her latest crusade for fresh air.

For two weeks now, she had made all the right motions while her heart hung heavy in her breast. If what she had done was right—and it was right—then why did it hurt so?

She and Patience had talked far into the night one night, and both were resigned to the rightness of Jo's decision. Now Jo longed for Doc's reply, so she could pack her things and be gone. She lived in fear that Mitch would come home before she left—and that she would not have the strength to leave once he came home. She would die without Mitch, but her promise to her mother was tarnished, and the only way she could make it bright and shining again was to become a real doctor.

Why didn't Doc's answer come?

This marking time was sheer torture. Now that she had given up, she wanted it to be over and done.

I'm giving up without a fight, she thought.

But she *had* fought. And when she left here, she would fight again. "I know I'm right," she whispered into the smoothness of her lonely pillow. "But when will the ache go away?"

The next morning another large envelope arrived. This one was postmarked St. Louis.

The certificate inside was large and white and very plain. It was handwritten. One corner held a coffee stain. One corner had been crumpled in the mail. *This is to certify that Jody Gates has completed an eighteen-month course of study and is fully qualified to engage in medical practice and to hold the title of Doctor of Medicine.* It was signed *Archibald Adams, M.D.* and was the most beautiful piece of paper Jo had ever seen.

Doc's note said, *This is something I should have done long ago. Sally used to nag me about it—but I couldn't think beyond her pain in those days. Now she is gone and life must go on.*

*Forgive me for taking so long to send something you earned years ago. You deserve it. And, incidentally, my Sal will rest easier now, too.*

*About your wonderful offer: I can't tell you how excited I am over the prospect of actually being a part of a small, private hospital. Of course, I know I can't expect the offer to hold now that I have sent your certificate and you will be staying in Oregon. Yet I can't help but hope you'll still want me as your partner. And I'll make it clear right off—I'm willing to try your soap and water routine, but I'll not be nagged about it.*

*But, be that as it may, I would like to join you. If you could still see your way clear to take on a partner . . .*

Jo held the mutilated, coffee-stained certificate to her breast. She felt as if she had just seen God. "I did it," she whispered. "I really did it."

She tore the banjo clock from the office wall and held the license up to admire. Never, never had anything been so gorgeous. Almost tripping over her skirts, she flew screaming down the hall, "Patience! Patience! Where are you? Come see! Oh, do come see!"

# 50

On March 18th, 1865, Jo celebrated her twenty-third birthday. Trudy gave a small party for her—Jo's first party ever.

The following week Mitch came home. There were lines around his eyes and streaks in his dark hair, as there had been that first time she saw him on the Little Blue. But these were streaks of gray.

Jo had just come in from house calls in the country and was wearing buckskins. She had dreamed of meeting him in the green dress he had given her three years ago when he went away, but after one swift, appraising glance, Mitch appeared not to notice her attire at all.

"You're looking well," he said, not looking at her.

"I've been well," she replied, her heart pounding. "And you?"

"Never better." The black circles and a hint of pain in his eyes belied his words, but his cold tone pulled the reins on her desire to touch him—to rush into his arms and tell him how desperately she had missed him—how much she loved him.

They were strangers.

Jo walked him through the hospital, the pride in her accomplishments tarnished by his disinterest. There were two new wings now: a ward for women and a ward for children, with the old eight-bed porch ward reserved for men. Patience—Nurse Harrow—still occupied a bedroom upstairs, but Doc Adams and Jo lived in quarters of a new building they called Staff Hall.

"I'm thinking of building a small house of my own," Jo told Mitch. "Perhaps this summer." She hadn't been thinking that at all. She'd thought he would come home and ask her to marry him, and they would build a house together. Why did he look so uncaring—so unfeeling?

"Very impressive," he said. She thought he sounded bored, and she was sorry she had spoken. "You've been busy," he said.

"I couldn't have done any of it without Patience and Doc." She wanted Mitch to look—really *see* what had been accomplished here. She was so proud and he appeared not to care.

His tired eyes rested on her certificate. "You must be very pleased."

"We are."

"I meant you, personally." Not after that one swift glance had he looked directly at her. "You have achieved everything you set out to do, haven't you? It must give you a great sense of satisfaction." His eyes still on the certificate, he stuck a briar pipe into his mouth and held a lucifer to it. She had never seen him smoke before.

"We are all proud." Her voice sounded stilted even to her own ears. He was taking the pleasure out of everything. Half her joy had been in knowing how delighted he would be to see what she had accomplished. How could he be so indifferent? What had happened to his love? What had happened to J—I'm Waiting?

She studied his face. He did look tired. And now he

469

was home—faced with years of company tangles. Harrow Lumber had never fully recovered from the flood and the wholesale desertion of loggers. Despite Trudy and Willie's best efforts, the company still operated in the red. Now Mitch was home, war weary, disillusioned, and faced with a complete overhaul of a floundering business.

There was plenty of time for him to see what she had accomplished, Jo decided. She mustn't be so selfish. Right now what he needed was rest and understanding. She wanted to go to him—wanted to cradle his head in her arms and be strong for him as he so often had been strong for her. Oh, Mitch, cried her heart, don't turn your back on me. Let me help. But her lips were sealed. He was a stranger who smoked a pipe and leaned against the wall and looked past her with weary, reticent eyes. What happened to our love? cried her heart.

He stayed only a few minutes more.

"He's not himself, Jo," said Patience. "Give him a little time to get used to being home."

Jo didn't see him again for almost two weeks. She thought about going to him, but decided to take Patience's advice and give him time to get adjusted.

Then one day, just as she was leaving the hospital for rounds in the country, Mitch cantered past on his big roan. He glanced at her, passed her, tipped his hat, and kept on going.

She was dressed for the country again, and suddenly it struck her: *That* was the reason for his coldness. He hadn't seen her in a dress, and no one had told him she had given up her masquerade.

She touched her mare's flanks with her heels, then thought better of it and let him go without speaking.

If Mitch's cold behavior was just because she wasn't wearing the dress he'd given her, he could go straight to hades, she thought with sudden rebellion. If he really loved her, it wouldn't matter whether she was in breeches or a dress. She wasn't going to start out her married life kowtowing to him just because he was a man.

Yet if she never saw him, never talked to him, how was she ever to find out why he was so changed? Where was he hiding himself anyhow?

To Jo's hesitant queries, Trudy replied that Mitch had spent that first week sleeping and eating, the second poring over the company ledgers.

"He comes in late and falls into bed," his mother said. "Then he's up again at dawn, at the books. Of course, business has doubled since he came home. I can't get over it. In just a few weeks, he's bought up stumpage on six hundred acres. He's hired two full crews and has orders enough to last us into next year. He's even talking of buying up federal script he can redeem in government-owned land. He'll soon have us in the black again." She looked at Jo over the rim of her china cup. "What's wrong between you two anyhow? I don't mean to pry, Jo, but I always thought you'd get married. I know you love each other. I thought it was your wearing pantaloons that kept you apart."

"It was."

"But that's all over. What's wrong now?"

"I guess he doesn't know I'm wearing dresses. But it doesn't matter," Jo said, miserable. "He's changed. He's so indifferent."

"Have you tried to talk to him?"

"We don't seem to be able to communicate anymore."

Trudy toyed with her saucer. "I'll admit," she said finally, "that his temper was as short as a pie crust when he first came home. But that's all over now. Jo—why don't you come for dinner? Then he'd see you in the

471

dress and know you've changed."

Jo looked up swiftly. "He'd see how *I've* changed? What about him? Why should it always be the woman who gives in? If he really loves me, he'll still love me even if I am in buckskins."

Trudy's desire to advise was plain on her face. "Of course, it's your life, Jo," she said, "but if you . . ." She stopped, studied Jo's tight face, then sighed. "Maybe all he needs is more time, my dear. A man needs time to get back to normal after he's been off killing other men."

Knowing Trudy was right about that part of it, Jo waited impatiently for Mitch to come to her. But he didn't. She had seen him only twice in six weeks: that first day in the hospital and the day he had tipped his hat and ridden on without speaking.

It was quite obvious that his feelings toward her had changed over the last three years. If only I'd given up my masquerade before he went away, she thought. But being a doctor was all I could see. I was so certain of what I wanted, so positive I could fix the world. And I couldn't even fix my own little corner. Fifteen years ago, when I was just a child in Ireland, I knew what I wanted. I wanted a family—a closely knit family like Mama and Pa and me.

Somewhere along the line, had she lost that need?

No, not lost. It was still there, still beating strongly. What she had lost was her chance to have Mitch and a family. She had put doctoring first when what she needed was a balance between the two. She knew now that no career would ever substitute for marrying Mitch and bearing his children.

Years ago, in St. Louis, she had seen a man in her dream valley. And five years ago, on the trail, she had realized that man was Mitch. How could she have let the knowledge slip away? Jo's heart was sick with wanting—wanting to be a woman, complete, and with Mitch. But she couldn't let him run her life. He had to come to her. She wouldn't run after him.

She sat in the office on Monday afternoon, finishing the last of her case notes and thinking that it would soon be night again, and she would lie sleepless as she did now night after night. Sleepless and alone.

She had just come back from Canyonville and was hot and sweaty. She looked down at the soft buckskins and wondered where she would find the energy to bathe, brush out her hair, and put on a dress before dinner.

The certificate on the wall mocked her. The light faded slowly.

Surrounded by the things that should mean most to her—the tools of her profession—Jo felt drained, empty. The office was a malevolent jail—her longed-for profession, a jailer—and Jo sentenced to waste her life in a prison of her own making.

She jumped to her feet and paced restlessly around her desk. If she had been wrong about Anne's abortion, she thought, what else might she have been wrong about? Had she lied to herself all these years about what was real, what important?

And Mitch—did his promise to wait mean nothing? Was their love all a figment of her overactive imagination?

Possessed with a driving need to see the carving on the mountaintop once more, she rushed from the office. She couldn't see it from this side of the lake, and if she didn't hurry it would be too dark to see it from the other side.

The light was failing. Shadows lengthened across the dusty lane as she ran up First Street toward the footbridge.

On the porch of the company store lounged the usual

old men and drifters. Mr. Yarnel waved at her and she waved back.

"Hey, Doc," called Mr. Redfield, "you got another emergency? Where you off to in them breeches?"

Zeke Redfield was a talkative old coot, the only man in town who still alluded to her occasional masculine attire. Folks said he'd make a good neighbor if you had a windmill. Jo cupped her hand over one ear and smiled, as though she couldn't hear the question.

She raced across the bridge, down Lake Road to her old office site. Two ginkgo trees had sprung up where her little cabin had stood. A soft April breeze fluttered the fringes of her buckskins.

She raised her eyes to the mountain; blue shadows crept across the face of the peak, and she could barely see the carving, let alone read it.

"What's the matter? You afraid I climbed up there and cut the message away?"

She hadn't heard Mitch come up behind her. She jumped and turned. "You scared the daylights out of me."

He was dressed for the trail, tanned and healthy, his dark hair sun streaked as it had been the first time she saw him.

His eyes sharpened as he looked at her, and something quivered deep within their electric blue depths. "You come over here often to read the old message?"

What did he expect her to say? If she said yes, she was admitting her love. If she said no, she was denying it. She wasn't ready to do either just yet. She had to find out how he felt first. Oh, why couldn't she just be honest with him? Why couldn't she just come right out and say, *Mitch, I love you*?

"What are *you* doing here?" she countered. "Checking to see how soon the carving will be obliterated by

474

the weather?"

He turned away, his sun-bronzed face tightening. "I'm not interested in a sniping session, Jo."

"What are you interested in?" she asked quickly.

Something moved again, deep in his eyes. "I saw you come across the bridge and thought maybe we could talk. I thought . . . I got the impression . . . that day at the hospital . . . that maybe you wanted to tell me about your life . . . your plans." His voice walked on eggs.

Jo's heartbeat quickened. "There's not much to tell. You saw it all when you saw the hospital." *He followed me across the bridge*, cried her exultant heart. So their meeting wasn't accidental after all. She took a quivering breath. "Oh, Mitch, I've missed you."

His glance flicked down to her legs and back again. "Has your success made you happy?" he asked, just as if her words didn't hang between them, screaming in the quiet dusk.

Why didn't he move? If he would just hold out his hand. Just smile. Anything to break this frozen distance between them.

He pulled a pouch from his pocket and began filling his pipe. She plucked a pine needle and stuck it between her lips. It was bitter, like green tea, only worse. She sucked on it, pushing the bitter flavor around in her mouth. Overhead, a crow cawed loudly. Across the lake, on the front porch of the company store, men's voices raised in a loud guffaw and Jo stiffened.

"So you do think about us sometimes." Mitch dragged a lucifer across his breeches and held the flame to his pipe.

"Yes, of course. Don't you?"

"What do you think about us?"

She looked at her feet. "I remember."

"What do you remember?" His voice was husky.

475

"How it was." She wondered why he was looking at her with that funny look—as if he were disappointed in what he saw—as though it hurt him to look at her. Was that why he hadn't come to her these past five weeks? Was he not indifferent after all, but hurt? Did he hurt, thinking that she didn't want him?

"Have you ever been back up to Number Three Camp?" he asked.

"No. Have you?"

"I've just come from there. We have a new crew moving in next week."

"Oh." The thought of dirty loggers sleeping in their beautiful camp was a sacrilege. She knew he had to fill the barrack, but it hurt.

"The calendar we kept is still on the kitchen wall," he said, watching her carefully. "And there are still pine needles on the floor. I guess we didn't clean up as well as we thought we did."

It hurt to breathe. She was sure her throat would split. The heat from his body touched her though they did not touch. Her flesh tingled.

Sudden, angry helplessness swelled within her. "You find yourself another camp whore yet?" She looked up at him, challenging, and saw his head rear back and his nostrils flare as if he'd been slapped.

"I did that four weeks ago." His voice was harsh. "How do you think I was able to hire three full crews on such short notice? You have to dangle a carrot if you want the jackass to perform. I thought you understood that."

He was deliberately being crude. Just to hurt her. Tears formed. "I don't understand anything anymore, Mitch." She clamped down hard on the inside of her cheek and felt a ragged edge of skin tear loose.

He puffed on his pipe. The smoke had a pungently sweet aroma. "You're not happy with all your success as a country doctor?" He inspected the pipe stem with a critical eye.

"Oh, Mitch." Tears flowed freely now. She couldn't seem to make them stop. Still he didn't move toward her, didn't try to touch her. His clinical analysis shifted from the pipe to her, and she felt like a fish impaled on a hook, being inspected to see if she was big enough to keep or be thrown back.

Suppose it *was* hurt that he was feeling? Suppose he thought she didn't love him and that's why she was still in buckskins?

"What is it, Mitch? What's changed you so?"

A muscle twitched in the side of his square, set jaw.

Suddenly it didn't matter. Nothing mattered except her love and her need. She couldn't go through life just half a person. She put her hand on his chest and looked him full in the face.

"I love you," she said with simple honesty. The breeze dried her tears. "I've loved you ever since I found you raging with fever in that tent on the Little Blue."

She leaned her head against his broad chest and heard the pounding of his heart. But his arms hung limp at his sides.

"What would you like to do about it?" Except for a rough edge to his voice, he might have been discussing the weather.

When she didn't answer, he held her away and smiled into her face. It wasn't a nice smile. "If it's another trip to Camp Three you have in mind, I'm ready for that."

Her mouth dropped open and she pulled back, aghast. "You think all I want is to go to bed with you?"

"All? I wouldn't consider that such a small offer. In fact, if that's what you have in mind, I'm quite agreeable." His voice grated and his eyes gleamed with dark mirth.

"I'm not about to go back to that place with you."

"You have some other place in mind?"

Her fist struck his hard chest. "Oh, damn you, Mitch Harrow! I'm offering to marry you!"

His eyes raked her, moving from the top of her head to the tip of her boot-encased toes.

Jo felt the blood rush to her face as she realized how hot and sweaty and unattractive she must look

"I'll tell you the same thing I told you the last time you brought up the subject of marriage," he said bitterly. "Wait until the guy asks before you accept or refuse."

"I know I'm a mess, Mitch. I'm sorry. I've been up to Canyonville all day." She tried to laugh. "I'm not much good at setting the stage for love scenes, am I? I guess Mama should have shown me how to catch a man instead of teaching me self-preservation."

His eyes roamed her body once more and his tone was dry. "Get this straight, Dr. Gates. When I marry— *if* I marry—it won't be to a woman in pants."

An angry reply sprang to her lips, but she bit it back. After all, he thought she was still masquerading full time as a man. He thought she didn't love him enough, thought her medical practice was still the only thing in her life. He still loved her, sang her heart. It was *her* love he doubted, not his own.

She turned away for a moment, cherishing the hot leap of joy within her breast, yet trying to hide it from him. So he wanted to take her back to Mountain Camp Three for a return engagement, did he?

She faced him again and tipped her cat's eyes up, her lashes fluttering ever so slightly. "Are you all through waiting, Mitch?"

"Did you think I'd wait forever?" He bent his dark head toward hers, his eyes pools of blue fire. "When I marry, it will be to a *woman*. Not a changeling in breeches."

"Don't you want me anymore? Is that it?" She moved closer, sure now of his love. "Don't you love me, Mitch?"

"Oh, Christ!" She thought it was more a prayer than a curse, but when his arms tightened around her, they were granite, unforgiving bands. Without love. Without gentleness. With a passion that rocked them both in its fierce intensity. His mouth took hers.

Her body molded willingly to his.

But he dropped his arms and thrust her away. "Get this straight, Jo, and get it good; I'll only say it once: I love you. But I'll not let you use my heart as a plaything to dangle and flip whenever the urge strikes. The world is full of beautiful women—women who aren't ashamed of their femininity."

"I'm *not* ashamed of my femininity," she shouted back, stung that he should accuse her of such a thing.

"If you want to marry me," he said implacably, "you'll strip off those damned pants and put on a dress. I want a wife, not somebody I have to meet on the sly because everyone else thinks she's a man." He pushed her roughly aside.

"Oh, Mitch! Darling . . . is that what you think I want?" She caught his arm.

"I've never been a patient man, Jo. I've shown you more patience than you deserve. Five years is long enough."

She stood on tiptoe and her arms reached for him. "Oh, Mitch," she whispered against his cheeks. "I stopped posing as a man years ago. I wanted it to be a surprise. I even made your mother promise not to tell. Oh, I was wrong, darling. But I'm all woman now— and I'm your woman if you'll still have me."

He held her away again, his eyes narrowed in disbelief. "If you gave up being a man, what in hell are

479

you doing in those pants?"

"I only wear them for calls out in the country. I swear, Mitch. People have known for over two years now. Look . . ." She swept back her red hair so he could see the dainty gold earrings, the proof of her femininity.

His arms pulled her close as the realization swept over him. His lips parted hers with the softness of remembered intimacy and the promise of bliss to come.

"In that case," he murmured against her mouth, "let's go up to our camp one more time before we hire the preacher. Cute as you are in breeches, darling, I can't wait to take them off."